SHAME OF MAN

SHAME OF MAN

Geodyssey: Volume 2

PIERS
ANTHONY

TOR

A TOM DOHERTY ASSOCIATES BOOK

NEW YORK

SHAME OF MAN

COPYRIGHT © 1994 by Piers Anthony Jacob

This book is printed on acid-free paper.

A Tor Book
Published by Tom Doherty Associates, Inc.
175 Fifth Avenue
New York, N.Y. 10010

Tor® is a registered trademark of Tom Doherty Associates, Inc.

Library of Congress Cataloging-in-Publication Data

Anthony, Piers.
    Shame of man / Piers Anthony.
        p.   cm.
    "A Tom Doherty Associates book."
    ISBN 0-312-85811-6 (hardcover)
    I. Title.
    PS3551.N73S55   1994   94-21747
    813'.54—dc20   CIP

First edition: October 1994

Printed in the United States of America

0 9 8 7 6 5 4 3 2 1

CONTENTS

SHAME OF MAN

THIS is the second part of the Geodyssey series, following *Isle of Woman,* concerning the evolution, history, and nature of mankind. It is based on research and speculation, and not all of its assumptions are approved by contemporary authorities. It explores aspects of our species more thoroughly than before and draws some new conclusions, some of which are conjectures of the author rather than accepted anthropology. For example, this volume sees the divergence of man from the chimpanzee as occurring about six million years ago, and the pygmy chimpanzees, or bonobos, diverging from the chimpanzees about three million years ago. The so-called Aquatic hypothesis is accepted, though it may not be in the third volume. And one reason for mankind's present ascendance may be—fleas.

The prior volume followed two seeming families through three generations. Blaze and Ember were ordinary people amidst the larger human adventure. This one follows one family through one generation, in similar fashion: it is as if its members are reappearing in subsequent times as they have been before. The point is that all human beings are related, and we can identify particular types throughout human history. Human nature has been fairly constant through recent millennia; it is the scenery and circumstance that have changed. *Shame of Man* shows the family of Hu or Hue or Hugh or Huuo, who would have been Blaze's distant ancestor or perhaps cousin. Other characters carry through in similar roles as the novel progresses, though they may not be perfectly consistent from chapter to chapter. Thus what happens in one chapter may or may not be part of the background of another, and characters who know each other in one may not associate the same way in another. They are only approximations, representative of types and situations. Each member of the core family ages a year with each chapter, though the action sequences may be continuous. As before, there are are maps and discussions surrounding each setting. Some of these notes become rather long and detailed, as in Chapter 7, because the subject is complicated. Those readers who prefer merely to enjoy the ongoing story may ignore these, and the somewhat technical concluding Author's Note.

Because this volume covers different aspects of the same larger story of mankind, portions skirt or overlap the prior volume. Some of the previous characters make appearances here as secondary figures. Because of the reduction to a single generation, the alignments are not perfect. But in a general way, the characters of each novel are presented as they are at whatever stage of history is represented. Since the larger picture has all people existing at all times, there is no anachronism. They are as they seem when shown.

The span of time explored has been expanded for this volume, and covers eight million years. Thus it begins well before true-mankind emerged from the line of primates. However, most of the characters are introduced early, and will appear again later in the novel. As a general rule, only the named characters are important.

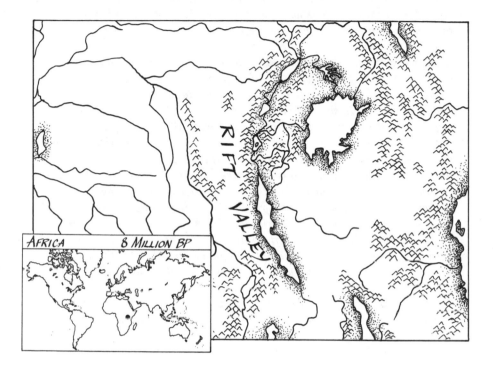

AFRICA   8 MILLION BP

RIFT VALLEY

C H A P T E R 1

GRACILE

The Great Rift of East Africa is a fascinating region. It is one terminus of a system of plate tectonics—that is, drifting continents—that traverses the globe of Earth. Our world seems to be boiling like a slow pot of mush, with hot lava welling up along a series of fault lines, pushing the existing surfaces apart, and in the process moving the continents around like ungainly checkers. If we trace that line of fire, we find it circles Africa clockwise, splitting in the Indian Ocean to send one rift looping around the Pacific Ocean, forming the "Ring of Fire" there and touching America to form the San Andreas Fault. Meanwhile the other fork proceeds from the Indian Ocean to complete its circuit of Africa, moving north to form the Mid-Atlantic Ridge, passing the North Pole, entering Siberia at the Lena River Delta, tunneling under until it surfaces again at Lake Baikal, then carries across Asia to Turkey and the Mediterranean Sea, where it plunges down through the Red Sea, and finally ties back into Africa at the Great Rift where it started. There has always been a whole lot happening along this fire line, and it may also account for mankind's emergence as the dominant species of the planet.

In Africa itself, the Rift proceeds roughly south from the point where the corner of Arabia almost touches it—that point being known as the Afar Triangle—through modern Ethiopia, Kenya, Uganda, Tanzania, Zaire, Zambia, and Mozambique. In simpler terms, it is a thirty-five-hundred-mile system slicing off the eastern segment of the continent. About halfway along, it divides into two branches, forming a great crude circle that encloses Lake Victoria. Geologists don't seem to know why it divides, but the answer seems obvious to the uninformed: this is the site of a meteor strike that tore up the landscape so badly that the Rift itself was fractured and had to detour around, leaving the crater to fill with refuse and water and form the lake. Something similar evidently happened at Iceland, which lies astride the Mid-Atlantic segment of the fire line.

This is rough country, with Africa's highest point—Mt. Kilimanjaro—and lowest point—in the Afar Triangle—both associated with the Rift. It is bounded by the great Sahara Desert in the north and the jungle of the Congo in the south. Within the Rift there is constant volcanic activity; its inlet in the Afar Triangle, lined with volcanic cones, is called "The Devil's Throat," and its low Danakil Depression has been described as the "Hell-Hole of Creation." Lions, hyenas, elephants, and the Cape buffalo range the Serengeti Plain southeast of Lake Victoria. Lake Malawi at its southern extreme has more fish species than any other lake in the world. What kind of primate would leave the protection of the jungle and choose to live here? Perhaps only one who was desperate, and hungry, and smart enough to survive its hazards. As it turned out, mankind.

But not quite yet. The time is approximately eight million years ago, and the place is central Africa near the Equator, on the eastern slope of the western branch of the Rift. Today the remnant of the mountain gorilla lives there, and it is part of the much wider range of the more versatile chimpanzee. But back then the two species were diverging from a common ape ancestor, and the smaller, thinner cousin—the "gracile" one—had to give way to the "robust" one. This led in some cases to a forced extension of the range. Most chimps were displaced westward; one band went where none other had dared, east over the volcanic ridge. This was not bravery but the luck of the draw; they couldn't get around the gorillas, so had to retreat where they would not be pursued. The immediate outlook was not promising.

HU lifted on his hind legs and gazed at trees on the slope below. The brutes were there, making threatening gestures. The trees of home had been occupied by stronger foreigners.

"Come!" Hu recognized his mother's urgent call. He dropped to four feet, turned, and scampered up the slope to join her. His little sister Be was doing the same.

They had foraged often on this slope, finding bugs and berries and caches of water in crevices. Hu was well familiar with it. But there were times when the mountain trembled and smoke spouted from its mouth, frightening them away. Now they were going toward that mouth. That wasn't safe, for no one could know when it might spout again.

But there was nowhere else to go, because of the brutes below. Hu's father, the dominant male, had tried to hold his territory, but the brutes were just too big. So he and several other males were taking their families away, seeking some better place. They had to move out before the brutes came after them, to take their women and kill their children. Hu had seen what happened to a neighboring band whose male had fought and lost. They all had seen. The women were not actually used by the brutes, but became tolerated outcasts, allowed to feed themselves until a brute female or adolescent male became annoyed and attacked. So the end was the same for the spared women; it just took more time, because they weren't deemed to be threats.

Hu and Be scrambled after their mother, just as the other children were after their mothers. She was no larger than Hu himself, but she ruled him until he chose to leave the family. Near them were Ra and Fa, following their mother. They were children of Hu's father, because the dominant male mated with all the women in the band. That made them close kin; they had the kin smell. Hu got along well with them, and they often groomed each other, picking out the bugs in their fur. When there was any alarm, and the mothers weren't close by, Hu and Be usually grouped with Ra and Fa.

The climb went on and on. The mountain trembled almost continuously, but they were getting used to that. They could tell when the mountain was feeling angry, and right now it was merely irritable.

As the day waned, they got beyond familiar territory. The group closed in together, becoming nervous; none of them liked strange land. There were too many dangers in the unknown.

But they were lucky, or perhaps the big males had been here long ago and knew where to look. There was a cave. It wasn't deep, but it was big enough to shelter the bands. There were several recesses, and one male took over each recess, putting his mates and children there. They would be safe here. It wasn't as good as a tree, but it was better than the open slope. Especially since the mountain was rumbling louder now, with smoke rising from its top, and some rocks were shaking loose and sliding down the steeper slopes. There was a pile of rocks before the cave, but not many inside. They would be good to heave at predators.

There were berry patches nearby, growing in furrows and gullies in the slope. They were rich with ripe berries because no one had been this far to pick them before. Immediately the women and children went out to eat. Hu dashed for the nearest patch, but a male growled him off. He had to go farther out. This was happening more as he got older; the big males were starting to notice him, and not with favor.

He moved on out. There was a cry, and Be was scampering after him. Hu was disgusted; she would slow him. She had been weaned only the year before. But she was his little sister, close kin, and he had to accept her. So he waited for her to catch up, and then they went on together.

Other young folk were spreading out, seeking untouched berry patches in the hollows of the slope. Those who first spied a good patch stood guard over it, reserving it for their own siblings. Hu didn't want to fight; he was already tired from the long climb. So he went on beyond, Be beside him.

Be was agile enough. She scampered up a steep ridge to a crevice above—and paused, with an exclamation of awe.

Hu knew that she didn't make that sound for nothing. Young as she was, she was learning the key danger sounds, and would not utter them randomly. But this was not quite danger; it was more like mystery. So he had to investigate. It might be something she didn't know was dangerous.

He mounted the ridge, grabbing handholds and hauling himself up. He reached her side, and followed her gaze ahead.

It was indeed different. Beside the ridge was a deep crevice, and from it warm air gusted. He squinted, peering into it. There was light in there, like that of the sun on a dim day. There was an odd sound, not quite like water running, and a strange hot smell. Hu did not understand this, and for that reason he did not like it.

But before he could warn Be away, she spied something new. Beyond the crevice was a fine patch with many large ripe berries. She bounded over the crevice and began to pick them, greedily eating.

Hu hesitated. That burning light in the crevice—could it hurt them? He wanted to know more about it before trusting it. Besides, he was curious. His curiosity had on occasion gotten him in trouble, such as when he had ventured too close to a copulating couple and put his nose in the way, but it had also enabled him to discover interesting things. So he had two reasons to explore this situation.

He followed the cleft, sniffing the fumes. It led down the slope, seeming to be a crack in the mountain, like an open cut. Was he seeing past the mountain's skin to the blood inside? Did the mountain hurt? Was that why it was rumbling? He knew how a deep cut could sting. But what could have made such a cut in so big a hill? No lion could have done it, and no elephant either.

There was a cry. That was Be's distress call. Hu spun around and leaped back toward the berry patch. What mischief had she gotten into?

He saw a larger form by the patch. It was Ss, the nasty child of one of the other dominant males, a year younger than Hu. He had never gotten along with her or her brother Bb, because they were always doing something mean.

Ss didn't see Hu. She was stalking Be, trying to drive her away from the berry patch. Naturally Ss wanted all the berries for herself. As Hu loped toward them, he saw Ss pounce on Be and lift the child into the air. Be struggled, terrified. Ss carried her to the deep crevice, about to throw her in. Be screamed, her arms and legs flailing helplessly.

Then Hu reached them. He snatched Be away, hugging her, keeping her safe. Ss screamed with frustration. She seemed about to attack Hu, but she was smaller as well as female, so could not win.

There was a sound behind Hu. He turned cautiously, so as not to leave Ss at his back, and saw her brother Bb advancing on them. Bb was Hu's age, but larger; he could win a fight. Hu and Be would have to give up their berry patch and flee, because they could not match the nasty pair. It was too bad, because the patch was theirs; latecomers were supposed to honor the choices of the early comers. Hu was hungry; he realized he should have started eating immediately, instead of getting distracted by the curious crevice.

But then two more figures appeared. Ra and Fa! They were kin and friends. They were a year younger than Ss, but both could fight well. Now the kin were more than the foreign ones, and they would be able to hold the patch.

Hu called, and Ra and Fa immediately scrambled up the slope to join them. Then the three of them stood before Bb and Ss, snarling, keeping little Be behind them.

Bb snarled in return, threatening to fight. But when Hu advanced, he retreated. He never liked to fight when he wasn't sure of winning, and he couldn't win against two males, even if neither was quite his size. Fa, though a year younger than Ss, could nevertheless prevent her from helping her brother fight. So Bb retreated, and Ss retreated with him. In a moment they turned and ran away.

Hu, Ra, and Fa smiled at each other. Then they settled down with Be to eat the berries. The little fruits were wonderful. The funny thing was that Hu used one forefoot to pick most of his berries, while the other three used the other forefoot. But all of them could use either foot, when they thought about it, so it didn't matter.

In due course the four made their way back across the hot crevice and down the slope to the cave. Their mothers were waiting for them. It was good to be home, even if it wasn't much like their trees.

❂

Next day they moved on up the slope, foraging as they went. The mountain was rumbling less, but they were getting closer to the smoke. Hu saw the others cringe as clouds of the smoke came out and spread toward the group. They were afraid of anything strange. Hu, in contrast, was attracted to oddities, and the more dangerous they seemed, the more he wanted to know about them. His curiosity warred with his fear, sometimes leaving him standing bemused, unable either to advance or to retreat. He was especially sensitive to sounds; they fascinated him, and odd ones could lure him beyond safety. He seemed to hear qualities of sounds that others ignored, so had given up on getting any support for this interest. The sounds of the fire mountain had power and resonance unlike others, as if a giant lion struggled within.

But smoke had never actually harmed him or anyone he knew before. It came from fire, and fire was hot and hurtful but could be avoided because it burned only on the grassy valley below their forest. And, perhaps, inside the mountain. So Hu wanted to know more about smoke, and was glad to be approaching it.

However, the leaders were wary, and when the slope allowed it, they moved around to the side of the mountain. There were more bugs and berries there, and it did seem safer.

But then they entered a high sort of valley between this mountain and the next. The slope above was steep and bare and hot in the sun; the slope below became a narrowing crevice. There was a bad smell that made them cough and choke.

They paused, milling. There did not seem to be anywhere to go forward. But there weren't enough berries this high to sustain them, and behind were the brutes.

Hu, as curious as ever, decided to explore the crevice. Be scampered after him, thinking he knew where he was going. He would not have signaled it, but he found her company reassuring. He could not take any bad risks when she was with him, because he had to protect her. That made it safer for him, too.

When the slope got too hot and steep, they moved down into the crevice. It was wider than it had looked from above, but scary too, because its walls were very high and close together. There was just room to walk at the base. But Hu saw that up ahead the walls became so bare that it would not be possible to climb them. If anything rolled down, he and Be would be crushed. Indeed, there was a pile of stones there that they had to climb over.

They stood on the top of the pile and looked on into the crevice. Wisps of vapor floated up from vents in the ground, and there was a faint but ominous hissing. The smell was bad. This was far enough to go.

Be tugged at his hand. She was frightened, and wanted to go back. That was a good enough pretext. So Hu shrugged and turned, pretending to humor her.

There was activity behind them. Someone else was following. At first Hu was glad, because he thought he could show off what he had found. Then he recognized Bb and Ss.

This was a problem, because he knew they meant mischief. They were still mad because they hadn't gotten the berry patch yesterday. Now they wanted to fight, and there was no grown kin to support Hu. What was he to do?

The sensible course was to run away. But they were blocking off the only escape. The walls did not seem any more scalable than before; only the bottom of the crevice was suitable. Bb knew that. He knew he had Hu trapped. He knew that no one else was close enough to intercede.

Hu turned again and looked forward. The crevice looked as forbidding as before. The evil vapor swirled in it, so that Hu could not see what was beyond. The hissing seemed louder now, like that of a restive snake. That was no place for a person to go.

There was a sound behind as Bb and Ss advanced. Normally females fought only among themselves, or to protect their children, but Ss often fought to support her brother. She was aggressive and vicious. Like her brother. Hu had little chance against Bb in a fair fight, and with Ss chomping his back, he had even less. She was really worse than Bb, because she was not being true to the nature of her gender.

Hu turned once more. He peered down through the steaming crevice. That might be doom—but so might a fight with Bb. He couldn't afford to get beaten, when he had Be to protect.

Bb was getting close. He leaped to the base of the rock pile. Hu leaped off it, into the crevice ahead. He called to Be to follow. This seemed to be the lesser risk, and now that he had made the decision, he felt his curiosity about what lay ahead. He had wanted to explore farther, but hadn't dared. Now there was as much of a threat behind as ahead, so it was easier to go on.

Be scampered close behind him. She was afraid too, but trusted Hu to keep her safe.

They came to the first vapor vent, and plunged through it. The air was hot but they weren't in it long, so it didn't hurt. But there was another vent beyond, with thicker steam.

Hu halted. Be stopped so close she was nudging him. He looked back. The prior steam masked the cleft beyond it. He couldn't see whether Bb was coming after them. But Bb couldn't see Hu and Be either. Would he come? Maybe he would just wait until they returned, then pounce.

Hu thought of the rocks that might roll down from above. He didn't want to wait here long. So he moved forward again, Be nervously pacing him.

He paused before the steam. The odor was bad, but it wasn't making him choke.. The hissing was steady rather than menacing. Maybe it was safe. Should he try to leap through it? He saw some of the path beyond, and it looked all right.

There was a sound behind. Hu leaped through the steam. He landed safely beyond it, with Be almost underfoot.

The way ahead was narrower than ever, and it curved. But Hu was recovering confidence. This path was not as deadly as it had seemed. Where did it go?

They moved on, passed through one more steam vent, and then the crevice got wider. The two mountains pulled away from each other and the steam vents stopped.

They went on, and the slopes on either side got less. Finally they were able to scamper out of the cleft. A valley opened out before them—and it was green with trees. They were through the mountains!

They made their way down the slope, and found a rich berry patch. They fairly gobbled the berries, which tasted wonderful. Their juice helped quench Hu's growing thirst, too.

But now the day was getting late. Shadow crossed the valley and reached up the mountain slope. It was weird, because it was coming from the wrong direction. This was morning shadow, coming at night.

Be began to whimper, picking up the subtle wrongness of this region. She wanted to go home. So did Hu. So they put down their knuckles and ran back to the narrow cleft.

But the shadow got there before them. The cleft was dark. How could they go there?

As Hu stared, he saw that the darkness was not complete. He could still see the bottom of the cleft. Soon it would be all the way dark, but there was time to get into it before that happened. So he bounded on down into it, with Be fearfully close.

Once at the base path, they ran without pausing into its narrowness, though the steam, along its close curve, through the next steam, and finally through the last one. There was the rock pile, and Bb was gone. They could get the rest of the way through!

It seemed only a moment before they were back where the band had been—but the band was gone. No problem; they sniffed out the trail and soon found it a short distance back, huddling under a rocky overhang. There was no cave, but this seemed good enough. Hu and Be had not even been missed.

❂

In the morning the indecision remained. No one knew where to go or what to do. Most of the band were hungry, for the berries nearby had all been eaten, including unripe ones, and bugs and grubs were hard to find. A foolish rabbit was spied, and was immediately circled and pounced on; soon the redly dripping fragments of it were being avidly eaten by the dominant males. But that merely made the rest of them hungrier.

Yet Hu knew where there was food. He tried to tell his mother, but she was distracted and did not understand. So he told his half-brother Ra. "Food!" He touched his mouth, then his belly.

Ra understood immediately. He and Fa came with Hu, following him down to the crevice. There they hesitated, but Hu plunged on in, and they followed. He ran over the pile of stones and plunged through the first steam cloud. Again they hesitated, but they were hungry, so they came on through. Both were frightened, but Hu's confidence encouraged them. They knew he would not lead them into mischief.

In a surprisingly short time they were through the narrow way and approaching the berry patch on the other side. There were other patches close below it with plenty of ripe berries. Ra and Fa pounced on the patches and gorged themselves. Hu found a separate patch, and ate too.

Then it was time to go back. They had to let the others know. Fa, with an intuitive insight, plucked a berry branch and clamped it between her teeth. Then they returned, no longer afraid of the steam path.

This time Bb was there at the rock pile. He bared his teeth as he spied Hu, thinking to attack him. Then Ra came up beside Hu and bared his teeth. Bb, alone, changed his mind and loped away.

Hu and Ra did not let it go at that. They bounded after him, screeching threateningly, forcing Bb to flee without dignity. It was fun. Fa followed close behind, enjoying the scene.

The three approached Hu's mother. "Food!" they cried. Fa showed off her berry branch. There were several ripening berries on it. That got the attention of the others. Where had she found that, when all the plants nearby had been stripped of all their berries, both ripe and green, as well as their leaves?

Hu's mother followed Hu, and Ra's mother followed Ra. Several other children came too. But the dominant males did not deign to pay attention. What could children have that could interest them?

The trip was not easy, for the women were far more wary of the steam vents than the children were. But when little Be jumped blithely through, evincing no fear, Hu's mother followed. She almost turned back when she saw the second vent, but again they managed to persuade her to jump through. Finally they brought her and the other female out to the berry patches. Then all was clear, and they all feasted.

Later that day they brought through more children and females. The word spread quickly: food! Soon all the young ones were running through the steam as if it had never been fearsome. Even the steady hissing seemed friendly.

It took time to convince the dominant males, but hunger finally compelled them. They navigated the cleft with extreme reluctance. Hu saw that their larger bulk made the passage difficult. In the narrowest section they had to stand and sidle along. It would have been impossible for one of the brutes who had displaced their band to squeeze through.

In due course the band moved down the new slope to the thickly growing trees below. There were no brutes there, and food was plentiful. They had found their new home.

In this manner the range of the chimpanzees extended beyond that of the gorillas. The graciles were not able to oppose the robusts, but the robusts could not go as far from their home forests. It was not just that the chimps could run better on ground or squeeze through narrower apertures, but that they could forage more efficiently in difficult terrain. Perhaps their constant displacement to the fringe of the joint range forced them to be more versatile, and that helped them survive when times changed. Thus those who were less specialized for a particular habitat became survivors in varied habitats. This pattern was to be repeated endlessly as our species evolved, and it seems to have been the graciles who usually outlasted the robusts. Thus perhaps their weakness was their strength.

Within our species, men are robust, women gracile. That may be significant.

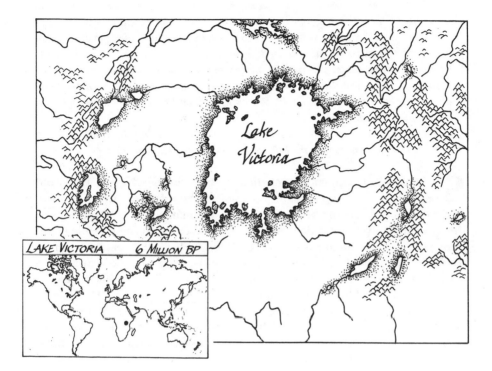

CHAPTER 2

GARDEN

Six million years ago Africa was in a relatively cool, dry phase. Lakes dried out and disappeared, and forests shrank. Savanna, the flat, treeless grassland, expanded. This was not good habitat for chimpanzees, and their range diminished. But one group fought to survive by adapting to the dangerous flatland to the east of the West Rift Valley. This led to a development that was to change the world, in time. But the significance of this physical adaptation might not have been apparent, being overshadowed at first by a social shift.

The actual social structure of those chimps that were to become human is not known, but there does seem to have been an increased sexual dimorphism: the

males became significantly larger than the females. That suggests the harem
style, with a number of small bands, each band with one dominant male and a
number of females and children, as with the apes. But human society was to
benefit from the development of larger bands, containing a number of males, who
had to learn to cooperate with each other. Thus the simple might makes right ape
formula was to become a more interactive society, with a leader governing not
merely by physical strength, but by the consent of the governed, or at least the
support of other males. The transition may not have been easy, but time favored
those who could form larger bands. Since a male with an established harem is
unlikely to give it up voluntarily, it may have been the juvenile males who led
the way to the new order.

The setting is Lake Victoria. But it wasn't a lake, in that dry time. The rich
sediment of its vast dried lake bed made it a very special garden.

S UDDENLY it happened: a challenger beat the band male. Hu could
hear the roars and blows, and it was the stranger who won. This was
real trouble, because the new male would systematically kill all the sons of
the prior male who didn't flee, even the babies. Once all the juvenile males
were gone, the dominant male would breed with all the females, and all
future babies would be his. As the female children grew up, he would breed
with them too. There would be no place for any of the existing males.

Actually it had been getting more difficult for youths like Hu before,
because their father did not care to have any other grown males in the
band. He tolerated them because they were his sons, but his tolerance had
been diminishing as they grew. So they had been foraging farther afield,
and some had been taken by the predators of the ground. Sometimes a
youth went out and didn't return. Since no neighboring band would admit
any male voluntarily, that meant they were dead. It was dangerous to stray
too far from home. But they were going to have to, in another year or so. So
Hu was not entirely unprepared.

Still, he dawdled, hoping that it would be different from what he had
observed in neighboring tribes. His sister, five years younger, did not want
him to go; he had looked out for her all her life, helping her to forage,
advising her what was good and what was bad to eat. In fact he had advised
a number of the other youths, because his unusual curiosity and sensitivity
to sound led him to discover things before they did, and he had gained both
good and bad experience. He also had sharp vision, improved by practice.
Thus when a new fruit ripened, he was likely to be the first one there to
pluck it. Of course the second one there would normally take it away from
him, because Hu was not large, and tended to use the wrong forefoot. Yet
often enough he was alone or with Be, and then it was all right. She didn't
mind what foot he used.

But the new male wasted no time. Within a day he made the round of all
eight women, snatching away their nursing babies and hurling them to the

ground to die. The women were unable to protest; they knew the way of it. They just had to suffer. Soon enough they would have new babies to take their attention. The males who had been weaned fled. It was better than being killed, though they would probably die anyway, being too young to protect themselves competently.

When the male approached Hu's mother, Hu fled. To his surprise, Be came with him. He realized that she, half grown, might not be spared; the new male was saving women and near women but not babies and children who would take too long to be breedable. As they left, they heard their mother scream as her youngest child was snatched and killed. Then silence, as she submitted to immediate breeding with the new male.

Hu paused down the slope, letting Be catch up. He hugged her comfortingly, but they both knew that they faced a very difficult time. They would not be allowed to return to their band's grove, and other bands would not admit them to their groves. Be in time could join a band, when she was nubile, but not Hu. He could join only by force, which meant not at all.

Another youth approached. It was Jo, the largest of Hu's half-brothers, not yet big enough to defend himself against a grown male, but quite able to dominate Hu. With him was Bl, who was small, like Hu, but smart. The two had different mothers but were close friends, with Bl suggesting what to do and Jo enforcing it. Hu had never much liked either of them.

But right now their plight was the same as Hu's and Be's: they had been cast out. That made quarreling pointless; they were all in too much trouble already.

Bl approached. He extended one forefoot, open, in the gesture of camaraderie. He wanted to be friends?

Hu looked at Jo, who was hanging back. But Bl persisted, and finally, grudgingly, Jo agreed, and held out his foot too.

Hu knew that if he accepted their offer, they would have a small band of half-brothers, which was safer than none, but that Jo and Bl would govern it. Still, this seemed better than the alternative. He had gone out playing and hunting with them before, on occasion, and they really weren't too bad. Not like Bb and his savage sister. So he extended his hand, touching first Bl's hand, then Jo's. Be did the same.

Two more approached: Ra and Fa, Hu's friends the twins. Bl extended his hand to them too, and so Jo did, and then Hu and Be. Hu was glad to have them.

Now they were six, and that did feel more comfortable. They moved downslope, looking for some unoccupied territory where perhaps they could set up a new band.

But every worthwhile grove on this slope was already occupied by a band. The only available trees had no fruit. There was no place for castoffs here. Hu realized that even with a band of six, the outlook was bleak.

Bl realized it too. He pointed to the path at the base of the slope, leading away. It went to the nearby pond, where they could go to drink when the fruit wasn't juicy enough. It was used by the bands along the valley, when there were fresh berries growing on the ground, and was considered to be neutral territory. Anyone could go where he wished, on the ground; only the trees were possessed by bands. At present there were few berries, so there was little activity along it.

They put down their knuckles and loped along, knowing that the day was waning and that they had to find a vacant grove with fruit soon if they were going to. Hu remembered seeing other youths go this way in past years. He had not before truly appreciated their situation. Now he wished he had thought about this inevitable time, and tried to make some advance plan for it. But somehow he had believed that it would never happen to him.

They spied an isolated grove and ran for it, but as soon as they came near there was a warning cry: occupied. They veered away, running on down the path, hoping for another grove. But all were full, right up to the edge of the baked mud. The pond had been larger, but was shrinking, so now it was just a small pool in a large patch of hardened mud.

They stopped at the pond and drank, putting their mouths down into it as they had so often before. But this time it was different, because they were not with their mothers, guarded by the dominant father male. They were outcasts.

They spread out along the edge of the pond, looking for things to eat. Hu found a fat snail, spotting it by its color. Snails weren't his favorite food, but would do in an emergency. He put the shell to his teeth and cracked it open, about to suck out the meat. Then he paused, seeing Be watching him.

She couldn't find snails the way he could. None of the others could. They could not see the distinctive colors under their coating of mud, as Hu had learned to do.

He handed her the cracked snail. She gobbled it down eagerly, spitting out bits of shell.

Then he saw others looking his way. They knew he could find snails and berries and edible roots better than they could. They were getting hungry.

Bl approached him. So Hu looked around, spied another snail by its masked color, fetched it up, and proffered it to Bl. Bl took it to Jo, who ate it. Then Bl returned to Hu.

Hu saw the way of it. If he wanted to be in the leader's good graces, he had to provide some more snails. So he got serious about foraging, scraping in the mud with his hands, digging out snail after snail. There were a surprising number of them, perhaps because few ate them by choice. That was an indication of how things had changed.

Bl gave another snail to Jo, then gave one to Ra and one to Fa. When each had had one, Bl gave one back to Hu. Again Hu had to pause to figure out the other youth's more devious thought: he meant that all of them should eat. Hu didn't have to give away everything. It was like a game they had sometimes played, sharing as if in a one-tree family, the mother giving her children food but not depriving herself. Now they were like a larger family, weird as the notion was.

For some time Hu foraged, and the others did too, watching him, learning how he did it. They had never cared before, but were apt enough now that they put their minds to it. So they found many snails, until they all were satisfied.

Then they moved on around the pond, looking for another grove. But the only one they could find had an uncomfortable type of tree. They just had to use it, settling into places on the branches to sleep. Be nestled beside Hu, and he held her close. He would hardly care to admit it, but she was providing him almost as much comfort as he was providing her. She was what remained of his immediate family.

In the morning they returned to the pond for more snails, then moved on beyond, looking for a really suitable grove. But this time they encountered several other youths, who swarmed down to taunt them while one grabbed Fa and another came toward Hu and Be. Hu recognized Bb, his nemesis from another band. Had he also been cast out? Or was he just making mischief? It hardly mattered, because Bb was coming to grab Be, whom he had bothered before. She was too young and small to breed, but Bb might try it anyway, just to make her scream. Hu shouted protest, trying to protect his little sister, but the malign youth was larger and stronger than he was. Ra and Fa were fighting back more successfully, but Hu was losing, as he usually did in altercations.

Then Bl was there, and Jo. Jo was bigger than the foreign youth. He grabbed Bb by the scruff of the neck and shook him so violently that he let Be go. She ran immediately to Hu's embrace, whimpering. In a moment Bb had had enough, and fled; he never favored an even fight, let alone one in which he was at a disadvantage. The other youth also retreated. When they fled, so did those who had merely cried out threateningly. The crisis was over.

Bl gave Hu a significant look, and Hu realized that Bl had brought Jo into the fray. Jo was big, but he had never before fought for anyone but himself or Bl. Now he had fought for Hu. That was the payback. Hu had foraged for them all, and shown them how to find snails, and Jo had defended Hu. They were a family.

However, other youths were appearing, and some looked desperate. This was not a good place to remain long. Bl nudged Jo, and indicated the path to the main berry field. Jo headed that way, exerting leadership, and the others followed.

The field was barren. It was out of season, and there were no berries.

That was a disappointment, because berries tasted sweet and were nice to eat, better than muddy snails. He had always liked this field for that reason; berry time was happy time.

However, he was able to locate some edible roots. He had discovered these the year before, when idly experimenting, and not thought much about it. They didn't taste very good. But now he realized that these were their best choice. So he dug them out, identifying them by the colors of the stems projecting from the ground. They were covered with dirt, of course, and that didn't taste good, so he rubbed them off on grass to get them as clean as possible.

Bl came over. Hu took a bite from a tuber, demonstrating its edibility. Bl tried a bite. He made a face. But it was food, so Bl took one to Jo and demonstrated. In due course they all were eating them and making faces.

Another youth from a foreign band spied them and loped over. He was very thin, and his fur was splotchy; he had not eaten well. Because he was foreign, and not large, Jo had no problem figuring out what to do. He stood up tall, beat his chest with his folded hands, and screamed challenge.

The foreigner immediately fell to the ground and rolled on his back, whimpering. He had not come to fight.

Bl went over to him. Bl extended a hand. Hu and the others were bemused: offering friendship to a complete stranger? The youth seemed almost as surprised. On his back, he reached out and touched the hand. Then he got up and followed Bl to Jo. Jo roared again, and the foreigner dropped to the ground again. Bl nudged Jo, and Jo reluctantly gave the stranger the rest of the root he had been eating. The foreigner had been adopted into the band. They grunted at him, exchanging names. His name was Vk.

After that Hu provided roots for the newcomer too, and showed him how to find them himself, by the colored stems. It wasn't hard, because there were many roots; no one else had thought to eat them before. Because Hu knew how to locate the succulent ones, it worked; without his knowledge, gained by sometimes bitter-tasting experience, it would have been an almost impossible task.

There was a clamor behind them. Hu looked back and recognized Bb and his spiteful sister Ss. They seemed to have organized the scattered other outcasts into another band, and were coming to interfere with this band. Now there were more of enemies than friends, so the enemies had courage.

Bl saw the problem immediately. He nudged Jo, and they moved on, away from the familiar home forest. Bb's band hesitated, not caring to brave the unfamiliar region, and was left behind. The groves became fewer, and the path faded out. Before them was a frighteningly open grassy plain. But how could they turn back? There was nothing there for them but mischief.

Some distance across the plain was what appeared to be a new forest. Bl gazed at it speculatively, then indicated to Jo that it looked promising. So Jo started toward it.

But Vk suddenly became agitated. "Bad!" he cried, pointing to the forest and cringing in fear.

Bl considered. But Jo, not deigning to respond to any suggestion by a scrawny newcomer, forged on, and Bl let it be. The others followed, with Vk nervously at the rear.

As they approached the forest, a swarm of youths dropped down from the trees at the edge and charged out to intercept them. Now the nature of Vk's warning was clear; he had already encountered this hostile region. Bl reacted quickly. He touched Jo on the shoulder and signaled retreat. Jo, seeing the number of the attackers, agreed. Their band quickly moved away from the forest.

But the foreign youths, once aroused, did not let it go at that. Five of them came on out, jeering and making insulting gestures. They spied the two young females, Be and Fa, and converged on them. Three hung back, not completing the charge, but two continued.

Hu realized that they wanted to breed. Both females were too young, and of course no band brother of theirs would breed with them. But these were foreign youths, of age to be interested, and they evidently were not much concerned with age. Fa, though young, had a nice form and smell, and the foreigners were eying her. Be clung to Hu for safety, and Fa stayed very close to Ra.

But this time Jo and Bl were quicker to react. Jo went to help Ra, and Bl joined Hu. Each attacking youth found himself opposed by two males. This was unusual and demoralizing to them; normally quarrels were one to one. In a moment each foreigner had been struck and bitten, and quickly disengaged and fled. Young females weren't worth such a fight.

Of the remaining three, two joined the two who had been defeated, and fled. But the last one hesitated. Then, hesitantly, he held out a hand in supplication.

Jo stalked over to him, growling. The youth rolled on the ground. Once more Bl interceded, causing Jo to accept the stranger. The others hardly knew what to make of this, but had to go along with it.

The new one was It. Unlike Vk, he was in good health. And he turned out to be useful, because he knew this new forest. He indicated where there was an unoccupied grove, and where there was water. Bl considered, and told Jo, and they went to it. There was some fruit in the trees, and they were good for sleeping in. This was an improvement.

They remained in this grove for several days, and two more foreign youths joined them. They were now a band of ten, which was a comfortable limit, because more could not be counted on the fingers of the forefeet. If it got much larger, they might have to fission into two smaller groups. Or maybe they would simply learn to count on toes as well. But the fruit of the grove was not enough; the last of it was eaten and they had to move on. That explained why no other band had taken it: it could not sustain a full band for long.

The new youths made clear that there were no good vacant groves in this forest. The situation was similar to the forest they had left, with every good place taken by a dominant male and his females and their children. The male youths who had been dispossessed had no choice but to scrounge around the fringe, trying to survive. That was why the new ones had joined the band; survival was more likely within it than without it.

Jo, prompted by Bl, led the band around the forest, going no farther into the grassy plain than necessary. Even so, there was trouble. Several big hyenas approached, and circled the band, considering whether it was suitable prey. But the moment the hyenas came, Bl picked up some stones and stood on his hind feet. The others did the same. When the animals looked as if they were going to come in close, the members of the band started throwing the stones. Their aim was not good, but some stones almost hit the creatures. The hyenas gave it up; these prey things were too numerous and too eager to fight back.

After that they moved closer to the forest. Hyenas were funny predators; sometimes they could be scared off, but sometimes they couldn't. It depended how hungry they were. It wasn't safe to go too far afield. Their newest member, It, had a nose for water, finding more for them to drink, but they remained hungry. They had to forage for grubs near the trees.

But this led to another kind of trouble. The dominant male of a grove they skirted spied the two females in their number and decided to take them into his band. He simply dropped to the ground and ambled out, knowing that no youth could stand up to him. He expected to take what he wanted without opposition. Indeed, in any ordinary situation he would have been correct; he was far larger than any of them, and muscular in proportion. He was old, but no less daunting. They sidled away from him, not daring to flee openly lest he leap and bite them on the necks, perhaps killing them.

He reached for Fa. She scooted back with a cry of abhorrence. He growled and leaped for her.

Ra jumped in to interpose himself. He was shaking with fright, but had to try to protect his sister. The male snarled contemptuously, lifting one arm to strike him out of the way.

Then Jo and Bl and Hu leaped, almost together. Two grabbed the male's powerful arms while Hu, directly behind, landed on the male's back. He put his face down and bit into the hairy neck. He got mostly a mouthful of fur, but his eyeteeth dug into flesh.

It wasn't enough. The male screamed with pain and fury. His two arms came up and back, lifting Jo and Bl off the ground. He was trying to get at

Hu, to sweep him away. But Jo and Bl clung tenaciously—and in the moment the male stood upright, Ra struck him in the face with a big stone. It smashed his nose and perhaps his front teeth. But it didn't kill him.

Hu saw Vk and It standing near, wanting to help, but uncertain how. There was no way to get into this fight without complicating it for the four already involved. But if any of them got injured or killed, then one of the bystanders could take his place.

Hu bit again at the neck, getting a better grip on the hot flesh. It still wasn't enough. The male was so strong that soon they all would tire and be thrown off. Then, if they didn't flee, they would be killed, one by one. They had gotten themselves into more of a fight than they could handle.

Ra struck again with his stone, at the top of the male's head. And again, and again. The male couldn't get his forelimbs free to grab the stone away. Blood spattered the dark fur. Slowly the male sank down under their weight, but Ra kept pounding, afraid to stop.

Finally Bl let go, and then Jo and Hu. They stood up, and Bl cried out to Ra. "Dead! Dead!"

It was so. Ra had finally beaten in the male's head. He lay stretched out on the ground. They had killed him.

They gazed with awe at what they had done. They hadn't planned on it; they had just reacted in the way they were learning, acting together when they had to.

There was a cry from the grove. A female was there.

The four victors stared at each other. The dominant male's women! They naturally belonged to the one who killed the male. But they were a group of youths, not a single grown male, and they had not had any such acquisition in mind.

Yet they were not so young as to ignore the potential. They had no sexual interest in the females of their original band, because they were sisters. But these other females were from a different band. They were available. That was an intriguing new prospect, especially now that they had proven themselves by defeating a male in combat.

Cautiously, they approached the grove. There turned out to be eight grown females perched in its trees, with more than that many children. They knew that their male had died; they had watched the fight from their trees. Now they were waiting for the new male to come.

Again the four original youths of the band hesitated. Someone had to take these females; they couldn't be left to try to fend for themselves. If this band didn't take them, other males would quickly move in, killing the young. Hu had no taste for such killing, having just fled that fate himself. He knew that the others had a similar sentiment. And who among them would take over? Jo was the biggest and strongest, but he wouldn't do it without Bl to guide him.

Bl's thoughts were as usual faster than Jo's or Hu's. He pointed to Jo, then to the nearest tree with a female. "Take," he said. That solved Jo's problem; he headed for the tree.

Then Bl pointed to Ra, and to another tree. "Take." Ra went off, with Fa going along.

Then Hu, and a third tree. There was a mature female with a child of about Be's age. Hu went there, and Be followed him. He heard Bl speak the names of Vk and It, behind him. Hu knew that Bl was assigning the other males to other females; there was one for each. They were sharing, again, in a way that only smart Bl could have devised.

Hu did not know what he would do with his female, for the prospect of copulation became daunting as he considered it, but at least he would get to know her. He saw her standing on one branch, and holding onto the one above. Her child stood similarly between two smaller branches. That was why these trees were good; they provided comfortable support as well as fruit.

Hu hoisted himself into the tree. Be followed closely. They faced the woman and her daughter. The child cringed, fearing she would be killed. The woman gazed stolidly, not opposing what was to be. She was only a little smaller than Hu, because he was far from full grown for a male, and small for his age.

Hu touched himself. "Hu," he said. He touched Be. "Be. Kin." There were words for individuals, and words for threats, such as hyena or lion, and words for relationships, such a friend, foe, and kin. But he wasn't sure that the people of this forest used the same words.

The woman touched herself. "Ll," she said, naming herself. Then her daughter: Le.

Be extended her hand to Le. The other paused, then touched it. They would be friends.

Hu still hesitated. What did this female expect of him? He was obviously not a dominant male.

Ll glanced at the two children, who were already playing a game of finger tag, trying to see who could touch the other's forefinger. Each held her other arm at the elbow, so that it could move only from that anchor. When one tagged the other, it changed over, and the other tried to tag the one. All children played it endlessly.

Then Ll turned on the branch, bending down to grip the trunk of the tree, presenting him with her bright bare rump. She had accepted him for mating.

Hu had not allowed himself to think this far ahead. He had smelled grown foreign females on occasion and gotten the hankering to mate with them, but they had always been protected by their dominant males. Mating was one thing; getting killed was another. Now there was no big male to prevent it. But was Hu ready?

Then abruptly the mature female scent of her struck him with new force, stirring his sexual response. He gripped her body from behind and his loin did what it knew to do, merging with hers. There was an explosion of joy from his groin, that spread out through his body, making it almost seem to float. He felt pleasantly dizzy, and hot, and out of breath. Never before had he felt so good, so swiftly. The few young females he had tried this with had lacked the smell and color of maturity, so that the act was more game than breeding. What a difference!

It was over in a moment, but it had been a remarkable experience. His life had changed. Yet little else had. Be and Le still played their game of tag finger on the adjacent branch, not concerned with the process of mating.

Ll turned to face him again, gazing appraisingly at him. She had accepted him, and he had accepted her, and her child lived. So it would be. Hu realized that she had done it to protect her daughter. Had he been going to kill the child, he should have done it before mating. Now he was bound to let Le alone. Which he was glad to do. In fact, he was relieved about that as well as about the sexual matter.

He looked across to the adjacent trees. He saw that Jo and Bl had done the same thing, the one surely guided by the other. No children had been killed. Ra had simply joined his female, being too young to really mate. The other youths had similarly abstained, but remained with their females. A curiously fragmented yet united band was emerging, with no single dominant male.

But the grove could not sustain this number of people. They would have to find another. And of course there was no other available. In fact, some other dominant male, seeing no similarly powerful male here, was apt to come to take the females for himself. They would have to fight him, and the next, and they might not be as lucky in the fray again.

Bl had figured this out first. He knew they had to move, and soon. He conveyed this to Jo, who did not understand the rationale but was amenable. They dropped to the ground, each youth with his new family, and followed Jo's lead to the grassy plain beyond the verge of the forest.

And there was Bb's band, evidently following their trail. It was still larger than their own, in terms of males, and in any event neither Hu nor the others were eager to fight. They had problems enough already. So they moved on, and the other band didn't follow. It was too interested in taking over the deserted grove.

But no matter how far they went, no open forest appeared. All the other groves were occupied. They couldn't even get trees to camp in for the night. Or food; there was nothing but grass visible on the plain.

Hu looked more closely, and found some colored stems. Be and Le joined him, eagerly digging out the tubers. They weren't the same kind as before, but they would do. Ll joined the others, tasting one tuber. Soon everyone was scrambling to get the roots they located. It wasn't a great meal, but it was better than nothing. Hu realized that it couldn't have been done without his understanding about the colored stems. But he wished he could have found something better to eat.

Meanwhile Bl pondered and came up with something. They would make a tree formation on the plain, with the women and children in the high center and the men around the low outside. No animal could attack without first encountering a man. Of course neither Hu nor the other youths felt comfortable on the ground, but they had no choice. Each took his position nearest the woman he had teamed with, and faced outward. Hu saw It and Vk on either side of him, conforming to the array.

But in a moment Ll nudged him. He turned, and she turned, offering her posterior. It was her way of thanking him for the protection. In a moment, compelled by the sight and smell, he was into her and feeling the marvelous pleasure. Then she clasped Le and went to sleep.

Be joined Hu, snuggling close, and again he drew comfort from her support. It would have been lonely indeed without her. The need to protect her gave him courage.

They were lucky. No bad animals came in the night.

In the morning Bl decided that there might be better food out beyond the range of the bands in the groves. Now that they had found that they could survive in the plain, they were free to find that food. So they went directly away from the forest, loping along on all fours, making good progress.

They did find a berry patch. They plunged in, picking and gobbling the sweet berries, most of which were ripe or almost ripe. Beyond the first patch was another, so they went to it and ate their fill. Hu found better berries, which he shared with Be and with Le. They were juicy enough to slake his developing thirst.

Soon Ll approached and offered him sex. Again his body did what it knew, gratifyingly. Then Ll took his handful of berries and ate them. Dazed again by the experience, he was glad to give them up. Sex was a new aspect of his existence, more wonderful than he had ever realized it could be.

At night they camped again, making their pretend tree. This time Bl searched out some stones and piled them near. Hu, remembering how effective stones had been against the hyenas, found some of his own. They might not be very useful in the dark, but he felt safer having them.

On the third day trouble threatened: a herd of elephants. These were huge beasts that no one wanted to approach. They usually didn't bother anyone who wasn't bothering them, but this was not reassuring when there were no trees near to use for escape.

But when they looked back toward their home forest region, there was Bb's band coming after them. Bb must have figured that if one band was able to survive in the field, then others could do it too. And perhaps the other males wanted to take over the females who had joined this band. Now that Hu had discovered the joy of sex, he didn't want to give it up, and he knew that Jo and Bl felt the same.

Bl considered, and made another bold decision: they would go toward strange distant trees they saw on the horizon. None of them had been to such a region, but of course none had been this far out in the endless plain either. They were learning new things. Maybe this time they would find a suitable unoccupied grove.

But the closer the band got to the trees, the less like trees they looked. They seemed to be small hills rising out of the plain. This was not promising. But Bb's band was still following, and the elephants were ranging near, and coming this way, so there was nothing to do but flee.

In two days of inadequate foraging they reached the hills. They turned out to be merely the line of trees growing on the bank of a dry river channel, and most of them were dead. But there were bushes with berries on them, and a few live trees with fruits. The youth It managed to sniff out a damp spot in the riverbed, and when he scratched out the leaves and dirt, water seeped in, so they could drink. Things were looking better.

They rested and feasted again. But then they encountered a lion. Suddenly the entire band was jammed into whatever trees were close. The lion ignored them. It was sated with a recent kill, not hungry, but suddenly they knew they had to get well away from this region. They had to find a safe haven.

There was nowhere to go but down the river channel. If lions came, they could scamper for safety to the dead trees there. Meanwhile they were able to eat some of the berries along the way. Maybe the channel would even lead to more reliable water.

But the channel wended its way slowly through the plain, remaining dry. There were no good trees here. After a while even the dead ones stopped, and there was nothing but grass and bushes. If it weren't for the berries and roots, they would have been entirely desolate.

Yet they still couldn't go back. They could see the pursuing band, and trees would not protect them from that, because the other youths could climb just as readily as their own people could. Their only chance for reprieve would be if they went where the others couldn't find them, or didn't dare go. The most fearsome thing was the barren plain ahead.

So Hu reasoned, and it seemed that Bl did too, because he nudged Jo in the direction of the bad plain. Jo hardly seemed eager, but headed on toward it.

By evening they were still nowhere. The dry river continued interminably. All it offered was a bed strewn with rocks. What use were they, when no bad beasts were attacking?

But there were many shrubs here, rich with their fruits and berries. They were of strange types, but tasted good, and their juice served to slake what thirst Hu and the others had. This was a good place for eating. If only it had more trees, and no frightening plain, it would be ideal.

Behind them the enemy band was relentlessly following. However, the gap between them would not be closed before darkness, and the others would not pursue them in the night.

They made piles of stones to throw, though they wouldn't be much use when no one could see. Still, it was comforting to have the stones ready. They settled down to sleep.

○

Next day they moved on more swiftly, wanting to find water and escape the pursuing band. They made good progress, but their situation didn't seem to change. The riverbed wound through the endless plain, and the band behind followed. However, the distance between them was getting greater. Hu thought it was because the others couldn't forage as fast or well, because his own group was eating most of the ripe berries first. Even so, Hu and the others were hungry; there just weren't enough berries.

They kept moving, day by day, getting used to it. Hu's knuckles had been getting sore from unaccustomed use on the ground, but he was learning to walk more lightly on his front feet. As long as they followed the dry river, they knew they were going somewhere. Maybe it would be a good place. Certainly where they were now was not; they never found enough berries or grubs to properly sustain them, and all of them were getting lean.

The riverbed broadened. The rocks diminished, being covered over by caked mud. That was easier to walk on, but what would they have to throw if a lion or hyena came?

Hu moved out of the channel, to see if there were more rocks there. There weren't; there was nothing but some old sticks. What use were they?

But when they camped again, Hu wanted something ready to throw. So he foraged for sticks, and made a pile of them. Bl noticed that, and did the same. Then the others did too. Wood might not be as good as stone, but it was better than nothing.

In the distance herds of big animals were grazing. They weren't predators, so probably would not bother the travelers, but the absence of protective trees made them nervous again. There was still no water, but It was getting excited, as if he sensed some near.

Next day the caked mud started getting sticky. Below it their toes touched cooler mud. Then there started to be a little water; they were able to find it by digging out the mud and letting it seep into the hole, as It had done before.

But more important was the plain. The grass was being replaced by marsh, and in the marsh were bushes with many berries. Not scattered patches, but a vast expanse: more than they could ever eat. They spread out and feasted. They had not found safety, but they had found food. At the moment, that was enough.

After they were full, they had time to think about things. There was food here, but no hiding place. Hu hated the fearsome wide openness of this region. If only there were some trees!

Bl considered the situation, and made their decision: they would remain here with the food. They all knew that they could not go back the way they had come, and there was nothing but plain ahead. So they made their camp, as before, in the form of a tree, with the males outside.

The enemy band caught up. But it, too, was distracted by the plentiful berries, and its members gorged themselves. So there was no immediate threat from that quarter. Still, part of Hu's concern, which he was sure the others shared, was about that other band. It was best to keep it away. With that in mind, he gathered as many sticks as he could find, and the others did the same.

But the first trouble came from a different direction. A herd of grazing beasts had been moving closer, and one day they came directly toward the two people camps. Several bulls came first. They were huge, with massive flat horns. They were not predators, but they were dangerous.

The great beasts moved on through, glaring menacingly. Hu and the others put down their front feet and loped out of the way. So did the folk of the enemy camp. But one bull, annoyed, turned on that camp. Suddenly it charged, catching one person by surprise. She tried to flee, but was struck by the bull's shoulder as it passed. She screamed and fell, rolling across the bushes. Hu recognized the voice: it was Ss!

The bull turned, searching for her. Ss did not get up and flee; she lay there, whimpering. None of her group went to try to help her. In a moment the bull would trample her, and she would be dead or badly injured.

Hu was in motion before he realized it. "Help!" he cried, making the scream of supplication. He ran three-legged toward Ss and the bull, carrying his stoutest stick with one hand.

In a moment he was there. The bull loomed huge and terrible, about to gore the trembling Ss. Hu lifted to his hind legs, shouted defiance and bashed it on the flank with his stick. The beast seemed not even to feel it. So Hu struck again, this time on the shoulder. Still the bull took no notice. It was intent on Ss, orienting its massive head and horn.

Then there was another person, with another club. It was Bl. He swung his club not at the bull's solid torso, but at one of its legs. This time the bull reacted. The head swung toward Bl.

And a third person was there: Jo. Jo clubbed the beast on the side away from Bl, striking at another leg. The bull made a squeal of rage and turned back—and Hu smashed it on the nose.

He thought that would really enrage the animal. But the bull just stood there a moment, blinking as if confused. Then it stepped forward. Hu threw himself to the side, but the bull was not pursuing him. It walked on to rejoin its herd, having forgotten the three of them.

Hu looked for Ss, to make sure she was safe. But she was gone. She had gotten away while the three of them distracted the bull, and now was back with the enemy band. She had shown no appreciation for their help, though they might have saved her life.

Hu, Bl, and Jo walked back to their own band. Vk and It were standing guard, protecting the group while its dominant males were occupied. The women and children were staring at them. Then Hu realized what they had done: they had attacked and driven off a monster beast, out in the open. They had fought, using their sticks, and won. Just as they had fought and beaten the dominant male, acting together. It was a good feeling.

Indeed, this desperate band of chimps had taken the first step, perhaps literally, toward becoming human. They had used the chimp abilities of standing briefly erect, using crude tools, and coordinating with others of their kind to defend themselves against a menace. Unable to flee or hide, they had stood like men and fought. These were keys to survival on the treeless plain, where they could not otherwise oppose creatures who would attack them or prey upon them. At first such activities were haphazard, but they became routine with repetition. It was necessary to stand erect in order to use weapons effectively, and they had to use weapons because their own teeth and claws could not compare to those of more specialized animals. They stood to fight—and later to move, because it was hard to carry weapons when moving four-footed. Thus the bountiful but exposed garden was the crucible that forged early mankind.

We shall call it the Garden of Eden.

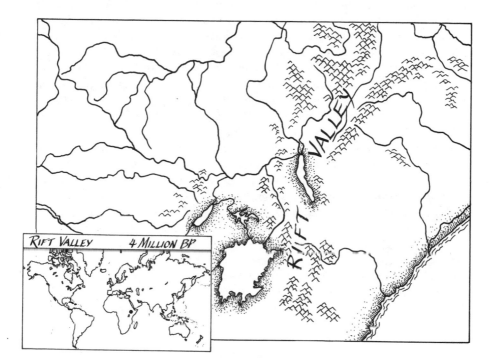

CHAPTER 3

RIFT

Four million years ago the global climate had become warmer and wetter. The forests of central Africa were expanding again—but so were the lakes. The Nile River, perhaps occasionally blocked by lava flows to the north, backed up, and once-tiny Lake Victoria expanded, and the marshy region around it spread. The creatures who had lived in the Garden retreated as the climate changed and their habitat was squeezed. The Flood was not sudden, and neither developed nor retreated in forty days; in fact it was several million years before Lake Victoria achieved its present size. But its effect was nonetheless decisive: mankind had to move on, periodically. This was probably not the Biblical flood, but it is tempting to credit it as the first of a series of water movements that helped define the species. The plain and Garden had shaped mankind considerably, but water was destined to reshape him, in due course.

Mankind's life-style had changed somewhat since he came to the Garden. At first men had to stand to defend themselves by wielding clubs with their hands. They had to keep their clubs with them, because if a lion or other predator came there was not necessarily time to hurry home for weapons. Thus it became easier simply to stay on two feet, and to develop the odd art of striding. In the course of two million years mutation and natural selection fashioned a creature who balanced habitually on his hind feet. Indeed, men grew proficient at this, and learned to extend their range so that they could stride for long distances without putting down their weapons or loads. This led to a crude but effective technique for hunting: They simply cut a wildebeest or other prey creature out of the herd and strode after it until it dropped from fatigue. Then they clubbed it to death. No science, no special skills, just endurance and single-minded pursuit. Thus mankind's legs grew big and strong, with distinctive buttocks, but not his brain. He was Australopithecus, *or the Southern Ape, and he resembled a furry chimp with long legs and short arms. His hands had become adapted to holding sticks rather than climbing trees, and he no longer knuckle walked.*

But with the expansion of the marsh, the "beests" moved elsewhere, and hunting grew harder. Mankind had to find a new hunting and foraging ground. He did it the old-fashioned way: by following the herds. But sometimes this led him to strange new lands.

T HE beests were grazing in the jerky way they had, turning one way and then another with seeming randomness. They were not the easiest creatures to hunt. But one of them represented a lot of good eating, and the berries were thinning. It was time to run one down.

Bil made the signal, identifying the beest to go after. It was a fairly fat young female who was grazing foolishly far from the main herd. She would be easy to start.

Joe hefted his club and walked slowly forward, so as not to spook the herd. It was possible to get fairly close to beests if no sudden motions or noises were made. They were rather stupid animals. But if the herd was spooked, there would be no stopping it. Once they cut out the cow, the herd wouldn't matter, so long as it spooked away and not toward them, but this first part was critical.

Bil followed Joe, moving as carefully, just far enough behind so that the two could close the gap swiftly if they had to. The cow continued to graze, not realizing what was starting. Then Hue moved out, similarly spaced, and Rae after him. Still the cow didn't react.

Vic and Iti followed, silently. After them came the women: young Fae, old Lil, and the others, interspersed by children such as Bee and Lee. They formed a long line that quietly stretched between the beest cow and the herd. The stupid creature still hadn't caught on.

Now the men turned and started walking toward the cow. The women and children did the same, keeping the line intact. They remained silent. They wanted to spook the lone beest, but not the herd, if possible.

At last the cow became aware. She lifted her head, alarmed. She knew these weren't her kind. Her first instinct was to run to rejoin the herd. But there were people between her and the herd, so she hesitated. If she simply charged through the line, they would not be able to stop her, especially if she picked a section with children. But the cow did not know that; all two-legged creatures were the same to her. So she walked away from them, and from the herd. Ideal!

They followed her. She retreated farther, growing more nervous. She could have galloped around the line and they could not have caught her, but she didn't know that either. They weren't charging at her, or making noise, or even moving very quickly; they were just advancing slowly and silently. So she retreated at the same rate.

By the time the beest realized that she was getting well away from the herd, it was almost too late, for the herd was moving in another direction, not liking this strange line of people any better than the cow did. She could still break into a run and crash through to them, but she still hesitated, and decided to retreat some more.

They followed, at a faster pace. She could spook now; the herd was safely away. But she kept thinking that she could somehow avoid them by taking a few more steps away. That was her undoing.

Soon they had her hurrying away from the herd. She broke into a run, but in the wrong direction: away. They strode after her, maintaining the line, but closing it up somewhat. When the beest finally summoned courage and made ready to charge them, they shouted and waved their arms, changing her mind. So the cow ran away again. She still could have looped around and run by too swiftly for them to intercept, but she just wasn't smart enough to figure that out. So she was doomed.

Hue, though a predator, nevertheless had some sympathy for the prey. He hoped that he would never allow himself to be maneuvered similarly to his disadvantage. He would try to take the necessary forceful action, despite his fear, if he thought that he were being herded where he did not want to go.

Now the chase was on in earnest. The big marsh had filled up much of their hunting ground, but there was hilly country ahead, and this was where the beest fled. The band had not yet explored that region, but the chances were that if the cow went there, there were no lions nearby. In any event, lions seldom advanced on a full band of people; they preferred to hunt down solitary animals, exactly as the band was doing now. So it was probably safe enough, and if it wasn't, well, it wouldn't be the first time they had fought such a creature. They never did it by choice, because the lion well might kill one of them before they beat it off, but enough men with clubs could sometimes make a single lion retreat.

The beest had lost the smell of the herd, and no longer knew where she was going. She wouldn't turn now; she would just keep going straight ahead, trying to leave them behind. And she could do so, for a while—but they would keep following her spoor, and would catch up in time. All it required was patience and good legs.

As the day passed, the terrain became irregular, with ridges and valleys. There were even some trees—and some berry patches. The women and children broke off to feed on these, and that was all right, because the full band was no longer needed to chase the beest.

In fact now another aspect of the hunt developed. The women not only fed themselves, they picked extra berries and put them in baglike patches of animal hide they carried. Then, when darkness came and the men had to halt the pursuit, they brought these bags to the men so they could eat without leaving the trail. Lil brought Hue a nice meal of berries, then gave him sex before joining the spot camp and going to sleep.

Hue realized something he perhaps should have noticed before: though Lil indulged him in sex as always, she was not in heat, and had not been for some time. Now her body was thickening, and she seemed to tire more readily than usual. She was old, of course, but he thought it was more than that. She was carrying a new baby.

He pondered that as he sought sleep, and concluded that it was time to find a new mate. A man normally had several. It was a sign of maturity. But he had no particular prospects in mind, and the matter wasn't urgent.

❂

In the morning the men moved out early, leaving the women and children behind. The men had to maintain the pursuit of the beest, giving her no time to rest by day, while the women foraged so as to sustain the men during the hunt.

They soon spied the cow, who had simply lain down to sleep when the pursuit seemed to stop. It had been safe to let her be, because her kind had no real initiative. Individual beests moved when the herd did, or to find better grazing, or to avoid threats. Otherwise they slept.

They closed on her, and she lurched up and away, still being driven from the original herd. She fled into the hills, not pausing to nibble grass, and they followed. Their striding was slower than the beest's running, but it was constant. The cow could not rest.

Hue looked around at the landscape as he moved, maintaining his place in the line. He was used to hunting on the plain, while the women foraged in the garden regions. These hills were eerie. Now he saw greater hills beyond them, with steep slopes, and clouds shrouding their tops. His people had seen a lot of clouds recently, with many days of heavy rain. The water had coursed across the land and into the lake, and the lake had grown, encroaching on the garden and their hunting range. Between rains the water ebbed away, but left muck. So at last they had had to search for new land, and that had taken them to this weird hilly country. Others disliked it, but Hue was intrigued. He wanted to explore those strangely steep slopes, afraid they would be gone before he had the chance. He almost seemed to remember terrain like this, though it must have been a dream.

But the hunt came first. They had not had solid meat for many days, and they were hungry for it. Berries were food for women and children; a man needed flesh. However, the beest was heading straight into the hills, so he would get to see some of them anyway.

All day they chased the cow, penetrating deeper into the alien territory. The hunt was going well. But there was one disturbing thing. They saw traces of their own kind. Was there another band in the region? There were old footprints near a berry patch, and the ripest berries were few, as if it had been well picked over a few days before. Who had been foraging here?

Yet they saw no actual people, and continued the hunt. The women spread out to find other patches. By dusk the beest seemed to be tiring; the next day should finish the hunt.

There was a good grove of trees on the slope. This provided them the rare luxury of safe sleep off the ground. Lil joined Hue in a large tree, with Bee and Lee sharing another branch. Rae and his sister Fae were in the next tree over. The feeling of security was wonderful.

Next day was mixed. They entered a broad valley with a small lake, surrounded by impressive hills. The beest was definitely tiring, having had no daytime rest or grazing; she staggered as she fled the line, and they were closing the gap. Soon they would make their final run, catching her and clubbing her to death. But here too the berry patches had all been picked over, forcing the women and children to go far afield in their foraging. Someone had definitely been here.

Bil looked at Hue. He was considering when it would be time to make the kill. Hue nodded; it could be any time, if the cow did not show any special reserve of strength. Soon Bil would signal Joe, and they would break into their finishing run.

There was a scream. Hue turned his head immediately, recognizing it: Lil. She was across the valley, by a berry patch, with Bee and Lee and another female. And—two strangers were near them.

Ordinarily Hue would go to the support of his woman, in the fashion of any male. But with the hunt so near to the finish, he hesitated. He wanted to be in on the kill. Lil and the others should simply run from the strangers, who probably wouldn't pursue them. This simply meant that the others had found the patch first, and were driving off intruders.

Then the other woman screamed. Rae jumped. That was his twin sister Fae. The strangers were grabbing her! They were going to hurt her, or rape her, or haul her away to join their band. Or all three. Lil and the children would not be able to fight them off.

Hue and Rae looked at Bil. Bil looked at Joe, then made his decision. "Go!" he grunted. He thought the remaining men could finish the hunt on their own.

Hue and Rae screamed challenges and ran across the valley. Now they were breathing hard. Striding tired a person slowly; running tired him quickly. But they could not let Fae, who was just coming into nubility, be stolen from the band. Mature women were too valuable.

The strangers heard the screams. They retreated, one of them hauling Fae along with him. She was struggling, but the strange male opened his jaws and bared his teeth warningly, and she was cowed. It was the nature of women to obey men, even strangers, because if they didn't they got chomped, and whatever they feared happened anyway. However, when they were together in a band, they could assert themselves to some degree, and things did not always go the male's way. So they were not eager to be taken into new bands.

By the time Hue and Rae reached the patch, the strangers were gone. But Lil and the children were there. "Bub!" Lil cried. "Sis!"

So this was that band! Somehow Bub and his spiteful sister always seemed to turn up at the worst times. Relations had been bad, because Bub kept trying to poach game in territory that wasn't his. Now they had hold of Fae, and her fate would not be kind if she weren't promptly rescued.

So they ran on after Fae and her abductors. It should be possible to catch them. Meanwhile the children were running across the valley to tell the others what was happening. Lil, wiser in the ways of things, slowly followed Hue.

The trail was easy to follow; the grass was pressed down and the ground scuffed in places. It led around a knoll to a thin forest. The trees were mostly saplings, not suitable for climbing, and there was a small stream.

Hue, always curious, looked around as he ran. Though the trees were small, it was not possible to see all the way through the forest. The irregular folds of land also hid much of the terrain from immediate view. Beyond, the enormous mountains seemed suddenly close. This was a nervous region, with too much hidden, compared to the open plain. Hue would be happy to explore it at leisure, but right now he didn't trust it at all. He liked to be able to see clearly to the horizon, in case there was a bad animal lurking.

There was a cry ahead. That was Fae again, by the stream; she was trying to get away, and Bub was hitting her with his closed hand, hurting her.

Rae reacted as if struck himself. But Hue was more cautious. It was almost as if Bub were trying to make Fae cry out, to attract attention. There should be other members of Bub's band nearby. This could be an ambush.

He caught Rae's arm, attracting his attention. "Danger!" he said, gesturing around at the too-close scenery. Rae understood, and controlled his impulse to go immediately to the aid of his sister. They slowed, and watched, looking for signs of others in hiding. They waited, not approaching, though Fae was taking a beating. It was a difficult thing to do, but they knew how devious the enemy band members were; they could have snatched Fae deliberately, to lure other members of the band into a trap where they could be pounced on and killed. Bub could readily have raped Fae and left her before other members of her band got there; instead he was making her hurt. Yet though Hue strained to hear the breathing or motions of the ambushers, he could not; his acute hearing was not good enough in this situation.

Then Bil and Joe ran up, followed by other males of the home band. Bill, too, must have realized that there was something suspicious about this, and acted. The tired beest would keep; they could run her down after handling this attack on one of their females.

They spread out, circling the three by the stream. They had numbers, now; they could flush out ambushers.

Bub saw them. He made a cry of rage and insult, and fled up the stream. Sis followed. Fae was left alone.

Hue was the closest to her. He ran to her, and she jumped into his arms, almost like a child. He hugged her close, reassuring her. He had always been somewhat protective toward her, for she was his friend's sister, and a nice person. Now he had grown huge compared to her, and was better able to protect her.

Rae glanced at them, and ran on. He wanted to get Bub. Joe and Bil and the others also ran on. There was no ambush, but they could still get the bad pair, kill Bub, and do to Sis what Bub had meant to do to Fae. For Sis, despite her meanness, was an interesting female. They would probably have to hold her down to stop her from biting and clawing, the first few times.

Fae's embrace became more intimate. She spread her legs, offering him sex from the front. She had the smell of a woman. Hue had not had this in mind, but now that she brought it up, he realized that he was interested. He had always liked her, and had enjoyed playing with her when they both had been children. Sex was another kind of game, and the idea of doing it with a longtime friend appealed. She did not care that he wielded his club with the wrong hand.

So he bore her down to the ground and drove into her tight body, experiencing phenomenal fulfillment. She moved with him, eager to oblige and to experience, and derived the same satisfaction he did. No biting or clawing here! Then she hugged him again, possessively, and he realized that he had found his second mate.

The others returned. Bub and Sis had eluded them, knowing this odd terrain better. They were frustrated, but satisfied that they had rescued Fae and driven off the attackers. It was time to return to the interrupted hunt.

Rae paused, knowing by the smell what had happened between his friend and his sister. He saw Fae standing very close to Hue, almost touching him, happy. Then he shrugged and moved on, accepting the situation.

They moved as a group back the way they had come. Fae stayed right with Hue throughout. When they returned to the berry patch, where Bee and Lee waited, the two children stared, immediately knowing the changed relationship. Then they too shrugged; these things happened.

Joe screamed with outrage. Everyone looked. There on the far side of the valley was a band of strangers consuming the beest. They had run down the prey the home band had worn out, and killed her, while Hue and the others were rescuing Fae. Now they were hacking and tearing off the most available portions, to carry away for slow consumption elsewhere.

The home band charged in a mass, eager to fight the interlopers. But it took time to cross the valley, and in that time the strangers were busily eating. Finally they retreated, as they were about to be caught, leaving the carcass to the home band. But the best parts of it were gone.

Hue realized what had happened. There had been no ambush. Bub and Sis had deliberately lured Hue, Rae, and the other males away from the chase, and kept them occupied while their other band members poached the cow. It was a marvel of sneakiness. Now the home band was left with the leavings, as if they had come across carrion. It was an insult, but there was nothing to be done. At least they had a good deal of solid meat remaining. All of them came to eat, their anger fading along with their hunger.

That night Fae joined Hue in his tree, bringing him further novelty of new sex and attention. Lil did not object; it was not her nature or her place. A man could have as many mates as he could govern, and Fae had always been nice to the children. Perhaps Lil was satisfied to avoid sex for a while. They would get along.

Sex among chimpanzees is frequent and universal; each member of a band may do it on an hourly basis, and every male has access to every female with the possible exception of his mother. Females can be quite forward about it, approaching males, giving them sex, then taking food from them. The competition for procreation occurs mostly in the testicles, which grow large and produce enormous quantities of sperm, so as to displace the sperm of rivals, rather than displacing the rivals themselves. It is a way of facilitating group social relations: a male did not fight with a female with whom he shared sex. Early humans may have followed that pattern, or shifted to the harem pattern, with dominant males reserving a number of females to themselves. Monogamy was a concept whose time had probably not yet come. But perhaps within the harem, man and women were reasonably loyal to one another, once they had made their choices, as they are today. Sex was not a matter of great concern, as long as it was among friends.

Lake Victoria probably expanded and contracted many times as the local climate shifted, causing the people living there to move back and forth more than they might have chosen. It is not surprising that some bands left it to range southeast through the neighboring geography. Hue and his friends did not realize it, but they had discovered a section of the Eastern Rift Valley, whose volcanic soil made for rich plant life, and therefore rich animal life. They left their footprints and their bones there, all the way north to the Afar Triangle. The great Rift system, including the Lake Victoria basin in its center, was the crucible that forged man. But it had not yet completed the job.

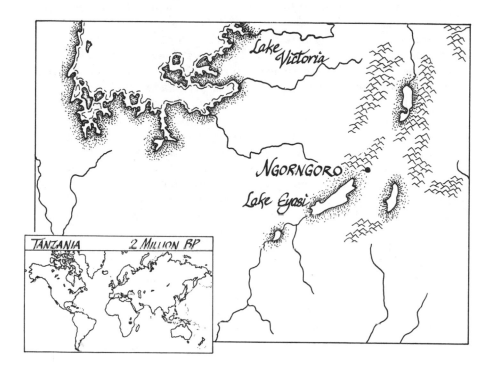

CHAPTER 4

FIRE

By two million years ago, mankind was using stone tools. He had always used clubs, which did not survive as fossils, and stones, which have not been recognized as tools or weapons because they were not modified. He simply threw them as they were. But now Homo habilis, *Handy Man, was pounding rocks into specialized shapes, and so was able to attract the notice of archaeologists. He was the gracile variant, competing with the robust variants of the Southern Ape for a million years.*

Several significant things were occurring at this time, and they may be related. The ice ages were in progress, mankind was using the hand axe, and his

*brain was expanding. So, probably, was his vocabulary. He was getting less like
a two-footed animal.*

BEE and Lee were almost like twins, always close together though they
weren't related. They were still children, but the next two or three
years would see them become women, and then things would change. They
didn't care. They were getting almost as curious about things as Hue, and
loved helping him explore new places. Lil was tolerant; after all, she had her
new baby, Hue's son, to keep her occupied. Hue had named him Jae.

So now the two girls raced ahead, seeking stones, while Hue followed as
closely as was feasible. Then came Lil carrying Jae, and Fae. Other
members of the band were foraging in other directions, not caring to go any
farther toward the huge smoking mountain than they had to. So it was just
Hue's family for this excursion. They would return to the band by nightfall.

The stones they sought were special: the kind that could be chipped to
form sharp edges. Vik had a touch with such stone; he could pound it into a
perfect hand axe. Every man in the band had his own axe, together with
lesser tools, but they wanted to have more, because there was a special use
for extras. The axe was the most versatile of weapons, and its use was
carefully cultivated.

But fetching suitable stones could be nervous business, because the best
ones were found near the smoking mountains. Those mountains were
dangerous; the band people had seen and heard more than one shoot
smoke and fire from its top, and often enough they dribbled burning red
spittle that flowed down the sides, setting fire to everything it touched, until
finally it settled and slowly cooled and solidified.

There was a scream of discovery. The two girls came running back. Bee
was holding a chunk of rock. "See! See!" she cried. "Tool! Weapon!"

Hue took the rock and turned it over, inspecting it. It was indeed the type
they needed, and would make a good axe. "Yes," he agreed. "Good."

Bee was so pleased with this success that she jumped up and down,
making little squeals of delight. Hue was reminded of Fae when she was that
age, before their father had been killed. Soon enough Bee would be a
woman, and would find someone to mate with. She wouldn't be his little
sister any more. That, oddly, made him sad.

Bee ran back to rejoin Lee. Hue put the stone in his sack. This search was
going well.

They continued on past mixed fields and trees. This was interesting
terrain, with mountains rising right out of the forests, and many clear
regions between.

Lee made an exclamation. Hue investigated. She had found a cave. It
opened into the base of a steep slope. It was fairly wide at the edge, then
narrowed into a dark tunnel. Hue had always been especially intrigued by
caves. He approached it cautiously, sniffing the air. There was no odor of

lion or hyena, and no manure. He peered into the tunnel. His eyes adjusted, and he saw that it wound deep into the ground, like a snake, and was cool inside. He made a sound, "Hoo!" and listened as its diminishing little echoes indicated the depth of the cave. He would have liked to explore it to its end, but he distrusted its darkness, and he had stones to find. So he reluctantly turned away, and resumed the search.

But he complimented Lee on her discovery. "Cave. Good." She clapped her hands together, thrilled.

The trees shrank into shrubs as they approached the big mountain. The hills grew oddly bare, as if recently burned. Hue would have known they were near a fire mountain, even if he hadn't been able to see its steep angry peak ahead.

Suddenly both girls went silent. They were standing on a ridge, looking down at something beyond Hue's line of sight. "What?" he called.

"Stranger," Lee replied.

Hue hurried to join them on the ridge, because strangers could be serious business. Normally they weren't hostile, but caution was essential.

It was a woman and a little boy. She was reasonably young and attractive, but the boy had an ugly red mark on his forehead, as if he had been recently injured. Yet he seemed healthy, so it must be a scar or a spirit mark. The woman was standing quite still, as wary of the girls as they were of her.

Hue knew what to do. "Fae!" he called, without moving.

In a moment Fae hurried up. "Trouble?" she asked.

"Stranger," he said, gesturing. "Woman. Fae talk."

Fae nodded. The woman would flee Hue, but might talk with another woman. It was the best way to handle contacts with strangers who might not be hostile. She made her way down the slope toward the strange woman, slowly. The boy, who looked to be about four years old, moved closer to his mother, who still did not move.

Fae stopped at a suitable distance, close enough to talk, not close enough to grab. She pointed to herself. "Fae."

The woman made a similar gesture. "Sue." Then she touched the boy's head. "Blaze."

Fae looked at the boy. "Hurt?"

Sue shook her head. "No." Then she made a gesture of something coming out of her body. "Blaze born scar."

Fae nodded. Then she gestured to Hue on the ridge. "Hue." She made as if to hug someone. "Hue Fae." Then she pointed to her belly. "Baby no."

Sue ventured more trust. "Sue lost. Stranger hurt. Flee. Home—" She made a gesture of bewilderment.

By this time Lil had caught up. Hue filled her in. "Stranger. Woman. Lost."

Lil went down the slope toward Fae and Sue. Fae meanwhile explained: "Lil. Hue Lil. Son Jae." And to Lil: "Sue. Son Blaze."

"Lost," Sue repeated. "Home?" Again she signaled confusion.

Lil looked at Fae, and the two nodded. They would try to help Sue find her home band. She was friendly, so should be helped, but they didn't want Hue to take her as another mate. Two mates, they felt, was enough for him. Of course he could overrule them.

But Hue had learned that women could be taciturn when crossed. He could discover urine or red ants in the food they brought him, and sex could become scarce. He could safely take another mate only with the concurrence of the existing mates. He would not seek to take the strange woman.

They were aware of his decision even as he made it. Women were uncannily sharp, that way. Even the stranger woman understood. She looked relieved. Had he demanded sex from her, none of them would have stopped him, but none of them would have liked the decision. Sex was normally reserved for more significant commitments, unless a person's usual mates were not around when the inclination came.

Now he descended the slope, flanked by the two girls. Sue made a ritual obeisance, bending down and presenting her rear to him, for he was a dominant male. He simply said, "No," freeing her of the obligation, completing the ritual. Sex was also a special social commitment, as people who shared sex did not fight. The offer and turndown were lesser commitments, suggesting an amicable temporary association. "Truce." That wasn't strictly applicable, because there was no question of combat here, but it was the way those of different bands agreed not to fight for a time.

"Truce," Sue agreed, relaxing.

Hue questioned Sue about the identity of her band. "Erl," she said, naming its dominant male.

Erl. He was all right. Joe's band had met Erl's band once on the range during a hunt, and agreed to go to opposite sides of the range so as not to interfere with each other's pursuits. Each band had honored the agreement, and each remembered that the other was being true. Hue had a notion where that band was foraging, not far from here. He could look for good stones as readily in that direction as any other. He pointed the way, and they began to move.

Little Blaze, reassured, was soon running ahead with Bee and Lee, who liked having a "little brother" to watch out for. Blaze, it soon was evident, was fascinated by fire. He kept looking toward the giant mountain cone that was smoking, as if wishing to go there and climb its slope. Hue knew the feeling; he was quite curious about that mountain himself. It was the biggest of its type he had seen. But it was never possible to know when such a mountain might get angrier than usual and spew out fire and dangerous burning rocks.

Indeed, the very thought of that chance seemed to alert the mountain, for it rumbled. Hue had been near such a mountain once before when it did that. He had gotten well away in a hurry—and nothing more had come of it. But if he hadn't done so, what might the mountain have done? It was only natural to assume that mountains, like creatures, had their concerns, and some did not like intruders in their territories. But after that there was nothing, so Hue wasn't concerned.

The children found something. It was another fine stone. They were more plentiful near the fire mountain, which was why Hue had come here to search. This one had even fractured of its own accord, so that it had one fine flat face. It was almost good enough for an axe as it was, though of course Vik would improve it. Hue added it to his bag. Stone hunting with these children was turning out to be good; they scampered into nooks he would not have bothered with, and found things for him.

There was a cry from ahead. This time it was little Blaze. He came running back to his mother, frightened. What had he seen?

Lee came back, clarifying it: "Stranger. Man woman."

Trouble, perhaps. Hue called back the children and strode ahead. This must be the stranger who had threatened Sue. If it was a man from his own band, he would explain, and there would be no more threat, because Sue was now under his protection. But if it was a foreign band—

The figures came into view. Hue stiffened. "Bub!" he cried, not at all pleased.

"Hue," the other man retorted. He spread his arms to indicate the region. "Bub land. Flee."

He was claiming this territory, and demanding that Hue go. But Hue knew that no band possessed this region. Bub was looking for axe stones, just as Hue was, and had no proprietary rights. So Hue challenged this. "No."

Sis appeared. She seemed never to be far from her brother, who was perhaps also her mate. She recognized Hue and grimaced. "Kill," she said. She always seemed to have a grudge against Hue, though he had once saved her from injury or death. It was too bad, in a way, because she was a well-formed woman he might otherwise have had an interest in.

Bub drew his axe and advanced. He held the weapon by its rounded base, with the chipped point forward. He could do real damage with that.

But Hue brought out the half-chipped stone. He hefted it, turning it sideways in his wrong hand. Bub saw that and laughed.

Then Hue threw the stone. It flew toward Bub's head. Sis cried out with alarm. Bub jumped to the side, avoiding it. But he had been caught by surprise, and had almost been struck. The ragged edge would have injured him, perhaps severely. Hue might use the wrong hand, but his aim was sure.

Hue strode forward, bringing out his second stone. It was clear that his aim would be even better when he got closer, and that Bub would have less chance to avoid the missile. The members of Hue's own band had soon learned that there was nothing funny about his wrong-sided throwing.

Bub reconsidered. He backed away, still holding his weapon, but not throwing it. If he threw it, he would have none, while he didn't know how many Hue had. He never fought when uncertain of victory. Hue continued to advance, holding the stone.

Bub circled behind a curved slope and disappeared. Hue followed, alert for any trick. But as he rounded the curve, he saw that Bub was now far away, leaving the region to Hue.

Hue went to recover his first stone. It was undamaged. It was imperfect for throwing, but had it been finished and balanced, he could have thrown it more accurately. Vik knew how to make them good for throwing, and all of the members of his band could bring down animals with their axes, if they got close enough. That was why Hue had not been afraid of the larger man. Bub would never have gotten the chance to strike with his axe; he would have been injured or killed by the stone before he got close enough. For Hue had used only the imperfect stones; he had held his good one in reserve.

The others came up. "Stranger hurt," Sue said, pointing where Bub had gone.

So that was the one who had frightened her, and made her run so that she had gotten lost. Bub had probably wanted to add her to his collection, after killing her son. No wonder she had fled with Blaze. Women could get very upset when their children were threatened.

They moved on. Blaze, going toward the big mountain until his mother called him back, found another nice stone. He brought it to Hue with a smile, an offering, and Hue accepted it. They were getting along well.

Then the mountain rumbled again, louder and harder. The ground shook. This was more serious. They needed to find Sue's tribe soon, and get away from here. Hue had three good stones, and those would keep Vik busy for some time, because chipping them correctly was no easy job.

But this time the mountain did not relent. It rumbled again, and smoke came from it—not from the top, but from the side. It was acting as if it were angry enough to do something. It was best to get away from it.

The way ahead was unclear. Hu did not want to risk getting lost in unfamiliar terrain. It was better to go back the way they had come, with the route clear.

Sue and Blaze came with them, knowing the problem and not wanting to be left alone. They could find their band after getting safely away from the nasty mountain.

But the mountain did not want to let them go. It rumbled almost continuously. Then it roared. There were undertones in that sound that perhaps only Hue could hear, but the menace was clear to them all.

They paused in their flight to look back at it. But all they could see was a boiling pile of smoke. Within that smoke the mountain was roaring with deafening volume, not yet satisfied.

They needed no further warning. They fled from it as fast as they could run.

The sky darkened as the smoke spread out. A terrible smell came. The ground shuddered so violently it was hard for them to keep their footing. Gravel slid down a nearby slope.

Hue realized that they weren't going to get away from the mountain. It was reaching out too fast. Already things were falling around them, glowing rocks and choking dust. If any of those rocks hit them—

"Cave!" Fae cried. "Hide!"

Good idea. "Cave," Hue agreed. It was on their way and not far distant.

They ran for it. More glowing things rained down. The leaves of trees began to smoke and burn as the rocks struck them. So did patches of grass in the glades.

They saw the cave. It faced away from the mountain, and Hue was glad of that. They ran into it, taking shelter from the falling fires. There was room for all of them.

Then two more figures ran in. Bub and Sis!

Hue grabbed his axe, ready to defend their place of safety. He would not have the advantage in such close quarters, but he couldn't let Bub and his savage sister just take over. Bub, seeing that as he reached the cave, put his hand on his own axe. So did Sis, who had a small but sharp stone, the kind used to cut meat from bone.

Blaze, recognizing him, cried and shrank toward his mother. Bee and Lee crowded back toward the tunnel with Lil, who held her baby tightly. But Fae stepped close beside Hue, snarling, holding another flesh-cutting stone. She hated Bub, who had once tried to abduct her, and meant to help Hue fight. This was unusual behavior in a woman, but not unknown. Considering that Sis often helped her brother fight, this was just as well. Hue would surely lose if both Bub and Sis attacked him.

"No!" Sis cried, surprisingly. "Fight no."

Both men looked at her, startled. So did Fae.

"Cave Hue," she said. "Bub Sis no."

She was correct. Hue and his party had taken this cave first. But since when had Bub and Sis ever honored such conventions? They had never cared much about anything except power and opportunity.

Bub looked out onto the landscape. Fire stones were falling more thickly, denting the ground and making the grass burn. There was no retreat that way. He would rather fight.

Then Hue saw that Bee and Lee had found sticks and come to stand behind Fae. They were small, but not as small as they once had been, and they knew how to club small animals. They could indeed help enough to enable Hue to prevail. Sis, more devious than her brother, had seen that the outcome of this fight was in doubt.

"Truce," Sis said, saying a word she seldom did.

But Hue knew better than to trust either of them. "No."

She considered just a moment. Then she tried another ploy. "Sex."

Both Hue and Bub looked at her, dismayed. Enemies did not engage in sex, unless it was rape, and there would be a fight to the death here before there could be any rape.

Sis put down her stone. "Hue Sis sex," she said. "Truce." She took a step toward Hue, her arms spread, hands open. She smiled, suggesting that she would enjoy it. Was it possible that her seeming grudge had masked desire? So that her brother wouldn't suspect her of disloyalty? No, more likely she was simply trying to deceive Hue about her feeling, to make him agree to it.

Bub looked at her, appalled. "No."

Fae echoed the sentiment. "Sex no." The last thing she wanted was such a connection between her mate and her enemy.

"Fight," Bub said, though without force.

Sis gazed back at him without flinching. "Bub Fae sex."

Now Hue was appalled. "Fight," he said, agreeing with Bub.

But Fae was coming to understand what Sis was proposing. Those who had sex together did not fight. Even enemies could make a truce by sharing sex. They would not fight until another day. Not even an untrustworthy person would violate that, because it went deeper than agreements. It was the way it was. Sis was offering a way for them to share this cave without fighting.

Still Hue and Bub demurred, not wishing such a truce. They had been enemies too long. They did not want to be even temporary, tacit friends.

Sis took another step toward Hue. She was very close, and the woman smell of her was strong. He found himself tempted. He had always hated her for her bad ways, yet always also been intrigued by her healthy body. He couldn't help reacting.

She took one more step, now almost touching him. She reached up to take his hand, the one with the axe. She brought it down and set the stone against her throat. She let go. He could cut her and kill her with one stroke. She had offered her life.

And of course he couldn't take it. Slowly he moved his hand, taking the knife away, dropping it to the ground.

Bub, seeing him disarmed, started to come forward. But Fae moved faster, dropping her own stone, intercepting him. Bub had always been interested in her, but she had never wanted him. Now she was offering. He hesitated, then dropped his axe. He knew this was the only likely way he would ever have her, and her acquiescence was better than rape.

"Sis want," she said, drawing Hue down to the ground with her. He realized with a shock that she was doing this not merely as a way to establish a useful truce, but because she desired him personally. He had not known she felt that way, but the smell of her suggested it was true. She had the heat of unfeigned passion.

Then it was sex, the two couples side by side, banging into each other, not caring. Hue's long-suppressed passion for Sis burst forth, and was met by her similar passion. He had never had sex like this! Their prior animosity actually enhanced it. If the grudge had been real at all; now it seemed more likely that Sis really had appreciated the favor he had done her long ago.

It was soon done. Hue looked up as they lay embraced, and saw the children looking down, interested in the details. Even little Blaze.

Embarrassed, Hue disengaged and got to his feet. Sis followed, not concealing her satisfaction.

Bub and Fae were also getting up. Fae showed no sign of satisfaction. She had done what she had to do. But it was clear that Bub was pleased. He didn't care whether she liked it, only that she cooperate. That much she had done.

Bub had desired Fae, and Sis had desired Hue. Both had gotten what they wanted, in this unlikely situation. Yet Hue could not hold it against them, because Sis had given him an experience like none other. It was surely better than combat would have been, though he still didn't like Fae's participation.

Now they were in truce. They picked up their weapons and put them away. Then they gazed out into the fire storm.

The rocks and ashes were piling on the ground. All the grass had burned away, and the nearby trees were still smoldering. The air was choked with smoke. They needed to get away from it.

They made their way into the dark recess. The women were afraid, so the men did it, with Sis and Fae close behind. Neither Hue nor Bub wanted close association with the other, but they were bound to the truce, as occasional words from the women reminded them. They picked up their stone axes and stepped cautiously into the darkness.

It was a disappointment. Not far beyond the wan light the walls closed up, leaving only small apertures they couldn't use. There was no good air here. Only a pool of water they could feel with their feet. It wasn't flowing, so surely wasn't good to drink.

But they had to have good air. All of them were coughing now, as the fumes increased. There was a strange, threatening sound outside. This was surprising, because the rain of fire was abating. What was making that sound?

Hue knew he should go outside and check. But there was still some ash falling, and he didn't want to leave the others alone in the cave with Bub. The truce existed, but was uneasy.

Sis solved that. "Hue Bub," she said, pointing out. Fae saw the logic and agreed.

That made sense. If both of them went out, neither could bother the women.

So they took their bags and spread out the hides as protection, covering their heads and shoulders. Holding their axes, they went out together.

They had to step carefully, because the fallen stones and ashes were still hot. Smoke was everywhere, especially above, making dusk of midday. But it was somewhat easier to breathe out here.

They went toward the sound, which was getting louder. It was coming from the other side of the hill, in the direction of the fire mountain. Hue was frightened, but would not show it in the presence of his enemy.

They crested a small ridge. Bub made a cry. "Fire!"

Hue looked. There in the valley between slopes was a river of fire. The trees and shrubs by its banks burst into flame when touched and soon were swept under. Hue had never seen anything like it, and was sure Bub hadn't either.

It was coursing toward them. Soon it would flow over this low ridge and on around and into the cave.

They turned as one and ran back the way they had come. They had to get the others out immediately.

"Run!" Hue called as they came into sight of the cave.

Fae and Sis peered out into the gloom, not understanding. The stones had stopped falling from the sky, but the women did not trust that. They thought the cave was the safest place.

"Run!" Bub cried, reaching the cave and hauling on Fae's arm so that she stumbled out. She made an exclamation of displeasure and fear, thinking he was trying to abduct her again.

Hue arrived opposite Sis and did the same to her. She was similarly confused, but she moved as he hauled, trying to step into him. He pushed her on out, though aware of her wicked appeal despite their recent mating. Then he moved on in. "Run! Run! Fire!" He hustled Lil and the children forward and out.

Meanwhile Bub reached Sue and Blaze. They shrank away from him, terrified. Then they ran after Hue.

The woman and children were milling around before the cave, confused. They did not know where they should run, or where. They thought the fire was still in the sky.

Hue got a notion. "Bee Lee!" he cried, making a come here gesture. But he was already moving back toward the low ridge, so they had to run to catch up.

He led them to the ridge, and pointed. The flowing fire was much closer now; he could feel its heat. They looked, saw it, and gasped together. Now they knew what they had to run from.

Meanwhile Bub was herding the remaining group as if it were so many grazing animals. They were moving up the slope to the side.

Bee and Lee hastened to join them. "Fire!" they cried. "Run!" The others reacted to the children's words better than to the male's words.

Then the fireflow reached the ridge. It paused, blocked for a moment, forming a pool. Then it surged on over in a thin bright stream. The very ground seemed to catch fire as the liquid flame crossed it. Acrid smoke puffed up.

Higher on the slope, they paused to look back. The fire water was swirling into the cave, scintillating ferociously. The inner wall turned bright from the light of the fire. There was a loud sizzle as the fire found the water, and a cloud of vapor puffed out. They watched, fascinated. Now they knew it would not have been good to stay in the cave.

They moved on, staying on the elevated slope. The air got better as they left the flowing fire behind. But they could hear the fire hissing along below, destroying any trees that hadn't already been burned by the flying hot stones.

Then they spied other people climbing the slope. None of the valleys were safe. Would this mean more trouble? There were several big males, who did not look friendly.

Sue cried out, happily. These were folk from her band. She ran toward them, then paused, ran back to Hue, touched his hand, and ran off again with Blaze. She had thanked him for helping her find them.

This meant that there would be no trouble, because Sue had identified Hue as a friend. The surly males paused, not attacking, letting Hue and those with him go on up the slope. Bub and Sis got the benefit of this, though Sue would not have let them go if they had been alone.

Now Bub and Sis decided to go their own way. Bub lifted a hand in parting, and Sis came over to rub against Hue one more time. She was trying to excite him sexually, so that he would be sorry for her absence. She succeeded. Fae glared. Satisfied, Sis ran to join her brother, and they were gone.

It took time for Hue and the others to find their own band, but they knew where it had been and were able to follow the high slopes to that region. Joe and Bil and the others were there, and glad to see those they had feared lost. There were many embraces of relief and camaraderie. It had ended well, and Hue still had the good new stones.

But somehow his mind lingered on what it shouldn't: his brief association with the enemy woman, Sis. He had two mates already, who were attentive and obliging; why should he desire one who was not available? It was a question he could neither answer nor forget.

The sexuality of mankind was shifting from the practices of the chimps, and constrictions were growing up around it, but it still had a way to go before becoming fully "manlike." It was used to defuse tensions and generate harmony, so that larger groups could assemble amicably. But the heyday of this sort of interaction was perhaps to come with the not deliberately punned Erect man, in the course of the next million years.

The volcano was Mt. Ngorongoro, in present-day Tanzania, in the East Rift southeast of Lake Victoria. It poured out its ash and lava about two million years ago and left a crater a staggering twelve miles wide. Today a complete community of animals lives within that crater, including a pride of lions and a herd of Cape buffalo; the vegetation has grown thickly in that rich volcanic soil. Perhaps this eruption helped form the fertile Serengeti Plain, so hospitable to mankind in the past. This type of event is typical of the Rift, which was formed by the constant upwelling of lava from the deeps.

The hand axe has been a mystery. It survived for two million years, hardly changing, while mankind progressed all the way from chimplike to modern, his already large brain doubling in size. What was the magic in this seemingly clumsy tool? It has been conjectured that the term axe is a misnomer; it was actually a throwing weapon, capable of doing significant damage to any animal it struck. But accurate throwing requires calculation — in fact, calculus, whose rules can be mind-stretchingly complicated to perform on paper. Yet we do it without conscious mental effort, every time we throw and catch a ball. Indeed, we like to try our accuracy in this manner, and many of our most popular physical games are ball games. Today we throw for money or fun, but then we threw for survival. More brain meant greater accuracy, therefore greater success in hunting or combat, so this weapon may have been responsible for boosting brain size. At first. More likely, the axe was simply a remarkably versatile tool, effective for throwing, stabbing, and carving, so its design was a compromise between its various functions. Actually, there were variations, with the point elongated in some, and the axe might be sharpened part way around or all the way around, suggesting specializations we no longer understand.

The brain is perhaps the most versatile organ of the body, and when it grew, it found additional uses for its power. Foremost among these was language. Today communication is vital to civilization itself, and superior ability in this respect brings considerable rewards to both individuals and cultures. But nature cares nothing for potential, and everything for the advantage of the moment. Better communication helped, but perhaps not as much as physical strength and accuracy. So mankind added words to his vocabulary, and his brain grew to accommodate them. This hardly showed in a single generation. Yet in the course of a million years this seemingly slow accretion developed considerable impact. As we shall see.

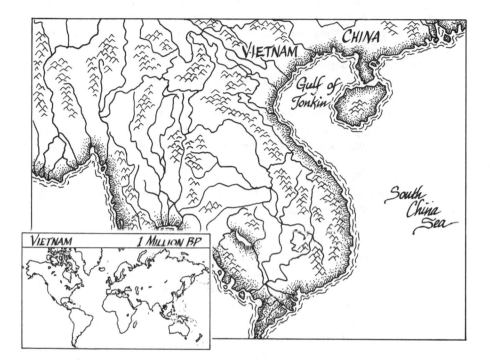

VIETNAM   1 MILLION BP

CHAPTER 5

GIANT

About one million years ago, mankind's then-variant Homo erectus, *Upright Man, found an avenue past the barrier of the Sahara Desert and moved into the continent of Eurasia. He was now close to modern humans in height, and more muscular. Soon enough he spread across the world as it was then available, in the process fragmenting into many subcultures and, in time, subspecies. He was probably somewhat xenophobic, fearing or hating all cultural variants differing in any way from his own. This was actually an asset to the species as a whole, for it promoted more rapid evolution in the small groups, enabling new traits to become established instead of being submerged by the much larger gene pool of the species as a whole.*

Some bands came to a strange region, southeast Asia, where a specialized grass grew very large and useful: bamboo. There they also encountered unusual creatures, such as the panda and the largest ape ever: Gigantopithecus. *This was a cousin of the orangutan standing ten feet tall, whose ancestors diverged from ours perhaps ten million years ago.*

Note: bamboo is a grass, not a tree—but to the people of the time who had migrated recently from forested land, it seemed like a tree.

HUE hefted his bamboo spear. Fae and the other women were grinding grain for gruel, but he was hungry for meat. It had been many days since they had caught any animal of good size. Maybe today they would have success.

Bil gestured. "See print," he said.

Hue and Joe looked, astonished. It looked like a crude human footprint, but it was twice the size of any they had ever seen. What giant had made that?

"Man big," Hue said, awed, making a gesture indicating a height twice theirs. "Hide." His signal indicated retreat from superior force.

Joe disagreed. "Kill," he said, making a thrust with his spear. "Enemy hunt men." He wanted to make a pre-emptive strike, to take out the monster before the monster learned of their existence and came after them.

"Big man smash," Hue pointed out, pantomiming getting struck and hurled back by a more powerful opponent. He didn't want to go up against a man who could surely destroy him with one blow.

They looked at Bil, the smart one. He would decide whether to pursue the monster and try to kill it, or to try to avoid it. "Follow, find," he decided. "Hide, see."

With this both Hue and Joe could agree. They would follow the giant tracks and try to spy on the huge man, keeping themselves hidden so that the man did not see them. Then they would know more about it, and be in a better position to decide.

The trail was not hard to follow, because of the size of the prints. It paralleled the river by which the band of people had camped. Hue noted another disquieting sign: where the tracks went, the bamboo was broken off. The small bamboo trees had been cropped close to the ground, and larger ones higher up. What remained were scattered stalks shorn of twigs and leaves, with teeth marks on the stems. The giant was eating the bamboo—and what he ate was as big in diameter as the spear Hue carried. How could they even hope to prevail against that?

There was a sound ahead. All three men paused in place, alertly focusing on it. Something was there, in the small bamboo by the bank of the river. Something big.

They advanced toward it, low and quiet, using the larger bamboo trees as cover. They came to a thicket and settled in the brush, staring out.

There were several giant apes foraging, the males twice the height of men and many times as massive. They were eating bamboo, breaking it off with their powerful hands and chewing it up with their similarly powerful teeth. Their fur was reddish yellow, or golden, perhaps silvery on their backs. They did not walk erect, but put their arms down so that their knuckles took much of their weight. Even on all fours, their heads were as high as those of men, and much larger. Their mouths were enormous, making the rest of their heads look smaller than they were. Their teeth were truly gigantic.

There was a stir of wind that ruffled those bamboo leaves that were out of range of the creatures.

One of the monstrous males sniffed the air suspiciously. He peered around as if searching for something. Then he stepped directly toward Hue. The giant smelled him! Hue was upwind, and the random gust had carried his odor to the ape.

His mind raced. Should he get up and flee before the thing reached him? But he feared the giant could outrun him. Should he stay in place, hoping the wind faded and the ape lost the smell? But the creature was already so close it could probably see Hue. Should he stand up and fight, trying to drive his spear into the thing's gross belly? That might merely madden it.

Yet the ape did not seem hostile. It was not baring its teeth or growling or waving its fists. It was just walking forward as if curious. So Hue compromised by doing nothing. He remained where he was squatting, unmoving.

The ape sniffed him out. It stood on its hind feet, lifted its torso, put its giant hands on the bamboo shoots masking Hue and snapped them off as if they were twigs. Its muscular power was frightening. But still Hue didn't move, and neither did Joe or Bil. Everything depended on what the monster did.

The ape parted the bamboo stems immediately before Hue, then broke them off and tossed them to the side. It peered down at Hue, an unfinished bamboo stem in its mouth. Like an animal, it seemed to focus on just one thing at a time, so it was forgetting to chew. Yet it looked a great deal like a huge man.

Hue looked up at it, and his gaze met that of the ape. Then the ape reached out with one big hand. It touched Hue's head with one finger, stirring his hair. It was indeed curious—and seemed curiously innocent.

Hue did something that surprised himself. Slowly he lifted one of his own hands. He touched the ape's hand, which dwarfed his. For a moment the two hands were together, like those of a parent and a child.

Then Joe jumped up, a short distance away. "Haaa!" he cried, hurling his spear at the ape. It was deflected by a bamboo shoot, and missed, but it spooked the ape. The creature reared back, then turned and ran four-legged away. The others did the same, and in a moment all of them were gone.

"Why Joe jump?" Hue demanded.

"Ape eat Hue," Joe said, going to recover his spear.

"No. Ape touch head. Hue touch hand. No eat."

"Ape eat bamboo," Bil agreed, joining them. "Chew teeth, no bite teeth."

A grazer of bamboo, Hue realized. Not a predator. The ape was like a panda bear, but larger. So he had not been in the danger he had feared. Unless the ape decided to smash his head with that giant fist.

They returned to camp, as there was no chance of having a successful hunt at this stage. But their news was exciting enough to make up for the meal of grain-gruel and soup made from bamboo tree shoots and boiled rat tails.

"Big, big!" Joe said enthusiastically, gesturing to show the creature's height. "Ape break big bamboo." He broke a thin twig to demonstrate. The others listened politely, for he was a man, but it was clear that they did not really believe, even when Bil and Hue endorsed Joe's description. They suspected that it was a joke, to make up for the bad hunt. That made Joe angry. "Tomorrow band see!" he said. "Hunt apes. Big meat."

The others were happy to agree. This meant that the women and children could in effect go on a hunt, and they delighted in the opportunity. The prospect of fresh meat was appealing too.

But Hue was ill at ease about it. He knew that Joe wanted to hunt the giant apes, and certainly such creatures would provide a great deal of meat. But Hue's brief contact with the one ape, the sharing of glances and touches, had impressed him with the creature's man-ness. This was perhaps not a real man, but it was also not an animal. It was a cousin-creature who meant no harm and should be left alone.

His mate Fae became aware of his distraction. She tried to tempt him to repeated copulations, but after the first two he lost interest. Seeing that, his young stepdaughter Lee came across to him, to see if he merely craved variety. Lee was his little sister's friend, and both of them were on the verge of nubility. His sister Bee would mate elsewhere, but Lee evidently thought Hue was a suitable prospect despite his lack of interest. She stood before him, bent over, and wiggled her rear, offering, but he merely turned his back. Still hopeful, she circled him and lay on her back in front of him, lifting and spreading her legs enticingly. He turned his back again. He wouldn't hit her unless she became too much of a nuisance, but he simply wasn't interested. She was too much like his sister. Finally she gave up, and departed.

Fae sniffed with satisfaction. It was not her place to say when or with whom he should mate, but she preferred to keep him to herself as much as possible, now that his first mate Lil had become too old to be alluring. A man was entitled to all the women he could handle, but it appeared that Lee was not just available for spot diversion; she hoped to become his regular mate. So Fae stayed fairly close to him, in that way not only being ready, but keeping clear of other males. Any female had to yield to any male who desired her, except when with a proprietary male. Thus Lee had succeeded in avoiding mating with any others, despite her growing desirability. She pretended that Hue wanted her, and others honored that pretense despite the fact that Hue denied it. Because Hue was one of the dominant males, and just might be biding his time with Lee. It was not wise to annoy a dominant male, even in some potential manner.

Hue walked away from the shelters of the band, seeking his own counsel. The females knew better than to follow him. They thought he was just going out far enough to defecate without having the smell bother the camp. And he did that, but it was incidental. He could not get the big apes out of his mind. He could not decide how to relate to them.

He passed a female who had made herself a separate shelter somewhat apart from the others. This was Ann, who belonged to the band because she had been born in it, but who made others uncomfortable because she had a defect of her fur. It was uncommonly thin, and parts of her torso looked almost bare. This meant that she had to wear a blanket much of the time, not just when the air was cold. She got cold much sooner than others did, though in the heat of day she did well enough. She was, overall, a rather pitiful figure.

Hue paused, scratching at a flea. Ann looked almost as different from regular folk as the big apes did. They were huge but fully furred; she was human in size and body, but awkwardly naked. He did not want to hunt either type.

The woman was about Hue's own age. He hadn't really been aware of her as a child, but thought she had been around. That might be because others teased her about her deformity, so she had mostly remained apart, always on the fringe of the group. So he knew of her, but had never really interacted with her. Yet now he realized that he felt a slight affinity, because he, too, was different, in his fashion: he wielded his club and stone with the wrong hand. Had he not had friends who didn't care about that, and had he not become a dominant male, he could have suffered ridicule or exclusion, as this woman had. He had a notion how she felt.

Ann remained still, neither fleeing him nor reacting to him, apart from watching him. She was wary of other members of the band, who might hurt her if she annoyed them. But perhaps she knew that Hue did not hurt people just because he was able to. So she waited to see what he wanted with her, not knowing that he had not sought her. He had just happened to take the path by which she camped.

He became aware of something else. Ann was not scratching. That was another oddity. He thought back, and realized that he could not remember ever seeing her scratch. Didn't the fleas bother her, as they did all normal folk? The only times a regular person wasn't scratching was when he was hunting and had to be motionless lest he alert the nearby prey, and when he was asleep—and many did scratch in their sleep. The fleas were a perpetual nuisance. The members of the band had to spend much time grooming themselves and others, picking out the fleas and eating them.

He peered more closely at her, in the dusk. He could see the surface of her skin clearly in many places, because of her defect. And discovered to his surprise that she didn't have fleas. Apparently they didn't like her taste.

Then, realizing that Ann might have misunderstood his attention, thinking he wanted to mate with her, he tried to make it right. He dug a finger into the bag he wore tied around his body, where he had stored a smoked piece of panda meat, a reserve for the time he might be on a long hunt and unable to forage when hungry. He dug it out and gave it to her.

Ann accepted it eagerly. She seldom got to eat meat. But she hesitated, holding it before her mouth. Was he giving it for sex? Actually he could have sex from her without any gift, because he was a grown male, but often men did feed women at the same time. So his gesture had been taken the opposite way intended.

Hue clarified the matter the simplest way: he turned from her and walked on down the path. He had peered closely at her only because of his curiosity about her odd lack of scratching, and had given the meat as much from compassion as interest. He was glad that he had no such defect of fur.

He returned to the camp, his mind still not settled. Now Fae approached him intellectually. "Hue sad," she said. "Say Fae."

To this approach he was receptive. "Big ape yes," he said. "Joe say yes. Ape tall man yes. Ape hunt no. Ape eat bamboo. Ape touch Hue head hand. Ape hurt Hue no. Hue hunt ape no."

Fae considered that, but did not comment. Instead she changed the subject by spreading her legs and drawing him into her. This time he was sufficiently interested to complete the act. His discussion and clarification of the issue had eased his mind.

The others wanted to hunt and kill the big apes. Hue did not. He felt a kind of camaraderie with the huge creatures, now that he had learned that they were harmless to his kind. How could he hunt them, as if they were mere animals?

❁

Next day the entire band went out in pursuit of the huge apes. Hue went along, of course, but remained doubtful. He almost hoped that they would not find the creatures; that the apes had fled to some distant place and would not be seen again. But that was not to be. They quickly found the tracks, and followed them to the place where the giants were grazing on bamboo.

The members of the band were duly amazed and impressed. They had never seen creatures like these before.

But there was something else there: two other people. "Bub Sis!" Hue said, recognizing them. "Tell Bub band."

Bil nodded grimly. The two were clearly spying in local territory, and would bring their band to hunt the apes, stealing what belonged to the local band. Perhaps they had been following the hunting party before, so had learned of the apes through no virtue of their own.

This had been planned as an exploratory excursion, to show off the discovery to the women and children. But now it became serious. "Hunt ape," Joe said. "Now." He meant that they could do it before Bub's band got here. Of course Bub's band would come anyway and poach some of the apes, but at least there would be good meat here.

"No," Hue said. "Ape hunt no."

Bil looked at him. "Why no?"

"Ape harm band no," Hue explained. But then he stumbled over a concept that the words were not adequate to address. How could he say that it was wrong to hunt a creature merely because it represented no threat to them? The rabbits were no threat, the pandas weren't, in fact most of what they killed and ate were not threats. It was clear that the other people did not share the affinity he felt for the apes.

Bil looked at Rae, who was with them today.

"Hunt ape," Rae said.

"Hunt ape yes," Bil decided. "Now."

But Hue couldn't do it. "No," he said.

Bil looked at him, not understanding. "Band yes," he pointed out reasonably enough. The consensus had been achieved; all but Hue wanted to hunt the apes.

"Hue no," Hue said, feeling bad. "Hunt animals yes, apes no." He wished he could get his feeling across to them, but he hardly understood it himself.

"Band hunt," Bil said. It was clear that the others agreed: once the decision was made, all of them should participate. What was the matter with Hue? For one thing, they normally used a formation of four or five when hunting big game: one ahead to block its escape, two on the sides to close it in, and one or two to pursue it. Otherwise it would break out on the sector not guarded, and they could lose it, or have a long chase. They needed Hue.

But still he could not. "Ape no," he repeated.

To make it worse, Bub had evidently been listening. Now he came forward, his hands lifted without weapon, the posture of negotiation. The others lifted their spears, not liking this; it was bad form to let an enemy or outsider see dissension in the band. But it was worse form to attack an outsider who came in peace, though no outsider was to be trusted. It was obvious that the home band was superior to all others, but the others had to be tolerated if they didn't infringe or attack.

Bub approached, and behind him came his disreputable sister, her hands also raised though of course it didn't matter because she was only female. She gave Hue a straight look, recognizing him. The two of them had shared shelter in a storm once, so of course they had mated, because that was the way of any man with any woman. Her look suggested that she would like to do it again, and that the event gave her some kind of claim on him. Hue was disgusted, because he didn't even like her. Yet she had undeniable appeal in her strangeness. Her chest fur was not only flat in the available manner, it seemed never to have swollen for the nursing of a child. That made her seem younger than he knew her to be.

Fae sniffed behind him. She didn't like the approach of the alien female either. He glanced back at her. Fae's chest was beginning to swell, indicating that it anticipated nursing. That meant that she had a baby starting in her. Perhaps that was why his interest in her was slowing; he hadn't been conscious of the swelling before, because it had happened slowly, but now he realized its significance. He would soon have to find another female for sex, because those with babies weren't much good. Breasted women were more interested in their nurslings than in their mates.

Then he saw that Fae was looking past him, at Bub. She was intrigued by the enemy male? Worse yet!

Joe addressed the intruder. "Want?" he demanded.

"Bad hunt," Bub said, glancing at Hue. "Man no." He knew their predicament; without one of the members of their hunting party, they could suffer loss of the prey, or even the death of one of more of their members. This was serious business.

Joe hefted his spear angrily. "Foreigner no," he said. The word foreigner had multiple meanings, among them distance, disapproval, and fecal matter. He was saying that it was none of Bub's business.

But Bub did not take offense. "Bub hunt yes," he said. "Share meat." He was offering to participate in the hunt, if they let him have some of what they killed. Such deals had been made before, on occasion; it was better than taking the risk of messing it up. The usual arrangement was for the stranger to be allowed to take whatever he could carry away in one haul, if the kill was big enough. In this case it would be, because of the size of the ape.

Joe was about to decline. But Bil was more calculating. He glanced at Hue. "Hue no?" he asked.

Hue was sickened by the whole business. If he didn't participate in the hunt, Bub would take his place and share the meat. They were forcing the issue. But he still was not willing to hunt the ape. "Hue no."

Bil looked at Rae. "Bub yes?"

Rae hesitated. He had always been Hue's closest friend, and his sister was Hue's mate. But he wanted to hunt the ape. "Yes."

Bil asked Joe. "Bub yes?"

Joe had always acceded to Bil's advice. With bad grace he agreed. "Yes."

Bil looked at Bub. "Yes," he said, completing the consensus.

Hue had been circumvented. With Bub to take his place in the hunt, they didn't need him.

But the decision was more significant than that. He had been shamed before the band. He had hoped to prevent the hunt, saving the ape; he had succeeded only in isolating himself from his band. There had always been a covert question, because of his wrong hand; now he had a wrong attitude, exacerbating his difference. The band's tolerance went only so far.

As a shamed man, he would have difficulty remaining with the band. The others probably thought it was cowardice: that he was simply afraid to face the huge apes. He was unable to explain the distinction between fear and conscience. He did not want to harm the apes because he was *not* afraid of them; they were harmless, and too much like man himself.

Sis approached him. She remained interested, despite his bad status. That stirred his emotions further. He didn't like her, yet he found her sexually appealing. He was tempted to copulate with her and then never see her again. But instead he turned his back on her.

The others set about the hunt. Soon they were gone, pursuing the moving apes. The remainder of the band did not follow; they would only get in the way.

Hue walked away from the group. He did not know where he was going, but he had to go. Somewhere else.

Fac watched him, but did not move. She knew how he had disgraced himself, and she did not want to be a part of it. Sis watched him, and almost seemed to start after him, but then must have remembered her brother on the hunt, and stayed put. Hue knew that no one would come with him, because no one felt as he did. To them, he had done a crazy thing.

Then there was a cry. "Hue!"

It was Lee, his little sister's friend. She had wanted his favor, and now thought she had found a way to achieve it.

He paused, letting her catch up. She was still too young to mate with, unless the need were great, but he appreciated her support. Should he reject her? But she would be tainted, now, because she had openly followed him; if she returned to the band, others would hold that against her. The damage had already been done.

So he resumed walking, taking no overt notice of her. That meant she could follow if she chose, but had no promise of reward. Perhaps she would give it up.

But she did not. She stayed with him, silently. Finally, far from the camp, he turned to her. "Lee hunt ape no?" He was asking her how she felt about the issue that had separated him from the band. Of course as a female she would not actually hunt anything, for that was man's prerogative.

"Hue hunt ape no, Lee hunt ape no," she replied.

So it wasn't that she had sympathy for the apes, but that she was ready to accept Hue's limits as her own. That would do.

They were entering the territory of a mountain. Hue knew that a hostile band governed the river region at the base, all the way up to the high pass to the region beyond, so unless he wanted to try to join that band, he would have to try to go another way. That would mean a difficult climb, and a problem foraging. But it had to be. Because the first thing the hostile band would do was to take Lee and make her the mate of one of their males. She would have no choice, unless Hue fought for her and won, and then he would have to mate with her himself. Since he wanted neither to mate with her nor to see her mated involuntarily to another, he had to avoid that band. She was his sister's friend, and needed to be protected.

The climb was arduous. They got beyond the bamboo trees, where the cold rocky face of the mountain ascended toward the sky. Hue looked at that, and considered the lateness of the day, and elected to spend the night in the forest. So they foraged, finding good bamboo sprouts and a number of fat bugs to eat. Then they made a shelter of bamboo sticks, for it was not good to sleep exposed. Hue made it so that a line of sharp sticks pointed outward, making it difficult for any large creature to attack. Then the two of them crawled inside, and he pulled the door into place, completing their protection.

As he lay down, tired, Lee snuggled close to him. She wanted to mate, as usual. He ignored her and went to sleep.

In the morning they resumed their climb. But the mountain fought them. There seemed to be only one place to crest it, and the route to that was so steep that they had to flatten out and crawl on their furry bellies. Lee, lighter, was better able to do it, so she led the way. She had always liked climbing, he remembered, and was good at it.

But then at a particularly steep place a rock suddenly pulled loose in her hand. Caught by surprise, she cried out and fell back, starting to slide down the steep face. Hue grabbed for her, caught her foot, and hauled her back to safety—but in the process lost his own perch and started rolling helplessly down the slope. He couldn't catch on to anything; all the rocks around him were rolling too. He heard Lee's scream. Then his head struck something, and he faded into a flare of pain.

Such was the fate of those who deserted their band. He had known it, yet foolishly done it anyway.

Some may have demurred, but the evidence suggests that Homo erectus *did hunt* Gigantopithecus *to extinction. Fossil deposits in southern China and north Vietnam show them together, and though Upright Man continued to be in the area, the giant ape did not. Mankind, in all his forms, was a devastatingly effective hunter.*

The irony, perhaps, was that it would have been in mankind's interest to preserve the huge ape. But those who might have understood this lacked the finesse of speech to handle complex concepts like conscience or conservation. The actual vocabulary may have been considerable, with a word for every animal, object, and thing, but syntax was primitive. The average person was practical on the immediate level: here is walking meat, how can it be killed? Early variants of mankind saw no need to wrestle with more sophisticated concepts that did not promise rapid gratification. That, in due course, was their downfall.

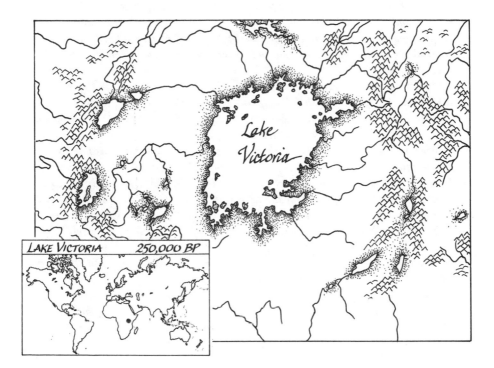

Lake Victoria

LAKE VICTORIA   250,000 BP

CHAPTER 6

FLOOD

Variation and mutations are constant. Variation within a narrow range is harmless; it doesn't matter too much whether a person's hair is light brown or dark brown, though geography and climate can make one preferable. Mutations are another matter; the great majority—perhaps in excess of 99 percent—are bad for survival, and those creatures unfortunate enough to have them are doomed. So a rat with a defective gene for fur may not survive; that fur is needed for warmth and protection against the direct radiation of the sun. This was surely true for mankind too, until a combination of unusual circumstances abruptly changed the survival qualities of nakedness.

Actually only one small segment of the species was affected, at first: the one that had remained at, or returned to, the region of the Garden of Eden. But it was no longer a garden. Geographic and climatic shifts had made it a basin that held much of the water flowing into it. It had become Lake Victoria. Most tribes of mankind shunned it, but one seemingly defective branch had no choice, being trapped there by mountains and the hostility of the neighboring tribes. This tribe learned not to escape the flood, but to live with it, being shaped by it. The water folk.

That tribe was squeezed into the shallow water. Its people learned to forage in a medium that others avoided. Their bodies were relatively gracile compared to those of Erect Man, but also became more fleshy, particularly those of the women, and more so in the legs than the arms. The previously deleterious mutation for hairlessness became an asset in the water, buttressed by subcutaneous fat. Unlike the females of most tribes, the grown women also had permanently swollen breasts, that helped warm their chests when they were between nursing babies, and also had become objects of attraction for men. The breasts identified the women clearly, even when their genital regions were concealed by the water.

These weirdly bare people were generally shunned by their normal neighbors. They were at one fringe of a worldwide array of mankind that was penetrating niches of ecosystems previously unknown, their bodies changing to fit. But they survived because of several factors: an uncontested habitat, a richness of available food, physical security from most threats, and a surprising freedom from the occasional terrible scourges of disease that affected other tribes. Wherever there was water, these fringe types endured: some on the Isle of Woman at the mouth of the Great Rift Valley, and some here in the Lake of Eden in the center of the Rift, about 150,000 years ago.

Yet an objective observer would have been unlikely to see in this isolated tribe the seeds for survival and success away from the water. Some of the elements of that success were so subtle that they would not become evident for the better part of another hundred thousand years. But the fact that these qualities were not obvious does not mean they weren't important. For the meek water folk were indeed destined to inherit the world, in due course.

At this time, however, they were anything but dominant. A conventional stranger coming among them would have been surprised by a number of their features, and would have had some trouble adapting to their ways. Yet there would be aspects of familiarity, too, and in time he might grow accustomed to them, and even discover a certain appeal in their way of life.

In this case, the stranger is Hue, led there by a girl of that tribe who befriended him in adversity. There are similar people in every band or tribe, so they are similarly named. But in this case the familiar names identify strangers to Hue; we know them, but he does not, and they do not know him. Yet perhaps some old affinities linger. At any rate, Hue has inadvertently left the robust Homo erectus *behind, and is about to join the gracile* Homo sapiens sapiens—*or fully modern man, physically. Thus his seeming loss of identity is actually his salvation.*

H E woke to pain. But someone was tending him, giving him water and food, covering his body from the cold. He faded in and out for what seemed like a long time, but finally recovered enough awareness to focus on his benefactor. "Who?" he asked.

She tapped him on the chest. "Hue." She tapped herself on her slightly swelling breast. "Lee." She spoke with a strong alien accent, but he was able to understand her. That meant that his tribe and hers were not too far apart.

Tribe? He struggled to remember. He was Hue—that made sense—but how had he come here? And Lee—she must be a relative. A daughter—no, she seemed too old for that—a sister, maybe. He had always helped and protected his little sister. Now she was helping him.

He lifted a hand to touch his head. He had a bad welt on it, distending the fur there. The skull seemed dented but not broken. "How?"

"Fell," Lee said immediately. Now he remembered that he had asked her that before, perhaps several times, as he woke and slept and woke again. She had grown facile with her answers. "Mountain. Lee fall. Hue catch Lee. Hue fall. Roll. Head, rock."

He had gathered as much: only a rock could have done the damage he felt. But what were they doing out here? "Where?"

That wasn't quite the right question, but he must have asked the right one before, because she had a competent answer. "Hue, Lee go mountain. Cross no."

So they hadn't gotten wherever they had been going; the mountain had been too difficult to cross. Now it did not seem wise to try. He wasn't sure he could walk, let alone scale the horrendous slope he saw.

"Why?"

Now she hesitated. "Trouble. Tribe."

He had gotten into trouble in his tribe? He couldn't remember what for. Lee evidently didn't know what kind it was, or didn't want to tell. But it seemed it had been enough so that he had to leave.

He slept again, and Lee snuggled close. Next time he woke, he was aware of two things: he now remembered her prior answers, so didn't need to ask again, which must mean he was healing; and her body was pressing against his side. She was definitely a maturing girl, and soon would be seeking a man.

She realized that he was awake. She rubbed against him suggestively. "Mate?" she inquired.

With him? But she was his sister! Men did not do sex with their own family members. Perhaps she didn't realize that. He did not want to hurt her feelings, so he simply said, "No," wincing to show that his head still hurt.

She did not pursue the matter. Evidently he had said that too to her before.

Hue took inventory, and found that he had a skin blanket, a pouch belt, and an axe. The axe was a good one, an all purpose tool suitable for stabbing, slicing, or throwing. It was his best friend. With this he could cope, even if he didn't know where he was or where he had come from.

"Hunt," he said, sitting up, wincing as his head responded to his motion by generating pain.

But Lee knew better. "Forage," she said.

In the days that followed, Hu realized that they would have to move, because they were exhausting the foraging of this limited high region, and were getting hungry. His strength was returning, but he really needed the support of others of his kind. Yet he had no idea where to go.

"Lee know tribe," she said. "Water folk."

A tribe living near water? She was on speaking terms with them? That would help. Some tribes routinely killed strangers, so it was best to have an introduction. Children could make contacts more readily than adults, because they were no threat to adults. Especially girl children, who might later come to join the harem of a male. So he let Lee lead him down the mountain, following a route she seemed to know.

Hue was staggering, but Lee managed to help him reach the region of an established tribe she knew of. Perhaps the region was familiar; he wasn't sure. It was a settlement on the shore of a large lake, where people were cooking fish at an open fire on the beach. It was evening, and the warmth of the day remained. The fish smelled very good.

A large, stout man challenged them as they approached the camp. But Lee interceded. "Joe no hurt Hue," she said, standing between them. She seemed to know the man, though Hue did not. She was an attractive nascent woman, which surely helped.

Joe looked disgusted, but let them pass. So Joe must know Lee, and be required to allow her to bring in a stranger if she chose to.

Lee brought him a roasted fish, and he chewed on it eagerly despite the bones. He saw that these tribespeople were so lightly furred they seemed ill, but apparently this was normal for them. The men retained fur on their scalps, chins, and crotches; the women's faces were bare but their clefts furred. And they all seemed to be nursing, for their breasts were developed. That was remarkable; most women finished nursing and became flat-chested and therefore sexually available until getting their next babies. Only a few babies were in evidence, but the other nurslings must be close.

There was an alarm. Immediately the naked people fled to the water, taking their roast fish with them. Lee tugged Hue along after them. Hue, realizing that he was in no condition to fight a vicious animal, realized that there might indeed be safety in the water. So he splashed in after them.

The water was warm, having been heated by the day. They waded out, following the gradually deepening contour of the muck below, until Hue stood chest deep and Lee chin deep. He noticed now that the women of the tribe were almost as tall as the men, so could wade out almost as far. That made sense, because it would not be safe for the women to be left behind during danger. But he also saw that no more were carrying babies than had done so on land. Where were their nurslings?

Now the danger they had fled appeared: the men of a regular tribe. They were large and muscular and hairy, in contrast to the men of the water folk, who seemed effete in comparison. No wonder they had to give way to the raiders.

The raiders charged up to the fire, searching for any food that might have been left, but none was. They stood on the beach and stared out at the folk in the water, but they were beyond spear-throwing range, and in any event their spears or stones would have been lost in the water. The men evidently did not care to enter the water themselves, which Hue found odd; after all, he was of their type, and he hadn't minded entering the water. So the water folk were safe, and after a moment the others moved away, disgruntled. It had been a harmless occasion, thanks to the protection of the lake.

But the water folk did not return to the shore right away. They simply stood, chest to chin deep, watching. The women nursed their babies; only the women's breasts and the babies' heads showed above the surface.

A man turned his head. "Lee," he said.

Lee, standing close between Hue and the shore, turned to him. "Hue stay," she said. "See." Then she forged to the shore, splashing her hands so as to make noise.

Hue wasn't comfortable with this. Suppose the raiders remained close, waiting in ambush? He should not let her go back alone. It was clear that the others were as wary as he was, but they wanted Lee to be the one to take the risk. Yet she had seemed confident. So, since he knew so little of the ways of these slender furless people, he did as told, and did not move.

Lee waded forward, passing several others. She did not go ashore immediately, but walked a bit to one side and then to another, looking around and pausing several times as if looking for something. But there was nothing there, just the level surface of the water. She paused longest by a thicket of reeds growing in the waist-deep water, splashing with her hands and kicking with her feet. What was she doing, besides stirring up clouds of lake mud? All the others waited impassively, seeming to be not at all impatient about this dallying.

Finally Lee went the rest of the way ashore. Hue saw her buttocks emerge, and her thighs. Her legs were fleshed in the manner of the women of this tribe, being thick and round. But she was not unattractive, because she had more fur on her body than the others did, though not as much as normal folk had. Hue suddenly realized that this could have been why she had approached him for mating: she wanted a man with some fur, rather than being weirdly bare like most of the others. Had she not been so young, and also his sister, he might have been interested.

Suddenly a man appeared, bursting from the concealment of the brush near the water. He charged at Lee. Hue was horrified and disgusted; the raiders *had* left an ambush, and Lee was the one who had sprung it. Apparently by the choice of the leader.

And not one of the other water folk moved to help her. Hue realized why: there could be a larger ambush waiting to catch those who tried to help the girl. They were vulnerable on land. The single man could be a lure to tempt them out of their safe water.

Lee screamed and dived for the water. The raider grabbed for her, but she spun and dodged, eluding him, and reached the shallow water. The man turned and pursued her. He was considerably larger and stronger, and in a moment he was almost able to catch her with his outstretched hands.

Still no one else moved. Hue started to—and Lee looked at him across the water, shaking her head no. Then she screamed again, and zigzagged toward the patch of reeds.

The raider splashed into the water after her. Apparently he wasn't concerned about the shallow water. Maybe the raiders had known that they couldn't catch any of the people in the deep water, so hadn't tried. But Lee hadn't had the sense to plunge deep immediately, and now was about to be caught by the reeds. If she tried to run through the reeds, she would be slowed, and the raider would have her in a moment. In fact he was about to have her anyway.

The man reached out and caught Lee's shoulder. Then he looked startled. He suddenly sat down in the water. He bellowed with pain. Yet there was nothing. Lee just stood there, looking down at him.

The man seemed to be unable to scramble back to his feet. His hands splashed, and for a moment his head ducked under the surface. Then he somehow moved past Lee, not toward the shore but toward deeper water. What was happening?

Two other men burst from the brush on shore. They forged into the water to rescue their companion. So there *had* been more of an ambush there!

Still neither Lee nor any of the other water folk moved.

The two men got knee deep, then abruptly fell forward, their faces splashing into the water. Both thrashed wildly. Then one brought out a flint knife and slashed with it, stabbing at something under the surface. In a moment he got back to his feet, holding a length of rope with clamshells dangling from it. The other man joined him, but seemed to be limping. Even from a distance, Hue could see a reddish tinge in the muddy water.

Hue was beginning to understand. That rope had been hidden under the water, and had tripped the men. That was why they had fallen. The shells were sharp-edged, cutting their legs. They had escaped the trap, but not without injury. It was a lesson; after this, they would be far more cautious about pursuing any water person into the shallow water.

Meanwhile the first raider, who had chased Lee, was now floating silently beside the reeds. His face was under water. He appeared to be dead.

The two raiders stared at the body, then shook their heads. They knew better than to try to wade out that far.

Then they turned to face Lee, who still stood where she had stopped. They had spears strapped to their backs, but they did not try to use them. It was all too clear that further efforts were likely to cost them a good deal more than their spears. They simply turned around and sloshed out of the water, defeated.

After they were gone, Lee moved. She returned by her devious route to the shore. Now Hue understood that she knew where the hidden ropes were, and was avoiding them. She had stirred up the water so that the raiders couldn't see what was under it. They had been the ones walking into the trap, not she.

Yet the whole tribe had waded directly into the water, before, not encountering any hazards. Where had the ropes and sharp shells come from?

Lee explored the shore, and found nothing. This time the raiders really were gone.

But the water folk did not go back to land. Instead they began moving along parallel to the shore, seeking some other place. They were finished with this region anyway. Two men approached the floating body of the raider and stripped it of anything of value. Then they pushed it to the shore and left it there.

Hue waited until Lee re-entered the water and waded up to him. "Rope no," he said, trying to express his confusion.

She smiled with secret knowledge. "Rope yes," she replied. And that was all.

They formed into a single file and headed toward the center of the lake. But though the shore receded, the depth of water did not. Hue realized that they were walking along a built-up path; his toes could feel the sloping sides of it. So the lake was getting deeper; they merely had a ramp. A ramp which surely could be changed, if an enemy learned its location.

But why didn't the enemy just swim, instead of trying to walk the path? Hue thought of the answer immediately: few regular folk were good swimmers, and they couldn't fight well while swimming. While the water folk surely were good swimmers—and could stand on their hidden ramps and use weapons effectively to stop any enemy swimmers. So the lake was proof against invasion.

They approached an odd island. It seemed to be made of a tangle of wooden branches. In fact it *was* such a tangle, extending well down below the surface. There seemed to be several domes in it, but no one was climbing onto them. Instead people were disappearing.

Disappearing? Hue watched the line ahead, and saw a man sink quietly out of sight, not to reappear. Then a woman with a baby did the same, pausing only to let the baby get a good breath. What was happening? No one seemed alarmed.

Finally the last person before Hue sank down. Now Hue saw that the man was swimming toward the stick island, going deep as if to pass under it. Then he disappeared.

Lee smiled. "Follow Lee," she said. Before he could protest, she took a small breath and dived low.

He had no choice. He ducked down into the water as well as he could and stroked after her. He was very glad that he knew how to swim; he knew that many did not. His curiosity about things had led him to explore rivers and ponds, and he had also liked to listen to the odd sounds under water. Sounds had always intrigued him. It was apparent that he was not nearly as proficient at swimming as Lee was, but she was not trying to elude him, and he was able to keep her kicking feet in sight.

Down she went, down, down. Then she swam into the base of the stick island and was gone. But in a moment he found that there was a way there, an opening in the mass of sticks. It was deadly dark within, like a deep cave, but that was where she had gone. So he followed, his breath getting pained.

The cave ceiling opened almost immediately, and he swam up. In a moment he found the surface and gasped his breath back. It was dusky here, beneath a dome of sticks; he was *under* the island! Had he had time to think about this swim, he would have been frightened.

Around him was a circle of legs, knees, and thighs. He was in the center of an interior pool, surrounded by sitting women. All of their legs were spread, showing their genitals as if inviting sex. But when he looked at any woman directly, her legs closed, denying sex. What was happening here?

He looked around the full circle until he located Lee. Her legs alone did not close. He shook his head, not trying to explain that this was not a thing he wished of his little sister.

She did not protest. She heaved herself up, and he saw that she had been sitting on a woven rim of reeds just above the water level. She moved on hands and knees away from the circle. "Follow Lee," she repeated.

So he put his hands on the rim and managed to heave himself up and onto it. That was just as well, because his arms, unfamiliar with this type of swimming, had been tiring. He was conscious of the women inspecting his body at close range, but none commented. He moved on hands and knees after the girl.

She led him down a short tunnel through the sticks that opened out into a chamber where many children were. Each seemed to have his or her place, out of the water but with the ceiling so low that it was not possible to stand up, or even sit up in comfort. There were many thick stick columns supporting the roof, and the resting places were around these columns. Lee had a section that was large enough for two, if they lay close together.

And that was what they did. They settled down for the night, and Hue was glad to sleep. He was worried that Lee would proffer him sex again, but now her legs were firmly closed; apparently this was not the occasion for that.

○

In the morning the women and children stirred, stretching and going to the water hole. At first he heard them in the dark, then he saw them. This reminded him that no babies had shown up for many women, just older children who were no longer nursing. Yet all of the grown women had full breasts. The mystery was not being resolved.

Lee had evidently awakened before him, but remained close. She saw him peering at the women. "Hue ask?"

"Breasts," he said. "Babies no?"

She laughed. "Breasts women," she said, cupping the halves of her chest with her hands so that its slight shaping was more evident. "Children no."

Hue shook his head. "Breasts, babies." He knew he had never before seen a breasted woman who was not nursing. When a woman lost or weaned her baby, her breasts quickly shrank into nubs, and developed again only when she had another baby in her. When men raided other tribes and captured women, they had sex only with the appealing breastless ones.

Lee shook her head in turn. "Breasts women."

So it seemed. "How babies?"

"Breasts babies," she said.

Women with breasts could get new babies? Hue was amazed and disgusted. These men had to take sex from unsuitable women? It was a wonder the tribe didn't soon die out.

Lee was quick to appreciate his revulsion, and to take advantage of it. "Lee breasts no," she pointed out, this time pressing her hands flat on her chest to diminish the swellings there. "Legs yes." She spread them invitingly. "Sex yes."

Hue realized that he would have to explain. "Lee sister. Sex no."

She looked perplexed. "Sister? Lee sister no."

Now he realized that she had not actually claimed to be his sister; he had simply assumed it, because it seemed right. He had a feeling, if not an actual memory, of a sister about her age, with whom he had always been close. And of course Lee came from a different tribe than he did, so she couldn't be his sister unless something quite unusual had happened. Why hadn't he realized that before? But if Lee was not that sister, who was she? "Lee who?" he asked.

"Lee water folk tribe child. Hue brother no."

Then how had the two of them come to be together? Normally men hunted with other men, or mated with their women, or protected their children or siblings. So she had to be his daughter or his sister. He was sure she wasn't his daughter. And now he strongly doubted that she was his sister, because of the difference in tribes and dialect. So if her claim not to be his sister was true, what was the explanation for their association? "Hue Lee how?"

She was ready for that question. "Lee woman need man. Lee—" Here she hesitated. "Lee hairy. Tribe men like no. Lee look hairy tribe men. Lee find Hue."

That made sense. Lee was the only one of the water folk who wasn't distressingly bare on torso and limbs. Her fur was light, but sufficient. And they actually rejected her because of that? So she had gone out to see if she could find a hairy man who would like her. She was evidently an enterprising girl. And she had had the wit to do so before she became adult, so that her growing breasts would not cause a hairy man to reject her. Hue was the one she had found. But that was not the whole answer. What had he been doing alone—or had she found him in a tribe? He would not have hunted with either a woman or a child, or gone out alone with a stranger.

"Find Hue where?" he asked.

"Find Hue walk alone," she clarified. "Hue stranger. Hue know land no. Lee know land by water. Lee tell land."

So he had agreed to let her walk with him, if she showed him the way. Because it was dangerous to go alone through the territory of another tribe. He had to avoid any party of hunters, lest they kill him without parley. He had wanted guidance; she had wanted a man. Their purposes had never been aligned.

Then they had tried to pass a mountain, using a dangerous path that others did not use, and had fallen. Now it was coming back. Lee knew the land near the water, but was less certain of the terrain high on the mountain slope where he had wanted to go. So there had been an accident. He had been helpless, because of his injury and his confusion, so Lee had led him home to her tribe. The tribe had had to admit him, because Lee meant to mate with him, and mating with a tribe member made a person a member. It made sense, from her perspective.

But not from his own perspective. Now he knew that Lee was not his sister, so she was legitimate for marriage. But he still thought of her as a sister, and had no sexual inclination for her. And he needed to make this clear to her. "Hue Lee sex no," he said firmly. That meant no mating, no marriage; he wasn't interested. In fact he wasn't interested in any of the water folk women, with their furless bodies and repellent breasts. This was not the place for him.

That hurt her. "Lee sex good," she protested, stroking her genital region. "Sex many. Sex any."

She was offering it as often as he wanted it, any way he might want it. She was ready to be completely obliging. But any woman was, with any man, willingly or unwillingly. But that couldn't make her attractive to him, or eliminate his perception of her as a person very like a sister. He still wasn't interested. "No."

Now she was angry. "Hue water folk Lee," she said, reminding him how she had been the one to get him admitted to this tribe. "Hue Lee mate day day day. Mate no, Hue go."

That made it quite clear: the water folk had let him in only because of Lee, with the expectation that he would mate with her. That was standard in any tribe he knew of, because often it was was better for a person to mate with one from another tribe. Neighboring tribes might not like each other, and might fight often, but they had to be tolerant of mating between them. It was the way it was. But there was a time limit: three days. If it didn't happen in that time, it was reasonable to suppose that it wasn't going to happen. No tribe wanted to have a noncontributing member, or one who was not implicitly tied to the tribe, so this was a reasonable limit. So he had to commit in that time, or be banished as the foreigner he was.

Since he didn't care to mate with Lee, there was no point in prolonging it. His head had stopped aching with the good night's sleep, and he was feeling stronger. He would resume his walk to wherever he was going. "Hue go." He got to his hands and knees and moved toward the pool.

Lee scrambled after him. "Go no! Land bad. Aliens bad. Kill Hue."

He ignored her. He was sorry that he could not do what she wished, for she seemed to be a nice enough girl, but he could not mate with anyone like a sister. He reached the pool, plunged in, and swam down to the exit hole. He was more confident now, knowing the route.

In a moment he was out of the stick hut and stroking toward the surface. Lee came out immediately after, and reached the surface the same time he did. "Path," she said. "Swim no."

Because there could be traps in the water away from the path, he realized. So he found the raised path and put his feet down. Lee came to walk in front of him, to show him the way, because the path was not straight. It wavered around like a moving snake, and now he saw that there were sharp shells and pointed sticks lining it, bad for any feet that strayed.

On the beach the women had a fire going, and were cooking more fish.

The smell wafted over the water, making him hungry. He had not realized how good fish was, having eaten little of it before this.

"Food," Lee said. "Hue eat." She was trying to get him to delay his departure. She was desperate.

But it wasn't right to take the tribe's food if he wasn't going to join it. "Hue go," he repeated. "Food no."

She turned to face him, walking backwards, as they emerged from the water. Her face was wet, and more water was coming from her eyes. "Lee bad?"

There were a number of water folk within hearing, but they seemed not to hear. They were declining to intrude on private business.

Hue realized that she was upset. How could he answer her? He paused at the edge of the water. "Lee good. Lee Hue help. Lee girl sister. Hue mate sister no."

"Lee sister no!" she cried, refusing to understand.

Finally he remembered the name of his true sister. "Hue sister Bee," he said. "Bee Lee. Hue mate no."

She tried another ploy. "Lee Hue help. Mountain. Hue owe."

That gave him pause. She had indeed helped him on the mountain, after the accident. He might have died there, if she hadn't tended him. He did owe her.

She saw that she had found a persuasive argument. "Owe. Mate."

This, too, was standard. Such a debt had to be repaid in kind. He had to save her life, or mate with her, or find her another man to mate with. Because she wanted a mate. It wasn't just a matter of joining the tribe, but of evening the score. But how could he repay her, when none of the ways seemed feasible?

"Hue think," he said, and walked inland, away from the lake and the food.

"Day day day," she said, following him. "Hue stay, think."

That was a fair request, in the circumstance. She wanted him to remain here as long as he was allowed, so that he might change his mind. But that meant he would be taking the tribe's food and shelter and protection, when he wasn't going to join it. That wasn't right either. "Hue think," he repeated, walking on.

Still she followed. "Show path," she offered, eager to please him even in this.

"Show path," he agreed with resignation. It seemed that she wasn't going to let him out of her sight until the issue was decided.

The forest thickened, then thinned. Lee grew nervous. "Path no," she said, pointing. "Tribe bad."

The territory of one of the raiding tribes. Obviously that would not be good, because they had lost a man in yesterday's raid. If any of them recognized Lee, they would impale her on a spit and roast her alive.

But as Hue turned, seeking another path, he noticed something. "Bee," he said.

"Lee no Bee," Lee said sharply.

He smiled. His true sister's name happened to match that of an insect, and Lee had thought he was confusing her identity again. "Bee buzz," he clarified, pointing as another bee flew by. Some names emulated creatures; some did not. He wondered fleetingly what had happened to his sister of that name. She must be with the tribe he had left. The tribe to which perhaps he should return.

"Bee," she agreed, shrugging.

"Bee bee bee," he said. "Hive near." He couldn't explain how he knew, but he had always been curious about things, and had learned how to fathom where bees nested. It wasn't just the direction they flew, or even the direction they flew when loaded. It was how many there were, and how the directions changed slightly. He and his sister had enjoyed the challenge of finding bees, and leading the tribesmen to the honey. He had seen several bees here, and the way they were flying made him sure they lived close by. "Tribe honey?"

"Torch," she agreed. Fire and smoke drove off the bees so that their honey could be taken. It was a chancy operation, but worth it for the wonderful stuff.

They pursued the bees. But then Lee's sharp senses caught something else. "Man, woman," she whispered urgently. "Near." She looked all around, trying to orient on what she had heard.

He heard it too. And they were near hostile territory. Those could be folk of the raider tribe. Yet the bee nest was so close. Did they have to give it up?

But perhaps they could return to it another day, when there were no enemy near. It was better to turn back now.

Lee's head turned. "Behind!" she hissed, realizing.

Indeed, it was too late. There stood a man and a woman, barring their path back. They must have spied Hue's footprints and followed, silently. The man was about Hue's size, hairy and grim; the woman was full grown, furred and sleek.

And—he knew them. Suddenly it came back. "Bub!" he said grimly, putting his hand on his axe. "Sis."

Lee stared at him. "Hue know?"

"Hue know," the other man agreed.

"Bub take Hue mate," Hue said. Bub had joined their tribe in a rare cooperative hunt that Hue had not been able to participate in, and when he departed with his share of the meat, Hue's mate had gone with him. That had been one element of a more complicated situation that had left Hue outraged and disgusted, and he had left the tribe. He would have liked to kill Bub, but it wasn't allowed; the man had been there under truce, and the woman had gone with him by her own choice. Fae—he had thought she hated Bub, but she had deceived him in that. His rage remained. Now they were on relatively neutral ground. There was no truce. Hue lifted out his axe.

Bub lifted his hands, empty. "Wait," he said. "Bub tribe males few. Bub take woman. Bub give woman. Sis."

And Sis stepped forward, smiling. Her woman scent surrounded her. Bub had no respect for her as a person, yet her sex appeal was strong. It would be easy to mate with her.

But it came at a price. He would have to join Bub's tribe, and be subordinate to Bub. And see Bub with his former mate. Maybe it was a fair trade, for Sis was certainly a compelling woman. But there were complications Hue didn't like, among them the fact that he neither liked nor trusted Bub or Sis.

Lee stepped forward to intercept Sis. She would not stand by and see her chance for mating be lost. But she was not yet grown, while Sis was not only grown but armed. That was one of the things about her: Sis could fight somewhat in the fashion of a man. She would destroy Lee.

Hue didn't want that. Lee was a good girl, and forthright about her wishes. She did not deserve this. "No," he said, pulling her back. Then "No," to Bub.

Bub considered. He could renew his offer, or he could fight with Hue, or he could retreat. He shrugged and retreated. He backed away, and Sis paced him, sending Hue a final sultry look before she disappeared into the forest.

Hue remained still, concealing his reaction. But Sis had achieved her aim; she had made him desire her, however guiltily. Somehow he knew that it would have been a remarkable experience with her; it was almost as if he had mated with her some time, so knew how it was. But his memory was not enough; it gave him no such encounter. It was probably just a fancy.

"Hue Lee protect," Lee said, pleased.

"No," he said gruffly. "Sis like no." Yet that wasn't really true. Sis had tempted him strongly; it was the situation he didn't like.

Then he realized that he had just denied doing Lee a favor that might have abated his debt to her: saving her life. Because Sis could have killed her, and he had stopped it. He had missed a useful chance.

But Lee did not let it go. "Lee owe," she concluded.

Maybe. But probably not enough for her to let him go. "Bee," he reminded her.

They moved on, and he oriented on the faint music of the massed bee buzzing, and soon located the nest. It was not a huge one, but it surely had a nice supply of honey. Lee nodded approvingly. "Tribe owe," she said.

Because he had found something good for it, he realized. So perhaps he was earning his keep, these three days. That made him feel easier.

They started back toward the lake. But Lee had more on her mind. "Day day day more," she told him. "Challenge."

The three days grace wasn't the limit? Provided he did something special to earn the extension? This was new to him. "What?"

"Lee owe. Lee show. Challenge."

As she described it, Hue realized that it was a ritual endeavor that could give a foreigner another three days with the tribe, before he had to mate with a water folk female. He had done Lee a favor, so she was doing him one. She would teach him how to do the ritual, so that he might have more time with the tribe before deciding about the mating. Of course he still wasn't interested in mating with her, but at least this meant that he would have more time to find some other way through. It wasn't as great a favor as she perhaps thought, since it only postponed the time of decision, but it was still a nice gesture on her part.

They returned to the beach, where Lee avidly reported on what had happened. The tribesmen were interested; a bee nest was always worthwhile. A man named Itt, who seemed to be the competent one in this respect, organized a small party. He led several men with torches to see about the honey, with Lee showing the way.

Hue now felt free to eat. There was still some roasted fish left. Most of the women had eaten and gone; they were foraging along the shore. As he approached the dying fire, there was just one other who it seemed had not eaten. This was a very thin woman with almost no sign of fur on her body, except at her head and crotch, so that her bulging breasts stood out. She carried no baby.

There was just one fish left in the hot ashes. The woman glanced at it, then at him, and stepped back. She was yielding the fish to him.

Hue shook his head. "Hue foreign," he explained, not touching the fish. In any tribe, the natives had precedence over the foreigners. Even the women. He was hungry, but he knew better than to violate the protocol.

"Ann outcast," she demurred. Outcasts were last for food, too.

He looked more carefully at her, seeing that she had another oddity: there was a wedge of flesh or bone just below her mouth, jutting out beyond the projection of her teeth. That must be why she was outcast in a tribe that didn't care about her breasts or furlessness: she was malformed of face. It didn't seem to interfere with her mouth, but it spoiled whatever appearance she might have had.

The foreigner and the outcast. It was not really coincidence that they each had come last to the meal. He was probably as distasteful of appearance to her as she was to him, because he was furred. So they had that in common: their deviance from this tribe's norm.

He brought out his axe, picked up the fish, laid it on a rock, and cut it into two pieces, head and tail. He offered the head to her. "Hue Ann share."

She seemed surprised. "Share," she agreed, taking the head. She smiled.

He returned the smile. He had done the right thing. It was better for both of them to be somewhat hungry than for one to take all of the fish.

They sat on two rocks and chewed on their portions. Hue realized belatedly that the single fish might have been intended for Ann, because they hadn't allowed for an extra person. But what would have happened if Lee had stayed to eat? Then, ordinarily, Ann might have gone hungry. That would explain why she was so thin.

They finished. Ann went to forage, and Hue went to relieve himself and then just wait, because he had no place in the tribe. He sat again on the rock and thought about Lee. How was he going to settle with her?

In due course the bee party returned. Itt was smiling. They had a wooden pot of honey, and were pleased, though sting-welts showed on the bodies of several of them.

Lee joined Hue. "Good," she said, licking her lips. She must have had some of the honey.

◎

That afternoon Lee showed Hue about the challenge. One section of the shore had been scraped out to form a pool closed off from the lake. A big fish would be driven into that pool, and he would have to catch and kill it. If he succeeded, he got the extra time; if he failed, he was banished. It was a simple and fair test of a foreigner's mettle.

But it was likely to be a problem for him, because he had no expertise in catching fish. Maybe a water folk native could do it, but Hue would probably fail.

"Hue swim good no," he said ruefully. "Catch fish no."

"Lee show," she said eagerly. "Lee fish. Hue catch." She waded into the pool, which was a little over waist deep on her. "Hue catch," she repeated, beckoning.

He laughed. "Girl catch yes," he said. "Fish catch no." Because no person had anything close to the swimming ability of a fish.

"Catch," she insisted.

So he waded in. He realized that she might just want to have him grab onto her, in the hope that he would discover her to be sexually desirable. She was endlessly inventive in that respect. Once he caught her, he would let her go, and he would not have to make the point again.

But the moment he approached, Lee swam away. She pretended to be the fish, swimming lithely in the pool, challenging him to catch her. He tried, changing course to follow her. But though he had swum into the stick dome well enough, he had none of the speed and maneuverability she did. She had been raised in the water, and could do things in it that were simply beyond him.

He leaped for her, thinking he had her, but she slipped past and was gone, leaving him with a double armful of water. She giggled right behind him. He whirled, grabbing, but she was gone again.

This was not as easy as he had anticipated. Still, he knew that it could not be all that difficult to catch a girl in a small pool. He had simply to stop being clumsy.

He stalked her, wading in the center, moving to the side when she did, getting closer. He trapped her in an irregular corner of the pool, so that she would not swim to the side and avoid him. He grabbed—and she sank out of sight.

So he plunged his hands down into the cloudy water. But they found nothing. She had swum around him under the water and was free again.

He turned to spot her, determined to be on guard against that next time. He would grab for her legs, so she couldn't duck down. There were only so many tricks she could use.

He didn't find her. She wasn't in the pool. The murky water was still. But she wasn't on the bank either. There hadn't been time for her to run out of sight. She must have flopped over the narrow ramp of sand that separated the pool from the lake, and hidden among the reeds.

He waded to the edge and out. He certainly had not done well! And a real fish would be much worse. He stood staring out across the lake. This was actually his second day with the tribe; after tomorrow he would have to move on. He might skip the fish challenge, knowing it was useless.

"Hue!"

He turned. There Lee was, in the middle of the pool. She could not have come in over the ramp, because he had been looking that way. But how could she have returned so quickly from the land?

"Catch!" she called.

He forged back into the pool, determined to get this done with rather than giving up. Lee sank down again, disappearing. He paused near the edge, waiting for her to come up, watching the whole pool.

She didn't come up. This time he knew she wasn't fleeing behind his back. Where had she gone?

Had she drowned? Suddenly alarmed, he dived for where she had been, searching for her body. If he could pull her out quickly enough—

"Catch!" she said behind him.

He whirled, startled. There she was, smiling. "Lee drown no?" he asked, though it was obvious that she hadn't.

She laughed. "Lee below."

Could she have held her breath that long? He was amazed. "Lee breathe?"

She approached him. "Hue see," she said. She lifted the end of her long head hair and put it in his hand. "Hold." Then she sank down again.

He held onto her tress, by this means keeping track of her though he could not see her in the dark water. She remained at the bottom of the pool, her hands hooked in the muck; he knew, because one of her fingers was touching his toe.

Didn't she have to breathe? Alarmed, he tugged at her hair. But instead of coming up, she swam on around him, making him turn in a circle as she moved.

It was impossible for her to hold her breath this long! He let go of her hair and reached down to lift her out of the water. But she slipped through his grasp and swam to another part of the pool.

Finally her head broke the surface. "Breathe no," she said.

Hue shook his head, bemused. She had proved it was possible to hold her breath much longer than he could, than he had thought possible. Thus she could dive into the murk and swim far away without being seen—just as a fish could. But he still couldn't catch her—or the fish.

He said as much. "Catch Lee no. Catch fish no."

But she had an answer. "Fish axe."

Use his axe? Not on Lee!

But she was more sensible than that. "Slow. Close. Axe. Fish smart no."

He couldn't stab the fish if he couldn't get close to it. But she showed him what she meant. She floated on the water, like a lazy fish, on her back. She had him approach her slowly, with his axe ready. Whenever he moved too fast, she stroked away, and he had to start over. But he saw that this made sense; he could never catch the fish by trying to pursue it swiftly, but he could fool it by being slow. It was stupid; it thought slow things were harmless. Then a sudden stab with the axe could catch it. Patience and surprise: these were the keys.

Maybe he did have a chance. Lee really had shown him how. He was pleased.

❂

Next day Hue tried for the fish. The man called Itt organized this, as he had the honey hunt; he seemed to be competent in special tasks. The water folk spread out across the lake and came toward the shore, splashing, driving before them what they could see and Hue could not: big fish. When one fish swam through the narrow canal to the pond, children quickly scraped sand to fill the canal, trapping it. They had indeed caught a big fish; it was almost as long as a man, and it circled the pond nervously, perhaps realizing that it was in trouble.

Hue entered the pond with his axe as many water folk watched. Among them were Joe, the leader, and Bil, the smart one, and of course Itt, the best swimmer. Also Lee, and Ann among the women. This was a diversion for them, as the women did not have to forage while the fish chase lasted. Actually he had noted that the water folk seemed to have more leisure than those of other tribes, as well as more security; they seemed generally happier and less pugnacious than the people he couldn't quite remember in his home tribe. Their life-style seemed easier, which perhaps accounted for it.

He stalked the fish. But the fish's circling around the pond had stirred up the mud, and the water was opaque, so that he couldn't see it. Every so often he saw a ripple as it moved near the surface, but he knew it wouldn't be there by the time he approached it in slow motion. This was a complication Lee hadn't thought of. She had stood, or floated on the surface, so that he knew her location. What could he do?

Then he realized that time would fix it. If he stood still, and the fish relaxed, the water would gradually clarify, and then he would be able to see the fish. So he moved to the center of the pond and stood, axe in hand, waiting.

But the fish did not relax. It continued to swim rapidly around the pond, keeping the mud stirred up. So Hue moved slowly back to the edge, so as to intercept the fish as it circled. He was getting a notion of its position, because it swam at a certain speed, and the ripples suggested where it was and in which direction it was going. If he could guess just when it would pass him, he could stab at it blind, seeing it with his mind rather than his eye.

But the fish was too canny for him. When he reached the edge, it changed its course to pass farther inside, remaining out of reach. His motion had alerted it, because he had moved too fast, thinking it couldn't see him any better than he could see it.

The watchers began to fidget. Hue was taking too long; it was clear that he didn't know how to get the fish. He shrugged and moved out of the pond, giving it up. He would have to leave this tribe. He didn't mind doing that, but he did mind failing.

Lee came to join him. That reminded him: he could still join, by mating with her. But he still didn't want to do that. But he wouldn't be able to stop her from coming with him, because he still owed her. That wasn't ideal either.

Itt took a step toward the water, but Joe stopped him with a gesture. "Watch," Joe said. He waded into the water himself.

Hue watched as the man took a stance near the fish's circle. He held his axe in one hand, and trailed the fingers of the other hand just slightly into the water. He stood so still he seemed dead.

Suddenly he moved, striking into the water with his axe. And he hit the fish! It thrashed, and blood colored the water. Joe grabbed it and tossed it out onto the land. Then he looked at Hue. "Hue do?" he asked.

Hue realized that the man must have sensed the fish with his fingers, picking up the vibration of its passage the way a man could put his ear to the ground and hear nearby large prey walking. But Hue was not trained for this; he had no such sensitivity. He could not see the fish with his fingers. "No."

Joe shrugged. He had given Hue another chance, but Hue couldn't take it. He had failed their challenge, and was not qualified to be one of the water folk. He turned away.

Then he saw a large shore bird flying close. It passed over the pond, winging up toward some distant perch.

Hue hurled his axe at it, using his favored arm, which wasn't the same as those of most other men. The axe spun as it sailed, glinting in the slanting sunlight. It curved, intersecting the bird. Then the axe struck the bird on the wing. The bird squawked and flopped down, landing in the pond.

Hue waded into the water to fetch it. He caught it as it struggled, wrung its neck, and tossed it beside the fish. "Bird eat," he said.

He left the pool and went to recover his axe, where it had fallen beyond the pool. There was blood on its sharp edge; he wiped that off in the dirt and returned it to his pouch.

Only then did he realize that the tribesfolk were staring at him. Itt's mouth was locked open. Had Hue done something wrong? Should he have tried to use his other arm, to be more like one of them?

Bil shook his head, seeming amazed. "Day day day," he said, and the others nodded agreement.

Hue had been granted his extension after all! "Bird easy," he protested. "Fish hard."

Several of the men shook their heads. "Bird hard," Joe said.

Now Hue understood. His tribe was apt at throwing; any man could bring down prey by air, if it was close enough and slow enough and small enough. The farther a man could throw with force and accuracy, the better valued he was as a hunter. Hue had not been the best or the worst thrower, but he was competent. The water folk were apt at swimming and hunting in the water; for them it was easy to track a fish, but hard to bring down a bird. So their routine fish hunt was beyond him—and his routine bird hunt was beyond them. But they respected his prowess as a hunter, now that they had seen it.

"Learn water," Joe said. "Woman show." He looked at the women seated around the pool.

Several of them got to their feet. One of them was Ann, the one with whom he had shared the fish. Lee went to join them. Hue realized that more was expected of him, in the next three days. He had to learn more about the water, and one of these women would teach him. These were the ones who were willing to do so. All were breasted except Lee, but none of them had babies. So they were probably unmated. Just what were they supposed to show him? He suspected that their willingness to do this meant that they found him to be acceptable for mating. Because of his unexpectedly demonstrated prowess for hunting.

He had become accustomed to their bareness and breastedness, and to their somewhat fleshy legs, but still was not eager to mate with any. Yet Lee was no better, despite being furred and almost flat of chest. He was beginning to see women through the eyes of the men of the water folk, and if he had to mate with any, it should be with a fully adult one who did not remind him strongly of his sister. Of course he could depart the tribe at the end of the time, not mating with any.

He was an outsider. One of the women was outcast. That was an affinity, of a kind. So he pointed to Ann.

She looked surprised. She looked around, as if to make sure he hadn't indicated one of the others. She had been willing to teach him, but hadn't expected to be chosen. So he spoke her name. "Ann." And smiled.

She smiled too, and came to him. The others turned away, except for Lee, who looked disappointed. But not grief-stricken. That was reassuring; it meant that mating was not what was expected.

Ann came to stand close before him. "Ann thank," she murmured.

He decided not to try to explain his reason for choosing her. But he appreciated her thanks. "Show?"

"Forage." She glanced up at him, and away, as she spoke. "Child forage. Woman forage. Man hunt."

But he had not been a child among the water folk, so had not learned how to forage their way. So he had to get that experience, if he wanted to join the tribe. They assumed that joining was his ambition. "Hue forage," he agreed. He would learn woman's work. After what he had seen of their way of catching a fish, and their stick shelters in the water, he knew that there was much he did not know, and he did want to learn it, because he was curious about everything.

She led him to the edge of the water, where other women were resuming work. Lee followed, evidently unwilling to give up on him yet. Hue wasn't clear why she hadn't been working before, but suspected that her job had been him: guiding him, keeping him out of mischief, so that no one else had to bother. If she got him to mate with her, all right, but until that time she had been responsible for him. Now it seemed Ann was responsible, so Lee had to resume ordinary work. But she could do it where she chose, and she chose to do it near Hue.

Ann kneeled in the shallow water, facing the shore, and leaned forward. Hue saw how her breasts became globular, almost touching the surface. Yet she wasn't nursing! He knew now that it was the way of the water folk, but he kept being surprised anew, and a bit repelled. Surely it was not pleasant for a woman to seem always as if she had a baby near.

Ann plunged her hands into the muck. She moved them slowly around. Hue imitated her, not sure what the point was. All he found was mud. Lee joined them on the other side, doing the same.

But after a time, Ann raised one hand, holding a clam. She showed it to him, then put it in her pouch. Oh—they were clam hunting. Hue had never done this before, because the mountain streams near his tribe didn't have clams; they had traded with neighboring tribes for them. This was interesting. He searched with vigor, now that he knew what he was doing. And soon he found a clam himself.

By early evening they had each found several clams, and Hue's back was sore from the constant bending over. They brought the clams to the cookfire, where they were added to those brought by other women. Roasted clam was a pleasant change from the constant fish. But there was also roast bird, because of Hue's throw, and there seemed to be much demand for that. Hue realized that the water folk didn't get to eat bird often. Probably the fowl of the water were wary of them, and were not as stupid as the big fish were.

Then they went to the island stick shelters for the night. But this time Hue went with Ann, not Lee. She had a different alcove in the women's and children's dome, but otherwise it was the same. She did not try to sleep against him, or to tempt him into mating, but the region was small enough so that they had to lie touching. Actually that did make it a bit warmer, in the absence of blankets.

○

On the following day Ann showed him how they foraged for reeds. These were hollow, but not perfectly so. They found good, large ones, and used small straight sticks to poke through them and get them clear. Hue learned how to do it, but was curious about the reason. "Reed why?" he asked.

She smiled. He was getting to like her smile, for there was no meanness or subterfuge in it, just pleasure. He had the impression that she liked his company, perhaps being flattered that he had chosen her to be his teacher. She put an end of the reed in her mouth and sank down under the water, in the way these folk could so readily do. She did not come up, and after a moment he realized that she was breathing through the reed, which stuck up above the surface.

And that, he realized, was how the men had been in ambush, when the raiders came. Breathing under the murky water, wielding ropes, catching the ankles of the raiders and pulling them down. They did not do it to friends, only to enemies, never showing themselves. So the raiders did not dare enter the water, lest they fall victim to what they could not see.

Lee laughed, seeing his comprehension on his face. Now he knew what would have happened to him, had he not had her protection as he entered the water, the first day.

That night there was a storm. The thunder was very loud, and the rain sounded on the domes, but only a few drips penetrated the tight mass of sticks. It was dark, but Hue felt Ann shivering beside him. He realized that she was afraid of the storm, as many folk were. So he did what seemed proper: he wrapped his arms around her and drew her in close against him.

"Storm hurt no," he murmured into her mass of hair by her ear. "Light, noise, hurt no." He felt her relax, comforted. In that embrace they slept.

He realized, coincidentally, that however odd this woman might appear by day, she was quite comfortable to hold by night. The softness of her flesh made up for her lack of fur, and her warm female body was appealing.

On the following day they foraged for sticks for the water shelters. It seemed that these had to be constantly maintained, so that they did not leak. He had appreciated the way they kept most of the storm off, so knew this was useful work. In the afternoon they used their sticks to repair damaged sections of the domes, and to shore up weak ones. There was an art to it that it was difficult for him to follow; somehow Ann and the other women were able to bend the thin sticks and weave them together with their attached leaves to make a blanket-tight layer. But there were also animal skins there, completing the job.

On the third day with Ann, Hue still had no serious expectation of joining the tribe. But he found he was getting more comfortable with it. The ways of the water folk were different from those of his own tribe, sometimes startlingly so, but he was learning that there was a certain underlying similarity. Hunting fish was perhaps like hunting birds, only in water instead of on land or in the air. Swimming was like walking—and indeed, much of it *was* walking, on the hidden paths under the water. The people seemed less odd as he got to know them individually; they were much like those he had known before. It occurred to him that it might after all be worthwhile to mate with a woman of the water folk, so as to join this special society for the rest of his life. But he still did not want to do it with Lee.

This day they were herding fish to the pond—many small ones. All the women and children and a few men spread out under Itt's direction to circle the school and splash, scaring the fish to the pond. Hue had a notion how that was done, though he still couldn't sense fish with his fingers the way the others could. But he could splash water with the best of them, and that did help herd the fish.

He was positioned between Ann and Lee, with other women and children spread out beyond. He was coming to know some of the others. He saw the child called Ember, so called because she was fascinated by fire and was always eager to help tend it. She was a small, thin girl, about ten years old, but nice of feature and an excellent swimmer; she would one day be a good woman.

Then something strange happened. The water rippled, though there was no wind—and the ripple went right down to the bottom. Hue could feel it throughout his body. The others did too; they looked at each other, and all around, trying to fathom the nature of this effect. It was as if some truly monstrous fish were coming, pushing the water before it—but there was no such creature. He saw that Ann on one side and Lee on the other were as baffled as he was. Little Ember looked fascinated rather than frightened by the oddity, while others seemed poised to flee the water. None of them knew what was happening. But it didn't seem to be dangerous, merely strange.

After a moment there was a dull sound from the distance, across the water and the land, as if something huge had fallen to the ground. That made Hue concentrate, remembering something he had forgotten. "Rock fall," he said.

Others turned to him. "Hue live mountain," he explained. His tribe had been near mountains, some of which had very steep slopes. "Rock fall." He made a gesture as of something dropping down. "Loud." Indeed, the neighboring avalanche had terrified the tribesmen. But it had stopped, and no one had been hurt. Later they had gone out to the region and found the new pile of stones in the valley, and realized that they had come sliding and rolling down from some high face of the mountain. So it was an ordinary event, just a rare one. Hue remembered the special sound of it, and what he had just heard was similar, though muffled by distance.

The water folk relaxed, understanding the principle. They could see the peaks of distant mountains, but had no experience with rolling rocks. This one must have been really big, because the peaks in that direction were barely visible, being far away. So the land and water had shaken with the impact, but no harm had been done.

The fish herding resumed. Hue realized that this was similar to the herding of rabbits and other small game that his tribe had done, driving them into a canyon where they could be slaughtered. The ways of the water differed from the ways of the land, yet had an underlying similarity when understood. He grasped only a small part of the water life as yet, but was coming to appreciate it better as he learned more. He realized that he would regret leaving it tomorrow.

Someone screamed. It was Ember, fleeing an ominous ripple. "Croc!" her mother cried, alarmed.

There was pandemonium. Women and children alike tried to escape the creature. The other men were on the far side of the skirmish line, too far away to help immediately. Itt started swimming strongly toward the commotion, but would not arrive in time to deal with it.

But Hue was close. He did not know what kind of a fish this was, but he knew the duties of a man when there was a threat. He brought out his axe and lunged for the ripple.

But Lee was between him and it. As he sought to pass her, the ripple veered toward her. A very long green mouth opened, horrendously toothed, and closed on Lee's arm. Lee screamed piercingly with pain and fear as the creature pulled her off her feet.

Hue swung his arm. He struck the green snout. The flesh was tough, but his edge cut into it. The jaws parted and Lee jerked herself away.

Now the croc focused on Hue. It was quick enough to know its enemy. Its mouth opened again, snapping at his head.

But though Hue had never seen a creature like this before, he had once fought a predator of the land. He knew better than to let those teeth score. So he oriented the point of his axe and stabbed it upward, into the descending upper jaw. He struck a tooth, and then the flesh around the tooth, and twisted, grinding the sharp rounded edge against whatever was there. An axe was a deadly weapon as well as a tool, and he did know how to use it.

The creature moved away, swimming far more swiftly than any person could. It circled, and came back for another attack. But in the brief respite, Hue realized that he had been doing it wrong. The thing had its horrendous long mouth, and that mouth was deadly; it was bound to chomp Hue if it kept trying. But the mouth had to open before it could close on anything. So Hue leaped to embrace the creature, wrapping his arms around its snout, squeezing it closed.

He might as well have embraced a lion! The croc whipped its head about, trying to throw him off, and its stout tail lashed at his legs. It hurt; the tail was not only strong, it was ragged, and it could do him damage. Hue had either to let go, or to get close enough to stop that tail. So he folded his body and wrapped his legs around the creature.

But this meant that he was no longer standing. The croc rolled, and Hue's head was under water. He couldn't breathe, but neither could he let go. So he did the only thing remaining: he let go of the snout with his axe arm, and struck where he hoped the throat was, digging the point in hard. The croc struggled mightily, but Hue hung on, carving with his axe.

Until his lack of breath overcame him, and he felt his consciousness fading. He felt his arms letting go of the croc, and felt the water coming into his mouth.

❂

Something was jamming down on his back, squeezing him unmercifully. Hue choked, and water poured out of his mouth. He coughed, and choked again. What was happening?

After an uncomfortable time he understood. He was on the beach, and Itt was beating the water out of him. He had nearly drowned, but Itt had hauled him out and done what he knew to do, shaking and squeezing until he started breathing again. Itt had saved him.

But as his body and head cleared, he remembered what else had been happening. "The croc—Lee—"

"Lee," Lee repeated. Now he saw her, with mud caking her arm where the croc had bitten her. That meant that the women were treating her, covering up the wounds. "Hue owe no." She looked sad, but perhaps it was because she was in pain.

She gave him credit for saving her life, as perhaps he had, and regarded his debt to her as having been acquitted. He would no longer have to mate with her, if he didn't want to. That was a relief, because though he might not remain with the water folk, he didn't like the notion of having an unpaid debt. He was now even with Lee.

"Croc," he said, now concerned about what other mischief the savage creature might have done. He didn't know whether he had driven it off.

Bil and Joe were now here. Bil pointed to a thing on the beach nearby. It was the croc, dead. It seemed much smaller, somehow, being no longer than a man. Its throat region had been so severely lacerated that it would not have been recognizable if seen alone. It seemed that Hue had managed to do the job before he faded out.

"Axe," he said, remembering his most valuable possession.

Ember stepped forward, the axe in her hand. She must have gotten it from the muck after they dragged Hue and the croc out. She gave it to Hue, smiling prettily. He remembered that she had been at one time in the path of the croc, so perhaps she felt he had saved her too. If he had, he was glad of it, because she was a nice child.

"Day," Bil said then, spreading his arms as if to include the whole land. That meant that the time limit was off; Hue could remain with the tribe as long as he wished, though he could not actually join it unless he mated with one of its women. They were satisfied that he was worth having with them.

Then the group dispersed. Ann came to tend to him, bringing him food. He saw the women returning to the water, reorganizing for the fish drive, which had been broken up. "Fish," he said, trying to get up.

She pushed him gently down. "Hue no," she said, and smiled to show that this was a privilege rather than an exclusion. He remained somewhat shaky, so perhaps this was best, because he might not be much good in the line. Evidently Ann was out of it, too, to take care of him.

Hue's head ached and his chest felt bad and his legs were scratched and bruised. But Ann made him lie flat on the ground, and she put her hands on him and kneaded his flesh, and that felt good. She hummed in the mode of healing. She knew the art of women, to make a tense or injured man relax. Her hands were thin, like the rest of her, but competent, and the pleasure they brought him made them beautiful. In fact as he lay there and let her massage him it was as if the pleasure spread from her hands to her arms and to her body, so that it no longer seemed badly shaped. Her legs were still somewhat thick, her hips too broad, and her waist too small, but now these proportions seemed right for her. Her breasts were still swollen, but actually not as much as for a fully nursing woman, and that partial development now seemed normal, as indeed it was for the women of the water folk. Even her jutting chin was not really ugly, and he realized that if she ever got struck on the mouth, her lower jaw would be protected by that buttress of bone so that she would not starve after such injury. He had seen the pitiful state of a man who had taken a jaw injury, able to eat only with pain, and knew that if he himself ever got struck on that vulnerable spot he would suffer similarly. So Ann, somehow, had a more sensible face.

That night, when he still did not feel good, Ann wrapped her arms around him and held him close, much as he had with her when the storm frightened her, and she hummed again, as if to a sick child, and he slept without difficulty.

❂

Next day Joe was waiting outside the shelter. "Come," he told Hue. So he left Ann and went to join the men. He had been promoted, and no longer had to learn the ways of women.

Now he began to learn the water ways of hunting. They used thin wood spears instead of axes, and sought to drive them into the larger prey of the region. Itt gave him a spear and showed him how, frowning without comment when Hue used what was considered to be the wrong hand. On this day they did not find any such prey, but they freely described how it was done. Hue also learned that they systematically hunted any crocs they found, keeping them out of the tribe's foraging region. The one that had attacked Lee had been an aberration, perhaps disoriented by the distant rockslide and shudder of water. The men felt that Hue had done a bold thing, fighting it alone with his axe. He was of stouter build than they, more muscular, stronger, so had been able to do it, but still they were impressed by the way he hadn't hesitated. It seemed that the women had told every detail, more than he remembered, of his fight with the reptile, with Lee being especially eloquent. He had shown courage on behalf of the tribe, when he had not been obliged to.

He learned how they set their rope and shell snares, so that when a stranger entered the water on hostile business, men concealed amidst the reeds—sometimes under water, breathing through the stems—had only to pull on those ropes to interfere with the legs. There were loops along the ropes, that could catch ankles. There were trench-pits, covered by fine nets and a thin layer of mud, some with sharpened stakes below. The women knew where they were, and avoided them; Hue had been placed between Ann and Lee not merely because he had been associating with them, but because they would steer him clear of mischief underfoot. They had not expected mischief to seek them out.

And they talked passingly about women. Hue, recognizing the opening, mentioned that he realized that he would have to mate with one in order to join the tribe, and that he was getting more interested in the ways of the water folk, but of the two women who had shown interest, one reminded him of his little sister, and the other was thin and odd-looking.

"Chin," Joe agreed, touching his own receding lower jaw, which was like Hue's. "Chin no, Ann yes." And the others murmured agreement.

Actually Hue had been more concerned with her thinness and almost complete hairlessness. But he realized that all the water folk were thin and hairless, except for their heads and crotches, so of course they regarded such qualities as esthetic. Their other women tended to be broad of hip and narrow of waist, too. And breasted, with rounded legs. So by their definition, Ann was indeed beautiful.

And he, having figured out the possible usefulness of the chin, had concluded that that need not be an objection. So it made her different from the others; so did his hair and build make him just as different. So in that sense they were reasonably matched.

"Lee young," another man said. He was Vik. "Vik sister no. Fur." He shrugged. That was Lee's liability; she was too much like Hue's tribes people.

"Fur bad no," Bil said, glancing at Hue.

"Fur bad no," Vik agreed. "Lee yes."

Hue felt good. Because they were accepting him, and he was furred, Lee's similar liability was diminishing. So she might after all be able to find a mate within the tribe.

The following day they did find prey, a baby hippo they were able to isolate from its mother and stab to death. Then they floated the carcass back to the home beach for butchering. Hue was getting more comfortable with the ways of water hunting, learning them quickly because of their underlying similarity to what he had known. He realized that he would never be as good at them as the natural water folk were, but at least he was making fewer errors.

That night there was another storm. Hue didn't wait for Ann to be frightened; he embraced her immediately. But the storm held off, not coming close.

Ann, close against him, smiled. It was too dark to see anything, but he felt her mouth stretching. He had embraced her without cause. He smiled back, not minding.

Then she put her hand on his penis and paused. She was silently offering him sex, in appreciation for his protection.

Surprised, he considered. His penis became immediately hard, indicating his body's interest. He no longer found her sexually uninteresting. But he wasn't sure he wanted to mate with her, with the attendant commitment. So he reached down and gently removed her hand. Then he held her close, to show that he was not rejecting her, only declining to go that far.

She relaxed against him, satisfied. Soon she was asleep, breathing softly against him. But he remained awake. Now that he had declined her offer, he wondered whether he should have. His penis remained hard. No, he did not find her unattractive, here in the night. But what of the day?

Then the storm abruptly moved in, and the thunder was loud, and the rain beat down. Ann woke, frightened, and he turned into her and tightened his embrace, to reassure her. She felt his hard member against her belly and paused in her fright long enough to inquire again. But again he declined—and then wondered why he had done so. He did desire her, and would desire her by day. But the major step of mating with her and joining the tribe—that put him into deep doubt.

The thunder eased, but the rain continued. Ann relaxed. But still his penis was hard against her. This time she slid up to put her mouth to his ear. "Ann tell no," she whispered.

So she would give him sex, and not announce it as a mating, leaving him free. In the steady noise of the rain it would be possible for them to do it, and others would not overhear.

He was sorely tempted. It would be so easy. But still he could not. "No," he whispered with regret.

She didn't question his decision, but neither did she withdraw. She went to sleep with his hard penis against her. And, finally, he slept too.

○

The rain continued the next day, sometimes light, sometimes heavy. When it wasn't torrential, they could tell by the sound of distant thunder and the sight of lightning flashes that it was raining just as hard elsewhere. The water folk couldn't hunt or forage during such a storm, because they were all wary of the thunder. In fact, none of them would go into the water while there was thunder. So they had to remain in the shelter, just clear of the water.

"Why?" Hue asked, perplexed. His tribesmen had hunted in the rain; it actually helped them for some prey, because it could confuse the animals.

"Water kill," Ann explained.

He could make no sense of that. As far as he could tell, it was an untested belief. Maybe something their shaman said, if they had one. But all of them were adamant; none would touch the water.

When there was a lull, they dived out in a long line, and swam for the beach, where they went into the brush to defecate. Hue did the same. Then they tried to make a fire so as to cook some of the hippo meat, but the moment it got fairly started, the rain returned, threatening to douse it. Ember was disgusted, evidently believing that she could make a fire that would survive the rain. But she was only a girl-child, without authority in such matters.

Hue had encountered this before. He broke a leafy branch from a tree and brought it to hold over the fire, so that the rain struck the leaves and ran down to the side, sparing the flame. It was still possible to cook. Ember clapped her little hands, pleased.

But the others fled to the water and to the shelters, so as to reach them before the thunder struck. Even Ember had to go, summoned peremptorily by her mother. She looked longingly back at the flame as she entered the water. Hue, disgusted, remained protecting the fire. Only Ann stayed with him, though she seemed reluctant. "Storm no," she said, looking fearfully into the sky.

He hadn't meant to get her caught out in it, knowing her concern. He lowered the branch. "Go shelter," he said.

But it was too late. Bright light flashed, reflecting from the water, and soon thunder came. She would not touch the water now.

So he did the next best thing. He broke off more branches, chopping with his axe when he had to, and quickly formed a kind of shelter by the fire. It was far from perfect, but it did deflect the brunt of the rain, so that the fire continued to burn. Then he carved off some chunks of hippo and impaled them on sticks so that the two of them could roast them. Anne joined him, somewhat comforted by the shelter and the fire.

But the storm got worse than before, and soon managed to extinguish the fire and soak both of them. Winds swirled, making leaves dance, and blew apart the shelter. They had to flee to the protection of the larger trees of the forest. They ate some of the meat, then huddled together in the sluicing water, gazing at the nearby surface of the lake.

Lightning stabbed down, striking the water. There was a sizzling sound. The thunder came at the same time, deafeningly. Ann screamed; he couldn't hear her, but felt her shoulders moving with it. He held her as closely as he could, but there was no way he could entirely stop her fright. The fact was, he was scared himself, though of course he could not admit it.

Then he saw something strange. Things were floating on the water. As he peered, trying to figure out what they were, Ann explained: "Fish dead. Thunder."

The thunder had killed the fish! He wouldn't have believed it if he hadn't just seen it. That was why the water folk stayed out of the water during a storm! They knew that they could be killed too. Somehow the thunder did in the water what it did not do on land, becoming not only deafening but deadly.

So they could not return to the shelter until the storm passed—and it showed no sign of doing that. On occasion a storm lasted for days, and this seemed to be one of those. So Hue left Ann huddling against a large tree, gathered more branches and rocks, made a better shelter, and plaited fine branches so as to overlap the leaves and make it as tight as possible. Large rocks weighted down the ends of the branches, and vines tied them together. Then he brought Ann to it and drew closed the small entrance.

Now they were insulated from the rain, except for some inevitable drips, and perhaps more important, from the wild appearance of the outside. He held Ann, sharing body warmth, and gradually she relaxed. He had restored some of what they had lost by being cut off from the water shelter.

But they were caught alone, isolated from the tribe, and he knew that Ann felt nervous about it. She was a creature of the tribe, and though she had been somewhat outcast within it because of her chin, she needed it. He had known first that he would have to mate with her to join the tribe; now he knew that he had to join the tribe to mate with her, because she could not exist apart from it. Lee was feisty and independent, ready to leave the tribe if she had to to get what she wanted, but Ann was a creature of her people. If he were ever to leave the tribe, he might not be able to take her with him. That could have been part of what made him hesitate, before. Did he want to be locked into the water folk?

What else did he have? His place in his own tribe had soured; he did not care to return there. Bub had offered to have him mate with Sis if he joined their tribe, but that didn't completely appeal either. So the water folk seemed best. All he had to do was commit to Ann—and he was about ready to do that. He was coming to like her very well.

But there was one more thing: how did she feel about him? She had offered to train him for the women's work, and had stayed with him when he went on to man's work, but that might mean just a continuing responsibility until he went to some other woman. She had offered him sex, but that might be from appreciation for his support, or just general courtesy. He needed to know how well she liked him for himself, and whether she wished to commit to him permanently.

He tried to ask her. "Ann Hue like?"

She glanced at him. "Sex?"

They were sitting beside each other. The reference made his penis harden, and she could see that. "No."

"Yes," she decided. "Owe." She shifted position, seeking a way to lie down in the cramped shelter.

"No!" But of course that wasn't clear. "Ann owe no."

She gave him a straight look. "Ann want."

But was she saying it to free him of obligation, so that she could give him this without committing him? He was not looking for appreciation, he was looking for love. "Hue want." She smiled acquiescently. "Hue want Ann want." She nodded. Finally he broached the dread notion: "Love." This was a seldom used, seldom understood concept. It signified the union of those who did it for reasons other than practical, sometimes at great cost.

Her eyes grew large. "Love," she repeated. "Hue Ann?"

"Ann Hue," he clarified. He wanted to know if Ann could love Hue.

She looked at him again. "Hue Ann love?" She touched her chin.

He turned his upper body, caught her elbows, and approached her face. She could turn away if she wished to. She did not. He kissed her projecting chin.

Her mouth worked, but she did not speak. Water appeared in her eyes.

He lifted his face and brought it close again. This time she moved too, bringing her mouth to meet his. They kissed. In that moment he knew that he could indeed love her, and that she could love him.

When he drew away, she remained unmoving. Her eyes lost their focus; she seemed to be gazing out beyond the shelter, into the sky. "Love day," she said. "Storm no."

She thought that love could not exist in a circumstance like this. She was afraid it wasn't real. She was afraid to believe.

But it might be days before the sun shone again. He did not want to wait that long. He wanted her to believe now. How could he persuade her?

He thought about it. Then he tried something he had never thought of before. He tried to pretend there was sun. "Ann eyes shut," he said. "Hue eyes shut."

She glanced at him, then closed her eyes. He did the same. "Think rain no. Think sound water splash. Think day yes." He had always been good at imagining sounds; could he enable her to do it too?

"Rain yes," she said, perplexed.

"Rain yes. THINK rain no. Think sun yes."

"Sun yes," she echoed uncertainly.

Carefully he took her through it: instead of being stuck in a leaking shelter in a storm, they were in bright sunshine. They were not alone on the beach, but together with the other members of the tribe. They had an audience for what they were about to do.

As he spoke the words, over and over, and heard her echoes, he did begin to see it. They were still on the beach, but in the brightest day, surrounded by a ring of all the water folk, waiting expectantly. Then he took Ann's hand. "Hue mate Ann," he said. "Join tribe."

"Ann mate Hue," she said, her voice charged with emotion. "Love."

"Love," he agreed. Then he kissed her. Then they did sex before everyone, the whole tribe being witness. And lay there hugging each other, just sharing the feeling. While the sunshine beat down loudly and steadily all around, and dripped on them.

✺

Hue wasn't sure how many times the sun shone on their unions, but it was a number. At one point they laughed together, realizing that the sun was shining just as brightly in the middle of the night. But at last they woke to real day, after a night, and the rain was gone. Hue opened the door.

And saw the water of the lake almost up to their shelter. What had happened?

They stared out across the lake. There were the shelters, but strangely small. They had been flooded out!

Now they saw the water folk swimming toward the shore. They had heard the sudden silence of the end of the storm, and come out immediately. But it must have been terrible in the shelters. Worse than on the beach.

They got the story in scattered bits: The rain had continued unremittingly, and the water had risen. At first the folk had simply drawn their feet back, having experienced such rises before; the shelters were made so that some rise could be accommodated. But this rise was worse than any they had ever encountered. The water crept across their sleeping places. At first they had to share the highest ones, but then these too flooded. They dared not let the water touch them long, for fear of the thunder-kill. So they took sticks from the domes and made higher platforms. These were uncomfortable, but they had no choice. Still the water rose. They had to keep building, until the domes began to collapse because of the weakening of their structure. By dawn their houses had become a cluster of islands, each crowded with shivering people.

At last the storm passed. As soon as they thought it was safe, they plunged into the water and swam for shore. Hue recognized Joe and Bil and Itt, Lee and Ember, and many others. They had lost their shelters, but at least there had been no deaths. Now most of them just wanted to find safe places to rest and sleep, for they had managed little of either during the night.

Hue exchanged a glance with Ann. They had thought they had been badly off, but they had survived the night in more comfort and a good deal more pleasure than the others had.

But something needed to be said. Hue approached Joe. "Hue Ann mate," he said.

Joe, distracted by other concerns, only glanced at Ann, who nodded. "Good," he said, and moved on.

So much for their fancied public ceremony. They had picked the wrong time.

Things were in sad disarray. Many people were badly fatigued from discomfort and fright, and stood somewhat dazedly, not knowing what to do. Some had been injured. One woman was about to birth her baby. And the storm was coming back.

Bil approached. "Joe enemy look," he said. That made sense, as the water folk were highly vulnerable now, being confined to the shore. They would have to hide if there were any enemy tribes raiding. "Bil island lead." So he knew of a new island the tribe could use for protection and residence; once he got the water folk there, they could afford to rest. "Hue food move."

Just like that, Hue was working directly for the tribe, with a responsible task. That hippo meat should not be wasted; they would need it to eat while they built new domes. "Where?"

"Island. Ann know." Bil looked at Ann. "Peninsula." He went on, seeing to other business.

Ann nodded. "Peninsula low neck," she said. "Water high, island."

Oh. Of course the water folk knew all the bypaths of the shoreline. They would simply float the carcass to the island. It would be a slow job for one man, but it was important.

But as the weary water folk followed Bil along the path around the expanded lake, the storm darkened and the rain resumed. Thunder crashed nearby. Ann cringed, and so did a number of the others. "Go go go!" Bil cried, not letting them dive for cover. He knew that the thunder wouldn't hurt them on land, but that enemies could. Their first priority was to get to the new island.

Bil was the actual leader of the tribe, Hue realized. Joe was the nominal one, but he wasn't as smart as Bil, so the key decisions were made by Bil. It seemed to work well enough, because Bil always made a show of consulting Joe and deferring to his judgment.

But now Hue had his own chore to handle. They couldn't enter the water while the thunder was threatening, but the hippo carcass was too massive to carry on land. What were they to do?

Hue pondered, and decided that a rope would do it. He foraged for vines, tied them together to make a long rope, tied it to the carcass, and shoved it into the water. Then he walked along the shore, hauling on the vine. It wasn't easy, because the carcass tended to snag on things, and there was no path here, but he did make slow progress. The thing also tended to swing back in toward land, until Ann got a long stick and kept shoving it out while Hue pulled. That helped a lot.

Ann told him the way, though she ran for the cover of a tree every time the thunder pealed. Hue did not comment; she was doing well to restrain her fear enough to guide him. Of course he might be able to find the island by himself, just by following the shoreline far enough, but this way he was able to skip inlets that she knew were wrong. There were streams flowing into the lake, and they had to gamble by forging across these, hoping the thunder would not strike when they were in the water. Ann was terrified, but did it when she had to. He grabbed her, held her, and kissed her, in this way shoring up her courage.

It was hard to tell in this unfamiliar terrain, but it seemed to Hue that the water was still rising. Certainly it wasn't sinking, because he saw no water marks on the tree trunks above the level of the lake. But there were a number of trees now growing out of the swirling brown water.

Late in the day they reached the island. It was hard to believe that it had ever been anything else, because it was separated from the land by a fair amount. But its central portion rose well above the lake, so it was in no danger of being flooded out of existence.

The rain eased off, and the thunder retreated, so they were able to swim across to the island, dragging the carcass behind. Ann was a real help here, because though she lacked Hue's strength, she was a much better swimmer. They heaved it onto the shore, and looked around.

The island was wooded, though there were no large trees. There was a crude dome shelter at the top of the hill, under which a number of women and children were sleeping. Men were building other domes around it, hauling bundles of sticks in from the mainland, floating them across the intervening lake. Women were plaiting roof material from prepared brush.

A small sheltered fire was going, and clams were being roasted. The woman had birthed her baby and was nursing it, while her prior child watched. The baby's head was huge, but that seemed to be normal for these folk. Overall, the situation was looking good.

Soon men came to work on the hippo carcass. They were smiling; there would be a good meal tonight.

Bil came down to them. "Hue Ann shelter," he said, pointing to a small open-sided dome. "Do."

"Work much," Hue said, looking around. "Hue Ann help." He was tired from his labor of the day, but much remained to be done.

"Shelter," Bil repeated firmly, seeming amused.

Ann caught Hue's hand and drew him toward the shelter. Then he understood: their mating. It was time to clarify it for the tribe. Then there would be no question.

They went to the shelter. They sat under it, and Ann brushed back her long dark hair and smiled at him, and he wondered that he could ever have thought her to be odd in appearance. Now her bare skin and full breasts seemed natural, and her chin gave her face distinction. After all, her face was small, and needed that extra brace of bone to keep it firm. Her broad hips were so she could birth a bigheaded baby. Everything made sense, and he was acquiring a taste for it.

He kissed her, and then lay with her, and it was wonderful to be close to her. The initial urgency of sex had been abated during the prior day and night, so there was no hurry, and he enjoyed it perhaps more. At length it was finished, and they separated and sat up.

The rest of the tribe was seated in a circle, watching, smiling. Lee was there, and she did not look jealous, while beside her Ember looked amused. This was their entertainment for a day that had not had much else to recommend it. Then, having seen that the couple had seen them seeing, they got up and returned to their various endeavors. And Hue and Ann returned to theirs: hauling bundles of sticks up to the shelters that were under construction. There needed to be shelter for all by nightfall, for the rain was coming back once more.

The fire increased, and the smell of meat spread. They went for their meal, and Hue realized that it was their first of the day. They had been so busy that they had never paused to eat—and there hadn't been much food available anyway. He saw Ember carrying wood; she was as usual delighted to be able to help tend the fire.

And there was Lee, carving out portions of hippo for the others with her uninjured arm and hand. She worked beside Vik, and there was something about the way the two related to each other that suggested that another couple was forming.

❂

The rain continued intermittently for several more days, gradually easing. But the lake continued to rise even when the sun was shining. The island grew smaller, but the center was high enough so that it could not be overwhelmed. Hue realized that Bil had required the people to build shelters high for this reason, so that rising water would not wash them out either. The island had become their shelter base, and if the water rose enough, they would be as before, with only the tops of the domes showing above the surface.

The neighboring enemy tribes did not attack. In fact there was little sign of them anywhere in the area. This was suspicious, and finally Bil decided to investigate it. Bil always anticipated problems, and tried to prepare for them in advance. Thus he had known where the tribe could be safe, if the waters rose; there had been no hesitation when he took them to the new island. Now he was concerned.

So Joe, Bil, and Hue left their women behind and went to where the nearest enemy tribe lived. It was a sunny day, so they were able to use the water when they got close, silently wading or swimming. They had reeds to breathe through, in case they needed to submerge. Hue knew that their pace was slower because of him, but Bil wanted him along because he knew more about the hairy folk, being one himself. He might recognize some aspect that the full water folk would not.

The region was strangely quiet. No raiders were out foraging near the shore. Of course they normally foraged away from the water; still, it was odd that there were none by the lake. But there was a fire some distance back from the shore. That would mark their camp.

The three moved quietly toward that fire, alert for enemies, for this was approaching the heart of raider territory. It was extremely unusual to have so little activity here. There did not even seem to be guard patrols.

Finally they came to the fire itself, peering cautiously out of the shelter of thick brush. And were amazed.

The fire was in a glade, and the glade was filled with hairy raiders. Most of them were lying on the ground. A few were afoot, but even those ones did not look lively. What were they doing?

"Sick," Hue whispered.

The other two nodded. That was why there had been no raids since the flood. Some terrible illness had come upon the raiders, and was wiping them out.

They retreated as quietly as they had come. But once they were away from the camp, they used land trails to return to the island. It was obvious that there would be no pursuit, no ambush party. The raiders had trouble of their own.

But Hue was worried. "Sickness—sometimes," he said, straining to remember what he had heard about it. "People die. Some live. Many no. All tribes." He had no idea why this happened, just that it did, every so often.

Joe shook his head. "Water folk sickness no," he said, and Bil agreed. Mass dyings were unknown among them.

None of them could fathom why this should be so. But it was. No sickness came to the water folk.

The water continued to rise, until the island was small. Itt had to supervise changes in their activity to keep their supplies secure. But they were safe there—and on the shore too, for there were now too few raiders to raid. They made their traps by the new shoreline, but never needed to use them. They began to expand their hunting and foraging territory beyond the lake, because the protection of the water was no longer critical. They accepted the new and better order.

Perhaps only Bil and Hue wondered why the lake had grown, and why the illness had so weakened the raiders. The others simply accepted it as the destiny of their kind, which was obviously the best fitted to survive and prosper.

And prosper they did, expanding in the course of thousands of years out from the fringe of Lake Victoria until they had taken over all of Africa, and then the rest of the world. But why did fate take such a turn, so that one of the seemingly weakest subgroups of mankind came to dominate and replace all the others?

Some questions are readily answered, in retrospect. The lake expanded because one of the frequent earthquakes caused a landslide that blocked the lake's northern drainage—today known as the river Nile. When heavy rains came, the lake filled, and this continued when the rains stopped because of the drainage into the lake from the entire area. Thus the territory of the land dwellers was flooded and diminished, while that of the water dwellers was increased. In time the river cut a new channel, and the lake drained and dwindled, but by then the balance had shifted, and the water folk were numerous and powerful, while the land folk were less populous and not well organized.

What happened to the Homo erectus *tribes? Perhaps fleas. Erect man was thickly furred, which meant he had fleas, impossible to obliterate. On occasion the fleas carried disease, and thus spread plague. The only people free of this liability were those who did not have fleas: the hairless ones. Modern man. Of course we Moderns do have body hair, but it is relatively slight, so that we do look bare, and fleas cannot survive on us. Hairlessness was originally an adaptation for the water, but it turned out to have survival value on the land too. On occasion Modern man did live in such dense communities, using clothing never changed or cleaned, and associated so closely with animals, that fleas could attack him, and so the pattern of plagues returned. The plagues of medieval times suggest what Erect man suffered in earlier millennia. But that later time there was no variant species waiting to take over, and mankind survived, pretty much by chance. The original change probably did not happen in just one siege; it may have taken tens of thousands of years for repeated sieges to weaken Erect man so that Modern man was able to displace him. The flooding of the Lake Victoria basin could have caused disruption as tribes were driven back, crowding them into smaller territories and making them more vulnerable to flea infestations and disease. Some survivors might have mated with the increasingly numerous water folk, as Hue did with Ann, but most furred tribes would have become slowly extinct. First in Africa, then in Eurasia, as the Moderns became overwhelmingly numerous.*

There was another aspect of the change in woman's body. Her great amount of time in the water made odor a poor sexual signal, so the emphasis became visual instead of olfactory. Her breasts became high and full, to be seen and used when she was chest deep in the water. With mankind's increasing intelligence came his awareness of the connection between sex and babies, and neither man nor woman always wishes to have babies. Thus nature conspired to conceal the woman's key time, so that it was never possible to be sure when she could conceive. The fact that a woman's breasts no longer shrank when she was fertile meant that she was continuously alluring and, as far as vision went, continuously impregnable. The risk of conception could not be avoided, if there were sexual activity. This led to chronic population pressure, and the evidence is that the Moderns did outbreed Erect man.

Breasts seem to be modified sweat glands, and sweating is something that only mankind and horses do for cooling—a dangerous mechanism, unless replacement water is freely available. But effective, enabling mankind to handle hotter climate, and to exercise longer without overheating. This was another powerful mechanism for survival, thanks to water.

The retention of pubic hair is more difficult to explain. Why did all the rest of the body go bare except parts of the head and the pubic region? The head needed hair to protect the valuable brain, and the hair on the face differentiated the males from the females. But both sexes grow pubic hair at maturity, and it really isn't needed to differentiate that section of the body. Hair can help spread odor, and this may be the case with genital hair, but could hardly have done so when women spent much of their time waist deep in water. Yet nature does not do things without reason. There had to be a survival advantage for genital hair. Perhaps it serves as additional protection of that region when the male's sperm cells are activated and possibly vulnerable to mutation or damage by temperature or the penetrating radiation of the sun. It may not be coincidence that only the brain and genitals remain protected by fur.

Modern mankind's head had modified. As his mouth and jaws got smaller and more nearly square, structural strength was lost, and some additional buttress was needed. Thus extra bone at the chin helped survival. The skull, too, changed shape. Modern man did not necessarily have more brain tissue than Erect man, but its distribution differed. This may have been because mankind's adaptation to life in the water, while not entirely leaving the land, required additional mental processes. People had to learn how to use the knowledge and reflexes developed for survival on the land to survive in water. This dual ability may seem elementary to us—but we represent the end result. It surely was not at first simple for mankind, who had evolved almost entirely away from the water. So some of the prior brain tissue at the rear of the brain faded in importance, and new tissue was added at the front. This is surely an oversimplification, but it may be that comprehensive memory gave way to better analytical ability. That turned out, later, to be a critical shift. Modern mankind not only looked different, he thought differently.

And, lest there be any confusion: though Ann may have looked odd to Erect Man, because of her swollen breasts, small waist, broad pelvis, thick thighs, furlessness, and even to her own tribes-people because of her bony chin, she represents physically the final human form. Today we appreciate breasted women, and males too have chin braces. For our tastes, she would appear to be absolutely lovely. She just might be the species template, Eve of Eden, the ancestor of all mankind today.

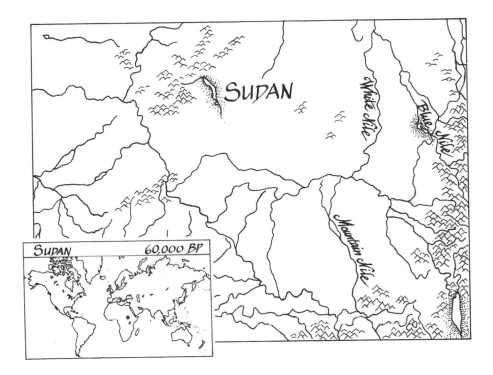

CHAPTER 7

DREAM

Mankind was physically modern when he emerged from the water to reconquer the land, but not yet mentally modern. One of the greatest mysteries of human evolution is what happened about 40,000 years ago. During the prior hundred thousand years or so mankind shared the world with other variants of Erect man, such as Archaic man in Asia and Neandertal man in Europe, and his life-style seemed similar. Then abruptly he made dramatic advances in organization, technology, language, and all the arts, and took over the world. The prior Geodyssey volume, Isle of Woman, *assumes that when a group of children were raised together, instead of individually by their mothers, they learned a new way of organizing their vocabulary, using superior syntax, and actually changed the organization of their brains in the process. Thus the origin of mankind's modern mind may have been in the Levant. That may be so, but this sequel volume assumes that it was more complicated than that, and developed more slowly in another region: Eden, or the Lake Victoria basin. That the intellectual breakthrough derives from the same place as the physical one, and followed naturally from it. That we owe our minds as well as our bodies to man's one-time adaptation to life in the water. And to our dreams. But to clarify this, we need to examine the nature of modern thinking and dreaming and memory. Much is not what it seems.*

The setting this time is not Eden, however. It is near the confluence of the Mountain Nile and the White Nile rivers in modern-day Sudan, about 600 miles north of Lake Victoria. The time is about 60,000 years ago. Because if this supposition is correct, the delay in the advance of modern mankind across Eurasia was not because of the resistance of Archaic man or Neandertal man, but because the giant Sahara Desert of Africa prevented the new thinking from reaching the fringe. Only very slowly could modern-minded man penetrate that vast hostile barrier, following the thin avenue of the great river where hunting and foraging remained good. It was slow because of the hostile primitive-mind modern-body tribes settled along that avenue; they would not let strangers by without trouble, and the terrain did not allow large-scale migration or invasion. The advantage that would enable mankind to explosively conquer the world may not have been enough for very small groups to prevail against set, conservative primitive cultures. Intruders had to accommodate themselves in whatever way they could, and most may have died. But some may have been lucky, and achieved a foothold. Only when their numbers increased in the world beyond the Sahara so that they could form complete communities, did the apparent transformation occur.

H UGH walked beside the river, reflecting on his situation as he watched for suitable prey to hunt. He realized now that Bub had done it. Bub had wanted Hugh to join his tribe, and take Bub's sister Sis as a mate, but Hugh had declined and married Anne instead. So Bub had bided his time, then struck. He had been maliciously cunning, waiting until a bad storm had destroyed much of the encampment and killed several people. Then he had told Chief Joe that this was the punishment of the spirits, because the tribe harbored one who was not properly a man. One who was a reverse man.

Joe would not have accepted the word of an outsider whose tribe was at times hostile, but it was a time of stress, and Bub offered to bring his tribe to join in a larger hunt that would bring in enough meat to support both tribes until the situation recovered. Bil had not liked it, but had recognized that a joint hunt would indeed be mutually profitable; it made sense. So he and

Joe considered it, while the privation continued and the people grew leaner. Bub refused to hunt with Hue, because of that bad hand. Bub's well-formed sister circulated, having private liaisons with men, and in her wake the hostility to wrong-sidedness grew. Hue came to understand, belatedly, that he had angered Sis by his refusal to marry her, and though men governed the tribes, the mischief of a woman disdained could be formidable.

No one before had remarked upon Hugh's preferred use of his left hand to wield his axe. Now the attention of the tribe focused on it, and others were too ready to believe that this was indeed the malice of the spirits. Hugh was one of the leaders of the tribe, but his position eroded, and soon he was unwelcome. Anne supported him, refusing to desert him for another man, though she used her right hand. Thus she too became suspect. Indeed, she had suffered a difficult childbearing, almost dying; now this too was brought forth as evidence of the mischief of bearing the baby of a cursed man. She had recovered and was now fully healthy, but the shadow remained.

"It isn't that we think you are bad," Joe explained, embarrassed. "But we dare not go against the spirits. If they strike again . . ."

That hardly mattered now. Hugh and Anne had had to leave with their baby son Chip, exiled. Anne had been devastated by the thought of leaving her tribe, but then had rallied and realized that she no longer needed the tribe, now that she had a family. They had fled down the great river, because that was the only direction that offered some hope of forage. There were always fish in the river, and if there were also more formidable creatures, these could be avoided. The plants by the riverside were lush, and of course there was always good water to drink. And there were inevitably people, eventually, for others also appreciated the advantages of water.

Unfortunately people represented one of the greatest dangers, because many tribes simply killed any strangers who intruded on their territories. So Hugh looked as carefully for signs of people as for animals and plants. He wanted to spy before being spied on. His life could depend on it.

The vegetation became tangled, and the water crossed rapids, which would be dangerous to enter, so he moved out somewhat, rounding the curve of a hilly slope. Then he stopped, because he heard something ahead. He remained quite still for a moment, holding his breath, orienting on the sound. Then he moved quietly behind a tree: one that would be easy to climb if necessary.

The sound seemed to be retreating. Whatever it was was moving away. Therefore it represented no immediate threat. It was probably some kind of antelope, a beest, too big and fast for a man alone to hunt. Hugh relaxed. There were many such false alarms in the course of an exploration or hunt, and each had to be taken seriously, because any one of them just might turn out to be lethally true.

By the time he skirted the thicket crowding the river he was in a ravine leading away from both the river and his camp. He picked his way to the clearest avenue to get back on course, climbing a steep slope. It was as if the animal had led him astray, or perhaps driven him off his original path. Or as if he were fleeing some horror of the valley, ascending the mountain, looking for food and safety. As indeed he was, in a larger sense.

He crested the rim of the ravine, and spied a rabbit perched near, its ears alert. He hefted his axe, conscious now as not before that it was his left hand that held it. But as he drew back his arm to throw, the rabbit bounded away. He followed it, mildly annoyed that he had not been alert for this. He should have crested the rim with his weapon ready to throw, and knocked off the rabbit the instant he saw it. But this was new terrain to him, and he didn't yet know the rabbit trails. One thing the episode demonstrated: rabbits in this region were not used to being hunted by man. That suggested that this would be a good place to remain for a while.

He pursued the rabbit, carefully, also watching for other creatures. How many men had been led to their deaths by focusing too narrowly on a hunt when in strange terrain? He could not afford to come to mischief, because Anne depended on him. She was more than competent, but she had their baby to care for, and needed his support.

Then the rabbit paused again, thinking it was out of sight. Hugh heaved his axe. The rabbit heard it coming and tried to jump out of the way, but the blade caught it flatside and knocked it unconscious. He closed on it immediately, picked it up, and checked: it was dead. Good enough. Now he could return to camp.

He put the rabbit in his game pouch, wiped off his axe, and angled for the river, whose voice he could hear not far distant. But as he crested another ridge he saw a distant plume of smoke. He stopped again, orienting on it much as he had on the animal sound. How far was it, and how big? Was it a distant volcano, or a near camp fire? Or an intermediate brush fire? All three were dangerous in their own ways. But as a general rule, the farther away it was, the safer it was.

He concluded that it was an intermediate fire, not big enough for brush, so probably a tribal campsite. He made careful note of its location; he would avoid that until he had no choice. When he encountered the people of this region—and the fire made it clear that they existed—he wanted to do so in a planned manner, with a good escape route planned. But he might be able to avoid such contact for some time, since they evidently didn't often hunt here. Now that he knew where they were.

Hugh resumed his quest for the river. He saw movement in the thicket. In a moment he identified it as a monkey. He could probably strike it with his axe, as it was regarding him curiously from what it thought was a safely high vantage. Monkeys, too, had not been hunted here recently. But he already had his kill, and there was something about its almost manlike aspect that made him disinclined to hurt it anyway. Monkeys were not men, yet they were not really far different from men, and the similarity bothered him a bit. Other men had regarded this qualm on his part as foolish, but it remained. He would not kill a monkey unless he had to.

He moved on, and soon saw the river, or rather the spray of water and mist it threw up at the foot of its rapids. As he come closer he felt the fringe of that spray like a light rain on his face, hands, and arms. He saw that the lay of the land was such that he would do better to cross to the other side of the river here rather than farther down where it might be deeper; there were rocky shallows here that he could navigate readily enough, with several channels running between them. He made his way down to the water.

There was motion on the near bank. Hugh stood still, his arm cocked, his eyes searching. It was a little crocodile, harmless and shy as far as he was concerned, though dangerous to smaller creatures. This was another creature he could have killed for food, if he had not already gotten his rabbit. This was truly a good hunting ground.

He used his axe to cut a sapling for a staff and made his way across the river, carefully, checking each rock before trusting his weight to it. He jumped across the surging channels after poking the landing sites with the end of his staff. It wasn't just firmness he checked for, but to make sure there were no bad snakes or bugs by them. One bad sting on a foot could be much mischief. He got soaked by the spume, at times plowing a seeming rainstorm, but that was the way of such things.

He completed his crossing, then paused to sniff the air. There was something. He searched the bank, checking every tree, snilling repeatedly until he had it.

"Anne," he said, facing the right tree.

She stepped out from behind it, the loveliest creature he knew. She was naked, with her dark hair swirling down around her very full bosom. "You took long enough to spot me," she said. "If I were a man, I could have attacked you."

"Men aren't in this region," he replied, advancing on her. "Except farther downriver where there's a camp."

She came to meet him, walking in the manner only she could. "Let me wash you," she said.

He let her strip away his loin-fur and pouch and set them on the ground. Then she led him back to the nearest thick spray-channel. It was a narrow one, with the water throwing up a constant barrage of drops and splash. Sunlight slanted through the vapor, making circular rainbows.

She stepped halfway across the channel and stood with her legs spread above the surging flow, one foot on each side. "Come to me, my ardent man," she said, smiling.

"Are you not concerned that I am wrong-handed?" he asked her, making a joke of what had become most serious. "That the spirits will strike you down for associating with me?

She answered him seriously. "I was virtually outcast myself, before you came and found me beautiful. If that was the mischief of the spirits, then I have no fear of them." She smiled again, spreading her arms and breathing deeply, inviting him with all her body. She was more than beautiful, with her swirling hair and phenomenally full breasts and sleek body and limbs.

How could he resist? He straddled the cleft of the river, facing her, feeling the water striking his legs and crotch. He moved forward to embrace her, bending his knees just enough to get his eager member into place. Her thighs were slippery wet; he slid in readily, and climaxed immediately, while she held him close and rubbed his back with flying river water. It was as if the entire river were flowing through him and into her, providing a force and ecstasy he could hardly remember experiencing before. She kissed him, her lips smiling against his. The rapture continued after his body was spent, and he just held her and held her, loving her in the wetness of it all. What did all else matter, with her here with him like this?

Eventually she whispered in his ear. "I would like this forever, my love, but my baby soon will wake, and I must feed him before he cries."

Of course she was right. "I will finish my exploration and join you," he said. He rubbed a hand across her slick bottom, then drew away enough to stroke a slick breast. "But we must do this again, soon."

"Soon," she agreed. Then she stepped off the channel and shook herself dry as she walked, in this manner holding his attention yet longer. She recovered her own fur and donned it, took his rabbit pouch, and walked into the forest beside the river, going upstream toward their hidden camp.

"Soon," he echoed, feeling his member hardening again already with the memory of the experience. What a way to do it! Anne must have planned it, waiting here for him. What a woman she was!

Hugh went to dress, then walked on downstream. He wanted to see whether there were any trails or other signs of human presence in this vicinity. The fire had been close enough so that this should be in the local tribe's normal hunting range, unless it was a temporary outpost for a more distant settlement. If they didn't hunt here, why didn't they? There had to be good reason. He needed to know this before he and Anne spent another night here.

He found a trail, but not human. This was hyena spoor. Hyenas were dangerous, but seldom attacked men unless really hungry. The presence of hyenas should not be enough to deter human hunters. Hugh's home tribe had driven the hyenas to the fringe of their territory. Hyenas were smart enough to know when they were overmatched, as they were by an organized human hunting party. So this simply was another evidence that the tribe did not hunt here. But not reason why. Anything bad enough to deter human hunters should also scare away hyenas. The mystery deepened.

He followed the hyena path, knowing that any of the big creatures near enough to smell him or hear him would move away. A wounded or sick man they might gang up on and attack, but he was neither. A group of them could overcome a single man like him, but they didn't know that. And any who did attack a human being were apt to find themselves relentlessly hunted until all were dead or fled from their territory. They wouldn't know that Hugh was out of his territory and therefore vulnerable. So he acted with boldness, knowing that the animals would respect that. But when he rejoined Anne, he would warn her. If she left the baby in a place a hyena could reach . . .

Then he heard something that made him pause. It sounded like the cry of a baby. Perhaps he had imagined it, because he had been thinking about his own baby.

The sound came again, and this time he was sure. It was the thin wail of a newborn human infant. But there was no soothing murmur of the mother's voice. It wasn't his own baby Chip; Anne would never leave him in a place like this, and he knew his own son's cry. This was another baby, and by the sound of it, alone.

What could a baby be doing by a hyena trail?

Hugh moved on, doubly alert for human presence, but could detect none. No sound, no smell, no traces. Just the baby.

There was light ahead. He left the trail and moved silently toward the light, for that was where the sounds were coming from. He made his way carefully through the thickening foliage near the light. He peered beyond it.

The forest opened into a glade. In the center of the glade was a cleared face of stone. On the stone lay a tiny baby swathed in a worn dirty fur wrapping. There was the faint smell of the crushed herb used to keep flies and mosquitos off. That was all.

Perplexed, Hugh studied the fringe of the glade. He saw a path entering the forest on the far side. That could have been where the mother had walked, bringing the baby. But she had to know that it wasn't safe here. Where had she gone?

Then he got a faint whiff of old carrion. Something had died here, some time ago. It could be the remnant of one of the hyena's kills. He sniffed, locating it. He saw a small bone. A human bone.

Then he knew. This was the tribe's abandoning ground. Where unwanted babies were left to die. That explained why hunters avoided this region. They did not like to think about what was here. People had spirits, and babies had them too, and the spirits did not look kindly on those who killed their bodies. So women would come here, leave their babies, and hurry away, and no one else would come at all. The rejection extended to the entire region, because it was not known how far spirits ranged. Any hunters who came too close could be attacked by the spirits and suffer injury. It would be made to seem that the injury was accidental, for the spirits arranged other causes for their malice, but no one was fooled. Bad fortune was sure to come to those who exposed themselves to it by coming here.

And Hugh had walked right into it. Now the spirits would be after him. Indeed, they might already be gathering, planning his accident. They would attack Anne, too, and Chip. No, not Chip, because he was a baby himself, one of them. But he would die when Hugh and Anne died. Spirits didn't necessarily distinguish between the living folk; they struck at any people who tarried in their domain. Maybe their urge for vengeance was so strong that they didn't care about individual guilt; any living person was considered culpable. Maybe his wrong-handedness made it worse. Could Bub have been right about that? If so, he and his family were doomed.

But there might be a way to fool them. Hugh was a hunter, but they might take him for a mother if he picked up this abandoned baby. If they killed or hurt the mother of a baby, so that the baby was left without a protector and died, they would be guilty of what they punished others for. So they normally didn't go after mothers with babies. So he had been wrong to assume that Anne would be attacked; she should be protected by her baby. Hugh needed protection too.

He entered the glade and picked up the baby, using both hands. It was female and seemed healthy. He wrapped the hide blanket about her more closely, put the bundle in the crook of his arm, and hurried back down the hyena trail. He would rejoin Anne, and they would flee this region before nightfall, getting clear of the spirits. Protected by their babies.

But when he came to their camp, where Anne had just finished nursing Chip, it didn't happen that way. Anne looked up and instantly recognized the nature of his bundle. "Where did you get that baby?" she demanded, amazed, as she set Chip down.

"This is the place of abandonment," he explained. "They are left out for the hyenas. We have to—"

"A girl," she said, taking the baby from his rigidly folded arm. "What are we going to do with a baby girl?"

"Protection," he said. "The spirits won't attack us if she's with us. We can flee this region now."

She looked sharply at him. "And what then?"

He was blank. "Then?"

"Once we get free of this region, what about this baby?"

He hadn't thought of that. "Maybe leave her somewhere else, and move swiftly away from there."

"And the tribe who left this baby—what of them?"

"We'll have to go away from them, because they won't like our interference here."

"Back up the river, the way we came?"

"No, we can't go back. To the side, perhaps."

"Where there is no river. No water. No easy path to follow."

She was right. This was a worse situation than he had realized. "But we can't stay here," he argued.

"With the baby, maybe we can. She will protect us here, as long as she lives."

"But she won't live long. She was abandoned."

"Unless we make her live."

"But we can't—" Then he understood her meaning. "But can you save her?"

Anne shrugged. "I have two breasts." She brought the baby to one of them.

Hugh realized it was possible. Chip had grown well on her full breasts, and was almost ready to start other foods. He would not need all her milk. There might be enough for the foundling girl. He watched the baby starting to nurse. He knew that sometimes babies couldn't survive with other mothers, but sometimes they could.

So perhaps the problem of the spirits had been forestalled, for now. But not the problem of getting past what could be a hostile foreign tribe—with one of its abandoned babies. What protected them from the spirits might put them into worse jeopardy with the tribe. Unless they could get beyond its territory without being discovered.

"Maybe if we travel at night, and hide by day—"

"No. We need to hunt and forage. I must eat well, and rest well, to keep up with two. We can't travel and hide."

"But what are we to do?" he asked plaintively, horrified by this disaster.

"We will stay here," she said firmly.

"But—"

"Who is going to bother us?" she asked.

And he realized that if the spirits let them be, so would the tribesmen. They could stay right here, for a time.

Except for one thing. "If the spirits discover my—" He paused, hesitating to say it, lest the spirits be listening. But his glance flocked to his left side.

"Surely they know already," she said. "Didn't they see you hunting? Maybe they consider you their friend."

Hugh was astonished. What she said made sense. The spirits would have seen him hunting, and they had left him alone. Perhaps they had even led him to the baby, testing him. When he had taken it instead of leaving it, the spirits could have known that he was their friend. And if that was the way of it, yes, he would be their friend.

"Make a fire," she said. "This baby needs more warmth than I can give her."

"But that will signal our presence to the tribe," he protested.

"So?"

And it wouldn't matter, because the tribesmen would not risk the wrath of the spirits. They would think it was a ghost fire, intended to lure them in for punishment. How neatly Anne had figured it!

He gathered tinder and brought out his little spark stones. In due course he had a fire. Anne sat beside it with a baby held on each arm, letting them nurse on either side as they wished. "Shall we call her Mina?" she asked.

Hugh was not ready to argue anything with her at this point. "Yes." He set up the rabbit for roasting.

So it was as the evening progressed. Mina did well enough, seeming to have no trouble with Anne's milk, and Anne knew very well how to care for a baby. Gaining confidence in the protection of the spirits, who were now perhaps their friends instead of their enemies, Hugh went about the business of making a competent shelter for the night.

As darkness closed, they entered a fairly tight hut, with the fire banked at the entrance, giving off just enough smoke to discourage insects and predators. They lay on a bed of fir boughs with the two babies between them, covered by warm fur blankets. The soft boughs were over sand that would absorb the babies' urine, keeping them reasonably dry. It was Mina's fortune that Anne was a practiced mother, well able to care for an extra baby, if her milk held out.

Hugh slept, secure in the knowledge that the spirits would protect them all from the tribesmen, and the babies would protect the adults from the spirits, and Anne would take care of the babies. Daytime might be a different challenge, but the night was secure.

❂

His dreams were scattered and not really comprehensible. In some he seemed to be furred like an animal; in others he mated with strange women and hardly noticed. His hands did not seem to matter; he used one or the other without preference. Sometimes he walked with his hands as well as his feet, turning his fingers under, and in the context of the dream this seemed natural. Sometimes he swung up into the trees with a facility that would have amazed him had he been awake. The dream did not care; it was just there. Whenever a thread of a coherent episode occurred, it broke off and something else formed. It was as if his wandering consciousness was not concerned whether he understood or remembered; the fragments were sufficient to themselves. Yet he tried to understand and to remember, suspecting that there was some vast importance that he was not quite grasping.

He walked through the forest. He heard something. He paused, orienting on it. Was it predator, prey, or acquaintance?

It was a huge gorilla, stomping toward Hugh's home. It growled and swung its monstrous hairy arms, and Hugh had to flee. Then all of his people were fleeing up a steep slope, women and children too. The apes had displaced them, and they had to find new territory.

They crested the slope, and it was a mountain, with steam issuing from vents. He had a little sister whom he protected, but at the moment he could not remember her name. They found more good trees on the other side, and moved into them. Life became much as it had been before, except that they foraged more frequently on the ground.

Then a foreign man came and took his mother. Hugh and his sister fled again, along with their friends. It was another exodus. They formed a band of their own. They fought someone. There were no trees, so they had to go on their feet all the time. They grabbed sticks and rocks to fight with.

There was the cry of a baby. Hugh remembered he had mated and there was a baby. But his mate took care of it.

He was walking again. A rabbit bounded away. He chased it, but it became large, a beest, and they were all chasing it for an interminable time. Finally it led them into a new, strange valley. Someone else got the beest, but Hugh found a new mate, and clasped her and penetrated her with sudden surprising joy.

He saw smoke. Was it a human campsite? He hefted his axe, which he had learned to throw, but discovered that it was useless. The smoke was from a mountain vomiting, spewing out monstrous roiling clouds, glowing rocks, and a red river that burned everything it touched. He and the others had to flee it and hide in a cave until the mountain's rage abated. He was with his new mate, but then he was mating with someone else, a woman he didn't like, and his own mate was mating with a man he didn't like. Somehow this enabled them to escape the fire mountain, and when they did escape it, they separated.

He saw a monkey in a tree. He approached it, and the closer he got, the larger it became, until it was an ape twice his own height. But he wasn't afraid of it, because it wasn't attacking him. It seemed almost friendly. Almost like a man. But then others wanted to hunt it, to hurt it, and he couldn't stop them. They didn't understand his reticence. Even his mate seemed disgusted with him. She looked at his left hand, and then they all were looking at it, and he realized that their unease with his difference was increasing, now that he was acting contrary to their wishes.

So he left her and his tribe and walked alone again, except for a girl-child who came with him. They passed a mountain, and fell, and then came to water. There were people there, odd ones, but he lived among them and learned their ways of the water. Hunting in water was like hunting on land, only different; he had to strain to discover the ways in which the disciplines

were similar, because it was better to adapt what he knew than to learn from
the beginning.

A croc attacked, and he fought it and killed it. Then the woman he had
protected came to him, and became beautiful, and it was An, or Ann, no,
Anne, and he mated with her and liked her, and it was much better than
what had been before. In fact the prior dreams were already fading, and
this was the only reality he knew. He was with Anne, loving her, feeling
emotion he had not known before.

He saw a baby lying in a glade. There were spirits around, threatening
him, so he took the baby and held the spirits at bay. He brought it home to
Anne, so there were two babies.

The babies grew, and more babies came, until there were children all
around. Anne nursed them, and sang to them, and taught them to speak,
and danced for them, and they learned well. They liked singing and dancing
and drawing, and that showed that they were real people instead of
primitives. Hugh took them hunting, as they got older, and they learned
that well too. They grew up speaking the language of the tribe Hugh and
Anne had left, not that of the tribe they had come from. They learned to
chip stone well instead of clumsily, and they were intelligent instead of
ignorant. One of them was like him, in appearance and manner, using his
left hand. Sometimes the others looked askance at that one, but he was
good in the things he did, so they did not object.

In time there were so many of them that they became a tribe of their own,
and Hugh and Anne were honored elders. They crowded the primitive
tribe, expanding their hunting and foraging territory. But they did not mate
among themselves; instead they went out and took mates from the fading
other tribe, and brought in those men and women, and tried to teach them
the ways of better speaking and organizing. In this they were really not
successful, but their children had no trouble learning the good ways. Some
went out to other lands, where they found their own places and saved many
abandoned babies, who in turn grew up to be like their adoptive families
instead of like those who had abandoned them.

In this manner the spirits saved many children, and conquered the world.
Not with any invasion, slaughter, or force, but simply by blessing their
children with superior ways. Whole subtribes grew up, honoring the spirits.
They spread everywhere, displacing the primitives, and everything was
wonderful.

❂

Hugh woke. Anne was nursing Mina and stroking Chip's head, keeping him
calm. All seemed to be well. He got up to tend the fire, which was down to
warm ashes.

Already the dream was fading, leaving only weird fragments. But that was
the way of dreams. They could be interesting and strange, but probably

meant only that the spirits were mischievously toying with the minds of the sleepers. If this meant that the spirits had no animosity for Hugh and Anne, as long as they took care of the babies, this was good. This was excellent hunting and foraging terrain, and they could stay here indefinitely, raising the children they acquired, teaching them the proper ways, just as the dream foretold.

It seems that primitive or cold-bodied creatures don't dream. When they sleep, if they need to, their brains shut down as well as their bodies. But warm-bodied creatures, notably the mammals, do dream. Why? Nature does not institute such procedures without reason. That reason is straightforward, though as yet generally unrecognized in science: the dreams represent important work being done. They relate to memory: a person deprived of dreaming suffers in the formation and retention of new memories.

Consider the situation: All day most creatures are active, hunting, foraging, feeding, mating, surviving. Life experience pours in pretty much randomly. Some are important, such as which berries induce vomiting or which bugs sting; such information needs to be recorded and made available for retrieval. Some are not important, such as how many times the third mouthful of food was chewed or the color of the wings of the fourteenth sparrow from the left in a flock of 100. Impressions have to be culled, lest what is important be buried under trivia. But it is not convenient to do this at the time; full attention needs to be available to the process of living, however tedious. Absent-mindedness on the hunt can be deadly. So the impressions are stored temporarily until they can be properly sorted.

Unlike cold-bodied creatures, warm-bodied creatures have a brain that is fully functional at night. This is its downtime: when new impressions are not pouring randomly in. So this is the time when those accumulating temporary memories are processed. The precise process is as yet not understood, but in essence those impressions are brought up into consciousness, considered, culled, cross-referenced, and filed as more permanent memories. Cross-referencing is vital, because this is the mechanism for recall at need. When a berry is seen, the associations relating to berries are traced, and the danger of some berries is recalled. But it may be that black stain is required to mark an item or a route, so the associations of black are traced, and the poisonous black berries are recalled: a convenient source for this purpose. Or it is necessary to describe a particular insect, whose size is about that of this berry, a useful comparison. It is not possible to know in advance exactly what connection will contribute to future survival, so all discernible attributes are referenced. It may be necessary to inspect the memory of tasting that berry from many angles, to do the job thoroughly, and it requires consciousness to make decisions as to what is relevant. So the whole experience of the berry is reviewed, and of the stinging bug, and of everything else in the recent day. It may be that the key to cross-referencing is not objective assessment of the qualities of experience, but relates to feeling about it. In the absence of the waking censor—the conscious critical facility of the mind—this feeling can get out of bounds and bring on a nightmare. But it may be necessary; fear, horror, and anger are powerful motivators, and it is important to have related memories clear. This process of summoning and reviewing may be the essence of what we call dreams. It is not necessary to remember this process; indeed, the process itself should be forgotten, or it, too, would become experience requiring processing, in an endless recursive sequence. So only dream fragments are remembered, as the waking mind tries to make sense of what are essentially random bits of experience and emotion. But the job, itself forgotten, is done, and key memories are strengthened and defined. The process of dreaming, if not our memory of the dreams themselves, is vital to our mental health.

Animals have relatively simple minds, compared to men. When anatomically modern human beings made the breakthrough to mentally modern status, between 40,000 and 100,000 years ago, their comprehension of the world and of their own society and capacities increased enormously. This meant that there was that much more information to process during the dream state. Thus dreams surely became more sophisticated and organized in their fashion, in order to do a job that other creatures could not, literally, even dream of. Modern man is a dreamer—and thus, paradoxically, more practical and realistic than other creatures.

What was the breakthrough that gave the Moderns such power as to conquer the world? How did it come about? This is perhaps the greatest untold story of mankind's history. The development of language with sophisticated syntax enabled man to communicate in far more effective manner. This facilitated his understanding of the world and increased his power to handle it, using complex symbolism that enabled him in due course to develop nuclear power and intricate computers, and to appreciate the arts also. That breakthrough, once made, could have spread slowly out from its origin in Eden, going first to the children, as shown in this chapter. That would account for a mental transformation that did not affect the genes: the existing people acquired new minds, quietly, tribe by tribe as those with such minds trained their children. Perhaps it seems incredible that those with old minds would not notice the change. But consider what is happening today, in America, where children exposed to the violence and short attention span of television programming grow up to form the most violent and rootless society of the world—without their parents fathoming why. As the twig of the young mind is bent, so the tree of the adult is inclined, on a massive scale.

What was this mental change? Why did it prove to be beyond the capacity of Archaic or Neandertal man? This may be associative thinking. When one segment of Homo erectus *entered the shallows of Lake Victoria and lost his body fur, he had to learn how to forage and hunt and sleep in the water, without sacrificing his abilities to do the same on land. He required a double set of reactions. He developed this by adapting: the ways of the land, developed over the course of millions of years, translated to the similar yet hardly identical ways of the water. This was a shortcut, far faster than starting from scratch. In so doing, he thus learned not only to survive in water, but the art of associative thinking. When he left the water to reconquer the land this mental facility was available for other purposes. Such as adapting the extensive vocabulary of anatomically modern man to new purposes, shifting the usage of words to apply not to the foreign medium of water, but to the foreign concepts of past, present, future, and supposition. Modern man learned "maybe": the tool of imagination itself.*

What was the key to this shift, that made it a survival quality? It may have been the development of self-consciousness. Ordinary consciousness is a remarkable quality that sets the animal kingdom apart from the plant kingdom. With consciousness, a creature can make choices, thus adapting his limited brain to many situations, instead of having to have every possible thing hard-wired. This is an advantage that enables conscious creatures to prevail when they otherwise might not seem well equipped for survival. Self-consciousness is another level, one that only mankind and perhaps a very few animals possess. Neandertal man perhaps had it to a degree, but he had diverged before the full effect of the water phase was felt, so was more limited in this seemingly incidental respect. It might seem to be no particular advantage, except for the chain of other things it leads to. High-level self-consciousness is probably what set the Moderns apart from the Archaics, and led them ultimately to dominance.

Associative thinking may have given man the capacity to appreciate more than the ordinary ongoing present tense of the animals. It may have been a mental tool, developed for one purpose, then applied to other purposes. It enabled him to ponder other realities: not merely land versus water, but today versus yesterday. How might things have been, had he taken another path and not trodden on that poisonous snake? He became conscious of time and choice. His language expanded to address such concepts. The connections between language and world view are substantial. When children learn such language, they learn the concepts too, and their understanding is rapid though the evolution of the concepts may have been slow. Just as the average child today has no problem with computers that completely baffle his grandfather, so children absorbed the significant change in man's outlook without difficulty, and retained it as adults. So perhaps in a single generation, or perhaps over the course of 50,000 years, mankind's new consciousness developed. He became fully aware of himself, aware of himself making decisions, of himself thinking, of himself thinking about thinking. He became aware of his own mortality. This sort of thing may be literally unimaginable for animals, but is easy for modern human minds. Self-consciousness: the ultimate awareness. It may have seemed as if this awareness was a thing apart from the body, a spirit inhabiting it, that perhaps moved on to another body when this one died. Perhaps the root of all religion was here.

Most creatures appreciate the company of their own kind. When man became self-conscious, he wanted the company of other self-conscious people. He was able to appreciate that if he could think about thinking, so could others. If he feared his own ultimate death, so might others. He wanted to share his special awareness with them, and to draw comfort from them. But how does one communicate self-consciousness to others? How can one be sure they understand? Words can convey concepts but not all feelings. There was a need to share what went beyond vocabulary, however sophisticated the language might be. This may have been where the arts came in. The sophisticated symbolism of language was only one ability of the new mind; it could appreciate the symbolism of a sculpture, or a drawing, or a dance, or music. Music, perhaps more than any other art, appealed directly to the aware mind, and stirred special emotions in it. When one aware person sang, and others listened, all of them knew that the others were experiencing similar awareness. They were sharing the feelings of their own kind.

And so self-consciousness may have led to complex language and all of the arts, including perhaps the art of love. Those of the new mind were not only able to communicate in ways others literally could not dream of, they were able to share feelings others lacked. This enabled them to congregate in much larger groups without quarreling, and in that unity was strength. A multitude could rest quietly, appreciating the arts. Listening to a tale of self-aware people experiencing unusual adventures. Watching a lovely woman dance, pantomiming hope, joy, love and sex. Singing together, feeling the united emotion. Sharing the dream. Sharing religion.

This change worked its way slowly through the minds and natures of the water folk, and slowly spread out across Africa until they all had it, until at last it reached that fringe in Asia Minor that was balked by the entrenched Archaics and Neandertals, who were well adapted to their life-styles and their terrain. When Modern minds made that conversion, they faced the vast terrain of Eurasia with potent new tools of understanding, technology, and social order. But this time their conquest was not by conversion, for the Archaics and Neandertals lacked the associative water minds, the camaraderie of the arts, the unity of group self-awareness; it was by conquest. For the first time they were displacing those whose capacities were not even close to their own. Thus the conquest occurred in a geological instant, and the other descendants of Homo erectus were gone. They had been replaced by the gracile dreamer.

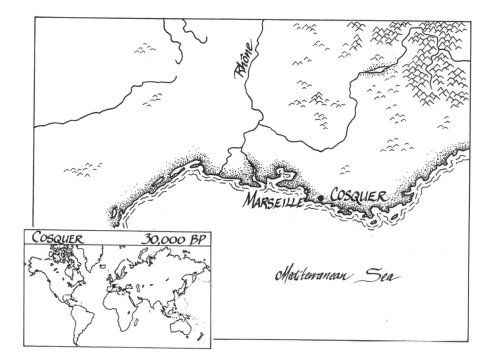

CHAPTER 8

MUSIC

To recap the complex development of the modern human mind: as anatomically modern humans spread out from Eden across Africa and leaked across the Sahara Desert to touch Asia Minor, the mind continued to change in the heartland. As with computer software that lags behind the hardware, the realization of the potential of the human brain took time. What had started as a way to address life in the water as well as on the land enabled the brain to grasp new ways of thinking. Self-consciousness came: thinking about thinking. The need to share such awareness with others, to know that they too felt it, led to far more sophisticated modes of expression. The vocabulary of nouns and verbs acquired better syntax, enabling people to address the past and future as well as the present, and to speculate on what might be as well as what is. The arts, speaking directly to the new sensitivities, became important, distinguishing mankind from all prior efforts. Perhaps the first of these were music, dance, and storytelling—none of which leave evidence for the archaeological record.

The time is about 30,000 years ago, on the southern coast of what is now France.

THE settlement was some distance in from the shore, but they had no trouble finding it because of the well-worn paths to the sea. Hugh led the way, carrying their supplies, with little Chip following close behind.

The natives knew they were coming, of course. No stranger approached a settlement without being noted, watched, and reported well in advance. But there should be no trouble, because they were obviously not a war party, but a family. And they wore the body paints of entertainers. They should be welcome, but if they were not, they would not be harmed. The spirits did not take kindly to those who harmed their messengers.

Indeed, by the time they saw the shelters, the folk were out awaiting them. The tribe leader was a large, gruff man, but though he carried a club he was not in a threatening posture. "Who are you?" he demanded as the family came to a halt before him.

"Hugh the flute and Anne the dance," Hugh replied in the standard manner. "We come to make you happy, for your hospitality, as long as you wish us to stay."

The man gazed at Anne, who was artfully posed with one hip outthrust. He nodded, needing no second glance to appreciate the aspect of a beautiful woman. "I am Joe. Accept our hospitality this night, and for other nights if our people like you."

"Fair enough," Hugh agreed, and Anne rewarded the man with a brilliant smile. Joe licked his lips, knowing that this was no more than artifice, but impressed nevertheless.

Joe turned and led them on into the settlement. There were about ten houses formed of poles and hides, and a central hearth well banked with coals and ash at the moment. The houses were in a rough circle, their door-flaps facing inward; space was cleared beyond them to allow people to be sure that no person or animal was close. Few creatures challenged man by day, but some did explore by night.

A woman approached. "I am Bunny," she said. "I will help you make shelter from our materials."

"Thank you," Anne said. This was a routine courtesy for invited guests; the tribe provided the makings and helped the visitors put up their house. When the visitors departed, the house was taken down again. Normally the poles or hides were marked, showing that they were for temporary residences. Visitors had a special status, not being expected to forage or hunt with the tribe, and not being privileged to participate in its decisions. Visitors depended on the good will of tribe members, and this was made clear throughout.

Bunny was joined by her son and daughters, Stone, Doe, and Weasel. Stone was five or six, Doe four, and Weasel a toddler of two. Now Hugh understood why Joe had assigned this woman to help: her children came close to matching Anne's children in age and gender. Chip was five and Mina was three. Of course these folk did not know that Mina had been adopted as a foundling, and it hardly mattered; she had been part of the family from her day of birth. Only her glossy black hair differentiated her from the others. There was no need to mention that Anne had proved to be barren after birthing her first baby.

The poles and hides were good, being made for this purpose, and soon the house was up. The children, at first abashed, were soon playing happily, running around the house in opposite directions and giggling.

But as evening came, it was time for the visitors to perform. The tribesfolk gathered for their evening meal, and sat in a circle around the fire. There was space for Hugh and Anne to do what they had to do. Now was the time of reckoning; if they were not entertainers, they would be denied food and sent away.

Hugh brought out his bone flute. It had a cutaway mouthpiece across which he could blow to make a whistling sound, and five holes he could cover with his fingers. It did not look like much, but he had practiced on it for years and knew his skill was good. He had always had a special ear for sound, and now was using that awareness to pay his way.

Anne got the children settled, then dressed for action. Now she wore a grass skirt, and removed her jacket, leaving her upper portion bare. Hugh's practiced eye noted the narrowing of the eyes of the tribe men, and the play of their tongues around their mouths as they got their first clear look at Anne's body. She was easily the most beautiful woman here, with her brown hair descending to her midsection and her tiny waist and broad hips. But it was her breasts that had the greatest impact; they were surprisingly large and firm for a woman with two children. Of course she had made a specialty of her appearance, normally veiling it with clothing and posture, then emerging like the brilliant sun from behind clouds. Few would have guessed that she was twenty; her face and body seemed five years younger.

After a suitable pause for the men to assimilate the sight, they started. Hugh blew a note on his flute, then another, going into a well-practiced song. There was a faint appreciative murmur from the tribesfolk; they recognized immediately that he was skilled. They loved music, as all people did; it struck through to their inner feelings.

Then Anne began to dance. She had been absolutely still, like a wood carving; now she moved her slender legs and swung her broad hips from side to side without disturbing her upper torso. The men smiled, instantly appreciating the sex appeal. The women were expressionless; it would not be suitable for them to evince similar pleasure. But they understood this art well enough, and perhaps were making mental notes.

Hugh's melody intensified, growing louder and faster. Anne moved with its beat, skipping, and now her breasts shook and bounced, and her special anklets rattled as her feet struck the ground. Her thighs flashed through the grass skirt as she lifted her legs high. She began to sing, at first matching Hugh's tune, then going into counterpoint. Hugh, still watching the audience reaction as he played, was gratified to see several mouths fall open with awe. They had never heard counterpoint before, but they felt its power. This was music beyond their experience.

When the song and dance was done, there was a light sheen of sweat on Anne's body, further enhancing it. It was clear that all of the men and a number of the women were sexually aroused. They were well satisfied with the performance.

"But anyone can do it," Anne said. "I can show you how. See, even my little daughter has learned." And she nudged Mina, who, ready for this, went out and made her bottom move. The effect was hardly as potent as it had been for Anne, but it was clear that if such a small child could project her hips that way, any girl or woman could. The audience was clearly impressed.

"And anyone can play the flute," Hugh said. He glanced at Chip, who brought out his own little flute. He proudly tootled a recognizable melody.

Joe stepped forward. "Eat, friends," he said. "And tomorrow—teach."

Hugh nodded. Of course the tribeswomen and elder girls wanted to learn how to make their bodies move like that, and the men wanted to know how to do counterpoint. Dancing was a woman's natural performance, and music was a man's; those who did these things well were valued anywhere. Hugh and Anne would teach them the fine points of their techniques. The process would require several days, and life would be easy during that period. That was the point. When the learning was done and interest waned, they would move on to another tribe and repeat the process. This was the nature of their livelihood.

They had a good dinner. Then a number of tribesmen came up to Hugh, asking about his flute; he let one of them try to play it, but all he got was an ugly whistling squeal, as Hugh had known he would. Tribeswomen approached Anne, inquiring how she had achieved such a good body. And the children were popular with the other tribe children. It was a successful evening.

"How do you play music so well?" a man asked.

Hugh gave his standard answer: "The spirits are with me." Anne said much the same, with respect to her ability to dance so provocatively. Of course they had both worked at their specialties long and hard, but so did some others, without having the same success. And they did respect the influence of the spirits; they seemed to have had good fortune since adopting Mina, who had been left out to die. It seemed the spirits appreciated their effort to keep the baby alive. Spirits had greater concern for the welfare of the very young and innocent than they did for relatively corrupt adults. So they were happy to give the spirits credit; that complimented the spirits, and kept their favor.

But at night, in their house, Hugh spoke of a disquieting note: "I saw one man who resented our popularity."

"And I saw one woman," she agreed.

"His wife?"

"More likely his sister. She is close to our age, but does not seem to have borne children. I don't like her."

"There are a few such in every tribe. Now that we have identified them, we'll be wary."

"But the woman Bunny is nice," she said. "So are her children. Her husband is away, searching for a new foraging area for wood. She says she is glad he is away, because she doesn't want him to see me."

"A nice way to compliment your appearance."

"Perhaps. But it seems he dreams of a woman, though he is true to Bunny, and so she fears the effect of any pretty stranger."

"Men do dream of pretty women," he reminded her. "I have not felt the need, myself; however—"

She struck him lightly on the shoulder. "Leave that unfinished. The odd thing is that Bunny doesn't think that her husband's dream woman is especially pretty. There's just something about her that captures his fancy. But perhaps a pretty woman might substitute for that mysterious quality. So Bunny prefers to play it safe."

"As she should," Hugh agreed affably. "If he saw you, and you *were* his dream woman, where would I be?"

"Oh, you would not be lonely. You could keep the children—Bunny's and yours."

"What delight," he said wryly.

"What's wrong with it?" Chip demanded from the other side of the chamber.

At that they all burst out laughing, and went to sleep.

◎

In the morning most of the men had to go out hunting, and the women out foraging. Bunny remained in the settlement, watching her children and others. She talked to them, encouraging them to learn new words, and did her best to keep them out of mischief. Anne helped by demonstrating her hip swing for the girls. The little ones couldn't do it, but they loved trying. They had more success when she showed them how to fashion anklets that rattled when they stomped their feet. Soon they were marching in step, thrilled by the massed beat.

Hugh, meanwhile, worked on another bone flute. He had found a nice hollow bone a few days ago, and carved on it when he had time. The holes had to be placed just so, or the notes were wrong. So he would make a small hole, blow the flute, then enlarge the hole in the direction required to get the note right. He had a special ear for it. This took time and care, but he enjoyed it, because he knew that few others could do as good a job as he did. Most folk could not even select a good bone, not realizing that the musical qualities of bones differed, so that each had to be tested. It would be a shame to waste a good bone with bad holes.

"Just don't carve any more holes in *me*," Anne said teasingly. "I won't improve, no matter where you place them."

He glanced at her appraisingly, about to make a suitable response. But at that point Joe approached, accompanied by the resentful man and trailed by a woman. Hugh paused in his carving, fearing trouble. "That is the man," he murmured.

"And the woman," Anne agreed.

"I don't like either of them." But that was only approximately true, in the case of the woman; there was a certain fascination mixed with the repulsion, for a reason he could not fathom. Had he known her elsewhere?

"Bub says you use the wrong hand," Joe said.

Oh, that. Usually no one noticed, but sometimes there was mischief when they did. "I use the correct hand for me," Hugh replied carefully.

"You hold your knife in your left," the man Bub said accusingly.

"Why should I not? One hand is as good as another." He hoped they would not come up with the worst answer.

"Because that's the bad spirit side," the woman said. "Everyone knows that those possessed by bad spirits are warped, and bring bad times to all with whom they associate."

That was the worst answer. But Hugh could not afford to let it stand unchallenged. "This is not something *I* know," he said mildly. His eye crossed the gaze of the woman, and it was as if something jumped between them. She had a brooding look, and considerable sex appeal. That might speak to her motive: she did not like being displaced for even a few days by another woman.

"Because you're warped," Bub said triumphantly. "You bring trouble."

Hugh looked at Joe, and saw that the man was in doubt. He evidently was not unduly smart, and could be guided by bad persuasion. "We have never had trouble with the spirits," Hugh said mildly, though he was angry and disturbed inside. "We travel much, alone through the forests, and they leave us alone."

"Because good spirits do leave folk alone," the woman said. "It's the bad spirits who hurt people. They don't hurt the ones they possess, but do hurt others. Those possessed by bad spirits can bring them into good tribes, and bring disaster. Our children are at risk." Such folk always brought children into it, though it was Hugh's impression that they hardly cared for children.

Joe wavered. "That is known," he agreed. "Sis is right." It was evident that he did not want to have to send Hugh and Anne away, because the tribe liked their show, but he didn't want to risk mischief from the spirits.

Anne got in on it. "This is nonsense," she said. "I use my right hand, and I have not suffered from my association with him."

Sis looked sneeringly at her. "The bad spirits use you to lead them in. They will throw you away when they are done."

Hugh saw that the two had rehearsed this, and would prevail unless he did something extraordinary. Similar complaints had gotten him exiled from his home tribe, starting his life as a wanderer. But he was getting less inclined to accept such charges without fighting back. "What would it take to prove that I merely use the hand I choose, and have nothing to do with bad spirits?"

"Go into the burial cave for a night," Bub said.

Hugh felt a chill. He did not like burial places, and not just because they could be littered with bones and smell awful. It was that they had rescued Mina from such a place, and he feared that if she ever went there again, the spirits would change their minds and take her back.

Sis saw his doubt. For a moment as their eyes met, he thought she wanted something else of him—that she found him as guiltily intriguing as he found her. But he averted his gaze. Then she spoke: "You can't go there, because you know it is filled with good spirits, and they would destroy you. They don't like the intrusion of bad spirits."

So that was it. Bub and Sis wanted to get rid of Hugh and Anne permanently by getting the spirits to kill them. All because the tribe liked the visitors and valued what they had to teach. The choice was now between death and ignominious departure.

Hugh looked at Anne, but before he could speak, she did. "We'll go to your cave," she said. "We know the good spirits will not hurt us."

Hugh winced. It was not at all smart to provoke the spirits like that. Spirits did not much like *any* intrusions, especially by night, especially by strangers. They could kill the family merely for being there, not even caring about who was left-handed. But he couldn't reverse what his wife had said; that would bring shame on her. So they would have to risk it. He nodded, not trusting himself to speak.

Bub smiled grimly. "Tonight," he said. "We will close you in so you can't sneak out before morning."

Worse yet! Hugh might be able to stand it if he could remain near the entrance and see outside, able to escape if the spirits attacked. But to be closed in—!

"The spirits like music," Anne murmured, reminding him.

So they did. But did they like it enough to counter their natural resentment of the intrusion? Hugh experienced a sick doubt.

"I will inform the tribe," Joe said, obviously ill at ease. He had been maneuvered into this as much as Hugh and Anne had, but had to play it through, as they did.

Sis stared at Anne. "You fool," she said witheringly. "You will never walk out of there. The spirits *know.*"

It seemed that it was Sis's jealousy that drove this. She had fastened on Hugh's left-handedness as a pretext the tribe would accept. As his gaze crossed hers once again, Hugh had the odd feeling that the woman, far from being repelled by his reverse-handedness, was perversely attracted to it. Again he felt the tug of her sex appeal, though it disgusted him. There was something about her, and her hate/love focus on him.

Then the day returned to normal, seemingly. But when others could not hear, Bunny spoke to them, quietly, while facing elsewhere. "Those two are the ones possessed by evil spirits," she muttered. "Bub and Sis—they are not really of this tribe. But somehow they got Joe to let them stay. They stop anyone else from being accepted. He's a tough fighter, and many men are afraid of him, and she seduces those who aren't." She snorted delicately. "Though I don't see what they see in her."

"Some men like willful women," Anne remarked. "Not to marry, but to dally with."

"I hope my husband encounters none such," Bunny said. "At least I know he can't stand Sis."

"How do you know?" Hugh asked, genuinely curious for more than incidental reason.

"His pupils narrow when she comes near, and his penis shrinks."

Hugh forced a laugh. "Those are apt signs."

"So why didn't yours?" Anne asked mischievously.

She had him there. She hadn't even been looking at him when Sis was close, yet she knew. But she also knew that he was in search of no other woman of any nature, however much he might react to them in passing. He already had the best. So she joked, having no concern on that score.

"I was standing too close to you, my love, to be repelled," Hugh replied after a moment. "If I met her alone, it would be another matter."

Both women laughed, appreciating an apt response.

But in the evening they had to go to the cave. "Why not sleep in the house?" Chip asked.

"We'll stay in the house again tomorrow night," Anne told him reassuringly. "But tonight we must use the cave. Don't worry; we'll have warm blankets."

"All right."

"All right," Mina echoed, as she tended to.

The cave was some distance from the settlement, as such places usually

were, because it was not wise to camp within the normal range of spirits of
any persuasion. The entrance was dark and low; they had to duck well down
to enter it. Hugh led the way, carrying his torch. He knew that the torch
would not last long, and then they would be in complete darkness. They
would have to find a suitable place to sleep before it guttered out. He
dreaded the occasion.

"Oooh, it stinks!" Chip exclaimed, intrigued.

"Because this is where their dead live," Hugh explained.

"Can I see one of the dead people?"

"Yes. Perhaps several." They had carefully taught their children not to be
afraid of the dead, because of Mina's origin; they did not want the spirits to
think they did not appreciate Mina, or that they had any objection to
anyone who had died. So they always spoke well of the dead, hoping to keep
the favor of the spirits, and so far that had been effective.

But privately both Hugh and Anne had some concern. These were the
dead of a foreign tribe, and their spirits well might be resentful of the
intrusion. There was no doubt the hostile spirits could and would kill
the living, if aggravated. Hence Hugh's dread. His first priority was to make
peace with these spirits.

He moved his torch around, exploring the cave. It widened and
deepened beyond the narrow entrance, so that there was room for them to
stand without stooping. There were no bodies in view; they would be placed
well inside the cave, for protection. But there was no doubt they were there,
as Chip's nose had ascertained.

The tribesmen were meanwhile rolling the barrier boulder up across the
entrance. It nudged close, closing them in. The seal was not tight, so that air
came in around the edges, but the space was not large enough for any of
them to get through. That air helped, for it carried the fresh outside odor
of the forest, pushing back the queasy stench of death.

"First we must introduce ourselves to the spirits," Hugh announced.
"Otherwise they might not like our bothering their bodies. So we shall play
and dance for them." He handed the torch to Anne. Its smoke was moving
forward, into the cave, as if this were the mouth of a huge beast that was
inhaling.

Chip nodded, liking the notion. He had seen how living tribesfolk were
charmed by music and dance, so it made sense that dead folk would have
similar sentiments. They had on occasion entertained the spirits of animal
skeletons, so that they could pass unmolested; the principle was clear.

So Hugh led the way deeper into the cave as it slanted up into the
mountain, playing his flute. Chip followed, playing his own flute. Then
came Mina, dancing in her fashion, and finally Anne, holding the torch
steady despite the gyrations of her body. They were making a procession
toward the chamber of the dead.

The cave went straight back into the mountain, on and on. Hugh had had no idea it went so deep. He worried that the torch would burn out before they found the bodies. He did not want that; it would be an awful affront to the spirits if he stumbled over a body. So he walked faster, still diligently playing his music. The others followed, continuing their playing and dancing. They all understood how important it was to keep the spirits pacified.

At last the passage ended—in a sharp upturn. They had to scramble up into a higher level. Hugh removed his pack and set it on the floor, and Anne did the same; no one would steal them from this place. He played one-handed as he wedged his way up, while Anne danced below, charming the spirits with especially luxuriant swings of hair and hips. He reached the top, and looked around in the dim fringe of light from the torch below.

There was a much larger chamber, with points of stone rising from its floor like giant animal teeth, casting living shadows against the receding walls. And here were the bodies, spread between the teeth. The smell intensified. The drift of air had stopped; this was the depth of the breathing beast.

He found a place where he could hold on and reach a hand down to help the others. "I must pause, O spirits," he said. "So I can bring my family up here to entertain you. I will play again soon." He hoped that the spirits were not impatient. They had listened very quietly so far, so he thought they understood.

He caught Chip's hand and hauled him up. "Oooo!" the boy exclaimed, spying the bodies. He was fascinated.

"Play for them," Hugh said quickly.

Chip settled himself and resumed playing his little flute, happily wrinkling his nose as he breathed. This was certainly a stink worthy of his appreciation.

Hugh hauled Mina up, and set her to dancing beside Chip. They made a nice miniature couple who would surely charm the spirits. Then he helped Anne up. She could not dance while scrambling, but she moved so lithely that the spirits might not know the difference. She held the torch in her free hand, and the rock shadows crawled weirdly as it came up.

When they all had secure footing among the dead, they did a full show for the spirits. Hugh played his flute as never before, and Anne danced so voluptuously that it seemed likely to lift any penises that hadn't rotted away.

When the show was done, they were quiet, waiting for the reaction. There was none. That was a good sign. The spirits were accepting them, having appreciated their offering of entertainment. Still, it was best to be sure that there would be no change of mind.

Hugh brought out some charcoal he used on occasion for drawing figures on outside rocks. Such figures had protective properties; spirits did not like to pass them. He would make a drawing here, to bar the spirits from descending into the lower tunnel.

He looked for a suitable place to draw. Then he thought of a better notion. Mina was a child of spirits, having been rescued from death; she had always been their real protection from spirits, ever since they had taken her from a death grove. The drawing should be hers. But she would not be able to do it effectively; she wasn't that skilled with her hands.

So he decided on a special technique he knew. He bit off a mouthful of charcoal. He chewed it up, getting it saturated with saliva. Then he guided Mina to the neck of the entrance cave. He took her tiny hand and laid it against the rough stone, the fingers splayed wide. And he pursed his lips and blew, spitting out a stream of liquid charcoal. She giggled at the feeling of it, but he held her hand firmly in place until he was done. Then he lifted it away.

There was her handprint—outlined in sprayed black. It was a marvelously spiritual effect. Mina was delighted, and Chip was jealous.

"But *your* hands must be clean, for playing the flute," Hugh told him. The boy recognized the validity of that. Mina's little hand was filthy with charcoal spit.

They made their way back down into the lower tunnel. There was no further need to play and dance; the spirits had accepted them, and now Mina's handprint would prevent the spirits from coming down after them. They would be able to rest, and to sleep.

That was just as well, because the torch finally guttered out. Anne had kept it going as long as she could, but now its spirit would join those of the people in the main cave. The family was in complete darkness.

They linked hands and walked toward the entrance. It would be more comfortable there, and the air would be fresher. They would curl comfortably together, and in the morning, when the tribesfolk rolled away the stone, the four of them would emerge fresh and smiling. The troublemakers Bub and Sis would be discredited, and the rest of the stay here would be good. The spirits were still smiling on those who understood and honored them.

This cave is now known as Cosquer. It can no longer be entered afoot; when the ice age ended, the level of the water rose, and the Mediterranean Sea expanded across lands that had been near the shore. The cave had been several miles inland, but now its entrance is more than a hundred feet below the surface. All of the access tunnel and half the main cave is flooded. So are the camps and hunting grounds of mankind in that region; you might say that mankind lived under the sea. We may never know the details of the lives of those coastal dwellers, because the sea washed them out.

Two thousand years after Mina left her handprint, using the "spitting image" technique that we have understood only recently, another tribe used the cave for paintings. They cleared out the bones and decorated the cave first with more hand stencils, then with the largest variety of animals and designs known in such a context. About a hundred animals have been found painted or engraved, including three auks—the only such depictions of this seabird known. But this may be only half the original total, because the rising water washed out the lower ones, including Mina's original handprint.

It seems natural that when self-consciousness brought awareness of similar awareness in other human beings, folk also suspected that it existed in animals and even in inanimate things, such as the surging sea, shaking mountains, and the dead. The spirit of self-consciousness seemed to exist apart from the tangible body, perhaps as an independent entity. If there was doubt, it was better to play it safe, and propitiate any spirits that might be in the vicinity. Thus, perhaps, another beginning of religion, with its attendant ceremonies. But the arts were also pleasurable in themselves, so they continued to flourish wherever mankind existed. It's too bad that music and dance left no tangible records in the way that painting and sculpture did. We have no evidence that musical counterpoint existed in early times, yet our deep appreciation of it can hardly have developed only in the past thousand years, so here it is assumed that it existed, though in limited form. We have surely missed man's most dynamic artistic aspects.

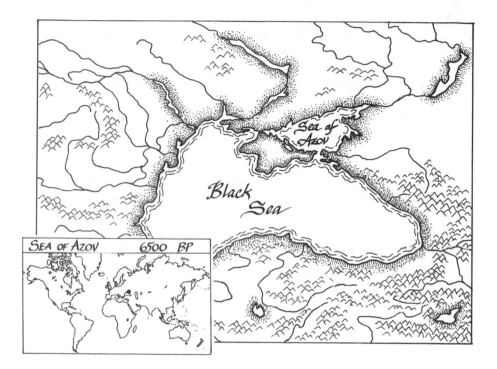

Sea of Azov   6500 BP

Sea of
Azov

Black
Sea

CHAPTER 9

HORSE

Start at the Atlantic Ocean. Pass east through the narrow Strait of Gibraltar to enter the smaller Mediterranean Sea, around which so much of mankind's political development has taken place. Pass northeast through the Dardanelles Strait and on into the yet smaller Black Sea, a region more important than many historians have credited it for being. Pass north through the Kerch Strait into the tiny Sea of Azov, widely unknown. This is surely a backwater of human activity. Yet here, perhaps, began one of the greatest ongoing conquests of all human history—one that is still in progress.

The time is about 6,500 years ago, and nothing much is happening. Yet retrospect can provide significance for even tiny events.

AS the dawn came, it was clear that the spirits had let them be. Perhaps it was the music and dance they had done by the burial ground at dusk, and perhaps the magic symbols they had drawn in the dirt. But Hugh believed it was mostly that little Mina had always been a child of the spirits, and that the family was safe as long as she was part of it. They had acquired her somewhat haphazardly, but it was clear that their lives had improved thereafter.

Rather than hurry out of the deep sacred grove as if afraid, they delayed, waiting for the tribesmen to come and find them. Anne served out crusts of bread, while Hugh cleaned up their campsite; it would not do to leave a mess in spirit territory. Then as the sun blazed hugely across the water of the great lake, they settled down to divert themselves as if without any concern for their locale. That, of course, was part of the act.

They were making toys for their children. Hugh fashioned a wheeled wagon, while Anne made a tiny pot. Naturally the children asked awkward questions.

"Why not just carry the stuff?" Chip asked. He was curious about everything, just as Hugh himself had been at that age.

"Because more can be moved on the wagon," Hugh replied. "If there is a level trail to push it along." He demonstrated by pushing the toy wagon with his finger. The carved wheels squeaked, and the wagon weewawed as it moved, but it did make progress.

Chip smiled. He pushed the wagon himself, liking the way it reacted.

Meanwhile, Anne presented Mina with the pot. It looked just like a real one, with its wide round top and pointed base. "Don't try to jam it in the ground yet," Anne cautioned her. "Wait for it to dry and harden."

Mina took the pot and turned it around in her hands. Though still tiny, she was already clever with her hands. She liked to paint pictures in dirt, and she could play the little wood flute Hugh had carved for her, making recognizable tunes. In fact she took after her parents to such an extent that no one would have guessed she had been adopted.

"I want mark it," she said.

"You can decorate it with a stick," Anne told her. "It is still soft. Just use the point to make your marks."

"That too long. I want nice mark, now."

Anne cast about for something. "Maybe you can roll it on something, to mark it."

"No." Then the child caught up the cord that tied her clothing together. She wrapped it around the upper rim of the jar, pressing it in. When she pulled it away, there was the pattern of the cord, impressed on the clay. "There."

Anne nodded. "That's very clever, Mina. Maybe I should decorate my own pots that way."

"Yes," Mina said decisively. "They'll look nice."

Then they heard someone coming, and waited quietly. It turned out to be the woman called Seed, with her three-year-old son named Tree. She had helped them get settled in the village two days ago, and her little boy had played with Mina. Hugh had a strange feeling for a moment that there should have been two or three small children, but of course that was a fleeting dream fragment. He found himself taken by such bits of unreality at times, and had learned to shake them off.

Seed was perhaps the most beautiful woman he had seen, apart from Anne. And of course Anne caught him looking. She laughed. "I will teach her to dance just like me; then you will know for sure."

Hugh did not reply. Anne was not the jealous type; she knew that he appreciated lovely women, and that he touched no other but her.

Seed looked relieved as she joined them. "Of course I believed that you had the confidence of the spirits," she said. "Yet I was concerned."

"We are charmed by the spirits," Hugh said. "Now we shall return to your tribe and teach you music and dance. There should be no more trouble with those who doubt us."

Seed still looked uncertain. "Sis is jealous of Anne's beauty, and seeks to undermine it. I know the way of that."

Surely she did, being lovely herself. "But they can't do anything more," Anne said, half in question.

"Those two are devious. You must watch out for them."

"We shall do so," Hugh agreed.

They went to the village center, with its clustered oval houses, where the women were suitably impressed to see them alive and hale. They went to work, with Hugh and Chip demonstrating the tricky art of flute playing, while Anne and Mina instructed interested women in the art of provocative dancing. A white-clad priest watched, but stayed clear; he was present only to show that this matter had been cleared with the priesthood and was not objectionable. Most of the villagers wore the brown clothing of the herders or cultivators. Hugh and Anne wore green, the innocuous color of travelers.

Seed was the first to try the dance, while little Tree eagerly attempted Chip's flute. The little wooden flute was expendable; Hugh had promised to make him a good one from a bird bone, similar to Hugh's own, when they found exactly the right bone. Seed was not only beautiful; she had a natural grace that facilitated her motions. Soon she and Anne were dancing together, matching step for step, hip for hip, smile for smile. Hugh stared, entranced; they were like twins in their beauty, one in green, one in brown, the very essence of all that a man desired. The one in green had brown eyes, and the one in brown had green eyes, the seeming contrast enhancing the symmetry of their beauty.

A crowd was gathering, similarly intrigued, though perhaps the reasons differed with the sexes. More women joined the class, and Hugh played his melodies for them all, because music gave form to dance. He put Chip on the taut hide drum he had made, keeping the beat. Some of the men joined the dance, unable to resist the lure of beat and melody. It was becoming an excellent session.

But it could not go on forever. The villagers had work to do. So they agreed to return in the evening, when there would be another show. In the interim, Hugh and Anne could rest. Food was brought for them: barley bread, fermented mare's milk, baked fish, and dried strips of pig meat. They were eating well.

Then a woman approached, and they became cautious: it was Sis, who had caused her brother to challenge their favor with the spirits the day before. She was a dusky, sultry creature, unsmiling, but possessed of a healthy body. Surely she did not want to learn to dance.

She came to stand before Hugh. "There is a crippled child who dearly loves music. His family begs you to come play for him. I have brought horses so that you can go there and return with dispatch."

Seed looked up and nodded; it seemed that there was such a child.

Hugh was taken aback. This was the last thing he had expected from this sullen woman. Yet it seemed it was legitimate. He looked at Anne. Her eyes narrowed, then relaxed. "Go," she said. "I will rest here with the children. You should get experience on a horse."

She knew what most others did not: that he was well experienced with horses, and enjoyed riding when he had the chance. So did Anne. On those occasions when they had access to horses, sometimes they raced each other. If it had been possible to care for horses adequately as they traveled, they would have trained their own. But because he did not trust this creature Sis, he did not clarify this. "You will have to lead me."

Sis tried to mask her contempt for his supposed inadequacy. "The horse will follow mine," she said. "You have merely to hold on."

He walked with her to the horses. They were good enough animals, well cared for. The Yamnaya folk took pride in their horses, for they were one of the few tribes who had domesticated them for riding. Elsewhere, tribes hunted horses only for meat, not understanding how much more useful they could be. As a result, the Yamnayas and related tribes were far more mobile than most, and controlled a larger territory than their numbers might have suggested.

There were two mares, hobbled so they wouldn't drift. They were grazing at the edge of the village. Either mares or stallions could be ridden, but the stallions were usually reserved for the warrior class, being larger, stronger, and more spirited. Still, Hugh knew that a good mare could run well enough.

"There is yours," Sis said. "She is well trained and docile."

Hugh could tell that by looking at the mare. But he did not try to mount her. He merely stood as if not knowing what to do.

"I will help you mount," Sis said. "Stand directly by her side and bend your left knee. I will heave you up."

"Oh. Yes." He lifted his left foot, so that it was behind him. Sis locked her fingers together and put her linked hands under his knee. She heaved, and he swung his right leg up over the horse's back, so that he landed solidly. "Thank you."

Sis then went to the other mare and mounted with considerably more dispatch. She knew horses, he could see, while she thought him a duffer. That was the way he preferred it. Just in case she was up to something.

Sis clicked to her mare, and the horse started forward. Hugh could have guided his animal similarly, but did not. However, after a moment she started on her own, following her companion mare. Horses tolerated people, but preferred the company of their own kind.

They moved at a pace at first leisurely, then briskly. Hugh got two handfuls of his mount's mane, making a show of hanging on, though he was not in discomfort. Sis was perhaps teasing him, trying to see how fast the horses had to go before he begged for a slower pace.

Actually she was doing him a favor, unknowingly, because he was able to get to know the mare in her different paces, and to have the mare get to know him. He did this by murmuring to her in a voice too low for Sis to hear, and by applying pressure with his knees, guiding her where he wished. She was responsive, and became more so as she developed confidence in his competence. Rapport with a horse was one of the most important aspects of training. But to Sis it looked as if he were barely surviving. After a time she slowed the pace, perhaps concerned that he would fall off, and she would get the blame.

They came in due course to the shore of the great lake. "Itti's family lives on an island," Sis explained. "We will leave the horses here with hay." There was a crude enclosure with hay piled within it, so it was clear that the horses would be all right.

Hugh dismounted clumsily, but patted the mare on the side away from Sis. "We shall be together again soon," he murmured, and the mare rotated her near ear in acknowledgment.

Sis led the way to a small stone wharf where a wooden boat was docked. "Do you know about boats?" she asked.

"Of course," he said, looking doubtful. He had not had the experience with boats that he had with horses, but he had used them on occasion. It was part of the business of traveling.

"Then take a paddle." She lifted a long wooden paddle from the boat and gave it to him.

He caught it on the paddle end and continued to look doubtful. Again he noted her half-masked expression of contempt. Yet there seemed to be interest, too, in the way she covertly assessed him. Yesterday she had tried to get rid of him, because he was left-handed; today she had some other notion. He didn't trust it. That was why he was playing stupid; he did not want her to know his abilities.

"Like this," she said. She took the other paddle and held it so that the flattened end pointed down. "Now get in the boat."

He climbed in and sat at the end that floated in the water, facing back. She gave the boat a shove so that it slid the rest of the way into the lake, then stepped in herself. She had to lift one leg high and then the other, showing her firm thighs under the hide skirt. He appreciated again that whatever this woman was or was not, she had a good body.

She settled herself, then stared at him. "Face the other way," she said shortly.

"Oh." He had wondered how long it would take her to appreciate this particular evidence of ignorance. He turned himself around clumsily, in the process losing the paddle overboard. Then he almost overturned the boat while reaching for the floating paddle. What a duffer he seemed to be!

They finally got moving, and his paddling improved somewhat under her tutelage. She had taken the rear seat on the assumption that he would not be able to guide the craft, and he had pretty well confirmed that assumption. It was a kind of game that he hoped she did not know was being played. He still didn't know what her own game was.

The island was a distance east as well as offshore. But it was easy paddling, once Sis's sharp corrections enabled him to get the hang of it. He noted that she didn't tell him how to scull, to guide the boat straight forward despite paddling on a single side. So she thought that he would be unable to move the craft efficiently if he found himself alone.

They came to another stone wharf, docked, and climbed out. In the process he was treated to another glimpse of her handsome thighs, but he couldn't tell whether it was deliberate on her part. She might simply hold him in such contempt that she didn't care what he looked at.

There was a path up to the house, and there was indeed a lame child there. Hugh did what he did best, and not only charmed the child and his family with flute music; he brought out one of the simpler wooden flutes he had crafted and gave it to the boy, teaching him how to blow notes on it. A lame boy should have a lot of time to practice, and the lad did seem to catch on readily. The family was most appreciative. The man, Itti, was of the warrior class, garbed in red, and surely prominent. He gave Hugh two sheep's knucklebones that would be excellent for gambling, and had fair value in their own right. It seemed likely that there would be no objections, the next time Hugh's tour brought them to this region.

Then it was time to return to the village. Hugh followed Sis back down to the boat, noting the way her hips swayed as she walked. Now he had little remaining doubt: she was doing it deliberately. He knew because Anne was expert in the art of becoming sexually appealing, whether in a dance or otherwise. So, it seemed, was this woman. But what was her interest in him?

They got in the boat and paddled back toward the mainland wharf. But when they were farthest from either the island or the mainland shores, Sis paused in her paddling. "Turn around," she said.

Whatever she was up to, now it was about to clarify. The mission to play for the crippled child had been legitimate, but Sis must have volunteered to do it, so that she could achieve her own purpose. He now suspected what that purpose was, but remained mystified by its rationale. He laid his paddle down and turned around on the seat.

She was in the process of stripping away her clothing. He watched as the top and bottom came off, leaving her naked body glistening in the light of the declining sun. She was splendid in all her physical parts. It was the mental part that kept him wary.

He eyed the whole and the details. "You plan to swim?" he inquired after a moment.

She got right to the point. "I have a desire for you, wrong hand. Play your melodies on this body."

She had called him "wrong hand." So she had noticed. The strangest thing was that he had a feeling that he had done something like this in the past, though it was not true. There was something about her body and her manner that not only attracted him, it made him seem to remember having sex with her. That was impossible, as he had never seen her before yesterday. So from where could such a memory come? Perhaps from the similar sultry women who liked his music and who found the distinction of wrong-handedness appealing.

Meanwhile his mouth was saying the obvious. "I am married. My wife is beautiful."

"But I can give you more. I am hot and lusty." She inhaled, licking her lips and spreading her knees.

"I need no more than she offers." But the woman was stirring his desire.

"Why not try me and see?" She leaned forward so that her breasts shifted form.

"My wife wouldn't like it." Especially not with a woman like this.

"Then she need not know." She got off the seat and approached him, squatting so as not to rock the craft. That made her even more intriguing, as perhaps she knew.

She had ready answers, having evidently rehearsed this scene. But what was her real motive? He had acted like an ignorant duffer in everything except his skill with music, a performance hardly calculated to incite a woman's admiration or romantic spirit. He suspected that she had had this in mind from the outset. It surely wasn't passing passion that motivated her, yet she seemed ready to give him what any other man—and Hugh himself—desired. Why?

He decided on a direct approach. "What is your interest in me? I know I have not come across as a masterful man."

Her eyes narrowed as she paused in her approach. "So you *were* pretending. I wondered. You know the ways of deceit."

"You have not answered my question."

"I am jealous of your wife. I want to take you from her." She resumed motion.

That seemed true, but only part of the truth. Sis was certainly jealous of Anne's beauty, but she should be just as jealous of Seed's beauty, and she wasn't going after Seed's husband. There had to be some other motive.

Meanwhile he had to act, lest she succeed in seducing him. It was time to turn this off. "No. I will not be with you."

She squinted at him again, and saw his resolution. "If you seek to avoid me, I will claim that you tried to force me. You are new to this tribe, and wrong-handed; they will believe me rather than you." Now she had reached him, and laid her hand on his arm. "You would not want that."

"Something other than passion for me motivates you," he said, casting off her hand.

There was a flicker of something other than anger in her face. But she quickly masked it. "Hit me, if you wish." She caught at him again.

Then suddenly it came clear. "Anne!" he cried. "You are decoying me away from Anne. So that she is unprotected."

Now her teeth showed in a snarling smile. "Too late for her, I think."

Hugh leaned forward, put his arms around her, clasped her close, lifted, and heaved. Suddenly she was out of the boat and splashing in the water. He grabbed a paddle and scrambled to the boat's rear seat, where control was better.

Sis surfaced, her hair plastered, spittingly furious. "You can't get away!" She reached for the boat.

He lifted the paddle like a club. "Touch it, and I'll bash you. Then you'll have reason to accuse me—if you don't drown."

Her eyes met his for a moment. Then her hand withdrew. "So you are indeed a man," she said.

"I am indeed." He plunged the paddle into the water and drove the boat forward. He stroked again, sculling, leaving the woman behind.

After several strokes he glanced back. She was swimming for the shore. She was moving well, as he had thought she might. He had harmed no more than her dignity—and perhaps not much of that.

Then he realized that her clothing was still in the boat. Well, he would leave it at the corral.

He readily outdistanced the woman, for even a clumsy boat was better than swimming, when managed competently. He moved on to the shore, drew the boat out, and went for the horses. He considered, as he approached them; should he free the other one, and send her running away, so that Sis had no mount? No, he had a significant lead; his business would be done before she caught up.

Soon he was on his mare, guiding her without words. She responded eagerly to his competence, fairly flying across the terrain. Such rapport between man and mount was wonderful; both enjoyed it. It was sad the way other cultures did not understand such use of horses. They thought that meat was all they offered.

He reached the village quickly enough, for he had wasted no time. Seed was there, minding his children and hers. "Where is Anne?" he called.

"Bub came to guide her to you," Seed replied. "To join you with the lame boy, as you asked. Didn't you see her on the way?"

"No." And he knew why: Bub had no intention of bringing Anne near her husband. His design was of a quite different nature. "Which way did they go?" He suppressed the echo of Sis's words: *Too late for her.*

"To the north, where he had the horses." Now Seed looked alarmed, but her voice was controlled so as not to alarm the children. "Bub has a house farther north."

Horses. Hugh's growing tension eased a notch. "So they were riding."

"Yes. Perhaps you can find them. The children will be safe here with me."

"Thank you. How long ago did they leave?"

Seed made an indication of two close fingers toward the sun, showing that it had not traveled far. "Not long." Hugh nodded, turned his mare north and put her into a trot.

Naturally Bub and Anne were not by the local corral. But Hugh could see the recent tracks of the horses going north. They were walking, because Anne would have had the sense to do what Hugh had, concealing her excellent riding ability. Bub would have told her that this was where Hugh had gone, but she would have been cautious, knowing that the man was of doubtful character. She would have taken time to get to know her horse. Then, if the trip turned out to be false, she would ride swiftly away, and Bub would not catch her.

But if the man had had the wit to get her to dismount, to separate her from the horse, and to attack her without warning . . .

Well, even then Anne was not a likely victim. Because she was a dancer. Still, Hugh fingered his dagger nervously. He did not want vengeance, he wanted his wife safe.

Then he saw dust rising to the north. A single horse was coming, galloping south, expertly guided. Soon he recognized the flowing dark hair of a woman, and soon after that he confirmed that it was Anne. They drew up together and reached out to touch hands. Then they turned their mounts south, walking.

"Sis?" she inquired.

"Naked in the lake. Bub?"

"Indisposed in a field."

No more needed to be said; they understood each other. They returned to the village.

Later Anne gave another class in dancing. She showed a new step, difficult for many women but beautiful in execution because of the flash of flesh it showed. It was a quick step away from the partner, a spin around, and an unusually high kick forward. "Take care that you are not too close to your man," she cautioned the women. "It could be unfortunate."

Hugh played the music, nodding to himself. He suspected that Bub had stood too close, and been the recipient of that swift waist-high kick. Then he would have been inclined to drop to the ground for a time, suffering the pain only a man could feel. He would be unlikely to speak of the matter to others thereafter. But he would probably never again approach a dancer carelessly.

While the adults danced, the children played with their toys. Chip showed off his wagon, and pretended to hitch it to a horse, being intrigued with the foolish notion. Mina was proud of her unique design, pressed into the hardening clay by her belt cord. The other children were impressed too, by both the notion of hitching horses to wagons and of decorating pottery in such manner. But of course they were too young to appreciate why such things weren't feasible for serious use. It was a good session.

The Yamnaya tribe was one of a group of proto-Indo-European cultures that had domesticated the horse. This made them highly mobile, and they expanded over a wide area of the steppes. They also had wagons, but it seems that these were at first moved by manpower; their horses were too small to be used for such brute work. However, in time they figured out how to connect more than one horse at a time to a single wagon, and this magnified their mobility. This may be the explanation for their subsequent greater expansion, not merely across the thinly populated steppe but into the settled agricultural regions. A change in climate may have helped shift the balance of effectiveness toward the pastoral peoples, making more grazing land.

At any rate, expand they did, all across western Asia and Europe and on to India. We know this because their corded ware spread out, identifying them, and their languages displaced those of prior cultures in these regions. Today the Indo-European family of languages constitutes about half of all languages in the world, and governs most of the world's territory. Only China, southeast Asia, the south Pacific islands, northern Africa, and Asia Minor are excluded, apart from isolated spot cultures such as the Basques of Europe. Were this considered an empire, it would be the greatest ever known. We conjecture that the use of the horse, at first to ride, then to haul, and finally in battle, gave such an advantage to the Indo-Europeans that they were able not only to conquer the more settled societies, but to dominate them indefinitely, so that their languages came to prevail, just as English (one of the Indo-European languages) is spreading today. The economies of power were Indo-European, not because of any particular leader or ideology, but because they had a better way. The horse culture was here to stay.

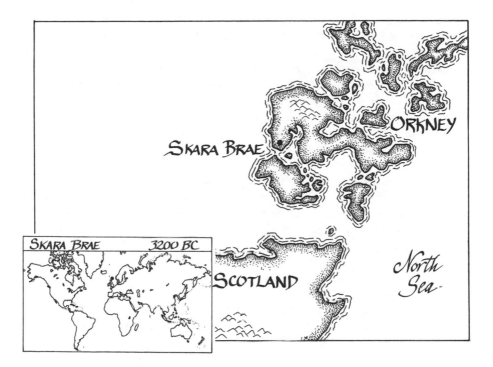

SKARA BRAE

ORKNEY

SKARA BRAE   3200 BC

SCOTLAND

North Sea

SKARA BRAE

A bad storm buried a village in the Orkney Islands north of Scotland about 1500 B.C. Another storm uncovered it more than three thousand years later, in A.D. 1850. Thus an untouched prehistoric community site was revealed. Its buildings survived because they were hidden—and because they were stone. Had there been enough wood there for building, we might never have learned of it, because wood disintegrates with time. Had it been exposed, the stone might have been taken for other purposes. So this was one of the accidents of preservation: a village of six to ten houses made of slate, beside the cold North

Sea. Skara Brae (not "Scary Bra"). They would not have called it that, of course, but we shall consider this to be our translation of their own name for it. This was the fringe of what we call the Megalithic culture, whose earliest monuments predated those of Egypt and spread across much of Europe. The best known example is Stonehenge in southern England, but there are others, and there were perhaps a larger number of Woodhenges whose ruins have been lost to history.

Who were these mighty ancient builders? What was the purpose in their circles of giant stones, some of which might weigh as much as sixty tons? How did these primitive people quarry, move, and erect such monsters? Gradually the wild speculations have given way to more solid conjectures. Skara Brae and the associated Stones of Stennes perhaps show the way. The time is circa 3200 B.C., near the beginning of this settlement.

ONE might have thought that things would be quiet the night before the annual Festival of Stones, in preparation for the strenuous activity to come. But there was too much excitement, especially among the children, for this year Chip and Mina were being allowed to attend. They were seven and five respectively, and had shown that they were able to walk a distance when they had to. So instead of being farmed out to their older neighbor Lil, to join Lil's grandchildren, they got to share the great adventure. They were supposed to rest, but were irrepressibly excited.

The sheep, however, were another matter. One had to be slaughtered and dressed, to be taken along; this was Hugh's contribution to the effort. The others Lil would watch, in return for the wool of one of them next season. And Hugh's eight-year-old nephew Jay would come to occupy the house, to care for the dog and see that no rats got into their supply of barley.

So all was ready. All they had to do was get a good night's rest. And that seemed to be almost impossible. The children could not relax. Anne served them a good supper of boiled limpets, because not only were the little shellfish plentiful and tasty, their knuckle-sized disk-shaped shells usually gave the children much entertainment. They would roll them at each other, and make high piles of them, and pretend they were jewelry or imitation teeth. But even this ploy was ineffective this time; Chip and Mina remained as animated as new lambs. They simply would not settle down on their cushion beds for long enough to fall asleep.

Finally Hugh did what always worked: he brought out his bone flute. He played, and Anne danced and sang, and both children were instantly enraptured. Of course they had to respect music, because it was special to the family, but it was more than that; they really did respond to it at a deep level. Soon both were asleep.

"And now what do *we* do to settle down?" Anne inquired as they let their music die gently away.

"What do you think, woman?" Hugh said, hauling her into him. So they made love, and it was effective; they slept thereafter.

In the morning Hugh was up first. He wrapped his sheepskin cloak about himself, called the dog awake, and went outside to urinate. They had a drained toilet closet inside, but he didn't bother to use it; it was for the convenience of women and children.

The house was joined to the next, and there was a narrow alley between them. There were six houses in all, each with its family of four to twelve people. In summer the interconnections didn't much matter, but in winter, when the fierce storms could last for days, they made community life practical. In fact it was this strong sense of community that enabled them to carry through the bad weather.

The dog led the way, long familiar with the route. They emerged from the tight cluster and walked out onto the shell midden against which the village was made. People had used this area for a long time before the present clan had occupied the site; they didn't know or care who those others had been. Their refuse had long since settled and become land, useful to brace the present houses. There were stories of harder times and stories of better times in the past, but all that mattered was how it was now.

He checked the house from outside, as he always did. The stone wall was secure, of course, but the thatch over the whalebone roof beams could get out of order and had to be watched. The last thing they wanted was a leak discovered only during a storm.

He saw Bil emerge similarly from the alley. Hugh gave the man time to complete his private business, then went over. "Your children settle well?" he inquired.

Bil laughed. "No more than yours!" Because Bil had two who would be going along too. The two men were close, for a reason that was not a fit matter for discussion: Hugh had had an early relationship with Fay, who had left him for Bub, but then left Bub for Bil. It was as if Bil had finished Hugh's unfinished business. Their children Wil and Faye matched Hugh's in ages.

"Start with the sun one fist high?" Hugh inquired, naming the time they had agreed on.

"Yes." Bil turned to check his own thatch, and Hugh returned to his house with the dog.

Anne was up now, wrapped in her sheepwool gown, breaking bread into chunks for breakfast. She hadn't bothered with a fire; there wasn't time. Her hair was in a loose tangle; she always made sure of the food before tending to herself. "You are beautiful," he told her.

She made a face, pulling her hair across in a momentary veil, then smiled. "Eat before the children get it," she said, setting out a chunk and a bowl of sheepcurds.

He sat at the stone bench beside the center hearth, in the wan light from the small window, and dipped the rock-hard bread into the soft curd. This was like the relation of man to woman, he thought, the soft complementing the hard. It was a good way.

Anne retired to the private closet to catch up on herself. He admired her rounded rear as she got down to pass through the low access portal. Any crisis that appeared now would be Hugh's responsibility, until she emerged.

As he gnawed on the softened edge of bread, he gazed around the chamber. He was proud of this house, which he had maintained since taking it over. It was large though his family was small, because it served also as a community center. He and Anne often entertained the others when it was not possible to work, and that diversion could be the difference between unity and fragmentation. The main bed was against the center of one wall, with its cushions and heath to soften the stone, and fleece blanket for warmth. The cupboard was against another wall, with its crocks of food and jugs of water and sacks of grain: their security against drought and freeze.

The children slept to the left of the main bed, in the corner by the closets. He focused on them for a time. Chip's brown hair matched Hugh's own, and indeed he was clearly of their family. But little Mina's glossy black hair was something else, shinier than Anne's tresses. Anne styled the girl's hair to match her own, and the two did have a similarity of appearance. But Mina was not a blood child; they had adopted her as a foundling baby, and never regretted it. She had been a delight throughout.

Yet it was more than that. Mina had an affinity for the spirits. Even bad spirits did not molest the family when Mina was there, and sometimes good spirits gave warning in subtle ways when mischief was brewing. That was an advantage they could never have anticipated when they saved the baby from death by exposure. They had no idea who her natural mother was; they had found her during a stone festival, when the whole island congregated. Perhaps she had simply been a gift of the spirits.

As if conscious of his gaze, the little girl stirred, waking. That jogged Chip awake too. In a moment the two were scrambling competitively to be the first to reach the private closet.

"Hold, people!" Hugh cried warningly. "Your mother's there now."

So they charged the bench instead, ready to gnaw on bread. "Are we still really going?" Mina asked, her eyes big and wonderful.

"We are still really going," he agreed.

She clapped her hands and flung her little arms around his neck, kissing him wetly on the cheek. Then she grabbed a chunk of bread and began to gnaw enthusiastically.

Anne emerged, her appearance improved. Chip charged the closet.

Mina, on the wrong side of the bench, seeing herself hopelessly behind, elected to ignore it. Her turn would come. Already she was learning to be graciously feminine when covering her losses.

They moved out before the sun was one fist high. Hugh lagged just long enough to be sure the dog didn't come. Other families were doing the same, making a rare crowding in the passage. They filed out to the gathering place.

Chip extended his arm and made a fist at the sun. "Hey—it's more than one fist up!" he exclaimed. "We're late!"

Hugh extended his own fist. "No we aren't. Your fist is smaller than mine."

"Oh." But the boy pouted only a moment. There was just too much excitement to allow small errors to remain long in mind.

When the sun was right, by Bil's fist, they set off: Six men, ten striplings, one woman, three maidens, and five children. Half the village, leaving behind most of the women, children, and old folk. Because this was not simply a celebration; it was the important working ceremony of the year. It was the Festival of Stones.

The distance to the ceremonial center was not far; a man traveling at a running jog could have reached it by noon. But though every person traveling was healthy, there were constraints. Two men were hauling a wagon loaded with food, blankets, coiled ropes, and special clothing made for the occasion, and sometimes that wagon needed extra hands, for the trail was narrow in places and steep in others. The children were full of energy, but would slow as the novelty wore off. The woman—Anne—and maidens would be tending to the children, so could not forge swiftly ahead even if they were so inclined. They were not so inclined, because they preferred to appear dainty—and the men preferred to have them appear so, at least for this event. Because their appearance at the festival could enhance their prospects for marriage. So it would be near dusk before this party reached the center.

They proceeded inland, roughly southeast, veering as necessary to avoid difficult terrain. The men shifted off on wagon hauling duty, making three teams; they, at least had no concern about getting sweaty. Hugh took the left side, so that his dominant hand was outside, in case of anything unexpected. Others in the village didn't care about his sinister handedness, but sometimes strangers did, so he masked it as a matter of course. Even so, Chip had been known to get into a fight because of it. Hugh had mixed feelings about that, but overall he was satisfied that neither child resembled him in that respect.

They stopped for lunch, and the women brought out smoked coalfish and fresh berries while the maidens fetched bags of cold water from a nearby stream. Anne made the children lie down to rest, and by this time they were tired enough to obey. It was a nice day, with just enough wind to make the heat of effort reasonable.

In late afternoon they reached the center. This was an open level region from which the hills all around could be seen. The children were especially impressed with the view of the steep cliffs of the large island to the south, which could be seen beyond a lake.

A great circle was marked on the turf, surrounded by a curving ditch enclosing a region fifty paces across. A single enormous stone poked upright from the ground, three times the height of a man. Tomorrow they would erect a second smaller stone.

The folk of other villages were arriving similarly. Bil directed his group to a suitable campsite, then nodded to Hugh. Hugh went in search of the clan leader, whose tent he thought he saw on the northern edge of the plain, by the lake there. He needed to check in and give the count of working men from Skara Brae, and also the maidens.

"Daddy!"

He turned, startled. There was Mina running after him, her black tresses flying. She was about the cutest little girl he could imagine, and in another decade would surely make a beautiful woman. But what was her concern? He waited for her to reach him.

"What is it?" he asked as she arrived. "Did you lose your mother?"

"No," she panted. "I think—I think you need me."

"I always needed you, precious child," he said, smiling.

"No, I mean really," she insisted. "For the spirits."

He looked back to the camp, and saw Anne. He waved to her, to confirm that Mina had reached him safely. "Then come along," he agreed, taking the little hand. Mina was at times unpredictable, but always agreeable, and she did indeed have a feel for the spirits. She was in her sweet way a haunted child.

They walked on north. As they approached the large camp, he picked Mina up and carried her in a sitting posture. She put her arm around his neck for security, facing forward.

Three youths were lounging before the big hide tent. "I come to see Joe, the clan leader," Hugh said.

They eyed him with expressions bordering on insolence. "Hey, it's the spooky one," one said. "With the wrong hand."

Hugh experienced a familiar surge of anger. Was he to be insulted by these striplings when he came on business?

Then Mina turned her face to look at them: first one, then another, then the third. And they blanched. "In there," one muttered, moving away.

Hugh concealed his amazement. The child had stared them down! He knew how big and dark her eyes were, at times seeming like infinitely deep pools of water, but this was new. The spirits must have shown through her gaze.

"Thanks, precious," he said, and carried her on into the tent.

Joe got up as he entered, and came to give him a bear hug that was gentle enough not to squeeze the child. "Welcome, Hugh," he said. "I'm always glad to see you. Did Bil come too?"

"Yes. And four more. And three maidens."

"And Anne, of course?"

"And my wife," Hugh agreed.

"And who is this little maiden?"

"My daughter Mina. She came to protect me from spirits, but all we encountered was three youths." That was as close as Hugh cared to come to reporting their insolence.

Joe looked Mina directly in the face, appreciating her aspect. "You will be a priestess one day," he said seriously.

"Yes," she agreed.

"Maybe already."

"Yes."

Hugh realized that Joe understood what had passed between Mina and the striplings. Joe had never been known for intelligence, but he recognized and appreciated power of any type. That was why he was the clan chief. Those who related to the spirits were respected.

Joe returned to business. "We have a good group and fair weather. We're going to try to erect two stones, flanking the Watch Stone. It's not right to leave it only half attended."

Hugh nodded. "Our men are ready. And our youths."

"But I want you on the drum."

"I understand," Hugh said, though he was hurt.

"No, it's not for your hand! That's nothing. Sometimes my own left works better. It's that there may be an attempt to hurt you or blame you for trouble. I don't know who, though I suspect. So I want you safe."

Someone wanted to cause him mischief? "Whom do you suspect?" Hugh asked.

"I must not say. Who kicked whom?"

Answer enough. There had been bad blood between Hugh's family and the brother/sister team of Bub and Serilda. When Bub lost Fay, he seemed to have gotten interested in Anne, perhaps in a notion of revenge, wanting to deprive Hugh of what he most valued. Last summer the man had tried to waylay her, and walked into a dancing maneuver he hadn't appreciated. Bub had never spoken of it, but news had gotten around. Serilda had never married.

Hugh was confident of his ability to handle Bub, should it come to violence. Bub was larger, but Hugh had greater finesse with the hand axe, and Bub knew it. So it wouldn't come to violence. But Bub had devious ways, so was dangerous. "I will drum," he agreed.

"Unless we have to have you on the rope," Joe said.

Hugh nodded. He left the tent. The striplings were gone. He set Mina down and they walked back to their own camp. It had been an interesting visit in more than one sense.

❂

In the morning Hugh was first up, as usual. But as he returned from the communal refuse pit, he discovered little Mina stirring. "Daddy, someone was here," she said.

He laughed. "Half the clan is here, precious. It's the Festival of Stones."

"In the night," she said insistently. "Doing something."

Hugh frowned. "A stranger? In our share of the tent?"

"Yes. I colored his shoe."

Hugh trusted his daughter's sincerity, but not necessarily her judgment. Someone could have blundered into the wrong section, and departed quietly upon discovering his error. But thievery was known, when so many people got together. "Show me exactly where he was."

She pointed to their piled family supplies. He checked, but nothing was missing. Their travel clothes, extra food, and his coil of rope were where he had left them. "It's all right, Mina," he said.

Anne appeared. "Something wrong?"

"Someone blundered by here in the night," he said. "Mina marked his foot."

Anne tried to be serious. "Mina, you shouldn't dye folk's feet," she said. But it was clear that she found it as funny as Hugh did. Someone in the camp might have a red boot. With luck, that person would not realize it soon, and would not know who had perpetuated the indignity.

After that it was rushed. Hugh set up his drum, stretching the leather across a big earthen pot and drawing it tight. It might not be the most melodic instrument, but it was loud and had a certain urgent quality of sound that was what they needed for parts of the work. He hauled it to the working area some distance from the camp, joining Joe and Bil. When Bil nodded, he began to play it, first lightly, then more firmly. This was the signal to get started, and all the working men and striplings converged.

The two great stones were lying on the ground near where they had been quarried earlier in summer. Quarrying was a somewhat tedious business, in which suitable boulders were located and separated into proper fragments by fire and water. Wood soaked in animal fat was laid along the line where the split was to be, and set on fire. When it burned out they cleared away the ashes and poured cold water over it, and the stone cracked along that line. They also pounded it with globular stone mauls, a number of men striking along the line in unison to break it farther apart. All this required special expertise and coordination, and the trained crew was the only group allowed to do such work, lest a good stone be ruined.

Now the men and striplings hauled timbers into place. There were not many suitable trees here, so these beams were saved to be used from year to year. They made a large sledge by fitting short cross timbers across long runner beams and lashing them together. This stout sledge was hauled into position beside the stone.

Now came the hard part. Hugh changed the beat of his drum, to get them perfectly coordinated, while Joe shouted the orders. Men with long stout poles levered up one side of the stone while the striplings hauled on a multitude of ropes from the other side. "On three," Joe cried. "One," matching the loud drum beat. "Two. Three!" All the levers and ropes went under tension together, and the giant stone heaved up on its side. Others shoved blocks in to hold the elevation when the levers were removed, but the boys on the ropes held steady. Then they shoved the sledge in close under it, and scrambled away before the ropes were slackened.

The stone fell back down, over the blocks, and crashed onto the sledge. It was now half on, but the worst was over. They used their ropes and levers to nudge it by stages fully onto the sledge. They tied it in place so that it wouldn't come loose no matter how it might be tilted.

Now round roller beams were laid beyond the end of the sledge, and the ropes and levers used to haul it onto the series of rollers. When it was fairly on them the work was easier; the ropes alone were enough to heave it forward, beat by beat. As it left rollers behind, men carried them quickly to the front and laid them down again. So it continued, moving grandly along its track toward the erection site. But the hauling was still hard work, leaving men and striplings panting, and glad to have the water the maidens brought to them during their rest shifts.

They brought the stone all the way up to its place of erection. This was a hole that had been well prepared, shored up inside by surrounding stones, with guide stakes driven in along the far side. They levered and hauled it to the brink, lifting the distant end so that the near end slid grudgingly into the hole and thunked into place at the bottom. They had to jam in more blocks at each stage, and lever it up a little more, so that its erection was actually rather slow. Hugh's drum made the beat throughout, keeping it coordinated, for any mistake could send the stone crunching dangerously wrong. A pyramid of cross-stacked planks formed behind the stone, from which the men kept working. Only when that structure was almost as tall as the stone itself were they able to get it all the way vertical, and fill in the rear of the hole with small rocks.

It was done—and though the work had seemed to move right along, the day was fading. It was time to relax and celebrate. Hugh beat a new cadence

on the drum, and the maidens of the several villages came out, provocatively dressed, and danced while the men finished their supper. Anne directed
them, for the dance was her specialty, and she led them through coordinated motions of heads, arms, legs, and hips that would have been perhaps
in bad taste on any less important occasion. But here the rules of behavior
were to a degree suspended; this was after all the Festival of Stones. The
men of course loved it, and there were no mature women to protest. Anne
did not count; she pretended for the moment to be one of the maidens, and
such was her figure that it was an excellent emulation. Her hair and torso
moved in ways that excited admiration and lust, as they were supposed to,
and Hugh was glad that she was his wife. The maidens emulated her
movements, shake for shake and kick for kick, making a most intriguing
array. Especially when the kicks were high.

Among the maidens was Serilda, who was qualified despite being older
because she had never married. She too had a figure to be reckoned with,
and her slippered feet seemed tiny. She oriented on Hugh with her stare
and did a dance that disturbed him because it made him react. He tried not
to look as she showed her thighs, but couldn't prevent it. Each summer she
did this, fixing on him though there were many single men who would
gladly have married her. He had once thought she would not have the
nerve, because Anne was here, but she clearly had no shame. Anne was
remarkably tolerant, evidently feeling no threat, but Hugh felt it. Serilda
acted as if she had some claim on him, as if there were some secret between
them. And the way his body reacted, it was almost as if it were true.

Worse, he had the feeling that her closest loyalty was to her brother Bub,
who had tried to rape Anne. Bub was here, but had remained well away
from Anne so far. How was Serilda's evident interest in Hugh connected to
that? How could Serilda dance in Anne's class while at the same time trying
to vamp Anne's husband? The pieces of this puzzle did not quite fit
together.

When the dance was done, it was time for the maidens to choose partners
for the evening. Everything was reasonably proper; they would merely keep
company with their chosen young men for the evening, in the view of
everyone. But such acquaintances could lead in due course to marriages.
Maidens could not marry within their villages, so this was one of their few
opportunities to meet the men of other villages and examine prospects for
the future. They had been watching the men as they worked, so now had
some notions about whom they would like to get to know. Anne herself
stepped back, doing a relatively sedate individual dance to cover the
interval.

The youths were seated separately. The maidens now addressed that
section, each closing on a particular youth and offering him the flower from
her hair. He could accept it and be with her, or decline. The maidens this

time were unusually pretty, and the dance had been unusually provocative, so it seemed unlikely that any would decline.

Indeed, the matchings were quickly made, and soon all the maidens except one had men to be with. They brought the men to their family groups for introductions. The one remaining maiden was Serilda, who had not deigned to offer her flower to any of the youths. Instead she cast her eye around a wider range—and it fell again on Hugh.

Oh, no! Was she going to try to shame him publicly by pretending to a relationship that did not exist? It seemed she was, for she forged toward him, lifting the flower from her hair.

His response should be clear: he would reject the flower. He wanted no part of this suggestive ploy. Anne knew he had done nothing with Serilda, but others might not know, and tongues would wag.

But as she approached, she did not offer him the flower. She tossed it to him, making it impossible for him to decline. The flower landed neatly in his lap. Since the moment a man touched the flower the date was made, he was stuck for it.

She sat down beside him, her hip touching his. Her body was warm from the recent exertion of the dance, and her breathing remained heavier than normal. He did not look at her, but her presence was dynamic. He knew that all around them the other families were marveling. They were surely conjecturing whether he had had a secret affair with her, that was now becoming open. Did she want to be his second wife? Such arrangements were rare, but not discouraged, because sometimes there were more women than men and it was best that all women be married. Did that explain why she had passed up those men who had expressed interest in her? Was she tired of secrecy, so she was forcing the issue now, shaming him into recognizing her? All these conjectures must be going around, and it would be difficult or impossible to refute them.

Now the grog was poured and circulated, and the party proper proceeded. Anne came to join them, bearing three mugs of it. She handed one to Hugh and one to Serilda, just as if the woman had been expected to join them. Then she sat with her own mug on Hugh's other side. Bub was sitting well distant, not trying to provoke any trouble—and this, too, might be cause for alarm.

Dusk was falling, and they watched the stars come out. The plan of the stones related to the sun, though Hugh understood that the right priests with the right circles could track the moon and even the stars with marvelous precision. So when the sun set on this center, the work was over.

The carousing continued far into the night. Hugh drank and danced with Anne, ignoring Serilda as well as he could. Serilda remained close, but did not make any additional scene. Apparently she was satisfied just to be near him. That, perhaps, was mischief enough.

At last they retired to their section of the tent, where the children had gone to sleep long before. Serilda did not follow, to Hugh's relief. Now he was free to be free with Anne, and they made love and sank into slumber.

❁

On the second work day they loaded and moved the second stone. But two men who had overworked themselves the first day turned lame and had to desist. Now Joe did what he hadn't wanted to do, and put Hugh on a rope. Hugh had his own rope with him, as he had the day before, in case of need; the need had come. He was privately glad of it; he wanted to do his physical share. A promising stripling was put on the drum.

They loaded the stone on the sledge, and hauled it down to the circle. All was going well. But when they made the supreme heave, starting the stone on its way to the vertical position, it didn't budge. This stone was heavier than the other one, and the men were tired after their prior day's work and night of carousal. So Joe joined Hugh on his rope. "Heave!" he cried as the drum beat, and both gave their utmost heaves.

And the rope snapped. Both of them took hard falls, amazed and disgruntled. The lifting came to a halt.

"I knew you shouldn't have put that weird hand on the sacred work," Bub said. "The spirits are turning against us."

There was a murmur. This was indeed holy work, for all of its festive aspects. The spirits had to support it. If they were annoyed, all would be lost.

"Hugh isn't bad for the spirits," Joe said. "It's just an accident. They happen."

"You say that because you're his friend," Bub said. The murmur supported him; the men were afraid that he was right. "He should be banished, so the stones will be sacred."

Bil came forward. He looked at the severed ends of the rope. "This rope didn't break naturally," he announced. "It was cut."

"How could it be cut?" Bub demanded. "He was using it right along."

"Inside, where it didn't show," Bil said. "I have worked with ropes; I know the difference between fraying and cutting. The inner strands were cut; the outer ones broke. Someone did this."

"You're his friend too," Bub said. "Your word is no good on this either." And the muttering was growing, supporting him.

At last it was coming clear: here was the mischief Bub had devised. Weakening Hugh's rope so that it would snap under stress, setting back the work, maybe injuring someone, and discrediting him. Because he was left-handed, and therefore under chronic suspicion. Bub had found a way to get back at him for what Anne had done. And if he managed to get Hugh banished, then Anne would have little effective defense against Bub.

But how had Bub managed to weaken the rope? It had been with Hugh all day, and in his home section at night.

Then he remembered what Mina had said. "Call for my girl-child," he told Joe. "Question her."

"That's a spirit child," Bil said.

Joe looked at him, surprised, nodding. Then he shrugged. "I must investigate this," he said. "I must know exactly what happened. Bring me Hugh's children."

The surrounding muttering became a murmur of surprise. What did children have to do with this? But the others did not object, because Joe was their leader and he had almost been hurt by the breaking rope, and he was investigating.

Anne came, bringing Chip and Mina. Joe addressed them both. "What do you two know of cut ropes?" he asked gruffly.

Chip gazed blankly back at him, but Mina jumped right on it. "Someone came! Night before last. By Daddy's rope. I marked his foot."

"Who came?" Joe asked.

"It was all dark. I couldn't see. But he was there for a long time. I put my dye on his shoe."

"There by Hugh's rope," Bil said thoughtfully, loudly enough to be heard. "Two nights ago. And he did not use that rope yesterday, so it didn't break then."

"What color dye?" Joe asked the girl.

Mina held up her little dye bag.

"That's a clue," Bil said. "But in two days that die could have been washed out. Still, if the man didn't know it was there—"

"Line up!" Joe roared. "All men! Striplings too. Show your feet."

Confused, the men obeyed. Almost all of them were sweaty and dirty, and their boots were soiled with dust and grease, but the bright dye should show on them.

Joe walked along the front of the row, and Bil along the back, peering intently at boots. And came up with nothing. None had the dye on them. "They can't have changed them," Joe said. "These are the only ones they have here."

Changed them. Hugh remembered how the maidens had brought changes of clothing, so as to do their dance. Today they were back in their working clothes. "The girls," he said. "Check them too."

Bil nodded. "It could have been a woman."

"Maidens!" Joe shouted. "Line up next!"

The maidens formed a line. Their boots lacked dye too. But two of the dancers were missing. "Where—?" Joe started.

There was a commotion. Then two women fell to the ground, scuffling. Anne had tackled Serilda. And there as they fought was the guilty boot: on

Serilda's foot. She evidently had not noticed the dye until now, or had not realized its significance. She had tried to sneak away, to get time to scrub it off, but Anne had stopped her.

In a moment the men broke up the fight and held Serilda captive. "You cut the rope!" Joe accused her. "To avenge your brother."

Serilda hesitated, and decided on a course. "I did it for myself," she said. "To get Hugh exiled. So I could have him."

She was protecting her brother, so that he would not get banished too. There was nothing they could do about that.

"Then you are banished," Joe said. "Leave this clan, and do not return, lest you be killed."

Serilda nodded. "I will fetch my things."

The men let her go, and she went to her section of the tent. Bub stood mute, giving no sign. But it was clear that his plot had turned against him, costing him what he most valued: his sister. And his vengeance against Hugh, who had been vindicated.

After that they returned to work erecting the stone, and by dusk the job had been completed. Tomorrow they would return to their home villages. It had been a good Festival of Stones.

> We don't know the details of the culture of the Megalithic builders, but it could have been like this. We do know something about the manner they handled their huge stones. No modern machinery, no aliens from space are required; they did it with their technology of the time. The Orkney isles were at the fringe of this culture, not as advanced as those settlements nearer its center, but their designs were similar. The site described was constructed at Stennes, with twelve stones in a circle, probably relating to solar observations. Later another was made nearby, the Ring of Brodgar, with sixty stones, probably a lunar observatory. There has been much debate on exactly what observations might have been done at such sites, and at their more sophisticated and famous cousin at Stonehenge in England, but there seems to be persuasive indication that rather precise observations were made over the course of many centuries. The natural cycles were very important to the ancient cultures.
>
> For perhaps three thousand years the Megalithic cultures endured, before being displaced by cultures with bronze and more productive agricultural techniques. Thus, in a literal sense, the stone age gave way to the ages of metals. But they left behind monuments like none seen since.

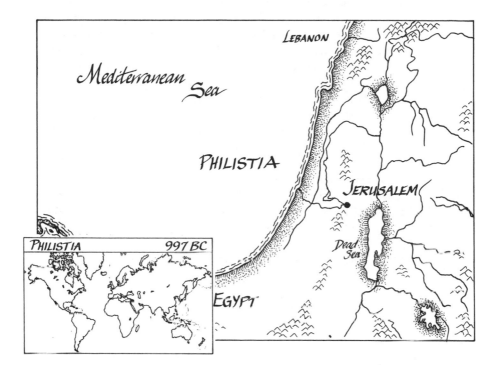

Mediterranean Sea

LEBANON

PHILISTIA

JERUSALEM

Dead Sea

EGYPT

PHILISTIA   997 BC

CHAPTER 11

PHILISTINE

The second millennium B.C.—*that is, roughly 2000–1000* B.C.—*was as busy and violent in the Levant—that is, the east Mediterranean coastline between Anatolia (modern Turkey) and Egypt where there are now the countries of Syria, Lebanon, and Israel—as the second millennium* A.D., A.D. *1000– 2000. More succinctly: things are always popping in the Holy Land.*

Homer's Iliad *describes a bold foray by the collected Greek city-states against the key city of Troy in Anatolia around 1200* B.C. *Forget the surrounding mythology, which is formidable, involving the Golden Apple, the abduction of Helen, and the ten-year effort to rescue her. The real motive for the war was political and economic: the city of Troy controlled an important trade route that the Greeks coveted.*

But this too may not be the real story. The Odyssey *describes the adventures of the Greek hero Odysseus on his way home after that war, when he encountered things like the forgetful lotus eaters, a one-eyed man-eating giant, and the luscious but dangerous sorceress Circe. This, too, may be a euphemism for a more practical reality. The Illyrians, who lived in the Balkans (present-day Yugoslavia—another chronic hot spot), advanced south into the Peloponnesian peninsula, displacing the Dorians of northern Greece, and the Dorians moved south to displace other Greeks, many of whom had to take to their ships to escape. These became the Sea Peoples, who ravaged Anatolia, Crete, Egypt, and the Levant. In fact it may be that the adventures of the* Iliad *and the* Odyssey *were merely the Greeks' version of what to all the other inhabitants of the eastern Mediterranean were destructive raids by barbarians on ships. The Hittite Empire of Anatolia was destroyed. The Egyptians managed to repulse a band of Sea Peoples, who then settled in the Levant, and thereafter that region was named after them: Palestine, from the Peleset, now called the Philistia. The Philistines do appear to have been Mycenaean Greeks; their shields and armor matched, as did their pottery, and a number of their names echo those of the heroes of the* Iliad. *So now perhaps we know where Odysseus went: to the Levant, where his people made a new nation, much to the frustration of neighbors like Egypt and Israel.*

Two hundred years later, about 1000 B.C., the Philistines were in firm control of the region, having thrown off any obligations to the Egyptians and subjugated the Canaanites who were the local natives. More was to happen in this region—much more—but for the moment let's consider the situation from the perspective of the Philistines.

HUUO kissed Annai farewell at the dock, and hugged his eight-year-old son and six-year-old daughter. He hated to separate from them, but this was a special tour where children were not welcome. Of course their loyal Cannanite servant and friend Crystalech could have cared for them this month; her daughter Desert Flower was Minah's age, and the children got along well. But it seemed best simply to let Huuo travel alone, while Annai and the children maintained the household. This occasion came only once a year, and that could be handled.

"Be careful, Daddy," Minah said as she let him go. Her eyes were great and dark, as if formed from the same midnight substance as her hair. She was not their natural child, having been adopted as a temple foundling, and the aura of the goddess seemed to cling to her. It was already understood that she would be a priestess when she came of age. Not one of the ordinary ones who gave sexual solace to male worshippers, but a ranking temple official with direct communion with the god. She was as different from her brother as night from day, but the family tacitly concealed this, lest some god decide that she was suitable grist for sacrifice. That was one reason they tried to keep the children home: so as not to attract undue attention.

"I will," he promised her. "You protect your mother from evil spirits while I'm gone." He smiled as he said it, but it really was not a joke.

"I will," she agreed seriously.

Then he turned and walked the gangplank to board the ship with its bird-headed prow and stern. He turned again as he stepped onto the deck, and waved to them. Some men clearly enjoyed this annual respite from their families, but Huuo did not; had it been feasible, he would have had them all come with him, including the servant and her child. But the expense would have been prohibitive. Huuo himself paid nothing, instead being well paid for his expertise, but the others would have counted as baggage.

Annai blew him a kiss as the ship put down its oars and stroked smartly from the pier. She was ethereally beautiful in the morning sunlight, her dark hair blown out by the breeze, her light dress alternately flattening against her shapely dancer's torso and tugging away from it. For a crazy instant he wanted to dive into the water and swim back to her. But the family needed the excellent pay he would receive for this tour. Certainly her love would keep; she was as constant as any woman could be, though she could have done extremely well as a woman of the temple. She simply preferred to allow no man but her husband to touch her, and Huuo was hardly inclined to debate that.

He made his way past the oarsmen and down into the hold, where the cargo was stacked under waterproof cover. The ship rowed out to sea, and there picked up a fair north wind. The oars were shipped; the galley slaves could catch up on their relaxation while the wind held. Huuo knew that they loved their games of dice and markers, and that the ship whore would get brisk business. Foreigners professed to be in doubt about the distinction between a whore and a temple priestess, but that merely showed how ignorant those of other cultures were. The priestess brought worshippers closer to the spirit of the goddess, while the whore merely sated animalistic passions. There was also a considerable difference in price, for those who chose to think of it that way. Actually there was no price for a priestess; there was a significant donation for the welfare of the temple. One might as well compare a field laborer to a noble: both did their jobs, but could never be confused with each other.

Huuo retired to his cabin, which was hardly more than a cramped cubby in the hold, and settled down for the ride. The ship was bound from Jaffa to Gaza, this leg of its larger route; he had boarded it at his home city of Mor. There would be other stops along the way. It might have been faster to ride overland, but the ship was both safer and more comfortable. Though the Canaanites of this region had become properly subservient, their wilder neighbors of the mountains, the hill folk who called themselves the Israelites, had never acceded properly to either authority or civilization.

Periodically they had to be put down, when they became too much of a
nuisance. The independent cities of Philistia would contribute to a levee for
mutual advantage, and a joint expedition would be mounted. Then things
would return to normal for a few years, until the savages forgot the lesson
and became obnoxious again. Sometimes one of their prophets would
rouse them to violence in the name of their cult god, pretending that it was
the *only* god extant; sometimes it was just their natural depravity. It had
been a while since the last punitive expedition, so the primitives might be
stirring; Huuo didn't care to risk riding alone through what the hill folk
pretended was their territory.

This festival tour was to celebrate the gods of Philistia, who had been
reasonably kind. Other musicians would gather from other cities, each
contributing its best; they would tour the principal cities, performing
together for each seren, or city lord, renewing the glorious history of
Philistia. The serens in turn would wine, dine, and offer blandishments to
the musicians, and the people of each city would throng in celebration.
Were it not for his separation from his family, Huuo would have enjoyed the
prospect greatly.

He found himself unable to rest adequately, so he brought out his double
flute and played, practicing for the big event. He hardly needed practice,
but the music always soothed him, and he realized that his tension was
because of the recent separation from his family. He closed his eyes and
imagined Annai dancing as he played the melody and descant. In his fancy
she languorously stripped away her scant items of apparel, until she
pranced naked, as she liked to do when feeling free. That gave him comfort.

"Sir."

Huuo paused, opening his eyes. A Canaanite sailor stood before him,
apologetically. "Yes?"

"Sir, the oarsmen—they overheard your playing. They bid me inquire—
if it be not too great an imposition—if you would honor them by playing
for them on the oar deck as they row?"

Huuo realized that the wind had died, so the oars were resuming. Music
could facilitate such labor. Flattered, he agreed. He got up and followed the
sailor to the head of the cramped deck where the twin rows of oarsmen sat.
The drummer was just establishing the cadence, so Huuo settled beside him
and adapted his melodies to that powerful beat.

The oarsmen grinned, and put forth extra effort, making the ship fairly
leap ahead. It was a good event for all parties, because Huuo appreciated an
appreciative audience of any kind, and the oarsmen liked the diversion, and
the ship's captain was glad of the extra speed.

The ship put into port at midday at Ashkelon. There it unloaded ingots of
copper and silver, and took on a quantity of fine textiles and assorted
jewelry. Huuo was sure that the local merchant-thieves were cheating the
pirate-captain, who was also cheating them, and that each was privately well

satisfied with his bargain, because it was the final buyers who wound up paying the most for the least. This was the name of trade. The cities of the seacoast flourished from it.

In an hour they were back at sea. A contrary wind appeared; the ship's priest burned incense, but the wind merely strengthened. Huuo shook his head; if he had brought his daughter Minah along, she would have spoken to the wind, and it would have changed. But then the captain would have schemed to acquire her, by devious means, and the situation would have become treacherous. Better a slow trip than that!

Now the captain approached him. He was a Philistine of middle age, grizzled, stout, but clearly possessing the competence of experience. "Captain Ittai here. My lord musician, do you play for the spirits?" he inquired brusquely.

Huuo smiled. He was wellborn but no lord, and the captain knew that. But Ittai was asking a favor. "I can play, but they do not necessarily listen," he demurred.

The captain lowered his voice. "I note you are bent to the left."

This could be trouble. Huuo had done his best to conceal his left-handedness, because superstitious seamen could have violent notions about the curse of such a person on a ship. He played more instruments than the double flute, but he carried that one now because it betrayed no handedness unless one were sharp enough to observe that he played the dominant melody on the left. But the captain was evidently an observant cuss, and had read the little signals that could never be entirely concealed: which hand lifted higher when he was startled, which way he preferentially turned, even the momentary angling of his head. Concealing all of these little traits was an effort that could give him a headache from the continuing tension. So, unconsciously, believing that no one was paying attention, he had given himself away.

"You choose to make an issue?" Huuo asked in a carefully neutral tone.

"By no means," the man said quickly, though of course his very mention of the matter had made the issue. "But there are those aboard who might react in an ignorant manner if the wind were unusually adverse. It seems best to me to negate the whole issue by seeing that the wind is not adverse."

Nicely put. "I will make an attempt to persuade the wind," Huuo agreed, getting up and bringing out his flute. "But understand this: the spirits, too, have been known to take note of particular things. Were my effort to annoy them on that score—"

Ittai laughed. "On a day like this? I have been at sea twenty years, and never seen a storm blow up swiftly in such weather. The adverse risk is minimal." He paused, then added: "Besides, the local waters are kind to the left."

That was a curious statement. But they were arriving at the incense site, and further dialogue would be awkward.

He stood on the deck and played the melody of the hymn to the north wind, which was the one they wanted. The south wind intensified. But he knew that these things were whimsical, and sometimes an increase preceded a reversal. He had no doubt that the spirits could change the winds, but suspected that they seldom bothered. Why should they do mortal men any favors? Minah could evoke their attention and cooperation, but she was Philistia's most winsome child. Huuo was simply a wrong-handed man.

As if the thought of Minah affected things, the wind dropped, then changed. It gusted east, then veered south. There was a cheer from the oarsmen. It was sheer chance, he was sure, but Huuo made a small bow in the direction of the oarsmen, then retired to his cubby. He knew he was lucky that something ill had not happened.

"Nice job," the captain said. "I didn't want to get delayed today, because things can get complicated after a battle, depending how it goes, and markets can tumble. I want to complete my deals in Gaza and be on my way before news of any kind comes."

"News?"

"About the campaign against the Israelites."

"Oh, yes," Huuo agreed, remembering. "There was a levee from Mor. But I wouldn't call it a campaign, just a routine cleaning up. The hill folk can't compete with civilized forces."

Ittai frowned. "You think not? That upstart they call king, David—he's a cunning one. That's the one who took out Goliath, remember. Now he's going for bigger prey."

Huuo was surprised. "The lucky lad? I thought he was a musician, not a warrior."

"The same. The little harpist. We put him on the throne of Israel, as a Philistine vassal, but now he's getting too big for his sandals and we have to take him out again. Remember, he learned warfare from us, from the years he served as our vassal. Achish, seren of Gath, trained him. So now the ungrateful lout will be using our own techniques against us. That's what makes him dangerous."

Huuo nodded. "Dangerous, indeed! Those wild hill folk have always been an annoyance. But still, their resources can't compare to ours."

"They took Jerusalem. That means they're more than rabble. This rebellion has to be ended before it gets awkward. Weird things can happen in the field."

"You speak as if you've had experience."

"Why do you think I'm wary of David? I was there at the battle of Ephes-Dammim, twenty years ago. We had the might to crush them, and should have done it, but the idiot generals agreed to a contest of champions. They figured no one could stand against Goliath. Then this sneaky shepherd used his sling to conk the champion on the forehead with a stone and felled him without ever coming close. I said then, may the gods forgive us if we ever give that little turd another chance. I retired from soldering when my levee returned, and have been a shipper ever since. The sea has always been my first love. But I've kept track of David, and I know trouble when I see it. But do you think they'd ever listen to someone who was only a foot soldier? Mark me, we'll be finding out the hard way."

"We surely will," Huuo agreed, not wanting to argue the case with someone who was obviously highly opinionated.

Then there was a call from elsewhere on the ship, and the captain had to hurry away to get it straightened out.

The wind freshened, filling the sails, and the boat moved south at respectable speed. Huuo lay back. Now he could take his nap.

For a time his mind wandered. The captain had reminded him of the encounters with the organized factions of the hill folk. More of that scattered history was returning to his memory. He had studied music, of course, and so had picked up information about musicians. David the harpist, said to have been a talented player when young. That man was now a king? He must be, for the name matched: King David. It wouldn't be the first oddity associated with the hill folk. There had been the time the hill folk had the giant. Instead of the Philistine Goliath, there had been the Israelite Samson, claimed to be the strongest man in the world. He was supposed to have single-handedly slain thousands of Philistines, though his first wife was a Philistine. Of course that had been a considerable exaggeration, but he had made a nuisance of himself. So they had put Delilah on him, and she fathomed the secret of his strength, and after that they chained him, blinded him, and used him for stud. Maybe Goliath was Samson's descendant, no brighter than his ancestor, falling for the wiles of a woman or shepherd musician.

Huuo drifted asleep, his dream picking up where his conscious thoughts left off. After Samson, Saul had come on the scene, anointed the first king of Israel. Huuo found himself in the body of the soldier Ittai, when the Philistines fought a pitched battle with Saul's crude army of hill folk. They beat the Israelis, of course. But then the enemy brought forth their fetish object, the thing they called the Ark of the Covenant. That made the Philistines nervous, because even primitive spirits could make a lot of mischief for mortal men. But the general urged them to attack regardless, and while the mischief of the spirits was chancy, the wrath of the general was certain, and they waded in. They slaughtered the hill folk and took possession of the Ark, and that was a real coup, because the enemy didn't dare attack as long as their sacred chest of artifacts was hostage.

They took the Ark to the temple of Dagon at Ashdod and opened it up. Huuo, though no priest, was somehow able to look over a priest's shoulder to see inside. It was just a few scrolls and things, a motley collection of items of supposedly holy nature. But the Israelites believed in it, so it wasn't destroyed. That was a mistake, for Huuo's invisible eye saw something awful seeping from it: the concentrated spirit of the hill folk, leaking out into the city. It squirmed its way into the sleeping bodies of the good citizens of Ashdod, and they turned dark and fevered and coughed their lives out onto the dirt.

So the authorities moved the Ark to the city of Gath—and of course the plague followed. Only Huuo, in his dream eye, could see the noxious spirit crawling in snakelike streamers from its crevices and seeking out the living people. So they moved the Ark to Ekron, and that city also suffered the ravages of the terrible plague.

Finally they realized what the nature of the problem was. So they returned the Ark, together with some token votive offerings, to the Israelites, and the plague ended. There was the lesson: never bring the enemy's spirit power into your home cities. Swords could slay physical enemies, but not malignant spirits.

And so Saul consolidated his new kingdom and harassed the civilized cities nearby. That was when they had to mount an expedition against him—and suffered the misfortune of the Goliath business.

At which point Huuo woke. Now he had a refreshed appreciation of the problem of the hill folk, and could almost believe Captain Ittai's dire concern about the current campaign. Those Israelites were slippery folk, and often luckier than they deserved.

The ship was pulling into Gaza. Huuo gathered his things and stood ready to disembark. The captain approached. "Thank you for your assistance; we are early."

"Thank you for your interesting review of the Israeli campaign," Huuo replied. "I hope I catch your ship on the return trip before any serious consequences appear."

"That would be best," Ittai agreed gravely.

A uniformed palace guard was waiting on the pier as Huuo accompanied Captain Ittai off the ship. He approached Huuo. "You are the musician? Seren Jaoch awaits you, sir."

"Awaits me?" Huuo asked, surprised.

"See, I told you the local waters are kind," the captain said wisely.

"But I'm only the flautist," Huuo protested.

"Exactly," the guard said. "Please accompany me to your place of honor at the palace."

Bemused, Huuo followed the man off the pier to a sleek riding wagon drawn by a sleek horse. This was the kind of treatment accorded to visiting dignitaries; what was he doing here? He did not quite trust this.

They got in, and the guard drove the horse smartly along the road toward the walls of the main city of Gaza. This certainly was easier than walking, but still felt strange.

"I would not question Seren Jaoch's decisions," Huuo said cautiously.

"But I am curious why an ordinary musician should be accorded such honor."

The man glanced sidelong at him. "You really don't know?"

"I really don't know. I have not been treated this well elsewhere."

"Seren Jaoch does not govern elsewhere."

Huuo realized that the man was not going to tell him, so he let it be. He satisfied himself with a good look at the approaching city. Gaza was larger and wealthier than Mor, and it showed; the ramparts were significantly more formidable. And while in most cities there was an uneasy coalition of ruling lords, it seemed that Seren Jaoch was clearly dominant here. Surely he was a good man from whom to receive favor—and a bad one from whom to receive disfavor. Huuo would have preferred to enter this city unremarked, because a despot's favor and disfavor could be separated by very narrow lines.

The guards at the main gate waved them on in, evidently recognizing the horse and wagon. They moved through the aperture, and on down the central street of the city. The city inhabitants crowded back to give the wagon room. The stone and mud walls of the dwellings and shops passed behind almost in a blur; Huuo simply was not used to traveling this fast.

Then they were at the grand columns of the central palace. The horse came to a smart halt and servitors rushed up to help Huuo down to the pavement. As soon as he was clear, the horse, wagon, and palace guard moved away, leaving him to the servitors. These hustled him into the palace and to a lavish suite complete with obsequious male and female servants. Huuo knew there wasn't any point in asking them anything, so he suffered himself to be stripped and bathed and garbed in clean, elegant robes. That meant that he would soon learn why he was receiving such special treatment.

He was ushered to a small but extremely well appointed banquet hall. There stood a heavyset man who seemed no older than Huuo himself, reminding him vaguely of the captain, though this was clearly a far more important personage.

The man stepped forward to embrace him. "So good to meet you, Huuo the Musician," he said. "I am Seren Jaoch."

Huuo hastily bowed his head in submission to a royal presence. "I am honored, lord," he said. "Yet I fear you take me for a far more important person than I am."

"Importance is as it seems," Jaoch replied. "You will eat with me, and we shall talk."

So it was no mistake. But what did this powerful man want of this routine musician? The strangeness had not abated.

They sat at the table, and the scullery servants brought in platters of lambsmeat and sweetbreads, and vials of wines so rare that Huuo could not identify them. There was nothing to do but eat well, hoping he was not in some way being fattened for slaughter.

But as he picked up his first morsel, he realized that Seren Jaoch was doing the same—with the same hand. He paused, assessing the implication.

Jaoch smiled. "Now you see it, musician. The hand."

"You are like me," Huuo agreed. "Left-handed."

"And like you, I do not proclaim it, but those around me know. We need not discuss the reason."

Indeed they did not. Huuo knew what Jaoch faced. For a man of power it was perhaps worse, because others were always scheming to diminish or pre-empt that power, and there was a stigma to the left side that could too readily provide them an opening.

"Captain Ittai remarked that these waters were kind to the left," Huuo said. "I didn't understand his reference."

"A man needs associates he can trust," Jaoch said. "My key personnel are all of this persuasion." He lifted his left hand momentarily. "They know that their positions would wither away without me. They support me with extraordinary loyalty."

Huuo nodded. No threats would be required; left-handers were normally discriminated against. Only when the leader was similarly inclined could they rise to prominence. "I am sure they do," Huuo said.

"But I lack one thing," Jaoch said. "It is my misfortune to suffer occasionally from insomnia. Sometimes my lovely mistress, also left-sided, gives me solace. Sometimes music. However—"

Suddenly it came into focus. "You have no left-handed musician! No one you can trust in your sleeping presence."

"Exactly. And you are acclaimed as the finest musician in Philistia."

"Oh, I would hardly make such a claim," Huuo demurred. "There are many who—"

"Of your persuasion of hands."

Huuo nodded. "That, perhaps. But—"

"Tomorrow is the day of the festival," Jaoch said. "I'm sure the music will be as fine as the rest of it. But tonight I will ask you to play only for me. I would like to hear for myself whether you are as good as your reputation."

"Of course I will play for you," Huuo agreed warmly. But behind the warmth was a chill. If he played as well as he could, he would confirm his reputation, and then Seren Jaoch might want him to stay here. But how could he ever play less than his best? That simply was not his way.

They finished the excellent meal, and Jaoch was a companionable host. But imperfectly concealed beneath that geniality was more than a hint of iron. At one point a subordinate entered with news of the capture of a wanted criminal. "Execute him this night, and leave his body for the birds," Jaoch said, and continued eating without pause. The lord of the city was perhaps deliberately showing the visitor two sides of himself: the best of friends, the worst of enemies.

Then Huuo fetched his double flute, and played several melodies of increasing intricacy. He tried to restrain himself, to avoid the prettiest, but his nature would not allow it. Seren Jaoch was a very good audience, showing real appreciation for nuance as well as directness, and his responses led Huuo into his best.

When Huuo paused, Jaoch made a small demonstration. "Play one more tune," he murmured, "and walk to the door as you do. See what you see in the adjacent chamber."

Perplexed, Huuo obeyed. When he came to the doorway, he saw seven or eight servants and guards standing there. When they saw him, they quickly dispersed, except for the one guard who was evidently supposed to be there.

Huuo returned to his place as he finished the melody. "I saw your household staff," he said.

"So I thought. They overheard the music, and were compelled by it, and remained to hear it all. That was not by my command, so I know that their judgment echoes mine: if you are not the finest, you are surely close to it. Your reputation is well earned."

"Thank you," Huuo said uneasily.

"But I am keeping you up, when you need your rest for the morrow. If there is anything you wish for the night—fine wine, a soft maiden—"

Huuo smiled. "My wife is said by some to be beautiful, and certainly she is to me. I live only to return to her."

Jaoch nodded approvingly. "In contrast to many musicians I see, who take this tour to revel in freedom from domestic constraints. Your attitude is like your music: excellent."

Huuo spread his hands. "If you saw her, you would understand, my lord. I thank you for your gracious hospitality." He bowed, and stepped to the doorway. There a servant was now ready to guide him back to his chambers.

✥

When the musician was gone, Jaoch pondered for a time, then spoke, seemingly to the air. "Zebub, appear."

Another man entered the room from a door concealed by a hanging rug. He was of rugged build, with a certain cruel set to his mouth. "I see you are satisfied, my lord."

"I am indeed. He is even better than you claimed. A man of both talent and honor, unlike so many I encounter." There was an incipient curl to his lip that hinted that his present company was not excluded from the generalization.

Zebub took no seeming note of that contempt. "A man you can trust, unlike some," he agreed. "You wish to add him to your court?"

"Indeed. But he lives only to return to his beautiful wife."

"You may remember that I warned you of that, my lord. She is as lovely as he is talented. In fact she is a dancer, like my sister, and very like her in appearance."

"But your sister schemed against one of my favored men," Jaoch reminded him grimly. "I had to banish her."

"I do not question that," Zebub said quickly. "You acted as a seren must act. The lesson is exemplary. Yet I think she has taken it to heart, and you know I would like to have her back with me, however chastened."

"And you think she can persuade the musician to join this court?"

"In the right circumstance."

"Despite the fact that he has a wife who is by other accounts lovelier than she?"

"I think Scylla might—if the reward were sufficient."

"The reward of residence in this city, and acceptance by this court."

"Exactly, my lord. She loves her own people, and longs for the return of your favor which she forfeited by her indiscretion."

"I will consider. It is possible that I will not need her assistance."

"As my lord elects," Zebub agreed. He exited quietly by the concealed doorway.

Jaoch sat for a time, meditating. He would prefer to win the musician by positive means, but was prepared to go another route if that were required. Zebub, an untrustworthy but sometimes useful officer, represented that other route. And it was true that the man's similarly untrustworthy sister also had certain qualities that could enable her to be useful on occasion. Jaoch had seen her dance, and might at one time have taken her as a mistress, had she not schemed foolishly against the captain of his guards. She had evidently developed a passion for the man, or perhaps for the power of his position, but he had disdained her. She had tried to get him in trouble, and almost succeeded. It had been chance as much as vigilance that had revealed the truth. Then Jaoch had had to act, lest a bad example be set. But if there came a pretext to forgive her—well, she was still a tempting woman who perhaps had the potential to become interesting for his bed. And it was true that at times diplomacy could be greatly facilitated by the presence of an alluring and unscrupulous woman motivated to get the job done.

Finally he rose and summoned his bedservants. Tomorrow would see what it would see.

❂

The other musicians were from all across Philistia, and were the best in their specialties. There were lyres, including a fine ancient one from Mycenae whose bowl-shaped soundbox was faced with a tortoiseshell.

There were drums, including a melodious one from Egypt. There were zithers, including a delightful one in the shape of a crocodile from an unknown land to the east. There were harps, including a bow harp from Sumeria with a dozen taut strings. There were great brass cymbals, and a number of ornate tambourines. And of course there were flutes, including Huuo's own double one. Huuo was delighted to be in this exalted company, for he seldom had opportunity to play with those who were as good in their specialties as he was in his.

He had met some of the others before, but most were new. There were politics within music as well as within cities, so that a musician might be in favor one year and out of favor the next year. But he knew there would be no bad musicians among them, for no city wished to be shamed at the festival.

The dancers were there too, of course, male and female, most of them young and healthy and well formed, but there were some for the elder roles. They looked like ordinary folk without their costumes, but that would change at performance time. It was said that the combination of talented men and comely women made for an extremely enjoyable festival for some of the participants, quite apart from the honor of the occasion.

And of course there were the historians, perhaps the most important members of this assemblage. Most of them were old men. Each had his own special aspect of the larger story, for this occasion, though of course all of them knew all of it. This was the occasion for the sharing of honors.

They rehearsed in the morning at a palace annex, playing the familiar melodies of the festival. The historians told abbreviated versions, mainly setting the scene, and the dancers did relaxed walkthroughs. It was coming together. A feeling of camaraderie developed, with strangers smiling at each other, and sometimes a young woman would embrace or kiss a historian or musician, and not protest when he goosed her pert bottom. This was the spirit of the festival.

A girl approached Huuo. She was possibly the youngest and cutest of the dancers; even in her deliberately drab day-robe the litheness of her body was evident, and her face was like that of a goddess who had not yet realized her power. "Your music is divine," she said. "Do you have company this night? I am Leda."

"I am married," he said gently.

"But this is the festival. Does your wife have this?" She opened her robe to show him her full body within, blindingly close to nascent perfection.

"I am also cursed."

"Cursed? How so?"

"This is my hand." He lifted his left hand.

Leda laughed, her bare breasts rippling enticingly. "They wouldn't let you play if you were truly cursed. Seren Jaoch isn't cursed, is he? I think it would be interesting to be with one like that. I have a left side too, you know." She stroked her left breast with her right hand. "Do you do it in mirror image?"

He had to laugh too. "No, there is only one of that part. But much as I would like to have a night with you, I must not risk it; my wife can fathom thoughts."

"But she surely knows what the festival is like. Love doesn't count, here."

Huuo did not want to offend Leda or hurt her feelings, because he would have to work with her for several days. Also, she seemed oddly familiar; it was almost as if she had invited him to sexplay before, though that couldn't be. So he finessed her offer. "You tempt me unmercifully. But I must not. But I think if you query that lyre player, he will not decline. I saw him watching you."

She sighed. "Very well. But know that you were my first choice, for the beauty of your melodies." She moved on to the lyre player, who was due for a pleasant surprise.

Actually, what Leda had said was correct: marriage vows had no special force during the festival, and men and women could indulge as they pleased. Annai accepted that, as he accepted her right to do the same. But his marriage had not yet progressed to the point where he craved that type of variety. Before meeting Annai, he had had some flings, but the appeal of those had faded like flowers in a drought once he loved her. When he returned he would tease Annai about the delights he had passed up for her, and she would tease him about his foolishness. They understood each other.

The musicians and dancers broke in due course for a light noon repast, none of them wishing to become weighed down with too much food and be clumsy for the presentation. Then it was time for the dressing and assembly, for the hour of the show was approaching. They got ready, with dancers changing openly before the others, a signal of their unity as a company, and of their confidence in the appeal of their bodies. Then they marched as a group to the temple of Ashtoreth, the mother goddess.

The common folk of the city were already thronged. The nobles had seats set up in front, while the others packed in behind, filling the square and streets beyond. There was a roar of applause as the performers made their way through the aisle reserved for them and mounted the outer steps of the temple. It was a fine sunny day, which was just as well, because it would have been impossible to accommodate the crowd inside the temple.

Seren Jaoch walked out in front as the performers found places on the steps and temple dais. "There will be wine for all at the palace gate after the ritual," he announced, and there was a cheer. "And the temple will be open for worshippers. Let the performance begin!" He went to take his seat at the front. No fancy speech was required; he had said what was necessary.

The first historian took the stage. The crowd went quiet, for all wanted to hear. "It begins with a beautiful woman," he said, his voice strengthening into a chant. "Her name was Helen, and she was of godly descent, the daughter of the king of Lacedaemon in the old country." Now the dancer who had approached Huuo, Leda, walked out from behind a concealing column, in a diaphanous gown that masked yet enhanced her figure teasingly. Again Huuo almost thought he knew her, perhaps from when she had been younger, when she had not yet developed her phenomenal beauty of form and face. It seemed possible, for he had played at many events, and encountered many children and youths. The splendor of her maturity must have burst from the dullness of her cocoon in the past two years, fuzzing his recognition.

The music started, first with a gentle background drum beat that matched the dancer's footsteps, then with a melody representing her. Huuo was the one assigned to that theme; he played point and counterpoint on the double flute, catching the swing of her arms and body. Leda twirled and flashed a smile at him, perhaps hoping that they would get together on another day.

"But Baal, chief of gods, spied her, and was intrigued by her beauty," the historian continued. There was a murmur through the audience: only a dead man would not be intrigued by the seductive vision on the stage. "Fearing that Ashtoreth would observe, he masked himself by assuming the form of his other nature, that of the bull, and approached Helen." Now the music of the harp came, augmented by that of the zither, as a dancer in a horned bull costume walked onto the stage, sporting a massive mock phallus. What followed was of considerable interest to the audience, despite the pantomimed distress of Helen and the piercing flute music that accompanied her attempted flight and struggles. That was of course why this mythical episode introduced the narration; there was nothing like a graphic animalistic rape of a lovely girl to work up an audience. Three times the damsel almost escaped, to the alarm of the watchers; but three times the bullheaded figure caught her and hauled her brutally back, bringing applause. He drew up her gown to expose her lovely body, turning it as she spread her legs so that everyone could have a fair view. Then the bull bore the damsel down on the pavement and pressed close to her in a dramatic rape, while the screaming flutes were dominated by the harp, zither, and intensifying drums. Both actor and actress did a fine job, making it look so real that even Huuo wondered. This was, after all, the festival, where such scenes could indeed be public.

"Thereafter," the historian resumed, after the commotion died down and the bull departed, "Baal abducted her and carried her away to a foreign city, where she lived in captivity and bore the bull's calf."

Whereupon it was time for a new historian and new dancers, taking the story through the Mycenaean expedition against her captors. The deeds of the heroes were given full play and dramatization, with suitably gory fight scenes. Some of the heroes, instead of returning home, decided to settle in the backward lands they saw along the way, thus bringing civilization to the natives. Unfortunately some of the natives were not properly appreciative, notably the Egyptians, and treacherously counterattacked. They sneaked up and trapped the fleet in the Nile River, and fired dastardly arrows at the heroes from the shore, then barged in with grappling hooks and overturned the ships. The dancers formed the semblance of a ship, and tumbled as it overturned. The audience groaned appreciatively.

The heroes of Philistia were able to beat them off despite their disadvantage, and keep possession of their fair new land. There was some thought of mounting a punitive expedition against the Egyptians, as they had before against the Trojans, but too many of their subtribes were more interested in consolidating their local resources. So in the end the five main tribes focused on their territories, and buttressed the great leading cities of Gaza, Ashkelon, Ashdod, Gath, and Ekron. These cities soon begat daughter cities, forming trading communities and spheres of influence. They labored diligently to civilize the backward Canaanites and beat back the savage hill folk who called themselves Israelites. Such nuisances were chronic, but progress was being made. And so came to be the present community of Philistia in all its glory.

The history play ended with a flourish of all the dancers jumping and whirling together, and all the musical instruments playing. The story of their culture had been presented once again, and the audience loved it, for all its familiarity. Then the exodus to the free wine at the palace began. A number of men headed instead for the interior of the temple, preferring to worship first in the arms of the attractive priestesses. There was more than one way to celebrate the occasion, and the re-enactments of the Helen story had surely whetted some appetites.

The musicians, dancers, and historians made their way separately to the palace, where a private banquet was being prepared for them. Huuo discovered cute Leda walking beside him. "Aren't you with the lyre player?" he inquired.

"We have a date for the night," she said. "But there is still the evening. You played just perfectly for me; my emotions were in your melody. I would just love to give them back to you in style. Are you sure—?"

He gave her a friendly goose, and she rode with it, smiling, though she desired a good deal more than this token familiarity. "Too much time with you, and I would forget my wife. I must not risk that."

"You have the quaintest way of turning a girl down. But there will be other days." Leda smiled again and walked off, moving her hips provocatively.

It was a good thing, he thought, that she hadn't realized how effective her approach had been. She was one delicious morsel that it would be all too easy to sample. He probably shouldn't have goosed her, though courtesy had required it; her tight buttock was almost unbearably compelling. The emotion of the play had worked him up, making him prey to speculations he would normally have ignored. Next year he would have to see that Annai came with him.

⊙

The banquet was excellent, and now the members of the troupe could eat and drink their fill, having completed their performance. Tomorrow they would be traveling to the next of the five major cities for their second performance. The complete tour would take ten days. Then they would be free to return with honor to their homes, having brought the festival to Philistia in proper fashion.

As he sought to return to his chamber for the night, replete with a full belly and somewhat dizzy from the copious wine, a servant intercepted him. "Seren Jaoch would talk with you."

Huuo was not so dazed as not to feel a chill. He had almost forgotten the interview of the evening before. Well, he would simply have to tell Jaoch no, as diplomatically as he could, and hope the lord did not take it too unkindly.

Soon he was back in the private room, this time without food set out. Seren Jaoch greeted him in hearty fashion. "I trust you found the repast satisfactory?"

"More than satisfactory, lord," Huuo agreed, rubbing his distended belly. "Your hospitality exceeds any elsewhere."

"I admired your playing today. Your flutes screamed so aptly for the maiden I almost thought it was her voice. You are excellent at more than melody."

"Thank you. It is a very special occasion."

"I would like you to join my court, to play for me. To be my chief musician. The style of life you have seen here would be yours throughout."

Now the crisis was upon him. "You are more than kind, lord. But my wife—"

"Your wife and children would be welcome also, of course. I understand she is a rare dancer."

"Yes. But her allegiance—our allegiance—is to our home city. Her family members, our friends—it would be very difficult for us to leave Mor. So while I very much appreciate your most generous offer, and have no wish at all to offend you by seeming ungrateful, I must say that I don't feel free to accept it." He braced himself for the likely consequence of his rashness in refusing this powerful man.

But Jaoch merely smiled. "I understand. I would not wish to cause any distress for such an admirable musician. Go with my blessing, and if ever you change your mind, know that you will be more than welcome here in Gaza as long as I remain in power."

"I appreciate that very much," Huuo said, vastly relieved. He had feared that it would not be safe to turn down the offer. "I shall certainly acquaint my wife with your invitation, and perhaps her mind will differ from my expectation."

"Perhaps it will," Jaoch agreed. "I wish you a good night, and a good continuing tour. I know they will appreciate you in the other cities as we have appreciated you here."

So Huuo found himself back at his chamber, his knees weak. Apparently his alarm had been for nothing; the seren's invitation had been complimentary rather that coercive. He knew that Annai would never have agreed to depart her dear home city. She loved to travel with him when they could, but always returned to their home. Her roots were there. And so, perforce, were his. No amount of good living elsewhere could make up for the slightest distress it caused her.

It was dark in his room; the servants must have been too busy with the banquet to attend him with a lamp. That was all right; he had relived himself at the palace refuse chamber, and now was ready simply to sleep off his overindulgence. He felt for the bed and climbed on.

And encountered a soft rounded body. "What—?"

"Ah, you are back," the dancer said. "Good."

"Leda, I told you—"

"The lyre player overimbibed, and finds himself not in condition tonight to perform as he had hoped. I am doing him the kindness of leaving him alone in his illness. So I am free to be with you after all. I thought perhaps—"

He would have to get rid of her again, and it wasn't getting any easier, either as a matter of politeness or one of desire. "No. I am in reasonably poor condition myself at the moment. I must ask you to depart, much as I know I will regret this in the morning."

She sighed. "You're a hard man to approach."

"No, I'm merely wary of getting involved with a creature so luscious she would likely make me forget my music and embarrass myself at the next performance."

"Oh, I wouldn't want that!" she said, laughing as she got off his bed. "But if you should change your mind, just give me a signal, any time."

"What, in the middle of a performance?"

She laughed. "Not unless you want to put on the bull suit. Then, however—"

"No bull suit," he said, lying down. "I am no Baal."

He heard her depart. Something about the encounter nagged him. He reviewed their dialogue as well as his somewhat wine-addled mind could, and managed to catch it: it was her comment about changing his mind. There were women who would be angry at being rejected, however politely, but she had merely acceded, perhaps being too young and nice to harbor much outrage. His vague prior image of her was as a most persistent girl, but that was obviously false. She remained open to his interest, should he change his mind. Very much as Seren Jaoch was. So twice in one evening Huuo had been surprised by amicable acceptances instead of ugly reactions. It was of course coincidence, and fortunate for him.

Reassured by that realization, he slept.

○

Zebub appeared at his lord's summons. "You were right," Jaoch said gruffly. "He declined."

"And the girl? What's her name, Leda?"

"Her, too. Three times today. She reports that even when he goosed her, his fingers didn't stray. The man is constant."

Zebub shook his head with wary appreciation. "I suspect he is the only man who ever turned that vamp down even once in a day. She looks so—"

"I know how she looks! I confess my defeat. You told me that the usual methods would not prevail with this musician, and he has proved your point. In the process he has shown me that I want him more than ever, for once he pledges faith with me, he will never violate it. So I must with regret go your route. But I am baffled how you think your sister can prevail where Leda failed."

"My sister is beautiful too, and more experienced, and she does not accept defeat as lightly as Leda does. Scylla can force a flush or a tear or a tremble of lip or hand at will. She can make her pupils grow large and innocent. She has a sense of timing and nuance that can lead a man opposite to the direction he thinks he is going. She can show flesh without seeming to that nevertheless incites instant hunger in a man. I myself feel guilty when I oppose her, though I know her tricks. Leda, in contrast, has not yet learned that that beauty must sometimes be buttressed by determination and cunning. She's too nice."

"I'm sure that is not a fault either you or your sister suffer from," Jaoch said dryly. "She will in any event keep trying. But you do have your uses. Do what you have to do to persuade him, but with one caution: no taint of it must adhere to me. The musician must never suspect that I had anything to do with it, other than being ready to receive him as supporter and friend." He glanced sharply at the other. "You do understand the consequence of failure in this aspect?"

"The same as failure in the mission itself," Zebub said grimly. "But we don't expect to fail. We expect to bring Huuo willingly to this court, and receive the rewards of success."

"I would despise you more than I do, were you not at times so useful."

"And I would not serve you, were I not sure of the manner you honor a deal, whether positive or negative."

"How very nice that we understand each other so well," Jaoch said with irony. "But you shall have your price, if you succeed: appointment as my tax collector, and the return of your sister to this court without prejudice."

"Thank you, my lord."

"My respect for the musician is such that I almost hope you fail."

"I shall do my best to disappoint you in that." Zebub made a half-mocking salute and departed.

Jaoch remained alone for a time, as he had before. The man disgusted him in much the manner of a rotting fly-ridden carcass. But the musician was a treasure he simply had to have: highly skilled, and trustworthy by both hand and nature. He had not asked how Zebub's sister Scylla hoped to change Huuo's mind and bring him here, but he was sure it was no way he would have arranged himself. He wanted to remain innocent at least to this extent, lest the knowledge poison the association he hoped to have with Huuo.

❁

Crystalech was uneasy. "Something evil is afoot," she told her husband Carverro. "I just know it."

"What, in the daylight?" he asked, looking up from his fine metalwork. "What could happen, short of a siege of the city?"

"I don't know, but I fear it."

"Then perhaps you should stay home today, Crystal, and not go to the market. We can get by." She had given up correcting him about her name, and increasingly everyone was calling her by the abbreviation, Crystal.

"No, today the hill folk bring in their cattle for sale and slaughter. I must be there to put in a bid while the meat is plentiful and cheap. Any other day I might skip, but not this one day of this month."

He nodded. "I had forgotten. You are right; we would go hungry if we did not shop expediently. Then perhaps I should come with you."

"No, for then we would have to bring Desert Flower along, and she would be exposed to the danger. I will go alone, and be alert."

"As you wish, my love." He had learned not to oppose her when she got a notion, for sometimes her premonitions became true. He had come from a hill tribe himself, and had abducted her as a lovely girl of the valley. But the men of her city had surrounded them before he could bear her away, sealing his fate—until Crystal had amazed him by claiming he was her lover on a tryst. She had saved his life, and married him, and even brought his aging mother to the city to live in comfort. From that time on he had been absolutely devoted to her, and never seriously opposed her will. And, she had to admit, she had made a good choice, for his talent as an artisan was now providing them with a secure if not wealthy life. His hill-folk ways had almost disappeared, and they had a fine lovely daughter in Desert Flower.

And, she thought as she walked through the native quarter of the city toward the market section, she had been fortunate in finding employment with a liberal Philistine family. Huuo and Annai did not treat Canaanites with contempt or condescension; in fact they had welcomed Crystal much as they would a family member, and encouraged her to bring Desert Flower to play with their own children. So just as Crystal had won her husband's complete devotion and loyalty by her actions toward him and his mother, so had her employers won her own respect and even love. They were good people, and never would she knowingly betray their interests.

She was early for the bidding, perhaps hurried by her vague concern. Her husband tended to doubt her intuitions, but she did not; something terrible was threatening. If only she knew what!

She crossed the market street and mall, seeking the shade of one of the trees that lined the public center. Beyond it she could spy the separate houses of the aristocrats and honored artisans; their villas had the place of honor closest to the ceremonial center, with its temples and the residence of the seren. The Philistines held music in very high esteem, and Huuo was a very good musician despite being reverse-handed. Sometimes he played his flutes at home when Crystal was there, and Annai would dance, showing her children how to do it. Chipp was becoming a fair little musician, and Minah a dancer who would be a marvel when she was grown. Desert Flower, the same age, was learning to dance too, though of course she would never be allowed to do it in a Philistine ceremony, being Canaanite.

She heard the tramping and lowing of the cattle, as they were driven into the city and along the street toward the market. The poor beasts didn't know they were to be auctioned and slaughtered. They would be fat from grazing the mountain pastures, and somewhat wild too, but the herdsmen and dogs would keep them in line. However, there were usually extra guards assigned to the section on cattle market days, bearing staves, just in case. Noise and staves could turn cattle back and set them milling, so that they didn't stray into the wrong section of the city. She didn't see any guards at the moment, but they were surely there. It was a normal precaution.

The crowd of prospective buyers was gathering. Crystal walked back that way. She would not get the first or best, but she would certainly be better off than those who waited for the cuts to be retailed by the greedy meat merchants. She didn't enjoy watching the actual slaughter, but it was the only way to be sure that an inferior carcass wasn't substituted after the sale.

Suddenly there was a stir on the street. Men shouted with dismay, and there was a scrambling as people tried to get out of the way. Crystal looked, and saw that the cattle were stampeding. Somehow the animals had been spooked, and the herdsmen were ineffective in controlling them. But the extra city guards should be ready.

The cattle charged down the street, throwing off all restraints. It was as if they had realized that this was their place of doom. Where were the guards? Crystal still couldn't see any. There were only the herdsmen, running along beside the cattle, screaming imprecations, unable to turn them back.

Then she had to scramble for her own safety as the lead bull veered toward her. She got behind the trunk of a tree and saw the beast charge by, followed by the others. She·heard the screams of townspeople as they realized that the animals were out of control.

Worse, this represented a breakdown of order. Immediately the criminals were appearing, using the distraction to rob unnerved people and break into houses to steal their valuables. It was a sad commentary on society that the moment there was any disturbance or confusion, the robbers and looters appeared. They were mostly Canaanites, she knew, claiming that they deserved anything they could get from the privileged conquerors. Yet the conquest had been 200 years ago; it was no longer an issue. It disgusted Crystal to see depravity in her own people.

Now fires were starting in the city, and she knew the cattle weren't setting them. What a disaster had been set off by the chance spooking of a cow! One fire was fairly close; it must be one of the villas. Naturally they were among the first targets of the criminals. They robbed, killed, and burned to cover their traces.

Fairly close? Crystal felt an ugly chill. Her employers' house was in that direction. Could it be?

Hoping it was not, but fearing that it was, she ran in the tracks of the stampeding cattle, looking for Huuo's house. Of course it would be a terrible thing for any house, but especially for that one. Her premonition . . .

She got a stitch in her side from running, and had to slow down, catching her breath. But she was already close enough to see that it was one of those houses. Dread surged; the closer she got, the more certain it was that it was Huuo's villa. She blinked her eyes, trying to make it some other house, but the terrible vision would not be shifted.

At last she stood by the blaze. It *was* her employer's house—hopelessly burning. Even if the fire crew arrived soon, it would be too late; the fire was too fierce. The looters must have torched it in several places, to make it burn like this.

Others joined her, confirming the worst. "Hill folk!" they cried. "They came through after the cattle. We came out to try to fight them off, but they had already pillaged this house, and they saw us and ran on toward the city gate."

"But what of Annai? The children?" Crystal asked. "They were home today; I know it. I was going to go there after I made my purchase."

A Philistine neighbor spoke. "They were there," she said grimly, "for I consulted with Annai within the hour." Her mouth grew tight.

"Then where are they now?" Crystal demanded, almost forgetting her subservient place before the Philistine woman. "Did they go before the trouble started? This will be a terrible thing for them to find on their return!"

"Annai was schooling the children in protocol," the woman said. "They were not going anywhere."

"But—" Suddenly Crystal's terrible premonition surged forth, almost overwhelming her. "They can't be in—"

The Philistine woman abruptly turned and walked rapidly toward her own house, her shoulders shaking. She did not care to show grief in front of people beyond her own household. Her Canaanite servant shook her head sadly.

"No!" Crystal cried. "They wouldn't stay in there!"

"Not if they lived," the servant woman said.

Crystal paused for a moment of utter horror. Then she leaped for the burning house. But two women intercepted her and hauled her back. They had evidently anticipated her reaction. "You can't help them," one said. "The hill brigands must have killed them first."

"And set the fire to hide the crime," the other said. "But we came out before they got away, so we know the crime. We saw them hauling rolled rugs of valuables. If we had had men to pursue them—"

"It can't be! It can't be!" Crystal screamed. But she saw the blaze, and knew the neighbors and servants weren't lying. They all knew and liked Annai and her children. None of them were as close to the family as Crystal, so they were more objective about it, but they were clearly appalled.

When they were sure that Crystal wouldn't charge the fire again, they let her go. She collapsed to the ground, sobbing. "I should have been there! At least to save the children   "

She must have stayed there for a time, for she saw that the fire had burned down, leaving only the stone ruin and mounds of smoking ashes. She was alone with her grief.

The hill folk had entered the villa, killed the people there, stolen whatever they could carry wrapped in the good rugs, torched the house, and run away. A crime of opportunity. The victims could have been anyone. And suddenly Crystal's employer and best friend was brutally gone. Others would soon forget the matter, for these things happened. But how could Crystal ever forget?

She picked herself up and trudged wearily toward home, her mission of the day forgotten. All she could think of at the moment was a meeting she knew would come: with Huuo. What could she say to him, when he returned from his tour and learned of this?

❂

The circuit of the festival was done. The troupe had returned to the city of Gaza and now was dispersing after a final banquet. Huuo knew he had put on weight from all the excellent eating. It had been a good celebration; he knew that all five cities were well satisfied. Now he was glad to be on his way home, his purse heavy with payment. Annai would be pleased.

When he boarded the ship at dawn, there was a surprise: it turned out to be the same one he had traveled on before. It was on its return trip from Egypt. Captain Ittai greeted him warmly. "Scuttlebutt has it that you charmed them all," he said. "And won the heart of the loveliest dancer."

"Perhaps I charmed them, with the help of all the other musicians," Huuo agreed. "But I did not touch the dancer."

"Come now, your secret's safe with me. With the license of the festival, and a creature all women envy choosing you, you surely must have been man rather than fool."

"I surely was the fool," Huuo said. "Perhaps I simply could not believe that her passion was true." He lifted his left hand significantly.

Ittai nodded. "Put that way, I comprehend your doubt. But what point would there have been in her insincerity?"

"None I can think of," Huuo admitted. "That does bother me. So let's just say that I love my wife beyond all else."

"I think you are a man I would like to know better," the captain said. "Perhaps we shall meet again, next year." He moved on.

The wind was good, and the ship made scheduled progress under sail. At noon they reached the port of Ascalon and put in for spot trading. And another Philistine boarded. A woman.

Intrigued by this unusual appearance, Huuo stood to greet her. She lifted back her traveling hood and smiled. "Why, it's the musician Huuo! I never thought to see you here."

"The dancer Scylla," he said, similarly surprised. "I did not know you were traveling?"

"Well, not by preference," she explained. "But it seems my family has inherited a house in Mor, which we can't use, so I must go there to arrange for its disposition. At least that will leave us in a good economic situation."

"I did not see you at the festival." He was being polite, though she was an associate rather than a friend. He had encountered her during various events, and she was an excellent dancer with a fine body. But she had a brother who was of dubious repute, and she herself—well, he was not one to credit rumors. He was nevertheless somewhat wary of her, perhaps because she was a beautiful woman who had on occasion hinted by her manner that she found him an interesting man. He had just been through that with Leda, and didn't care for more.

"I wasn't there. It seems that one of the serens objected to me. In any event, I couldn't have danced, because of my injury." She lifted her right hand, which was heavily bandaged.

"What happened?" There wasn't much to do except talk with her, as they were the only two Philistine passengers on the ship, and the passenger section was small. So they sat half facing each other by his cubby. And he had to admit that she was good enough company; maybe he had misjudged her.

"An accident during a dance. I took a tumble, and put out my hand to break my fall, foolishly. There was something sharp there." She shrugged. "It will heal, eventually. Meanwhile I am having to learn how to use my left hand. Have you any idea how awkward that is?"

"You forget that I am left-handed."

Her eyes rounded. "Oh! My apology. I didn't mean—I never thought—I meant no offense." She colored, looking flustered.

"No offense taken," he said quickly. "I make no issue of it anyway. At the festival I used the double flute, which diminishes my apparent difference."

"You are kind. I did know you were—I simply forgot, being absorbed with my own state. Yet perhaps our meeting is fortunate for me, because you could help me adapt, if you have the patience." She smiled, looking very pretty as her flush faded.

"I shall be glad to help in any way I can," he said. "It's no imposition. We have several hours of boredom before us anyway. What problem do you have?"

"Everything!" she exclaimed. "The most trifling, simple things become so infernally clumsy. Things I have always known how to do, suddenly I can't do without botching them. I've been spilling wine and—and I can't even tie my sash." She indicated her trim midriff.

Indeed, her sash was loosely knotted, and sagged. This was not a disaster, as it served mainly to enhance the contrast to her clothing, which sagged nowhere, but it was surely an annoyance to her. "If you will permit me—" he said, extending his hands.

"No, don't do it for me," she said quickly. "Show me how to do it myself."

"Well, it isn't just the change of hands," he explained. "It's that you normally use two, and now have only one. Naturally it's difficult."

"Oh, yes, that's true. Still—"

"So let me tie it for you. There are other things that may be done single-handed." He took hold of her sash, untied it, then retied it properly so that it was snug without being tight. In the process he was reminded that her body was in fine form. She was a dancer, of course, so her torso and limbs were slender and lithe. But there were differences in dancers, and hers was about as good a body as he had seen on any woman other than his wife.

"Thank you so much," she said, smiling with a somewhat endearing human relief. His prior mistrust of her dissipated; she was a nice woman, now that he was interacting with her. She wasn't coming on to him the way Leda had, but was just being sociable.

Now he saw that her hair was sloppily braided. She had concealed it under the hood, but in the heat of the day she threw that back, and her fair hair fairly sparkled in the sunlight. But the braids were bad. So he redid those too, with her acquiescence; that was another thing that normally required two hands. Her tresses were almost silken in their length and lightness, and quite clean.

They spent the duration of the sailing reviewing and rehearsing the left-handed way of doing things. It was clear that Scylla would have to practice a good deal before becoming apt, by which time her right hand might heal, making it all for little. But she was trying hard, and making good progress. She was also extremely appreciative of his assistance.

When the ship came into the port of Mor they were surprised to see another female passenger waiting on the pier to board. No, it was a Canaanite—in fact he knew her. It was his servant Crystalech. Probably Annai had sent her to intercept him; perhaps there was something he was supposed to bring home.

But as the ship docked and he and Scylla walked the plank to the pier, he saw that Crystal's mien was serious, almost gloomy. "What is it, Crystal?" he inquired as he reached her. "Is something wrong?"

"Master, your house is burnt," the Canaanite said.

He was taken aback. "My house—there was a fire? Then where is my family?"

The woman's mouth opened three times before she got the words out. "They are—gone. Raiders—a stampede—looters—they come through and your house was on their route to the gate—"

Huuo felt an ugly chill. "What do you mean, gone? Gone where?"

Crystal rolled her eyes heavenward. "Gone—to the gods. Master, I had to tell you, before you got there yourself. The brigand hill folk—"

"To the gods?" he asked, stunned. "Do you mean they are—" He could not say it.

The woman nodded grimly, tears flowing. "I saw the fire. No one came out from it. The hill folk—to hide their crime—they were gone before they could be stopped."

"Annai—the children—?"

"Master, they are dead," Crystal said, finally speaking the dread word.

Huuo would have doubted it from any other source, but he had known Crystal for years, and trusted her. Her daughter Desert Flower was almost like his own daughter Minah. Crystal would never knowingly deceive him. She was the city's most loyal servant, because she was also friend.

He found himself holding her, sharing her tears, not caring what others thought of a Philistine embracing a Canaanite in public. He had been so eager to get home to his family, and suddenly it had been destroyed.

Then he saw through his bleary vision the other woman standing near. Some numb semblance of propriety returned. "I apologize for this scene," he said as they walked along the pier to the land.

"By no means," Scylla said. "How could you have known? But perhaps I can help."

"No, it is no concern of yours. Go and forget this unpleasantness." But his ear heard his mouth, and was appalled at this seeming dismissal of the disaster of his life as "unpleasantness." His formal self was honoring the rules of protocol, while his inner self was struggling to come to terms with what could not be accepted. An observer might have supposed that he did not really care about his family; instead he cared so much that he could not express it, and could let only part of the grief out.

"You have been kind to me," Scylla said. "Allow me to repay the favor. You will need a house. Take mine—the one I am here to sell."

"No, I could not," Huuo said. "I must not impose. But I thank you for your concern."

"But the house is empty," she protested. "Use it until you can get another. Let me lighten this small portion of your burden, as you have lightened mine." She lifted her bandaged hand.

He started to protest again, but Crystal intervened. "Master, you need a house. You have so much else to concern you. If this lady is your friend—"

"An acquaintance," Scylla said. "I am a dancer. I know—knew Annai, professionally. But I want to help. It will take a month to arrange the sale of the house, and it makes no sense to waste it when there is such need. Perhaps you, Crystal, can serve him there as you have done before."

"Yes, certainly," Crystal agreed. "It is fortunate."

Huuo could not oppose her. He needed his Canaanite servant more than ever, in this time of crisis. She could not assuage his grief, but she shared it, and that represented vital support. She also knew how to take care of him. His sensible mind, operating apart from his feeling mind, knew that she was vital to his survival right now. "Do as seems best," he said.

"I will hire a wagon," Scylla said. "I will bring it here." She hurried off.

Time seemed both interminable and instant, depending on the focus of his consciousness. He was aware of the wagon, which held the three of them as well as its driver, as it bumped along the streets through the city. Then he stood before the ruin of his house.

It was nothing but ashes settled around the projecting stone walls. Long shadows shrouded the interior and reached across the land beyond. It was clear that nothing had survived the conflagration—no furniture, no possessions, no people. They had probably, as Crystal said, been murdered before the house was torched; only their bones would remain. Those bones were undisturbed, because only the next of kin could handle them with honor for their spirits. Huuo would have them rescued and properly interred in due course. But not today, not this week; it was more than he could face at the moment.

Then he was being conveyed by the wagon again, as the sun sank low in the west, until they stopped at an unfamiliar house. Crystal took him by the elbow and guided him inside. There was a bed there, and he lay down, leaving the two women to handle the world; he had to handle himself, if he could.

He must have slept, for he dreamed: Of Annai, smiling. Of Chipp, running happily. Of Minah, her great round eyes seeming eerily knowledgeable. She had always related well to the spirits; now she was a spirit herself. Perhaps she would be the one to communicate to him from the spirit realm. But in his dream she did not; she was merely a picture, as were the other two.

Evening faded into night. Scylla lit lamps and set them in the rooms of the house, and a candle beside the bed where Huuo lay. He got up to use the lavatory chamber, then sat on the bed, lacking ambition to do more. His dream extended part of the way into his waking state, and he thought perhaps Annai would appear, having taken residence in another house after the fire. She would come when she learned that he was back, and she would find him, and all would be well. At any moment he would hear the laughter of his children. Crystal would lead them here.

But Crystal knew they were dead. Had known before he knew. Had had to tell him at the pier, to try to cushion his fall some to some slight extent. So the dream dissipated, and for a moment he mourned it. Illusion was better than reality, right now.

Scylla entered the room. She bore a tray. "I prepared some food for you, Huuo," she murmured. "You must eat."

"I have no interest in food."

"You must be whole for the funeral. You would not want to dishonor the spirits of your loved ones, perhaps sending them astray. You must be ready to do their final honors."

She was right. Death was terrible, but death without honorable burial was worse. Those he loved were dead, but their spirits depended on him for guidance to the next realm. So, listlessly, he took the food she offered, and mechanically consumed it, unaware of anything else about it. Then he lay down again and wept himself to sleep.

○

Crystal tuned in on the local news. The Philistines were in control of the land, but the Canaanites had their own gossip network that covered things few Philistines knew of. Such as exactly which of the master's liaisons the mistress of a house knew about, and which she did not. Which temple priestesses were favored by which nobles, and the peculiarities of their interactions. Which noble, in the guise of a visit to the temple, fornicated instead with a heifer, believing this form of worship to be holier than the other. Which lesser lords were skimming grain from the tallies of which greater lords. And where every Philistine, of any level, traveled, and for what purpose, legitimate or illegitimate. The Canaanites knew, and did not tell. Because if they did, their masters would realize that their supposedly dumb witnesses were dumb only in the presence of Philistines; they shared everything with their own kind. That would be a disaster. Life was already hard enough without destroying their chief amusement: watching the follies of the masters.

Most of the stories were routine. But some were not, for Crystal. She was especially sensitive to two threads of the ongoing tapestry of news: the background on Scylla, and the actions of the hill folk who had made the deadly raid on Huuo's house. Because she did not trust Scylla, of whom some truly juicy tales were told, and she wanted very much to know exactly who had destroyed her kind master's life. Crystal's loyalty went beyond death; it extended to vengeance.

Scylla, it turned out, had been exiled a year ago from her native Gaza because she had schemed to corrupt a left-handed noble by seducing him away from his wife. The seren had learned of it and banished her from the city. Since then she had lived alone in a daughter city, on the largess provided by her brother Zebub, who remained in the favor of the seren of Gaza. Occasionally she danced for someone's party, receiving due pay. She was an excellent dancer who would have been in the festival but for her banishment. In exile she had done reasonably well for herself, economically, because of the finesse with which she rendered personal favors to wealthy men; it was said that even the temple women could not match her in certain respects. But seven days ago she had abruptly bandaged her hand and gone to the port city of Ashkelon, where she had waited until boarding the ship on which Huuo traveled. There was no evidence that she had actually hurt her hand; no Canaanite had been involved in that, as the lady had used no servant. It had been assumed by some that she lacked the wherewithal to afford a servant, but Crystal suspected otherwise. What happened to what she got from those wealthy clients? Scylla certainly hadn't wasted her resources in riotous living. The lady was good at keeping secrets, and perhaps knew that secrets were not secure with servants. So perhaps she had indeed taken a fall and hurt her hand—and perhaps not. Almost certainly her boarding of the ship was no coincidence; she had known that Huuo was aboard it. So what was her interest in him?

What else but the man himself! She had headed for the port city the moment the raid occurred. She had to have known that Huuo had lost his family, rendering him open for remarriage. He was a prominent musician, honored despite his handicap of hands. As his wife, she could surely live well, without suffering the indignities required by certain men. Huuo was known to be straight, in every sense other than his handedness; he would be easy to accommodate. So she was capitalizing on her opportunity, giving no other woman a chance to attract his attention first. Crystal couldn't really fault that, because the opportunities of women were limited, even Philistine women, and Scylla's reputation was none too savory. She had to be sharp to gain a good husband. And perhaps she would make him a good wife. She did seem to like Huuo; Crystal had watched her without seeming to, and caught the way her pupils dilated when she gazed directly on him. She probably admired his music; as a dancer she would know his skill. There was a certain sexual appeal to good music, and to those who made that music, and Scylla was by all accounts a lusty woman.

But what of the house burning? The reports were that the hill-folk herdsmen had been in complete control of their livestock—until suddenly the stampede had occurred. It had happened because they had abruptly incited it, then pretended to be overwhelmed by it. It had evidently been a plot to generate a distraction so that they could then pillage the city. Of course they knew that the guards would soon make their appearance, so the effort was fast and limited; they had charged almost directly for the front gate, knowing that if it closed them in, all would be lost, especially their heads. It had been their fortune that there had been few guards in the vicinity at the time; the guard captain had given most of them leave to sample grog, expecting no trouble. And Huuo's house had been right along that exit line. They had pillaged it, without a doubt, and torched it, perhaps as a secondary distraction. But had it been chance that that particular house had been attacked, and so few others? The hill folk had been seen carrying away items from the house, shrouding them with drab cloth so as not to attract any more attention than they could afford. But there were wealthier houses in that vicinity. Had the raiders been unlucky in choosing a medium house instead of a rich one? Perhaps.

So Crystal kept following the news, trying to gain the exact identities of the hill folk, which was no easy task because they were neither Philistines nor Canaanites. And she continued to serve Huuo with utter loyalty. If she were ever able to complete the picture of his disaster, she would give him the information so that he could have the city guards make a punitive raid and execute the guilty hill folk. Vengeance wasn't as good as prevention, but it was better than nothing.

✿

In the morning Huuo woke to find Scylla sitting beside him, fanning his somewhat fevered face. She was wearing a light smock whose filmy texture clung to her body, and her tresses hung loose around her shoulders. She was in dishabille, but was incidentally lovely.

"You need not take such trouble for my comfort," he said, embarrassed. He had not realized that she would be with him in the house, and attending him like this; that was not the business of an unrelated Philistine woman.

"It is no trouble," she murmured. "You are in need, and are a good man."

At any other time, that might have seemed like an invitation. But of course it was innocent. "Thank you," he said, and sat up. His head was logy, as if he had overimbibed, but he hadn't. He remembered the horror of the prior evening, but at the moment it was somewhat distant, as if there were a stone wall between him and it.

He got up and dressed. He didn't remember undressing during the night, but must have done so, for he was in night clothing. He used the lavatory, and emerged to find that Scylla had set breakfast for him.

"But you are no servant!" he protested. "Crystal will serve me, in due course."

"She is out shopping," Scylla said. "I told her to buy your favorites. You will need new clothing, too; you lost your wardrobe in the fire. She will see that you are provided for."

"But I gave her no money."

"I gave her some. Have no concern."

"Then I must repay you." He reached for his bag of gold pieces, which he had found undisturbed beside his bed.

"Please, no," she said. "I am not entirely destitute. It pleases me to help you in your hour of need, as you helped me in mine. See, I am doing better now." She held up her left hand. "I was able to prepare the food and to dress myself competently."

He gazed at her. "Except for your hair," he said. "I will braid it for you, if you wish."

"There is no need, unless the sight of it undone distresses you."

"By no means. My wife wore hers loose—" He was caught by a sudden choke, and could not continue.

Scylla turned away, sparing him the embarrassment of being seen in bad emotion. But in a moment he recovered. "Please, I should not eat alone. Join me, since you have done so much, so graciously."

"As you wish," she murmured, and fetched food for herself. She sat opposite him, and smiled as she ate. In any other circumstance, this would have been a pleasant interlude. He appreciated the manner she had relieved him of the burden of caring for himself during his distraction of grief; she was going well beyond the normal parameters of acquaintanceship, and perhaps even of friendship. If news of her presence alone with him in the house spread, her reputation would suffer, undeservedly. He would have to find a house of his own today, and spare her that.

Crystal appeared later in the day, bringing his favorite foods and new clothing made to his measure. He was now ready to go out about his business, but the thought of formally declaring his wife and children dead disturbed him, and he delayed. Scylla catered constantly to him, brushing off his attempted demurrals, repeating that she was happy to help a friend, and he argued the matter perhaps less than he should have. He still lacked ambition to get anything of substance done, and she made it easy for him to postpone it. He did at least manage to prevail on her to the extent of braiding her hair for her, and she thanked him warmly for the fine job. He felt guilty for closing his eyes and pretending that it was Annai's hair he caressed.

Somehow several days passed. He wasn't sure how it happened, but the calendar marks proved it. His grief remained intense, but was becoming less unbearable. Scylla diverted him with games of words and dice; she was surprisingly apt with the latter as they played for imaginary points. Once her robe fell open as she leaned forward during a throw, revealing her unbound breasts beneath; he could not help glancing. When she realized, she closed her robe more carefully, apologizing. "I still am imperfect, dressing myself with the other hand."

Crystal, too, was attentive, trying to see to his comfort in every possible way a servant could. It was almost as if she wanted to be alone with him, surely for no untoward purpose, but was unable because of the constant presence of Scylla. Had he been more alert, he might have arranged a private dialogue; she was after all his servant, and the one he trusted most. But his distraction of grief prevented that.

Yet he knew he could not dally forever. He had to get out and find his own house, and see to the funeral arrangements. He wasn't sure he wanted to live, but he did want to send the spirits of his dear family on their way in proper order. So he would have to do what he dreaded: sift through the ashes of his former residence and find their bones, so that these could be buried with proper honor.

The problem was that this would also confirm absolutely that they were dead. He had been dreaming that they lived, deluding himself. Now he would have to end the delusion.

So he marshaled what mettle he had, and prepared for the inevitable. "Crystal, it is time for me to get the bones," he said. "I must do right by those I have loved."

"Of course, master," she said, seeming almost eager. "I will help you."

"But you shouldn't go out yet," Scylla protested. "You are weak from your ordeal."

He wavered, knowing that her reasoning was specious, but distinctly uneager to actually find those bones. "Still, it must be done, and only I can do it."

"Maybe Crystal can facilitate the task," Scylla suggested. "While only you can handle the bones, your loyal servant might locate them for you by poking with a rod. Then your chore will be simplified. You will not have to sift your fingers through all the ashes and dirt."

"I could not ask—"

But Crystal surprised him by agreeing. "I will go and poke the ashes, master, and mark the places. I would not have you soil your hands needlessly. I can do that now, and return this afternoon, and show you exactly where."

Again he knew he was being too weak, but his reluctance guided him. A few more hours of illusion. "If you would, dearest friend," he said, relieved.

Crystal departed. Scylla did her best to cheer him. "You have not played your flutes since you returned," she said brightly. "Perhaps you should practice."

Normally he had played while Annai danced. That was another font of pain.

She saw his reaction, and was immediately contrite. "I should not have suggested it. Is there anything I can do to ease your condition?"

He looked at her, becoming aware of their situation. He was seated on a couch, and she was kneeling before him, leaning forward. Her inefficiently tied robe was falling open again, so that he saw the rondure of both her breasts. Her loose hair curved down around her face before spreading across her shoulders. Her eyes were great and concerned.

Suddenly he wanted her. But immediately his rational self condemned the illicit urge. This was not his wife; this was another woman, whose concern for him allowed her to become careless. He had no business eying her body. "No, I think not," he said. "You have been more than kind to me. It is time I stopped imposing on you and found my own residence."

"I understand your sentiment," she said. "But in truth, you have been no burden to me. Your wife was a most fortunate woman. I think I would have found it exceedingly dull and lonely in this house, were it not for you. Instead it has been a pleasure." Then she paused as if struck by a new thought. "I wonder whether *this* house might be suitable for you? You know I am here to arrange its sale. It never occurred to me that you were a potential buyer."

Huuo considered that, surprised. "It is true. This is a good house, and I do need one. It never occurred to me that you were catering to me in order to sell your house."

She laughed, and her breasts shook, attracting his gaze again. "I should have used that as a pretext. But I simply wanted to help you when it was easy for me to do so, and the more I have been with you, the better I like you. Do you realize that with any other man I would have been afraid to sleep without a guard?"

"Oh, I would never—"

"And yet my respect for you is such that if you asked me, I would agree," she continued. Then she flushed, prettily. "I just heard myself speaking. I should not have said that. I apologize."

"I understand. You are a Philistine lady. You would never—"

"Oh, I would do it. I merely should not have spoken it."

Because appearance was at times more important than reality. "Then I will forget it." But if she had inadvertently spoken her true thought, he was speaking a false one, for he desired her again, more strongly, and knew he would not forget her words. His guilt for the thought might rage, but at this moment he wished he were free to clasp her evocative body.

"Perhaps you should look at other houses," she said. "Or possibly visit the temple."

The temple—where worship was accomplished by making sex to a lovely priestess. He wasn't ready for that either. "I'm not sure I need to do the one, and I don't wish to do the other," he said. "I realize I am a drag on you. Go out about your business; I will wait until Crystal returns with news of the bones. I thank you for allowing me to stay here, and I will consider whether to buy this house."

"As you wish," she said. "I do have shopping to do."

"And I must repay you for what you have already spent on my behalf," he said, reaching for his purse.

"No, no," she demurred. "I think I do not care to take any money from you. There could be an implication. I am enjoying your company so much, and you have been such a help in teaching me the way of the left hand." She glanced down at herself. "Even if I do still dress sloppily," she said, drawing her gown together.

He smiled. "I had hoped you wouldn't notice."

She laughed again. "Do you mean that while I was trying to console you, you were looking at my body? I will take my robe off, if that will cheer you." She opened it wide, baring her breasts. They were unbound marvels of symmetry, neither too slight nor too heavy.

"No, I would not ask that of you," he said. "I had thought to leave you innocent, unaware of my glance."

"A charming notion. You surely know that I am not innocent in any sense. But I thank you for the thought." She closed her robe. "Do you know, I regretted missing the festival because of its special conventions. Not only does it honor our gods and rehearse our glorious history, it provides us opportunity and freedom to indulge in our delights without shame. Had I encountered you there—"

"There was already a girl. I turned her down. I just wanted to get home to—" He choked off again.

Scylla shook her head. "I keep trying to make you feel better, and I keep making you feel worse," she complained, her lip trembling.

He reached forward to half embrace her. "No, no, no fault of yours! These memories come upon me by surprise. I understand your regret at missing the festival."

She leaned against his knees, setting her head down on his legs. He felt the softness of her bosom as she breathed. "You are kind, Huuo." Then she got up. "I must go shop. Is there anything I can get for you?"

"I think not. But I thank you."

She went to her room, donned a street robe, and left the house. He lay back on the couch, resting, though it was not physical fatigue he felt. He

realized that he needed to find diversions, because otherwise he simply
dwelt on what could not be mended.

He did sleep, again, because again he dreamed. It was of little Minah
running, her midnight hair flinging out behind her. Perhaps it was her
spirit, sending him this vision. If any spirit knew how to communicate, it
would be hers.

Then Scylla was back with her supplies. "I hurried; there is a storm
coming," she said. "I found fresh fruits at the market, and rare pastry. Try
this." She held a piece of sweet bread out.

He reached for it without rising from the couch, but she dodged his hand
and speared his mouth with it. He had to take it between his teeth or get it
rubbed across his face. It was very tasty.

She proffered another, before he had finished chewing the first. This
time he caught her wrist. She brought up her right hand, spied the bandage,
and put it down again. But in the process she lost her balance, and fell into
him. "Oh!" she cried as they both were pressed into the couch and against
each other. She was on top, her torso on his, her left thigh caught between
his thighs. Her hair was strewn half across his face.

"Are you all right?" he asked anxiously. "I shouldn't have grabbed you. I
forgot that you are awkward while left-handed."

"Never better," she replied, lifting her head. "I didn't drop the pastry." Her eyes flicked to her hand, which still clutched it. She made as if to
feed it to him, but was prevented because his right hand still held her
wrist.

There was something about the position or the situation. Her face was
almost touching his. He lifted his head and kissed her mouth.

She kissed back. Then, as they broke, she stifled further dialogue by
bringing her hand down to feed him more pastry. That was just as well,
because his sudden guilt was threatening to overwhelm him.

There was a sound at the door. Scylla scrambled off him and wrenched
herself into order as she went to see who it was. Huuo straightened back
into a proper sitting position. It was becoming plain to him that not only did
he desire the woman; she desired him. She was not and could never be
Annai, but she was here, and his grief was muted while he was with her.
Maybe the fall had not been completely accidental, on either side. Maybe he
should simply divert himself with her and be done with it. He had to orient
on his future existence and set aside what was lost in the past.

Yet neither could he let it go, yet. His emotions were unstable, veering
wildly from one extreme to another. In one instant he wanted to die so he
could rejoin his wife; in the next he was gazing at the body of another
woman with desire. It was better to wait, lest he do what he regretted in the
following instant.

Scylla came back, with Crystal. "The storm—" Crystal said. "I couldn't
finish."

"And you will have to hurry home now, or you will still be caught by it," Scylla said. Indeed, the house was darkening, as if night were arriving early.

"Yes." But Crystal lingered as if wanting to say something more. Then she changed her mind and walked to the door—just as the storm struck.

The wind buffeted the house, seeming eager to carry the roof away. Rain beat against the wall. Thunder crackled sharply overhead.

"You can't go out in that," Huuo said. "The spirits are really stirring."

She had to agree. "I will go as soon as it passes."

Scylla did not seem entirely pleased, but she handled the situation gracefully. "You are surely hungry, after your labor. Have some food."

"Oh, no, I must not. I will wait by the door."

Huuo saw that Crystal feared she was intruding on something. But he preferred to have her company, partly because of that. "No, eat and be with us. You would not have been caught here by the storm, had you not been doing me a favor."

Reluctantly she yielded, and took the seat he indicated. With Annai she had never been so diffident, but of course this was not Annai's house.

Scylla brought out bread and berry jam, and they ate. It wasn't much, but this was an impromptu situation.

The storm did not pass. Scylla lit a lamp to brighten the room, but things remained awkward. Huuo had the impression that each woman would have preferred to be alone with him. Scylla, perhaps, wanted to pursue the interplay they had fallen into before the Canaanite's arrival. Crystal—he didn't know what was on her mind. But she wouldn't tell him in Scylla's presence.

"This is awkward," he said. "Maybe we can do something together, to pass the time while we wait out the storm."

Both women looked at him questioningly.

"Could we tell stories?" he asked, floundering.

"I am no storyteller," Scylla said. "Are you?"

"I play music for historians, but I don't narrate myself," Huuo admitted. Then he remembered something. "Crystal—once I heard you telling a rare tale to the children. What was it?"

"Oh, I couldn't tell that to adults," she protested.

"Why not? As I recall, the children liked it."

"Yes," Scylla said, perhaps enjoying the woman's discomfort. "What are adults, but grown children?"

"It was the Poem of Baal," Crystal explained. "The myths we Canaanites tell our children. But Philistines don't like them."

"Because they're heathen," Scylla said. "You people should have given up those false notions long ago."

Crystal didn't argue the matter. But Huuo chose to, in part because he felt the need to defend his loyal servant. The festivals he played for portrayed the bull god as unpleasant, but this was merely their orientation.

"I would not call them false, merely different. We honor the true Mycenaean gods, but before we came here, the Canaanites had their own gods, which I think were similar to ours in certain respects. I've always wondered just how close the relationship might be, if we considered it carefully. But I've never studied those other gods, so I don't know."

Scylla, seeing his interest, attuned her own. "Yes, let's hear about Baal, then."

Crystal was surprised. "You really want to hear it?"

"Yes," Huuo said. "I think this is the occasion."

So Crystal began to speak, telling the tale. After a while, intrigued by it, Huuo got his flutes and softly played an accompanying melody, as he normally did for the stories told at festivals. Scylla, joining in, began to dance, her body making grotesque shadows in the lamplight. The narration became a presentation, before an audience of no one—or perhaps the spirits.

❂

In the early days the supreme deity was El, the bull god, and all was well. But in time he aged and weakened, and others came to rival his power. One of these was Yam, the dragon god, prince of the sea and ruler of the ocean currents. But El's position as chief of the gods continued to be recognized.

Then Ashtar, god of irrigation, foolishly demanded that Yam be deposed in favor of Ashtar. El might have been inclined to make the change, but he knew it would precipitate a crisis with Yam, and he was uncertain of the consequences. So he declined, saying that Ashtar was inadequate to fill the exalted position of lord of all the waters of the world.

Yam, vindicated, made a display of his power. He sent his minions of the sea to the court of El, arrogantly demanding tribute. El, intimidated, acquiesced. Then Yam grew bolder still. He demanded that El's favored son Baal be included as part of the tribute as a slave.

"What?" Baal demanded. He was young, but strong. He was the rain god, and the spirit of fertility. "I will be a slave to no one! Least of all to such sludge of the sea as this."

Yam's minion eyed the impetuous youngster. "Yam will use thee to cultivate his oysters," he said derisively. "Until thou learnest some manners before thy betters, in a few millennia, assuming that thou art less stupid than thou lookest."

Others tried to calm Baal, to warn him of the perils in challenging the might of the sea, but he had been put on his mettle. He leaped up, drawing his knife. "I will cut off *thy* oysters!" he cried, striding toward the envoy of the sea.

But his sister Anat, the goddess of war, intercepted him. She alone could calm his fury, for she loved him as no other did, and was herself a formidable entity. She was garbed in the manner of the temple, though she was a virgin, with bells on the hem of her robe to ward off evil spirits. "Thou must not do this," she protested. "It would be a terrible violation of protocol. No mischief must come to an envoy in thy father's house."

She was correct, and Baal allowed himself to be restrained somewhat. But he couldn't resist taking a whip in his left hand and lashing the buttocks of the departing envoy. That was an indignity that Yam himself felt, for an insult to his minion was an insult to the god of the sea.

Naturally Yam did not take long to react. He challenged Baal to individual combat by the edge of the sea. Now Baal, the heat of the moment dissipated, had some caution. The god of the sea was indeed formidable, and Baal was merely the god of the tiny drops of rain that fell to encourage the crops. So he sought some advice from a divine metalsmith.

"Have I not told thee, O Prince Baal, that thou shalt prevail?" the skillful craftsman said encouragingly. "Behold thy enemy, whom thou shalt smite. Thou shalt subdue all thy adversaries."

"But I lack a weapon to match the trident of Yam," Baal protested.

"Thou shalt have that weapon," the smith said. And he went to work at his forge and crafted a mighty double mace. "Thy name is Driver," he told the mace. "Driver, to drive the sea from his throne. Thou shalt soar and swoop in the hand of Baal, even as an eagle takes its prey. Thou shalt strike the shoulders of the prince of the sea, and break his power."

Encouraged, Baal took the mace and went with his sister Anat to meet Yam at the appointed place. They performed the leaping dance as they went, to encourage their health and strength. The minions of the sea came out of the surging water and surrounded them, but Anat showed her weapons of war and made them retreat. "If thy lord can't fight his own battle, he proclaims his inadequacy," she said.

Then Yam emerged in his glory, a towering figure bearing his mighty trident. He shed so much water that it eroded the sand of the beach, putting Baal at a disadvantage. But Baal waded in, swinging his mace. It struck the breast of the lord of the sea, a blow that would have killed any mortal man.

But Yam was not mortal. He laughed, showing no impairment. "Callst that a blow?" he demanded. "Such a toy can't hurt me!" And he struck the mace with the three tines of his trident, and knocked it out of Baal's hand, and it fell to the ground in a twisted mass.

Then Anat rushed to her brother. "The celestial smith made another weapon, in case of need," she said. "I saved it for thee, and here it is: Expeller, to expel thine enemy from the field."

Baal kissed her and took the new weapon. Then he went after Yam again, and this time the battle was long and hard. When he struck at the lord of the sea, his blow was met by the metal of the trident and repelled; when Yam struck at him, he parried with the mace, and it neither broke nor left his hand. At last he succeeded in catching Yam unguarded, and swung his mace with horrendous force, and struck the god between the eyes. Yam looked surprised, and tried to laugh, but the blow had addled him, and he fell like a tremendous tree and crashed to the ground. His minions looked on, horrified; they had never anticipated this outcome. In truth, Baal was somewhat surprised himself, for the lord of the sea had seemed invincible. Only with the magic aid of the second weapon had he been able to prevail, and now he realized how tired he was.

Anat was jubilant. "Scatter him, O mighty Baal!" she cried. "Scatter him, O thou who mountest the clouds. Yea, the sea himself is our captive!"

"Let Baal reign!" cried the people. And, indeed, from that point on, Baal was considered to be the proper ruler of the land, for he had proved his valor. They celebrated his heroic victory in their songs, and declared that this was the New Year festival, in honor of Baal's accession. They divided parts of Yam's old dominions into new lands and waters and kingdoms, and made up the Tablets of Destiny, that all might forever know and honor the new order.

But at the moment Baal just wanted to retire and rest, for he knew that he had not won by much of a margin, and he suspected that Yam was not completely defeated. This had been a battle he had won, rather than a war. "Just take me home to sleep," he told his sister.

"But thou must not return to our father's palace," Anat protested. "Thou art now the supreme god, and must have thine own elegant residence."

"I don't care about that," Baal said. And he went to El's palace and to his private chamber there, and fell down on his bed and slept deeply and long. Anat covered him with a blanket and stroked his brow and took care of him, seeing his enormous fatigue. But to others she said that Baal was merely considering how he should rule the world, and what changes he should make in the existing order. She did not want anyone to know that her brother was anything less than invincible.

When Baal woke, recovered, his sister's words returned to him. It was true: he should have a palace of his own, so that he could live in proper style for the chief of gods. Only from such a residence could he be what he was destined to be.

But only El could authorize such an edifice, and it was uncertain whether the creator would allow a palace to be constructed which would rival his own in splendor. So for a time Baal and Anat busied themselves with other things. Anat made a temple wherein she indulged herself in the pleasures of the sacrifice of young mortal men, for she as goddess of war delighted in dismemberment and blood. Then she sanctified the temple and retired to her toilet, scooping up water and washing with the dew of heaven and the rain that poured forth from the stars. Then she sprayed herself with the perfumes of a thousand mountains, and cast her slops into the sea. Yam might have protested about that, but he no longer had the power to enforce his outrage.

She did not neglect the welfare of her beloved brother. She brought him to her temple, where she made a sacred marriage for him with three marvelous beauties, ushering in the fertility of spring after the sterility of winter. She gave him a love charm, and delivered to him nymphs called Plump Damsel, who would produce the fattening of the land and its produce; Dewey, the Daughter of Showers, who brought the vital rain from the sky; and Earth-Maiden, the Daughter of the Wide World, whose soil nourished the growing seeds.

But even these marvelous creatures diverted Baal only so long. The time came when he remembered his lack of a palace of his own. "I must build the House of Baal," he said.

"And I must help thee," Anat said loyally.

"I will demand of my father that he let me build the palace."

But his sister had the caution born of occasional reverses in battle. "No, it is better to be circumspect. Let's get our mother Asherat to intercede for thee; then El will surely agree."

Baal realized that her counsel was good. So they foraged throughout the lands and assembled a vast array of precious and wonderful gifts, including especially things that Anat knew a woman would appreciate.

They loaded the gifts on pack animals and made their way toward Asherat's residence. The mother of the gods was a gentle creature who saw the long caravan of camels and horses bearing their burdens and was frightened that this was a war party. But Anat reassured her, and when the woman saw how rich the gifts were she was entirely won over, and agreed to present Baal's case to her husband El. And El, moved by his wife's plea, agreed that Baal could have his palace.

Now they sought an architect. This could be no other but the Skillful and Percipient One who had made the powerful maces for Baal. He designed a truly marvelous edifice with many great windows. But Baal was reluctant. "Suppose Yam peers into them, and sees my beautiful young brides, and steals them away to the sea?"

"But thou didst defeat Yam," Anat reminded him. "He is no threat to thee anymore."

Still, Baal was doubtful. He had defeated Yam at the margin of the sea, but would hesitate to challenge him in the deepest depths of it, where there was no place to stand. Still, perhaps he could cow the god of the sea, so there would be no incidents. So they went out to the edge of the sea, and Baal brought forth his terrible mace and hurled a challenge to Yam to come out and fight if he dared. Yam was there, but he knew he couldn't win that battle, so he lay low under the water and did not answer the challenge. So Baal was reassured, and agreed to have the windows.

The palace was built, and it was the marvel of the ages. The workers went to Lebanon for its choice cedars, and used flame to forge silver into plates and gold into blocks. The building took seven days, and on the first six days the mansion was bathed in fire, and on the seventh day the fire was doused and it was complete. They slaughtered sheep and oxen, bulls and rams, and fattened calves, celebrating the achievement.

At last they installed the roof shutter and the palace was complete. When Baal opened the windows, the heavens also opened, and rain fell to fertilize the earth. Baal, his power complete with this grand palace, thundered out his challenge to all enemies, real and potential: "O enemies, how dismayed art thou at the weapons of my strength?"

For a time all was well. But Baal realized that his power was not complete. He had defeated Yam, but there was another god whose power was greater and far more sinister. This was Mot, the god of death and sterility, whose abode was in the underworld. Baal ruled the land, but every year the land grew arid and the plants withered and died, leading to hunger. The land recovered each year, but his favored wives and servants grew old and died, showing that the power of Mot was present. There was no mortal who did not in the end descend to that dread realm. Baal concluded that his position would not be secure until he made an end to Death. Then the season of growing would last forever, and people would prosper without dying.

But this was no easy thing to accomplish. Mot was insidious, not standing where he could be attacked. Baal sent a messenger to challenge him: "I alone am he who will reign over the gods, yea, be the leader of gods and men. I call thee to thy grave, Mot!"

And Mot returned the message: "Though thou didst smite the primeval serpent, and vanquish the lord of the sea, the heavens will dry up, yea they shall languish. I shall pound thee, consume thee. Thou shalt be cleft, forspent, and exhausted. Lo, thou art gone down into the throat of the god Mot, into the gullet of Death, O beloved of El."

Baal demanded that Mot come to the surface of the land and meet him in fair combat. But Mot, ever devious, countered with an invitation for Baal to come below and discuss the matter. "And thou, take thy clouds, thy wind, thy rain, thy Plump Damsel, Daughter of Mist, and Dewcy, Daughter of Showers, and set thy face toward the Mountain of Concealment. Grope thy way under the earth and descend to the House of Corruption in the underworld. Thou shalt be numbered with those who go down into the earth. Yea, thou shalt know annihilation, as do the dead!"

This was a summons, whether it was more truly an invitation or a challenge, that Baal could not ignore, lest he be shamed as a coward. So he accepted the dare, and agreed to travel into the underworld to meet the lord of death.

"But thou must not go alone!" Anat protested. "I will go with thee, to guard against betrayal."

But Baal did not accept this. "It is my courage Mot challenges," he replied. "I must show him and all the world that I fear nothing—not even the lord of death in his own dominion. I will go alone."

She saw that he would not be moved. "Then at least prepare thyself, my beloved brother, for Mot is both crafty and treacherous. Cover thyself with red ocher to ward off demons, and exercise to enhance thy virility and strength."

Her advice was good, so Baal did as she suggested. He smeared ocher all across his body until he was orange throughout, and the iron of it was like armor against anything the underworld might hurl. Then Anat brought forth a heifer, the fairest of virgin cows, and Baal undertook the ritual of copulation with her. So great was his virility that it was barely diminished by the first effort, so he repeated the act again and again, until he had done it eighty-eight times and begotten on her a calf-son, whose birth and growth would generate a bull the like of no other, to be worshipped seasonally by all the people. Now he was as strong as he could be, in every sense, and ready for almost anything.

He bid parting to his virgin sister Anat, who loved him so well that she was jealous of the heifer, and set off for the underworld. His route was through a vast deep cave that no others dared enter, for it was said it could be traveled in only one direction. He promised his sister that he would return in three days, allowing one day to descend, one to meet Mot, and one to return.

So concerned was Anat that she remained the whole three days at the mouth of that cave, so as not to miss an instant of his return. But when the third day came, Baal did not emerge. With growing alarm she continued her vigil through the fourth day, and the fifth, fearing the worst. She began to despair on the sixth day, and on the seventh she knew that her brother was lost. Mot had defeated him, and Baal would not return to the world of the living.

With heavy heart she reported the sad news to their father El. "Verily Baal has fallen to the earth," she said through her tears. "Baal the mighty is dead! The prince, the lord of the earth, has perished."

Then El the Merciful, the Kindly One, came down from his throne and sat on the footstool. Then he got off the footstool and sat on the ground. In grief he let down his turban from his head, and put his face in the dust. He tore asunder the knot on his girdle and made the mountains echo and re-echo with his lamentation. He rent his chin and cheeks, and the forest resounded with his cries. He lacerated his arms, his chest, his back, letting his blood flow. "Baal is dead!" he cried. "What is become of the prince? My son is dead! What of the multitudes of men? Shall I too go to the underworld?"

Anat mourned her brother as passionately as El did. She rent her clothing and tore her hair, ranging across the land and crying out her grief to every mountain and every hill and field. But this hardly abated her sorrow.

After the period of mourning, Anat resolved to recover the body of her brother for proper burial. She enlisted the aid of Shapash, the sun goddess, for after the sun passed over the Earth by day, it passed under the Earth by night. Thus the sun saw everything, and knew where Baal's body was. Shapash told Anat, so she could go to fetch it.

Anat ranged again across the hills and fields, and past every mountain, until she came to what she had not seen before—the pleasant land of the Back of Beyond. It was the fair tract of the Strand of Death. There she came upon Baal, fallen to the ground, unmoving in death.

She wept anew, drinking tears like wine. When at last she was sated with weeping, she lifted her face and shouted to the sun, to Shapash, the light of the gods. "Lift my brother upon me, I pray thee! Let me carry Baal the Mighty."

And so she carried Baal back to the land he had ruled in life, and there they made a great funeral with many sacrifices of prize animals, and had a funeral feast. They put him in a coffin in a crypt, and closed him in, and it was done.

Now Baal's throne was empty. Who could fill it? Ashtar thought he could, for he was the god of irrigation who had sought to displace Yam before. So El allowed him to try the throne. But when Ashtar took his seat on the throne of Baal the Mighty, his feet dangled, not reaching the ground. Not reaching even the footstool. His head did not reach the top of the throne.

At last Ashtar himself was convinced. He got off the throne. "I must rule from the ground."

Meanwhile the goddess Anat kept vigil by the vault where her brother was entombed. She saw that though the body did not move or breathe, neither did it decay. It remained unchanged, though many days passed. It was as if Baal were simply in a deep sleep, unable to be roused.

Then Anat concluded that her brother could not truly be dead. "Mot must have captured him by some stratagem, depriving him of his body," she said. "If Baal is released, he will return to his body, and live again."

The others did not credit this, thinking her grief-maddened. But Anat would not be dissuaded. She searched the Earth once again, this time for the spirit of Baal. She called to the god of death, pleading with him to release her brother.

Mot came to stand before her. "Why should I release Baal?" he inquired. "He sought to challenge my dominion. For that arrogance I have set him down."

"But thou canst not rule the land," she said tearfully. "Only my brother can do that. I beg thee again, Mot, free him!"

Mot pondered the matter. He studied the beautiful virgin goddess.

"Perhaps I might, for due consideration," he said cynically. "What wouldst thou give me, for that favor?"

Anat did not at first catch his implication. "Anything, O Lord of Death! Anything in my power. What dost thou wish?"

"Come to my dominion, and be my concubine."

"But I could not do that!" she protested. "I am the virgin goddess of war! I would lose my power."

Mot shrugged. "No doubt I would tire of thee soon anyway. So depart, foolish creature; since thou dost refuse to yield to my desire of thee, thou shalt not have thy desire of me. Thy brother will remain forever cold in that crypt."

Outrage overwhelmed her. "Thou wallowing pig!" she cried. "Thou didst never intend to free Baal!"

"Have it thy way." Mot turned contemptuously away.

The underworld knew no fury like that of a goddess scorned. Anat reached out and seized the god of death. She clasped him in her arms and threw him to the ground. Then she drew her deadly iron sword and cleaved him in twain.

But the halves came back together. "Thou darest attack *me?*" Mot demanded incredulously. "Thou foolish girl!"

Anat took up a shovel and caught him on it, and winnowed him, separating his head from his body. But the head fell back onto the neck. "I shall surely punish thee for this impertinence," Mot said grimly.

Anat struck flint stones together and made fire. The fire bathed the lord of death, parching him. But he did not die. "Thou art going to regret this, thou wild heifer," he said, becoming annoyed.

Anat fetched millstones and ground him between them. Mot was squeezed and rendered into powder. "This is beyond reason!" he exclaimed as his head was drawn into the mechanism. "What makes thee think thou canst kill Death?"

Anat took the powder and scattered it across the field. "Come, creatures of the wild!" she called. "Come feast on Death, who used to feast on thee!" And the birds came to eat his remains, and the wild creatures consumed his fragments. They sundered remains from remains.

At last the last of Mot was gone. He could not reassemble himself, because the parts of him were scattered in the bellies of many living creatures. Anat had indeed slain the lord of death. Of course in time the animals would defecate those remains, and one fragment would cling to another, and eventually all the portions would be drawn back together, and Mot would be whole again. He might stink, but his power would be restored. But that would take a year, and meanwhile he would not be able to interfere with Anat's pursuit of Baal.

She returned to report the news. El was gratified. He slept well for the first time since Baal's loss, and dreamed that his son was alive. The worshippers were thrilled. "For Baal the Mighty is alive! The prince, lord of the earth, exists!" But no one know where Baal was. The lord of death had hidden him somewhere, and they could not find him.

This did not prevent Anat from wreaking savage vengeance on Mot's allies, now that the lord of death could not protect them. She made wastelands of their territories. "Just be thankful I'm not really angry," she told them, "now that I know my brother will return. Otherwise I would treat thee unkindly." But the truth was that she remained somewhat miffed about the continued absence of her brother. Possibly some of those wasted allies suspected that.

However, Anat's conquest of Mot had already freed Baal's spirit from its magic confinement, and he was busy in the underworld. He wrought vast desolation in Mot's realm, and emerged at last to reclaim his own still body in the crypt. When Anat returned to her vigil there, she heard him rising, and quickly let him out. "O my brother!" she cried, embracing him passionately. "Thou hast returned!"

Indeed he had. Baal resumed his throne, and the land prospered. The skies rained oil, the wadis ran with honey, and prosperity returned. Until Mot managed to get together again and make more mischief, and Baal had to destroy him again. So it went, from season to season, from year to year, with neither force remaining forever in control.

○

The story of Baal ended. Huuo found himself embracing Scylla, for they had animated the roles of Baal and Anat. And the afternoon was gone, the storm passed.

"But I must confess there is a small difference," Scylla murmured, her eyes demurely downcast. "I am not your sister."

He remained holding her a moment longer. "True. You are not. Yet you played the part of the raging goddess well."

"I am a dancer," she reminded him. "I am experienced in animations. You are the one who did well, for you normally merely play the music. Which you also did very feelingly."

Huuo looked around, remembering Crystal, who had told the tale. But she was gone. She must have left as the story concluded, seeing that the way was clear outside. He would have to thank her for a fine afternoon's entertainment. He had never realized how detailed and interesting the Canaanite mythology was. He had viewed it with a certain disdain; now his tolerance was expanding. Baal was a better god than he had credited, and worthy of worship.

"I thought it would be a dull afternoon," Scylla said, not trying to disengage. "But your servant is quite a storyteller."

"Yes. Now I understand why the children were always so fascinated. I never really paid attention before."

"We should separate."

"Yes," he agreed absently, not acting on it. There was something else about the story of Baal that nagged him, but he couldn't quite fathom it.

"If you do not release me," Scylla murmured dulcetly, "I will not be responsible for the consequence."

He looked at her. She was of course very close, being in his embrace, and lovely in the candlelight. "Consequence?"

"This." She lifted her face to his and kissed him, lingeringly.

After a time their faces separated slightly. "This is how you show annoyance?" he inquired with a smile.

"It's how I show desire. It is clear that Anat's love for Baal was more than sisterly, though she could not express it. Similarly my interest in you is more than neighborly, though I have tried to spare you its expression. But enacting that story of Baal and Anat has stirred me beyond the bounds of propriety, and if you do not free me very soon I shall perhaps do with you what I should not."

She was describing his own surging feeling toward her. "Why should you not?"

"Because I sought only to render the assistance to you that a friend would, despite finding you most attractive as a man. I know that you do not wish to—"

"Let me be the judge of that. Act as you wish."

She flung her arms around him and kissed him with doubled passion, her tongue finding his.

There were no words after that. They went to a bed—he wasn't sure and didn't care which one—and got their clothing off and embraced naked in complete sexual congress. Scylla kissed him throughout, never pausing even in the final throes of fulfillment. Her hunger was a scourge that drove him on, so that when it was done it wasn't done, and he was trying to emulate Baal's performance with the heifer. He did fall somewhat short of that, he believed, but wasn't sure.

The darkness closed about them, and they slept. At least he did; when he woke he was alone, and that was just as well, because he remembered that Annai was dead and not yet buried, and he had lain with another woman. What had possessed him? He felt his face and body burning with shame.

Unable to return to sleep, he got off the bed and groped his way to the lavatory. He was, it turned out, on his own bed, so the way was familiar. Scylla must have gone to her bed. There was some light from the candle in the main chamber, which it seemed had never been extinguished; that helped. He cleaned himself up, then found a fresh robe, and went to put out the candle.

There was Scylla, sitting beside it. "Oh—I did not realize you were here," he said.

"I could not sleep," she said. "I am mortified by what happened."

"You mean I—I took you when you did not wish it?" he asked, surprised.

She smiled, wanly, in the light. "Oh, no! Because *I* took *you* when you did not wish it. You are in mourning, and I—I should have left you alone. I would apologize, were the matter not beyond apology."

Huuo found himself arguing the other case. "You tried to demur. I gave you leave."

"I *pretended* to demur. I desired you so much I could not pull myself away. I kissed you. I pressed my body against you. I seduced you, not giving you time to reflect. I am guilty."

"But I am not a mindless animal!" he protested. "I should have withdrawn."

"I should have let you withdraw. I knew you were not in your right mind."

"My mind was right," he insisted. "But not my emotion."

She lifted her head, evidently coming to a decision. "I will move out tomorrow. I will find another temporary residence, so you can be alone."

"But this is your house! I have no right to it, but for your sufferance."

"I give you that gladly. I must leave you alone, and I may not do that while remaining so close. I do not want you to hate me after this is done."

"I don't hate you! You blame yourself falsely. I take responsibility for my own action."

"You are very kind. But I must spare you further mischief. I will seek another—"

"No!" he said, surprised by his own vehemence. "This is your house. You must stay. I must be the one to go."

She shook her head. "I would not cast you out, Huuo. I want only to smooth your course, not complicate it."

"Then let there be no change," he said. "What happened, happened; let's place no blame for it. There is no need to dwell on this, if neither of us wishes to."

She smiled, falteringly. "You are so generous. If you truly are satisfied to forget—"

"There is no fault," he said firmly. "Now let's retire to our rooms. We need our sleep."

"Yes. Thank you." She rose and moved toward her room.

Huuo watched her walk, before snuffing the candle. For an irrational moment he wanted to follow her. Then he put out the candle and made his way to his own room. He thought he might have difficulty sleeping, but soon enough he was dreaming again. Of Scylla.

❂

Crystal was disturbed. She had wanted to tell Huuo of her findings, suspicions, and conjectures, but none were sure and she didn't want to rouse his hope only to dash it again. In any event, Scylla had been there with him throughout, so there had been no way to talk privately with him.

So she braced her husband instead. "Something is amiss," she said. "I don't know what to do."

Carverro had had a hard day working at his metal sculpting, but he knew better than to try to balk his wife. "Tell me. Maybe I'll have an idea."

"You know how the raiders burned out Huuo's house and killed Annai and the children," she said.

"Of course. You have been depressed ever since. It must be about time for the funeral."

"Yes. Huuo asked me to locate the bones without removing them, so that he will find them promptly. This morning I went there and poked all through the ashes with a staff, dreading what I would find."

Carverro waited, but she was silent. "And you found them?" he prompted her.

"No."

After another pause he prompted her again. "You looked more carefully then?"

"I looked as carefully as I could without putting those ashes through a sieve. I found no bones."

"Could someone have taken them?"

"No. There was a light rain not long after the fire, wetting the ashes in place, and they have been undisturbed since. I watched that fire die; I do not think anyone was there, ever."

"Was the fire so hot it burned even the bones?"

"Not that hot. Not to entirely burn up fresh bodies."

Carverro looked at her. "Something is amiss," he agreed.

"Where are the bones?" she asked.

"From what you tell me, there are no bones. That suggests something remarkable."

"It suggests what?" she asked, not volunteering anything. She wanted him to say it.

"That the hill folk did not slay the family. That instead they took them away to be slaves or hostages."

"Then they could be alive," she said.

"They could be alive," he agreed.

"And I couldn't tell Huuo," she said.

"Just as well. They could have been carried away, wrapped in cloth to fool the gatekeeper, but you know that Annai would not have submitted to slave-girl use. No highborn Philistine would. So the barbarians might well have killed her."

"And what of the children?"

"Better we not inquire. Death might be preferable."

Again he had echoed her concern. "But before I returned to try to talk to Huuo, at that woman's house, I inquired." She paused, but this time only briefly. "There is still no news of any marauding hill folk in this area at this time. They have been minding their own primitive business. In fact most of their men are with that upstart ruler, Damon."

"David," he said. "King David. Upstart he may be, but he did just defeat the Philistines in battle. I hear it was a grievous loss."

"Yes. So it wasn't a raid. It was just a cattle trading day that got out of control. But would such ruffians, suddenly running wild, have taken the trouble to carry away a Philistine family?"

Carverro opened his mouth, and paused, considering. "No," he said after a moment. "That's not the way the hill folk are. They don't plan ahead; they just rampage when they get the chance."

"Then why no bones?"

Carverro shook his head. "Something is very strange, here. Very strange."

Crystal gazed at him. "So what could I tell Huuo?" she demanded.

He spread his hands. "Your observation. Your suspicion. He must be the one to judge."

"That is what I concluded. But that woman was there, and—"

"You think she could have something to do with it?"

"I don't know. But she met him so conveniently, and just happened to have that house to sell, and she's so interested in him. She's even trying to be left-handed, because of her pretended injury to her right hand. I almost wonder if she didn't buy that house, so she could pretend to have inherited it, so she had a pretext to come here at this time. But that suggests such a monstrous plot—"

"Monstrous indeed," Carverro agreed. "But it does fit your observations. Some plot to abduct Huuo's family, making it seem that they were dead—"

"So that woman could seduce him," Crystal concluded. "I have hesitated even to imagine such a thing, yet—" She shrugged.

"And you couldn't tell him, in her presence," he said. "Yet there must be a way, because this is too important to let pass."

"I thought I had found a way. I was caught there by the storm, and they craved diversion, so they prevailed on me to tell a story."

"Prevailed on you?" He laughed, "As if you could ever be shut up!"

"They did ask me," she said, somewhat stiffly. "And I realized that there is an aspect to the history of Baal that might relate."

"When he seems to be dead, but returns to life!" Carverro exclaimed. "As just might be the case with Annai!"

"Yes. So I told them that—they took it as fantasy, of course—and dwelt on the aspect of the seeming death. But I fear it had a different effect than I wanted."

"Different?"

"When I left, they were so interested in each other that they didn't notice me at all."

"Well, you must admit that the goddess Anat is as fair a morsel of sex appeal as any woman, and if Baal did it eighty-eight times with a heifer, how much better to—" He broke off, seeing that his wife wasn't with him. "Evidently the male perspective differs. But I can say that if I were a widower in the presence of a woman as healthy as that Philistine is said to be, a veritable Delilah, and I heard a rousing rendition of the loves of Baal, I would be interested. We must be realistic, Crystal."

She realized that he was trying to be helpful. "But suppose Annai lives? Then what of such seduction?"

Carverro assumed a serious expression. "If I thought you died, and a woman seduced me before your funeral, and I then learned you lived and that she was implicated in the ruse, I would kill her. To redeem my honor."

And so would Huuo, she realized. "I think I had better not tell him. Not without proof. But how can I, a mere Canaanite woman, ascertain the truth?"

"I think it is time for a mere Canaanite man to get involved," he said, picking up the hint. Actually, he was intrigued by the mystery, and he did have good regard for Huuo and his family, so it was an easy decision to make. "I will see what the menfolk can learn. Meanwhile, you continue as you have, giving no hint that you suspect anything. For surely if there is a conspiracy, for what ultimate purpose we don't know, and they think you suspect, your life will not be safe."

"Oh!" She had not thought of that. But she had accomplished her immediate purpose: to get her husband involved. Because though the women were adept at learning secret news, the men were adept at doing things, and something needed to be done.

○

In the morning Huuo woke somewhat refreshed. He reflected on what had happened in the evening, and realized that while his horror and grief for the loss of his family continued, he did have to orient on his future. It had been indiscreet to bed Scylla, but perhaps inevitable. She was certainly a winsome woman. Never would he consider her in lieu of Annai, but as a temporary creature, akin to a session in the temple with a priestess, she was more than adequate. Still, he felt guilty for weakening, and intended not to do it again. He would see to the funeral for his loved ones, and she would sell her house and return to wherever she had come from, and then he would see about making a new life.

How sensible it all seemed! But only because he was walling off the sea of his grief, so that he could do what had to be done. When he had acquitted his obligations, then he would also be free to grieve fully.

He got up, cleaned up, and went to the main room. Scylla was already there, preparing breakfast for them both. Her robe covered her body completely, yet somehow did not conceal its pliant nature. Whatever else she was or was not, she was a most attractive woman.

"Do you know," she said as they completed the meal, "while I am of course chagrined by what happened last night, I must also confess that it was my private delight. You are an excellent lover."

"I thought we had agreed to forget last night," he said gruffly.

"Oh! I am sorry. So we did. It was just that my dreams were so—I just couldn't help thinking how delightful it would be to—but I have said too much." She turned her face away.

She was right, and he knew he should let it be. But she had inadvertently intrigued him. "Delightful to do what?" he asked. Because he suspected that she was not talking about mere sexual activity.

"No, it is foolish and impossible. Come, you must see to your arrangements, and I must see to mine. I have not begun to market this house."

But, perversely, he pursued it. "What is impossible?"

"Please, Huuo, do not press me. There can only be embarrassment for me."

Which made it even more intriguing. "How can a mere dream be embarrassing?" he asked, though he knew that this was certainly possible.

She faced him, flushing slightly. "You intend to have this of me? I would rather take you to bed again."

He had resolved to avoid that, but now he was tempted. "I don't think that would be fair to you, considering that soon we will part and not see each other again. This is not the festival, or a chamber in the temple."

"True. But we might pretend it was. Shall I be a priestess of Ashtoreth for you?" She opened her robe to show her breasts.

He smiled, though the sight stirred a desire for just that. "You are trying to divert me from the subject. So you won't have to tell me your embarrassment."

She hung her head. "Yes. It was a transparent ploy." She closed her robe.

Something about her fascinated him, though there was guilt behind it. She said she wanted to bed him again; he wanted the same. The more she tried to divert his sexual interest, the more she incited it—and even when she tried to use sexual appeal to divert him from something else, his interest increased. He knew he should depart this house, leaving her behind. And knew he wouldn't. "What is your secret thought?"

She made a little sigh of resignation. "I knew I shouldn't have let any hint slip. You are a musician, bound to follow the melody to its end. But my fancy is not simply told."

She was still teasing him. "We have time. Tell it as it needs to be told."

"I was originally a citizen of Gaza. But I committed an indiscretion, and was exiled by the seren."

"Would that be Seren Jaoch? I met him."

Her eyes widened. "You know him? Then I really must not tell you this!"

He smiled. "Be at ease. We are not friends. Merely acquaintances. How did you annoy him?"

"I seduced one of his favored officers."

"I can imagine." She had never made a secret of her propensity. "But surely that happens routinely."

"He was married to a woman with political connections. When she learned of our relationship, she required her husband to charge me with trying to discredit him. The seren believed it, and sent me away. She had her vengeance, sure enough, for I do love my home city, and long to return there."

"That's understandable. But what has this to do with me?"

"I think Lord Jaoch suspected that I was innocent of that particular crime. But he had to support his officer. I think Lord Jaoch would let me return, were I in other guise."

"Other guise? How can you ever be other than yourself?"

Her flush deepened. "If I were someone's wife. Particularly if that person were prominent."

"Then your course seems simple. You have only to beguile a noble, and—"

"I have affairs passingly. But I have never married. Because I could marry only a man I truly loved. Only to him could I be duly subservient. And I have never encountered a man with qualities compelling my love. Until now."

Suddenly her meaning struck him. "You—you find me such a man?"

She met his gaze. Her eyes seemed large, with depths of innocence. Her lower lip trembled. "Must I answer?"

Flattered but confused, he found only one response. "I think you had better."

A tear appeared at one eye, and trickled down across her flush. "I love you," she whispered. "I dreamed of marrying you. There: I have said it at last."

"But I am—" He broke off, appalled. He was no longer a married man.

"You are not ready for this," she said softly. "I didn't want to tell you. And it is indeed a foolish dream. Why should I marry to return to my home city—when I would not care where I was, were I with you? So it makes no sense. We shall part and be strangers soon enough."

"I suppose so," he agreed. "In any event, I wouldn't care to leave Mor." But as he spoke he knew it was not so. What was there to hold him here, now that Annai was gone?

Scylla got up and went to her bedroom. Huuo remained where he was, trying to make sense of the chaos of his thoughts. He was in a situation he would never have chosen. But he could not escape it. Suppose he went his own way—who would see to his comforts? Since he had married, the routines of the world had retreated; Annai had taken care of them. He had focused on being the best musician he could be, and making the family living thereby, with considerable help from Annai's supportive dancing. Even the children had not been a burden, for she cared for them too. Though Minah might have found a home in the temple, with her prettiness and her affinity for the spirits. Chipp might have found employment as a musician's helper, for he had learned useful things. But now they all were gone, and he was alone, and he had little notion how to cope. Go out alone? He wasn't sure he could.

So regardless of his grief, he needed a woman. Crystal would help him all she could, but there were sharp limits. She was a servant, and she had her own family. He needed a Philistine woman—yes, a wife. And Scylla was offering. This was not something he wanted to face while his grief was raw, but he knew that there were decisions he would have to make regardless of his grief. It was possible that Scylla would be an appropriate choice. If she wanted to return to Gaza—well, Seren Jaoch had asked him to go there. He could have a good situation, and Scylla, as a native of that city, would certainly know how to handle its ways. Marriage between them? It could be a rational choice.

But not yet. He simply wasn't ready. The memory of Annai was too strong.

He became aware of something. A curious faint sound. He oriented on it. Then he realized that it was Scylla. She was lying face down on her bed—he could see her through the doorway—and sobbing.

Because he had shamed her by making her express her secret thought. He had been cruel, though her dream was not unreasonable, when considered cautiously.

He got up and approached her room. She did not know of his nearness. He hesitated, gazing at her. Her robe was in some disarray from her haste in throwing herself down, so that one of her thighs showed fairly high. He felt guilty for considering her body when she was in such misery, yet the sight did stir his desire. Somehow he desired her each time he was close to her, and the sexual urge mixed with and colored his impression of her situation. What did he really want of her? A temple priestess? Or a woman to take care of him? Who happened to be a dancer, as Annai had been.

He went to kneel beside her. "I am sorry I made you tell your dream," he said. "But you need not be shamed. It is not unreasonable."

She heard him. After a moment she turned her tear-stained face to him. "You are such a kind man."

"No, merely a man trying to find his way. I regret making you unhappy."

"I make myself unhappy with foolish notions." She shifted her position, getting her feet to the floor so she could sit up. In the process she showed a good deal more thigh and breast than she realized. "But this is inappropriate. You are the one in grief. I must stop holding you back from your business."

She was right. He had chores to do. But her inadvertent exposure was having an illicit effect. Suddenly he was reacting more than he might have to the full open exposure of her body. There was something extraordinarily compelling about the partial view. "I wish it was last night," he murmured.

"Last night?" Then she glanced at herself. "Oh. This is nothing. You are welcome to whatever you want. It is a gift gladly given. But surely you know that if you borrow it, you may in time want to buy it."

An incitement to marriage. Again, she was surely right. She was giving him fair warning. "He who handles vipers risks getting bitten," he said.

She laughed. "How apt an image. But I have another. He who handles fresh fruit at the market risks having to purchase it." She caught his right hand with her left hand and brought it to her exposed left breast. The touch of that not quite forbidden fruit abolished whatever restraint had remained to him.

He moved into her and kissed her. She met him eagerly. Then they were on the bed, and he was on her and in her, doing what he had resolved not to do. And she was weeping, but not with grief. As before, they remained clasping each other long after the physical passion was spent. They did not separate until they heard someone approaching the house.

Then they had to go into a flurry of repairs, mutually administered, so they could meet the visitor in good order, though they knew it was only Crystal coming to be of assistance. Today, Huuo resolved, he would go to take those bones for the funeral and burial ceremonies.

❂

Annai despaired of getting herself and the children presentable. They had only the clothes they had worn when abducted, and those had been roughly treated. "At least get us some clean robes!" she cried to the mute woman who guarded them.

She expected no more response than she had gotten on any of the past days of their confinement. But this time there was something else. "Give them robes," a man's voice said.

There was a pause. Then the woman appeared at the tiny window normally used to introduce their food and remove their refuse. She shoved in a pile of cloth.

Annai took it eagerly. "Thank you," she said politely, for this was behavior she wanted to encourage. When she unfolded it, there were three robes: one large one and two small ones. Exactly what she and the children needed.

She got the children changed, then changed herself. Because she had heard the man's voice, she was cautious, and faced into the stone corner so that no more of her body showed than was necessary. The changing took only a moment. Then she brushed out her hair with her fingers and braced herself for whatever was to come. Because she was sure this was no incidental visit.

The man's face appeared at the window. "I would like to talk with you, not quarrel with you," he said. "You are a Philistine lady. Will you give me your word not to behave in an uncivilized manner?"

"Uncivilized!" she exclaimed. "My house gets raided, the children and I get knocked on our heads and bound and hauled for days we know not where, wrapped in coarse blankets so we almost suffocate, and finally dumped in this bare cell like so much garbage, and you expect civilized behavior? That woman never even speaks to us, just shoves in food every so often. Fresh robes can't fix the mess we're in or the stink of which we reek."

"You seem remarkably clean and sweet, regardless," he says. "Your class shows."

Annai had used tearstrips from their old robes to make clothes, and had dipped them in the water left over from their meals, to wipe herself and the children as clean as was feasible. She had spoken somewhat hyperbolically in her distress; she certainly hoped they did not smell. But in these close confines it was hard to be sure. "If you behave, we will," she said.

"That suffices." The man went around to the barred door, and it a moment it opened. He entered and stood a moment outlined by the light beyond. He was a tall, solid, armed man, obviously too strong to be overcome by any ordinary woman. In any event, she had pledged no mischief.

"Who are you?" she demanded. "Are you the one responsible for this outrage?"

"I admit I am, to a degree," he said. "Lady, do you know me?" He removed his helmet.

She stared at him. "Why—you are Zebub, the nefarious schemer. We have met on occasion during the festivals."

"True. In this case it is perhaps well that I am such, because an avenue was open to me that would not have been to another man. Are you aware of the fate of your house and husband?"

"The fate of—" Her hand flew to her mouth. "No."

"Then I have unfortunate news to impart. You were the victims of a chance raid by hill folk, who rioted when their cattle stampeded in your city. Seeing their opportunity, they ravaged several houses on their way out. Evidently taking you for nobility, they took you and your children for hostage, so that they would not be pursued too closely. They burned your house as an additional distraction. Evidently this was effective, because there was no effective pursuit."

"My husband," Annai said tightly.

"He was on his way back to your city after the festival. He learned of the raid, and went after the hill folk, not waiting for a proper expedition. That is perhaps understandable, as expeditions can take forever to mount. He had been told you were dead, but he refused to believe it. But the hill folk ambushed him and killed him."

"Oh!" Annai cried, and both children screamed.

"But once they were home without complications, the hill folk were not certain what to do with their captives," Zebub continued. "They were too ignorant to know how to negotiate for ransom. You did not speak their language, and did not know their ways, so they feared you would make poor slaves. They did appreciate the fact that one captive was a beautiful woman, and realized that perhaps she could be sold to some man who desired her for the obvious purpose. That left the children, whom they deemed to be too old for full assimilation into their tribe. So probably they would have killed them."

Despite their mutual shock at the news of Huuo's death, Annai and the children listened attentively, realizing how relevant the man's discourse was. Annai sold as a sex slave, and Chipp and Minah killed? That had not happened, but they still did not know what their actual situation was.

"Fortunately I was in the vicinity, dealing in sundry items of trade," Zebub said. "I have learned their language. They asked me whether I would be interested in a lovely female slave. The truth is that I do dabble on occasion in the slave trade, which can be lucrative. But when I learned that this was a Philistine woman and two Philistine children, I knew this was no ordinary situation. Apparently the good folk of Mor did not even realize that this family was alive, or there would have been a reprisal and recovery expedition. But if a highborn woman turned up on the slave market, there would be severe repercussions. Philistines do not tolerate the enslavement of members of their noble class. I realized that something had to be done, or she would find herself not only enslaved but with her tongue cut out so as to conceal her identity, as is the case with my personal slave women here."

Suddenly Annai understood why the woman never spoke. "Her tongue—?"

"It is a routine precaution in some circles, just as is gelding or blinding male slaves. So I knew I would have to act. So I bought her and the children, though uncertain how I might recoup my investment. It seemed to be the prudent thing to do. I had them delivered to my residence. Now imagine my surprise to discover the identity of these captives: the Lady Annai of Mor, whom I have encountered socially."

There was something disingenuous about his story. He must have known their identities before this. Why, then, had he not freed them? But she hesitated to ask, lest she not like the answer. "Yes, I am Annai, and these are my children. We have been held here, uncertain of our fate."

"That was unfortunate. But I had business elsewhere, and could not attend you sooner." He studied her. "May I speak with candor?"

This was mischief. She feared that she knew what was on his mind, but also knew that a direct rebuff might well result in getting her raped before the children. If it was going to happen, she wanted to spare the children the sight. "That depends on the nature of your concern."

"I confess that you have always struck me as not only a beautiful woman, but a sensible one. My sister is a dancer too, and so I appreciate the art of that form, and know you to be a very fine practitioner."

"Thank you," she said guardedly. "I have danced with Scylla, and she is very good."

"In fact, I deem you to be the equal of my sister, the only woman I have encountered to be so."

"Thank you," she repeated, even more guardedly. What was the man working up to? He was being surprisingly social, considering the situation. She knew his reputation, and therefore trusted this not at all.

He glanced at the children, who were tensely quiet. "Perhaps these two are hungry. They could go and eat with the slave while we converse here."

This was definitely trouble, but she needed to know its nature and extent. "Go with the slave woman," Annai told them.

Chipp seemed to want to protest, but Annai silenced him with a glance. Reluctantly he and his sister went out of the cell to join the waiting slave.

"You are indeed sensible, and your children well disciplined," Zebub remarked. "I appreciate that."

"Say what you have to say," she said, schooling herself not to clench her teeth. Did he intend to rape her now, knowing she would not scream lest it alert her children? Yet why should he care about their reactions? His ultimate motive remained a sinister mystery.

"You are now a widow. You would do well to remarry, after a suitable interval. I have perhaps understated my admiration for you. Do you understand?"

Annai's jaw dropped. "You can't mean—!"

"My sister is the finest woman I know. But I can not marry her. You, however, I can. I realize that you lack a similar interest in me. But I point out that if you marry me, I will adopt your children and guarantee their success in life, exactly as I will those I have with you. You yourself will have all the privileges of the lady you are."

This was worse than anything she had feared. But now she had to ask. "And the alternative?"

"I think we need not explore that."

"I think we do. What gives you the notion that I would ever in life accede to such a relationship?"

Zebub shook his head. "I feared it would come to this distasteful discussion, which is why I preferred to have it private. I will of course give you time to consider, for you are in mourning for your husband. But you are surely aware that your children, however important to you, would be something of an encumbrance to me."

"My children!" she said, experiencing the worst of chills.

"I see we understand each other. If, after a reasonable period of consideration, you appear to be unreasonable, we should have to test the issue with one child. If that did not suffice—"

"May I speak with candor?" she inquired, emulating his phraseology.

"By all means."

"You are an unspeakable son of a beaten dog, grandson of a festering pig, and cousin of a rabid bat. The dung beetles would sicken on your refuse. The stench of your personality causes the underworld itself to recoil. When the criminals of all time are reckoned by the gods, your name will surely be listed seven times, and the very parchment will smolder with indignation at the insult of bearing it."

Zebub smiled. "I appreciate your felicity of expression, which indicates a ready mind—something I value almost as much as a lovely body. I take that as the commencement of your consideration of the offer," he said, making a small bow. "I am gratified that you are not turning it down."

He departed, leaving her to her consideration. The notion revolted her, but he was in essence correct: short of killing herself and her children, she would probably in the end have to accede to his desire. The alternative would be to see first one child tortured and killed, and then the other, and then to be ravished until he tired of her, after which her tongue would be cut out and she would be dumped in some distant slave market to finish her life in degrading menial work under the whip. It might actually be better to let him marry her and sire his brats on her. She would ponder the matter. So for all her emotional "felicity of expression," she had indeed not actually turned him down.

Soon Chipp and Minah returned to the cell. They had been fed, and not hurt. But Zebub had made his point: they were hostage to her cooperation. She could stall only so long before giving him an answer, and he would accept only one.

He knew, of course, that once she gave him her word, even under cruel duress, she would honor it. She would be given more freedom. But he would probably keep the children confined for a while anyway, just to be sure.

Suppose she attacked him before giving her answer? She had once used her skill as a dancer to foil a man's untoward advance, but she suspected that Zebub would be alert for just such a move. She would have to catch him by surprise, with a weapon he didn't anticipate.

What she needed was a knife. Since there was no prospect of getting one, she would have to see whether she could make one. It was her only realistic chance.

With that decision made, she was able to focus on her emotion. It was time to morn for Huuo.

○

Crystal brought fruits and bread and set to work preparing the noon meal. Huuo was diffident about talking with her, fearing that she would realize that he had been intimate with Scylla. He knew she would not approve, and he agreed with her nonapproval; she was in a sense the embodiment of his conscience. But guilty as he felt, he now recognized that he was in a fashion smitten with the lovely dancer, and would be bedding her again. It was the only way he could experience any part of the joy he had felt with his wife.

And Scylla wanted to marry him. By coincidence, her home city was Gaza—the same one Jaoch had invited him to go to. He could go there and have a good life, and he could take her there. She was probably right: she would be allowed to return, if she were with him. It would be an easy situation to step into, and he would not be left floundering.

But first he had to conclude his business here. So he braced himself and approached Crystal. "You could not finish your search for the bones yesterday, because of the storm," he said. "But did you locate any?"

"No. I shall have to search again today."

"I will go with you, since this is my duty." It was a duty he dreaded, but he was resolved not to continue in his dereliction.

"There is no need, master," she said quickly. She always called him that, in this house, rather than betraying the informality of friendship they had. "I will do a better job, so that you will not be burdened."

"As you will," he said, relieved.

Crystal completed the preparation of the meal, and departed on her mission. They ate, and it was good. "Your servant is competent," Scylla remarked.

"Yes. I trust her completely."

She half smiled. "Yet you did not tell her what we did."

"I am less trustworthy than she is, I fear."

The day passed, and Scylla persuaded him to play his flutes, and she danced for him, her art marred only by her bandaged hand. Then they retired to the bedroom again, inevitably.

But when another day passed, and Crystal still did not locate the bones, Huuo knew that something was wrong. "They must be there," he said. "I will find them."

"No, master," Crystal begged. "Give me one more day. They can't hide from me forever."

"I don't understand this," he said after the Canaanite left. "She should have found them by this time."

"They must be deeply buried," Scylla said. "I am sorry that this agony is being prolonged for you."

"It allows me to postpone the awful confirmation," he said. Then one thing led to another, and they were making love again.

On the third day Crystal admitted defeat. "Master, I have poked repeatedly through every part of the ruin, and have not found the bones. I think they are not there."

"But where else can they be?" he asked, his dismay mitigated by the faintly flickering hope that his family had somehow escaped the fire.

"Maybe—maybe there are no bones," Crystal said.

"No bones?" Scylla asked, startled.

"If the fire was so hot it burned them all up," Crystal said.

"I don't believe that," Huuo said, appreciating reality once the foolish notion had been uttered aloud. "Now I will find them."

"I am so sorry to have failed you in this." Crystal looked really upset, as if her emotions, too, were mixed.

"They must be there," Scylla said. "You must sift through every ash."

Huuo went with Crystal to the site of the burnout, for the first time since the night of his return to Mor. The ashes had been badly disturbed. It was evident that she had gone through them extremely carefully. It would be pointless for him to look; he could not find what she had not. "What does this mean?" he asked.

She glanced around, as if to make sure that they could not be overheard. "Huuo, it means there are no bones."

"But there have to be!"

"I had to get you alone, to tell you," she said. "There are none."

He stared at her. "Are you suggesting that—?"

"Huuo, when I couldn't find them on the first day, I suspected something was wrong. I told my husband, and he agreed to search more widely. Today he told me what he learned. A terrible, devious plot. Your family was not killed. Annai, Chipp, and Minah were carried away by the raiders. They are alive in another city."

He was stunned. "Alive?"

"We think it was a plot to deprive you of your family."

Huuo's world was turning over. "Where are they?"

"In a daughter city near Gaza. Captives of Scylla's brother Zebub."

"Scylla!" he cried. "She's part of this plot?"

"Yes. She wants to bring you to Gaza to serve Jaoch. But I think she does not know that Annai is alive. Your wife was supposed to be killed."

"This is a plot by Jaoch of Gaza, to get me to serve him?" Huuo asked, his anger building like a terrible storm. "To kill my family, and have Scylla bring me there?"

"That is as it seems to us," she agreed. "But Zebub coveted Annai for himself, so instead of having her killed he bribed the hill folk to secretly abduct her. And the children too, to be levers against her."

"But how could such a thing happen, here in Mor?"

"We think Zebub bribed some hill folk to spook their cattle on market day, and to strike directly at this house. He also bribed the chief of guards, so that there were no guards assigned to prevent the stampede or rioting. But the real purpose was to destroy your family, freeing you to move."

"And when Scylla met me on the ship, it was no coincidence," he said, working it out. "Her constant kindness to me—all part of the plot."

Crystal nodded wisely. "Actually I think she does like you. I see the signs in her. So this plot did not go against her grain. But she is laboring on behalf of her brother."

"And what is his reward for this?"

"We understand he will be promoted to chief tax collector."

"Where he will squeeze the people unmercifully, and retire extremely rich," Huuo said. "Yes, that is sufficient motive for him." He put his hand on his knife. "But as for Scylla—I will slay her today."

"No, Huuo, you must not!" Crystal cried.

"Why not? She was satisfied to see my wife and children slain, so she could seduce me."

"Because Annai and your children remain captive of her brother. If you kill Scylla, Zebub will know you have learned the truth, and will kill them."

He froze. It was true. "Then what am I to do?"

"My husband believes he can rescue them, with your approval. Let him do that. Then you can settle with Scylla."

"But how can I delay, knowing what I know?"

"You must make Scylla believe you do not know. Only thus can you protect your family."

"But that means—Crystal, do you know I have bedded her? When I thought—"

"As Anat thought Baal was dead."

"But Anat did not—oh, I should have been constant! But now, with this news, after what has passed between Scylla and me—"

"Then you must bed her again," she said.

He sat down in the ashes. "This is a wonderful and awful thing you have brought me to, my friend. My wife alive—and I must embrace her enemy!"

She kneeled beside him. "I know, Huuo. I delayed telling you until I was sure. But if you do not deceive Scylla, what you believed may well come true. You must make yourself do it."

"Oh, Crystal, I am ashamed of this," he said. "Were it any other person than you who told me this, I would not believe it. But you I must believe."

"I know." She put her arms around him, and held him while he wept.

Then they forged a suitable story, and he covered himself with ashes, and returned to Scylla's house.

"You searched thoroughly," Scylla remarked, eying him.

"No, I covered myself with the ashes, overcome with chagrin for what has happened," he said. "My wife not yet sent to the other realm, and I have dallied with another woman. How great is my shame!"

"Do not blame yourself," she said quickly. "I desired you though I knew you were in mourning. Blame me." She dropped her gaze, coloring.

Now, with the scales from his eyes, he saw the art of her presentation. She was a dancer, skilled in miming emotions, even to a blush of shame. Her act was perfect. Her robe, supposedly forgotten, had fallen slightly open in front so that the curve of one firm breast was revealed, and it fell away from one thigh. All pretense, so cleverly done that he had been deceived despite having seen similar mimes many times. Had he not been blinded by grief, he should have seen instantly through the show.

Yet to the extent that her attitude promised immediate physical rapture, it had been no pretense. She had delivered in full measure, the cup overflowing, time and again. Her body was excellent, and her performance delightful. No man could have had more satisfactory sexual experience, not even in the arms of the head priestess of the temple, a truly experienced and talented woman. Could it be that Crystal was right, and that Scylla did have genuine feeling for him? In times past she had hinted that she found him intriguing, but he had dismissed it as artifice. Now he saw the artifice, and could not dismiss the possible reality. She loved her home city, true, and sought to use him to achieve her return, but she could also find him compatible.

And so, despite what he knew, he found his desire stirring again. Just as he performed music for plays at festivals many times, and was stirred anew each time, the sight of a beautiful body and appealing manner stirred him despite his awareness of the falsity behind it. He had to hate Scylla for what she had done—what she still was doing—but also to give credit to the finesse with which she did it.

She became aware that he had not automatically reassured her, as he had done when she used a similar ploy before. She thought that the depth of his renewed grief had dulled him to such nuances. So she proceeded smoothly to the next ploy. "But come, Huuo; we must make you comfortable." She fetched a damp cloth and began to wipe his ash-grimed face, her touch gentle. More of her body showed, seemingly coincidentally, in her supposedly exclusive focus on him. He thought he should strike her down, but he knew he must not; he must let her seduce him yet again, so that he could deceive her as she had deceived him. So he let her do it.

Soon she had his face clean and was working on his body. She stripped away the soiled robe and washed him naked, and when she had him clean she brought him to her bed and down on it with her so naturally that it was as if they had been married for years. He viewed the process in the manner of a spectator, but his body responded as it had to, and soon he was in her again, his passion undiminished. But this time he appreciated the other level of it, and the quality of the manner in which she managed him. She was good at it—as good as he could imagine any woman being. Better than Annai, because Annai never pretended a passion she did not feel. Scylla had made seduction an art.

And so he realized that he did not need to pretend. He had merely to let her carry her pretense through, while he reacted as any audience would. Until the time of revelation arrived, and Baal was clear of the underworld.

❂

Annai's quest for a knife was not going well. She had found a chip of stone, but it had chipped because it was weathering, and its point would crumble when used. She needed metal, and even if she got it, she would not be able to forge it into anything effective.

She had also sought a way to escape, but the stone was solid and the mute slave woman watchful. With a sledge she might have pounded out a stone from the wall, had she the strength and endurance to do it, and if the noise of the effort did not bring the slave to disarm her. But she lacked any such tool. Her prison was tight.

Meanwhile Zebub was growing impatient. He had been away again for several days on some illicit business, but when he returned he intended to have her answer, and she knew that her son Chipp would be made to scream horribly as he died, if that answer was wrong. Without a knife she had little hope of hurting her fell captor, and if she tried and failed, Chipp would be punished in lieu of her. Realistically she had no choice: she would have to agree to Zebub's repulsive suit.

Yet somehow she hoped that the gods would deliver her from this terrible strait. "Oh, Huuo," she murmured. "If you lived, this could not endure!" For the news of his death had shriveled the heart in her, depriving her of much of her will to fight. Were it not for the children, she would have strangled herself on a rope made from her torn-up robe. But she had to do whatever she could to preserve them in body and spirit.

She lay awake in the closing darkness of dusk, beside her children. She had, she hoped, succeeded in shielding them from the worst of it, but she feared that Chipp suspected what was wanted of her, and she feared that Minah, with her attunement to the realms of the spirits, knew. For the little girl was strangely sanguine. "Don't worry, Mommy," she had whispered. "Daddy isn't dead."

Ah, if only it could be true! And Annai realized that she had only Zebub's word that Huuo was dead—and Zebub was a liar. He could have made it up, to accomplish exactly what he had accomplished: weakening her resolve to oppose him. For he could not marry her if her husband lived. But if she believed that her husband was dead, and gave her word to Zebub, then he would be able to do with her as he desired. The fact that it had no legal standing would not matter; what did Zebub care about legalities? He just wanted her cooperation for his lust, and her assurance that she would neither harm him nor flee him. He was not content with mere forcible rape; he wanted complete domination.

But this was a speculation based on mere hope. Minah might believe, and Annai would not try to spoil her belief, but she herself had no such confidence. And even if Huuo lived, the threat against her children remained. She would have to let Zebub ravish her, to protect Chipp and Annai from harm.

There was a sound at the door. It was a male grunt. Oh, no—Zebub was coming by night! To take her while the children slept. She would have to let him do it, to protect their innocence. The horror was upon her.

The bar lifted and the door opened. "Annai."

Resigned, she got up quietly, not disturbing the children. She went to meet him. "I have not yet given you an answer," she reminded him in a whisper, forlornly hoping for another delay.

"Annai, it is Carverro," he whispered back. "Will you trust me?"

She stifled an exclamation. It *was* Carverro! Crystal's artisan husband. She recognized his voice. He had come to the rescue. "Yes."

"Fetch the children and put them in my wagon under the sculptures. Dress your hair in the fashion of a Canaanite woman. You must pretend to be my wife, and the children must be silent, or we all could die."

"Yes." She went back and put her hand first on Mina's shoulder, waking her, because the girl had instincts of secrecy. "We are escaping. Wake your brother silently and go with Carverro."

Without a word, Minah sat up and then leaned over Chipp in the dark. Annai rearranged her hair, quickly binding it in the manner Crystal did, and shifted her robe to emulate the servant style. She bowed her head and assumed the posture of a lesser person. Because of her long association with Crystal, it wasn't hard to emulate the woman's mannerisms.

They went out with Carverro, and the children climbed into his little hand-drawn wagon. Annai covered them with a cloth, then carefully buried them in elegant copper pots and statues. The ride would surely be bumpy and uncomfortable, but Minah would keep Chipp quiet.

Finally Annai was able to ask the question uppermost in her mind. "Huuo—"

"Alive and well, but in the company of Scylla."

She knew what that meant. If Zebub had a lust for Annai, so also did his sister have a lust for Annai's husband. Huuo had seemed not to notice, but Annai had; the woman would have done almost anything to get him into her bed. Apparently mostly because of the challenge of it; Huuo was one of few men genuinely disinterested in her. Naturally she had moved in on him the moment Annai had been moved out.

"But—"

"Your house was burned. He thought your bones were there."

So Huuo thought she was dead, just as she had thought he was dead. What a vile plot against the two of them! Yet what had happened seemed beyond what the evil brother-sister couple should have been able to manage. Something more was going on.

"Now follow behind," Carverro said. "There are not many abroad at this hour, but we must not risk attracting any attention. This is a hostile city."

They moved out, Carverro pushing the wagon over the stony pavement, Annai walking meekly after him. There were some torches at the street corners, and some men heading home late. The traveling trader was ignored.

Until they came to the rear gate. It was already closed. "Go around to the front gate!" the gatekeeper called.

"My wife took sick and I have to take her home," Carverro called back. "I'm sure it's not the plague, but—"

"Pass!" the guard exclaimed, cranking the gate open.

They hurried through, Annai hunching even more and affecting a weak coughing spell. The very mention of plague was enough to make anyone nervous. Had they wanted to enter the city, they would have been barred, but leaving was another matter. Let some other city take the risk.

When they were well clear of the wall, the children were allowed out, bruised but satisfactory, and Annai indulged her curiosity. "How did you get by the mute slave woman?"

"I slipped bhang into her beer. She is peacefully dreaming in her chamber, not caring what occurs elsewhere."

How simple! Bhang was supposedly a mild intoxicant or hallucinogen, but samples differed; it could be made strong enough to put a person into a delirium for hours. The slave would enjoy her sleep—until the morning revealed the empty chamber she guarded. Then, if she were smart, she would hasten from the house and the city, never to be seen again, for Zebub would be furious.

"How will we return to Mor?" Annai asked. "It's a long walk, and I am not in the best of strength." For the confinement had wearied her in body as well as spirit. She had not practiced her dancing, fearing that that would lead only to more interest by her captor. "And there may be pursuit."

"You and the children will be Canaanites."

And they would be looking for a Philistine woman. It would be impossible to check every Canaanite family; there were too many of them, and they supported each other too firmly. No Canaanite would oppose a Philistine directly, but the indirect resistance could be overwhelming.

Carverro led them to a Canaanite village off the main road. They entered a lowly inn. "I have brought my wife and children," he told the proprietor. "Will you grant us sanctuary?"

"Let me look at them," the man said.

"Stand up straight and do not speak," Carverro told them.

The three of them stood straight, though Annai had a misgiving of the wisdom of this, because all of them had significant Philistine features.

The man studied them carefully. "Canaanites," he said, nodding. "They will have to work for their board."

"They will," Carverro agreed.

The man beckoned to his plump wife. "Put these Canaanites to work," he said.

Annai knew better than to protest. Canaanite men treated their women with no more respect than Philistines did. She hoped the work would not be unduly arduous, because what she wanted most was to relax with the feeling of freedom.

"You'll need uniforms," the woman said. She took them to a back room where she had them don the dull clothing of the lowly. Then she smeared grease and dirt on their faces and arms. She tied a cushion to Annai's midriff to make her appear fat. She poured coloring over Annai's head and rubbed it into her hair, changing its color. "Never speak," she cautioned. "Always obey. My husband will not hit you unless he has to."

Then Annai know that the woman knew. If a Canaanite man asked that a Philistine woman be hidden, and she was not protesting, they would hide her. By making her one of them.

Soon Annai was sweeping the dirt from the floor of the main chamber, while Chipp was cutting fish and Mina carrying ale to customers. They had hardly gotten to work before a horse galloped up. They heard its hoofbeats stop and the thump of a man jumping down.

In a moment the rider appeared in the doorway. "A Philistine cavalryman," the proprietor exclaimed loudly, so that everyone knew. "We are honored! Girl—take his cape."

There was a pause. Then the proprietor whirled on Annai, lifting his fist. "Must I beat you again to make you mind? I said take our guest's cape!"

Oh. Annai hurried up, reaching for the visitor's cape. "Get away from me, slut!" he snarled, whipping it clear of her reach. "This isn't a social call. I'm looking for a woman."

"I will have a young and pliable one brought to your room," the proprietor promised.

"Idiot! I'm not staying in this hovel. I mean a fugitive. A beautiful Philistine with two children. Have they passed this way?"

"A beautiful Philistine?" the proprietor repeated, amazed. "In a place like this?"

"I must search your premises. Stand aside, dullard, or pay the consequence."

"By all means satisfy yourself," the proprietor said, bowing as he backed off. Then he shot a glance at Mina. "Bring this fine man a mug of ale!"

Minah dashed to the kitchen area, where the wife poured out the ale. Minah brought it to the Philistine. The man hesitated, then shrugged; free ale was worthwhile at any time. He took the mug without even looking at Minah.

Of course the search turned up nothing. Soon the man was on his way to check the next inn. The three fugitives had been hidden the most effective way: in plain sight.

And not one of the customers at the tables, all Canaanites, had said a word, though all had seen the party arrive and change. For the first time Annai appreciated the solidarity of the Canaanite culture. She had trusted them not to betray her, and they were trusting her never to betray them in turn. No word of this would be spoken to the authorities.

Now Carverro and his party were served good food. "Will you tell us your story?" the proprietor asked.

"This is my wife's mistress Annai of Mor," Carverro said, startling Annai by his sudden openness. Yet she realized that this was part of the payment for their protection. Odd happenings were always of interest, in the dull outlying villages. "Her husband is Huuo, the renowned musician." There was a murmur of recognition. "They have always been good to us; we owe them. Lord Zebub abducted her for himself." He continued with the story, while they ate.

When it was done, there was applause. The folk at the tables approved of what Carverro had done. But there was a question: "Will she dance for us?"

"She has been confined, and is tired," Carverro said. "She can't—"

"No, I'll do it!" Annai said in a sudden exultation of abandon. The folk of the villages seldom got to see the presentations of the central temples. "You have protected me; I will reward you." She got up and hauled out the pillow from under her robe and unbound her hair, while the men scrambled to move the tables so that there was dancing space in the center. One of the men produced a tambourine and made a melodic beat with it, while others clapped their hands in unison.

Then Annai began to dance, at first slowly, limbering her limbs, then more swiftly, twirling and leaping with more vigor than she thought she would have. Finally she flung off the dirty robe and danced completely naked, making a scene that they would never forget. For she was indeed beautiful, and the dance enhanced her, and she knew it. This was her expression of gratitude and freedom.

When she stopped, panting with the wild exertion, she was satisfied to see stares of mesmerization all around. She had suitably impressed her audience.

The proprietor brought her a clean robe. "I never liked Philistines," he murmured, "until this night. Your name is not Annai; it is Anat."

The Canaanite goddess of war, she remembered from Crystal's stories to the children. The most volatile and beautiful of women. "Thank you."

There was more, for it took them several days to make their way to Mor with covert Canaanite help, but that was the occasion that remained in

Annai's mind: her dance of freedom, with the dazed support of the Canaanites, who might never again behold such beauty of motion. She knew that later in her life she well might encounter some of the men who had seen her here, but that not one of them would speak of it to any Philistine. It was a good kind of secret.

○

Crystal was late. It was near noon. Scylla had already seduced him for the morning. He had hoped that Crystal would arrive in time to interrupt that, but when she was late he had been caught for it. Because all he could do, while Annai and the children were captive, was maintain the pretense.

The irony was that he was now playing the same game Scylla was, deceiving her as she deceived him. If she was despicable, what was he? She drew him into sexuality, trying to win his commitment by both inciting and satisfying his passion. He acceded to it, trying to keep her ignorant so as to protect his family and win his freedom from her. Yet he could not be certain that Scylla didn't truly desire him, apart from her scheming—or that he did not desire her, apart from his own scheming. Whatever else she was not, she was one phenomenally alluring woman. So was there a core of genuine unity of desire? The notion bothered him.

He stood at the doorway, looking out, while Scylla attended herself inside. Then he saw Crystal, hurrying up. He stepped out to meet her. "When you are late, I have no protection from—"

"They're safe!" she cried. "Carverro rescued them. They are entering the city now! Soon they will be here!"

An invisible weight lifted from his back. Huuo turned and strode back into the house.

Scylla was just emerging from the lavatory. She looked beautiful, but now he wanted none of it. He wanted to do what had to be done before his family arrived. "You lied to me!" he said, lifting his left hand. "You conspired against my family!"

Her mouth and eyes went round in perfect emulation of astonishment. "What do you mean? Your family died! The hill folk—"

He struck her backhanded across the face. "They took them to your brother—while you told me they were dead."

She fell half on the couch, this time in a disarray that was not esthetic. "My brother—did that? He didn't kill them?" Her surprise seemed genuine, and it was tinged with a trace of anger. It seemed that she herself had been deceived in that respect. But it hardly lessened her guilt, if she thought Annai had been killed.

"So you could trick me into marrying you. Now I will kill you. It is my right." He drew his knife.

Scylla twisted by the couch so that she was sitting with her back against it, her legs splayed on the floor. The bruise where he had struck her was starting to show, and there was blood on her lip. She flung open her robe, baring her breasts and all else. "Then kill me!" she cried. "Stab me through the heart! I will not flinch. I am guilty." Tears flowed down her cheeks, too copious to have been forced. "But know two things, my lover: I did it for love of you and would have been a true wife to you throughout, with an excellent situation for you at the court of Jaoch in Gaza. I would never have deceived you again." She paused, fixing her eyes on his, her dishabille and wild hair making her weirdly compelling for this instant. "And when you kill me, you kill also your child within me." She touched her bare abdomen.

Both of her statements had impact. She was neither trying to escape him nor reviling him; she was professing her love for him. That could be artifice, but he couldn't be sure of that. The time of incipient death was a time of truth, and she knew he wasn't bluffing. And a child in her belly? How could she know, so soon? That much was probably a bluff. Yet he couldn't be certain. Women had ways of knowing about such things.

He covered his hesitation by grabbing her right hand. "And you pretended to be injured, to play on my sympathy for your left-handedness," he said. "Bandaging an uninjured hand." He sliced at the material, and unwound it. She did not resist.

But when the last of the swathing came off, it was caked with old blood. Her hand was now bleeding freshly, from the violence of his stripping. The injury was real. Perhaps she had done it herself, deliberately, to ensure that this aspect not betray her—but again, he could not be sure.

He couldn't kill her. Maybe she knew that her words would have that effect; maybe she had rehearsed them for this occasion, in case it came. But evil though her plot had been, and terrible as the grief it had caused him had been, she had given him what in any other circumstance would have been a man's perfect dream. Now, in her openness, her confession of defiant guilt, she was pitiful.

And, indeed, her plot had failed. Neither she nor her brother would be welcome in Gaza after this disaster. His best vengeance on her was to leave her alone.

He spat on her, and turned, and stalked out of the house, carrying only his flutes.

And there were Annai and Chipp and Minah, just arriving. He ran to meet them.

Little is really known about the Philistines, apart from generally negative Biblical accounts and more recent archaeological excavations. But they do seem to have been maligned by history. They brought a more advanced culture to Palestine, and indeed that name derives from them. Their expertise in shipcraft seems to have transferred to the Canaanites, who learned well. When the power of the Philistines was broken by King David of Israel—a nation once dismissed as rabble or hill folk—the seacoast fringe of the Canaanites took over the sea trade, now being called Phoenicians (Philistine Canaanites?—a tempting juxtaposition, but probably invalid), and became the chief rivals of the Greeks in spreading their culture around the Mediterranean Sea. The Philistine or sea people tribe of Dannuna migrated inland and may have become the Israelite tribe of Dan. The story of Samson and Delilah, vaguely echoed here, may have originated with a Philistine in the role of Samson. Indeed, the celebrated exodus of the Israelites may not have occurred as such; it could have been an aspect of Philistine history, passed along as they assimilated with the Canaanites and the Israelites, for the Philistines did indeed escape Egypt. The increasing sophistication of Israelite military and economic capacity may have derived from the Philistine model. We have surely lost much because we could not record the Philistine oral histories, which were probably kept in poetic verse. Here the validity of the David and Goliath is assumed, but there is doubt that it actually happened. It might have been a military victory later rendered into a mythical individual encounter attributed to King David to enhance his reputation. Later the Philistines were destroyed by the empires of Assyria and Babylon, as were the Israelites, but the Phoenicians remained, thanks to their distant sea trade, apt fortifications, and savvy politics that recognized tribute to the powers of the moment as the lesser of evils.

The Canaanite Poem of Baal was found on recovered tablets dating to about 1400 B.C. Aspects of it shed light on the Bible's Old Testament and on the mythologies of Greece and Egypt. The Philistines seem gradually to have adopted the Canaanite schedule of gods, so that the Bull of Baal became their hero instead of the nemesis it was to the Greeks and others. When the Philistine power was broken, Baal was reviled as an eater of babies, but though there may have been child sacrifices, these were hardly unique to Baal. Certainly Baal was originally an honorable and powerful god, as portrayed here. As for the temple prostitution—this was a standard form of worship in much of the region, and was socially proper. The Israelites, with a forbidding single male god, found it difficult to keep their people in line in the face of the sexual delights of Canaanite worship—until they hit upon the notion of making sex itself reprehensible. That may have been the beginning of a long association of religion with the condemnation of sexuality, which continues to the present, requiring the intercession of assorted religious rituals to detoxify it. The Original Sin may have started as the evil of sexual indulgence—in the temples of the gods.

Thus this seemingly inconsequential region and time may have had considerable impact on the subsequent course of human history.

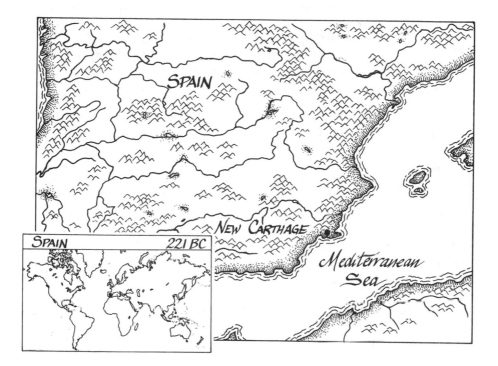

CHAPTER 12

PHOENICIAN

Once the Phoenicians, who were in a sense the seafaring arm of the Canaanites, got established, they quickly rivaled the Greeks in explorations, and may have gone considerably farther. They are thought to have circumnavigated the continent of Africa circa 600 B.C. and explored as far north as the British Isles circa 450 B.C. They founded colonies around the Mediterranean Sea and established an extensive trade network. Their language was Punic, and it spread widely. The leading city was Carthage ("New City" in Punic), a colony founded by Tyre in 813 B.C. on the north coast of Africa across the sea from

Italy. Carthage developed a formidable commercial empire, and in due course come into conflict with another developing empire: that of Rome. This was Rome's greatest challenge. Carthage lost the first Punic War (264–241 B.C.), and had to pay heavy damages, which provoked rebellion by its allies and eroded its African commercial base. But Carthage recovered by exploiting Iberia (Spain) as a resource, founding Cartagena (New Carthage, or "New New City") in 228, and rebuilding its military strength. But the politics of the day could be ferocious: Iberia was tamed by savage conquest, and the natives did not submit meekly. As was clear in 221 B.C.

HUCAR ran to meet Anice. He could see that she was worn and tired from her ordeal and travel, but she was still the loveliest creature on his horizon. They embraced and kissed, and she wept for relief. Then he bent down to sweep a child in with each arm. "I thought all of you were dead!" he said.

"And we thought you were dead," Anice said.

"Our house was burned."

"We know."

Then it stalled. There was an awkwardness. They had been apart for a month, and much had happened that they didn't want to discuss in the presence of the children.

Hucar saw the man standing nearby. "Who—"

"This is Vik, who guided us here," Anice said.

"But I thought—"

"My master had other business, so he asked me to attend to this," Vik said. He was an Iberian who bore the slave mark.

Anice had traveled with a strange man? Hucar decided to let this aspect rest for the moment. "We thank you for your service. You may now return to your master."

"My service to my master is not complete until I see you safely to New Carthage," Vik said firmly.

"He has been very good," Anice said. "We Iberians are loyal to our own."

"To the death," Vik agreed.

That brooked no refutation. The man would have to be allowed to complete his mission to the letter, lest he be severely punished on his return to his master.

"We must find a place to stay the night," Hucar said.

Anice glanced at him. "I thought you had rented a house."

Hucar looked back at the house. "That one won't do," he said tightly.

"Why not?" their son Chipu demanded. "It looks like a nice house."

"We must not know," their daughter Minih told him.

The boy accepted that. But Hucar felt uneasy; what had the spirits told her?

"The temple will give us a room for a night," Anice said. "Tomorrow we must travel on toward New Carthage."

So they walked to the temple of Tanit, where Hucar had often played his music and Anice had danced. They were known there, and would indeed be granted lodging on a temporary basis.

"I do not know whether I can afford a new house here in Baria, when this is done," Hucar said. "Everything was in the old one." This was a matter that had not concerned him during his wife's absence, because the family was so much more important. But now it loomed more formidably.

"Where do you think it would be better?" Anice asked.

"New Carthage," he said. "Perhaps we should remain there, after we have reported to General Hasdrubal. We could entertain more important families, and the rewards would be greater."

She was hesitant. "Perhaps for you. But you are Punic. I am Iberian. They might not accept—"

"Hasdrubal himself has an Iberian wife!"

"But she is a princess, whom he married for political advantage; she has to be accepted. And she is his second wife."

"But his brother-in-law Hannibal also married an Iberian woman, and she's not a princess, and not his second wife either."

"Himilce," she agreed. "From the town of Castulo. I had forgotten her. But she is beautiful."

"And you are not?" he asked challengingly. Actually at the moment she was grimy from travel, and her robe and hair were dull. But she was still the creature of his dreams. He had married her for reasons other than her appearance, but no one believed it. As a dancer, it was her business to be beautiful, and she fulfilled the requirement well. He was surprised by her information on the general's brother-in-law's wife; evidently she was aware of any other beautiful Iberians who had married Phoenicians.

"Perhaps I could dance in New Carthage," she agreed. He realized belatedly that she had sought his affirmation, perhaps supposing that he might find her unattractive after their ordeal. That was so far from the case that it might as well have been across the sea.

And she had tacitly accepted the notion of living in New Carthage. He had been afraid she would not. He wanted to get away from this city of Baria, because it had become a place of disaster and shame for him. "I am sure you can," he agreed warmly. "They will love you there."

They continued walking toward the temple. There was so much they had to say to each other, yet it was so difficult to say, and not just because of the presence of the children. After all, the children had been with Anice during her captivity. What horrors might they have seen?

For it was in his mind that she could have been raped. Such an event was almost inevitable when a lovely young woman was in the power of her enemies. He knew that she might have died, rather than submit—except for the children. To spare the children, she would do anything. But what would the sight of such a thing mean to them? She would spare them that sight if she possibly could, but she might have had no choice.

But if she had spared them the sight, she could not say so before them. They must remain innocent. So the two of them would have to be alone before they could discuss it. Then—he did not know.

They reached the temple. It took only moments to explain their situation, and they were ushered to a private suite. Far from being the bare chamber he had expected, it was a lavish miniature complex of three rooms and a bath: the type of accommodation normally reserved for a dignitary or extremely generous supporter. Probably it was not supposed to be used for a mere musician's family, but this was a slow time for visitors, so a friend in the temple had made it available. But they would have to be sure to be out before it was needed by a legitimate party. The slave Vik was given inferior lodging in the stable. He did not complain; this was the place for one of his station.

Anice had a luxurious bath, and emerged looking much improved. She donned a robe provided by the temple personnel, and worked on her hair while Hucar saw to the children's bath. He saw that they too were grimy from travel, but without bad bruises: they had not been mistreated. "What happened?" he asked as they splashed in the warm water, enjoying it much as their mother had.

Chipu launched into a from-the-beginning narrative, as was his fashion. Minih let him talk, as was her fashion. She took after her mother in appearance and manner, though she had been adopted from the temple, and it was clear that she was the dominant child despite her tendency to leave the action and expression to her brother. Hucar had often wondered whether that, too, was an accurate echo of Anice's relation to himself.

"And they wrapped us in blankets, and carried us to a wagon or something," Chipu was saying. "It was bumpy. Then they tied us up, and this man came and took us away to his house and locked us in, and his slave woman fed us. And he came and talked to Mother while we ate, and she was sad."

The man had met with Anice alone. That could mean anything from a threat to a rape. She would conceal its nature from the children, of course, but her emotion would suffer.

"And in the night Mother's Iberian friend came and rescued us," Chipu continued. "We hid in his wagon, and Mother pretended to be his wife, and we sneaked out of the city, and she danced naked in an inn. The men really goggled. Next day Vik was there, and he showed us the way and brought us here."

Anice had danced naked before strangers?

"It was all right, Father," Minih said. "They were keeping the secret."

Hucar now had a sufficient notion of their time in captivity. The children had not been abused or unduly frightened, but he wasn't sure about Anice. But one other thing bothered him. "The man who showed you the way back—Vik—what is he like?"

"He's all right," Chipu said brightly. "He showed me how to gamble with bone-bits."

"I don't like him," Minih said darkly. "He has a secret."

"He might hurt you?" Hucar asked sharply, completing the pattern of their dialogue. His son was usually cheerful, while his daughter had a streak of foreboding that was at time eerie in its accuracy. Thus Hucar paid close attention to her, but tried to seem otherwise, so that there would be no favoritism.

"No, he doesn't care about us," she said. "But there's a big pain in him."

"People do have pains. It surely isn't our business. He will go to deal with it, once he has seen us to New Carthage."

"Yes." But she continued doubtful.

When the children were ready, Hucar cleaned up too, making himself presentable. He carefully shaved the sides of his head with a razor, and reworked his single braid to be even throughout. He shaped his beard so that no hair was out of place. Then he emerged from the lavatory.

Anice was still tired, but she was beautiful again. She wore blue eye shadow, her cheeks were rouged with cinnabar, her lips were reddened, and her fingernails and toenails were orange with henna. She had applied fine perfume, and her hair was lustrous.

All of them looked good. This was necessary, because a person did not dishonor the goddess Tanit by appearing at her altar poorly garbed.

They went as a group to the main hall of the temple. This section was architecturally elegant, with massive columns, high arches, and a lovely mosaic floor. There they presented themselves before the altar. "O Tanit," Hucar said. "I come to thank thee for thy beneficence, and for saving my family from captivity, and I bring to thee this gem in token of my appreciation." He dropped a small pearl, part of his pay for a recent performance at a festival, into the altar cup.

He stepped back, and Anice approached the altar. "O Tanit, I think thee for preserving me and my children from adversity among the pagans," she said. Of course she had been pagan herself, before she married Hucar, but she had converted and worshipped primarily the Punic gods ever since. She dropped a smaller pearl into the cup, because Hucar's was the main one for the family. "And for allowing my family to stay in the temple for this night."

She stepped back, and Chipu came to the altar. He repeated the ritual, and donated a tiny grain of silver. Then Minih came, and dropped her own grain of silver. "I am with you always, my lady Tanit," she said, smiling.

There was no direct sign from the goddess, but that was good; it meant that she accepted them and their offerings. They withdrew quietly, and went to the temple mess hall for a meal. Then at last they were able to retire to their suite to catch up on rest and personal matters. It was only late afternoon, but there was no question about it: it was time for a long sleep.

The children were so tired they were asleep almost before being undressed. That left Hucar and Anice.

"We should do the same," he said. "I know you are fatigued, and tomorrow may be difficult in its own way." He was suggesting that he would not demand sex of her.

Anice smiled. "The journey was wearing, but reunion with you restores my strength." She was indicating that she was nevertheless amenable to it.

"I want nothing so much as just to hold you, and know that you are really safe and well," he said.

"Hold me close!" she agreed. She came to him and embraced him passionately. "Oh, Hucar, I feared I would never see you again."

"When I saw those ashes of our house, and believed your bones were there—"

"He told me you had come after me, and been ambushed and killed," she said, her tears flowing. "I should have known better than to believe it!"

"What did Minih say?"

"She said you were not dead. Yet I so feared—"

"We each believed foolishly," he said.

"We each tend to trust others," she agreed. "Even when we know they are not trustworthy. I should have realized that Zabub wanted only to—" She broke off, unwilling to say what was clear enough regardless.

"And that his sister was of the same stripe," he said. "There was no truth in her." Yet there was a tinge of doubt. He *hoped* she had lied throughout.

"Now we are free of them both," she said, kissing him.

He felt her warm body against him, simultaneously lithe and voluptuous and altogether wonderful. She was inviting his physical love. Yet he was conscious of the violation he had committed against her only that morning, before confirming that she was safe. He had been afraid that if he did not conceal his knowledge of her survival, she and the children would after all be killed. So he had pretended, and the seductive Scilla had done her business with him. How could he now embrace his true love similarly? There had been logic in his action, yet there was also guilt. How could he reconcile the two? So he held Anice close, but did no more.

She did not insist. She kissed him again, then relaxed. He did the same, and in due course they slept.

❁

In the morning they dressed in traveling clothing and left the temple. The Iberian slave was waiting, and joined them without a word, walking behind. Hucar had rather hoped that the slave would conclude that safe delivery to the temple of Tanit sufficed, and not insist on accompanying them farther. But evidently he had his orders, and would honor them literally.

The merchant ship was loading in the port as they got there. It was almost forty paces long and eight paces wide, with a stout mast in the center and a single bank of oars along each side. Chipu ran along it, counting the number of benches for the oarsmen: seventeen, he announced with pride. At the moment the oarsmen were on leave; their rough relaxation could be heard at the port tavern. They were not actually slaves, because slaves could not be trusted to do their best when there was need, but they were not far above slaves in status. A good oarsman was known for his muscle and his lack of imagination.

Carthaginian guards watched as Iberian laborers carried the heavy bags of silver ore and cinnabar aboard. New Carthage was located near the most productive silver mines, but it still paid to haul in the ore of lesser mines for processing there, increasing the total output. It was of course a lot of work to transport the ore, but that was what the native workers were for. The armies and labor forces of Carthage were mercenary, and generally untrustworthy, but the officers and supervisors were citizens whose loyalties were civilized. It was a feasible system, and Carthage and its colonies prospered despite the onerous reparations they had to pay to Rome. Hucar knew that the time was coming when Rome would have to be dealt with; it had won the war, but could not be tolerated indefinitely. Soon, when Punic strength was sufficient, there would be another reckoning. When Carthage was ready.

"You are thinking of war," Minih said.

"Well, these are warlike times," Hucar said.

"Tell us a story of war!" Chipu exclaimed excitedly. "With lots of blood!"

Anice shook her head. "I think your son will be an officer rather than a musician."

"It must be that Iberian blood in him," Hucar replied, teasing her.

"Don't start getting friendly with Mother," Chipu said. "You have her at night. Now it's our turn."

So it seemed. So while they waited for the loading to be completed, Hucar told them a bit of Carthaginian history, couched in dramatic terms. "Eight years ago, General Hamilcar besieged the rebellious town of Helike, not all that far from here," he said. Actually it had been part of a campaign of conquest, but the official view was that any resistance in Iberia was rebellion. "But King Orison of Helike was a cunning leader. He had oxen hitched to carts filled with hay. Then they fired the hay, and that panicked the beasts, and they charged into the Punic lines, wreaking havoc."

"Yes!" Chipu agreed, loving the action.

"Then, when Hamilcar's formations had lost their integrity—that is, got confused by the charging oxen and flaming haycarts—the Iberians launched a furious counterattack. It routed the besiegers. Hamilcar had to retreat suddenly across a river to safety, but he was wounded in the fighting, and drowned before he got across."

"But—" the boy said.

"But the Carthaginians mounted another mission and subdued that town on another day," Hucar said. "Of course. But my point is that the military life is not an easy one; there are real risks, and not just for the mercenaries. Carthage had to select a new general, and Hamilcar's son-in-law was appointed. Do you know who that was?"

"Hasdrubal!" Chipu cried. "Who we're going to see!"

"Exactly. Maybe he'll make you an officer."

"Awww—" the boy said, realizing that he was being teased.

"Hasdrubal was in Carthage at the time, subjecting some rebels in Libya, but he wrapped that up and left immediately for Spain. He was more peaceful than Hamilcar, and preferred diplomacy, and when he lost his wife he—"

"Married an Iberian princess!" Minih put in, hugging her mother's arm. "Just like you!"

"I'm not a princess," Anice protested.

"You are to us," Chipu said gallantly.

They boarded, proceeding to the stern deck where the captain was overseeing the loading. The stern post rose high and curved gracefully back over the deck. Hucar paid the captain one small gold coin for their passage and that of the slave. "Good to see you again, musician!" the man said heartily, evidently remembering Hucar's prior ride on this ship. "This time you brought your family."

"We are moving to New Carthage," Hucar agreed.

"If the wind dies, maybe you will play for the oarsmen again."

"Pray to Tanit the wind does not die," Hucar said as they moved toward the hold.

"Next thing, he'll want me to dance above the oar deck," Anice murmured, smiling. Such a performance would allow the oarsmen to peer up under her dancing skirt. Sometimes slave girls did it, but never Punic women.

The captain blew his piercing summoning whistle, and the oarsmen emerged from the tavern and came to the ship. There was no question of any skipping out on this work, because the pay was better than the men could get elsewhere, and each had his assigned place. Soon two men sat at every bench. The ship pushed off, giving room, and the oars came out and down. The cadence keeper beat his drum, and the oars moved in lovely synchronization, propelling the ship forward and out to sea. But when it was far enough out, the oars were shipped and the sail handlers took over, taking advantage of the wind. The children found the whole process fascinating, as they had never before traveled on a ship this size.

Then the guardship appeared, and now the children were truly awed. It was a trireme, a sleek warship with three banks of oars, one above the other, each bank as big as those of the merchant ship. It forged swiftly through the water, its deadly ram leading the way. It made a pass at the merchanter, as if to ram it amidships, and the children screamed. The captain was not amused. "Veer off, oafs!" he bawled, shaking his fist.

The warship lifted its oars and turned, passing so close that the oars of both ships would have been sheared off if they had remained in the water. The wash of its passage rocked the merchanter. "Oooo!" Minih cried, delighted, as the merchant oarsmen chuckled.

The captain turned away. "The fools will have their sport," he grumbled. But his scowl lacked force; he was used to this, and perhaps had even allowed it in order to give the children a thrill. One thing was clear: it would be a foolhardy pirate who thought to attack this vessel, protected as it was by a first line warship.

Safely ahead, the trireme benched its oars and spread its own square sail, satisfied to loaf along at the lumbering velocity of the merchant ship. They could see her oarsmen, now off-duty, drinking their cannabis tea. Chipu waved, and several men waved back, giving the boy another thrill.

Because silver ore was heavy rather than bulky, compared to a cargo of wood or crockery, there was room in the storage chambers. The slave would be able to sleep in one section, and the children in another, and Hucar and Anice in a third. But they were well rested now, and the children preferred to run along the decks, screaming. The slave got into a game of dice with some oarsmen. Hucar and Anice practiced their music and dancing. For them this was no chore, but business and pleasure. A number of the oarsmen were watching as Anice moved and turned and spun and leaped, but it didn't matter; her dance was meant to be seen, just as his music was meant to be heard.

Meanwhile the shoreline passed slowly by, as the ship proceeded northeast. The wind did change, and the oars did have to be used for a while, so Hucar did play. Anice didn't dance, then, but little Minih did, doing a credible job of it. She was only seven years old, but a lovely child, and she did know the moves. The trireme drew alongside so that their men could view the dance too. "They are watching her too closely," Anice said, her eyes narrowing, and Hucar could only agree. The humor of tough oarsmen extended only so far; when they watched the dance through to its end, Hucar knew that they were seeing something that interested them. Minih's thighs were thickening and her waist was thinning; when she whirled, her hair and skirt flared together, becoming suggestive. Had the child been any older during the abduction, she would have been in the same type of danger as her mother. It was a sobering thought.

Captain Ittui came to join them for a while. "I am glad to see you and your wife safe," he said to Hucar. "And your little girl," he added, squinting at Minih. "I admit I was concerned, when the news came."

"The news?" Hucar asked blankly.

"Did you not know? When General Hasdrubal learned of your wife's abduction, and confirmed that it was the work of an Iberian faction, he not only sent a spy to rescue her; he had the headman executed. The whole thing was done in a day."

"That was where our rescuer went!" Anice exclaimed. "To kill the chief."

"Or to carry the order to the appropriate authority," Ittui said. "The forms must be followed."

"So the slave guided you instead," Hucar agreed. "And said nothing."

"That was just as well," she said. "If I had realized what was going on, I would have been terrified. That chief's people must be extremely frustrated."

The slave approached. "They are," he agreed. "There has seldom been such anger."

"I never knew a thing about it," Anice said, amazed.

"Neither did I," Hucar said.

"That ignorance protected you," the slave said. "But it will not protect the guilty one." He walked away.

"I *knew* he had a secret," Minih said triumphantly, returning from her dance.

"Yet I wonder whether justice was done," Hucar said musingly.

"Howso?" Captain Ittui asked.

"As I understand it, few knew that my wife remained alive. The abductor's own sister seems not to have known. So probably the chief didn't know either. I was supposed to be the target of that mission: they wanted to bring me willingly to the chief's court."

"So the chief was guilty," Ittui said. "The one who gives the orders is responsible, no matter how they are carried out. I know. When I order a man overboard, I don't pitch him myself, but I am responsible."

"But what of the man who actually abducted me?" Anice asked.

"He's guilty too—for not killing you," Ittui said firmly. "For private lust he compromised his orders, and caused the mission to fail. But he probably disappeared the moment word got out. The sneaky ones are hard to nail."

Anice nodded somewhat wanly. "He was guilty," she agreed.

"I am glad of that guilt," Hucar said, shaken. "It saved your life."

"The gods work in meandering ways," the captain said, and moved on to see to other business.

"That slave is angry too," Minih said.

"Everyone should be angry about such a plot against a Punic family," Hucar said. "It brought us endless anguish."

"Yes," the child agreed, but she seemed doubtful.

A suitable wind reappeared as evening came, and the sails came out again. They would travel through the night, rather than risk the valuable cargo in a port. It was safe enough, with no storm threatening and a competent captain and crew.

After the others were asleep, Hucar and Anice settled down together, effectively alone. The gentle sway of the ship was pleasant. She snuggled close, and this time he had no pretext to avoid making love. Yet still the guilt weighed on him. He had lain with another woman during his wife's absence, and though there had seemed to be a rationale at the time, it poisoned his outlook now.

She knew it, of course. "Last night you let me rest," she whispered. "But tonight I am rested. Am I not desirable to you?"

"Oh, yes! But—"

"Let's not speak," she said. She was now naked beside him under their blanket, and he was too. She embraced him, and he felt her smooth breasts and thighs against him.

But there was that aspect of him that did not react. Appalled, he did not know what to say. This had never happened before.

"Or perhaps we should speak," she said, drawing a little apart. "For it seems that I am not after all—"

"No! You are beautiful!"

"You believe that I was raped," she said. "It has destroyed your love."

"No!" he exclaimed, newly appalled. She thought that the failure was in her rather than in him. "That would not—"

"And you suppose that I would conceal this from you, so you can no longer trust me." Her words were becoming blurred, and he knew she was crying.

"No!" he cried a third time. "That's not it at all! You could be raped a thousand times and I would still love you. And I do love you, no matter what—"

"Your body gives you the lie. Oh, Hucar—"

He realized that he would have to expunge the guilt between them; it could not be hidden. "Anice, I swear to you by the goddess Tanit and my honor as a man—" He realized that was invalid, for his honor was tarnished. "Anice, will you believe what I tell you?"

"Of course," she said doubtfully.

"I love you. I desire you. There is no fault in you. But I—there is fault in me. I—the Iberian woman—"

"You have evinced a taste for Iberian women," she said, with a trace of humor admixed with the tears. "It seems the plotters were aware of that."

He realized that that could have been a factor. Scilla had been like Anice in some respects, being a beautiful Iberian dancer. But that did not absolve him. "I lay with her. Now I don't deserve you."

She was taken aback. "You don't deserve me? But I am the one who has been compromised. I was captive of a man who desired me."

"And forced you," Hucar said. "But you can not be blamed for that."

"He didn't get to that. But he threatened to kill the children if I didn't submit. And I resolved to submit, rather than—"

"Of course you did," he said. "You would do anything to save the children, and I would not have it otherwise. But I did not have any such excuse. I thought that you and the children were already—"

"So nothing remained to hold your loyalty."

"But then I learned that you were alive, and I lay with her again."

She was silent a moment. Her body was abruptly tense. She had finally discovered his point. But she didn't give up. "Why?"

"Because you were not yet free."

There was another pause. Then she relaxed. "If I had lain with Zabub, lest he kill Chipu, would you condemn me?"

"No! But—"

"And if you lay with Scilla, lest her brother kill me, should I condemn you?"

His guilt began to thin. "But she—I—"

"She was good at it?"

"Yes."

"I can not think of any man who would not enjoy being in her arms. But did you love her?"

"No. But—"

"You did what I was prepared to do. You said you would not condemn me. So do you condemn yourself?"

"There is more," he said tightly.

Her body tensed again, then relaxed; she was learning control. "What more?"

"She—when I knew you were safe, and was about to kill her—"

"You killed her?" Anice asked, horrified.

"No. Because she said she—she carried my child."

At last she appreciated the whole of it. "Oh, my."

They were silent for some time.

At last Anice spoke again. "That woman is beautiful, but she would lie to gain advantage, and certainly to save herself. You threatened to kill her. She knew how to protect herself. So perhaps you were a fool. But it clarifies how you felt about her."

"Yes."

"I am glad there is no such blood on your hands. Let's yield this night to this discussion, and let it be forgotten tomorrow."

"Agreed," he said, much relieved.

They kissed, diffidently, and lay back. It did not take them long to sleep.

✪

Hucar woke to Anice's kiss. It was dark, with only the wan suggestion of false dawn. "It is tomorrow," she whispered.

For a moment he was confused. Then he took her meaning. They had agreed to leave his guilt behind with the prior day. There would be no more discussion of it. She had paid him the compliment of approaching him early rather than late. His love for her swelled explosively. He clasped her, and this time his potency was phenomenal. They had resolved their separation, in the closest way.

Just in time, for the moment the first glow of color showed across the sea, the children scrambled to join them. "You made up!" Minih exclaimed happily.

Hucar exchanged a silent look with Anice. That child was eerie!

The ship had made good time, and soon approached the harbor of New Carthage. They disembarked, and the slave followed.

The city was huge, compared to Baria, with people thronging the streets. All four of them gazed around in wonder. There certainly should be a good market here for the skills of a competent musician and dancer.

They made their way to the court of Hasdrubal. "Ah, Hucar!" the official at the entrance said. "And your family, all safe. The general wants to talk with you about that plot, to be sure complete justice has been done. He is at the altar now; you can see him the moment he is through."

It was not surprising that General Hasdrubal was at worship. Religion was extremely important to civilized Carthaginians, and the many gods were constantly consulted and propitiated. Most of the ceremonies that Hucar and Anice performed at were religious in nature.

They followed the official, and the slave followed them, being part of their party. They came to an elegant temple annex, where there was a massive silver altar to Baal Hammon and Tanit, the leading male and female gods. Baal Hammon was nominally the most powerful one, but Tanit, as his wife and the Earth Mother, was perhaps the one most worshipped, and certainly she received the greatest number of human child sacrifices, the most valuable kind. Foreigners tended not to understand this aspect of worship, but the fact was that while small commercial offerings sufficed on a day to day basis, blood was required for ceremonial occasions, so animal sacrifices were standard. That was the *mulk 'immor,* a lamb or kid. But when there was a very special event, the goddess required a very special offering, and there was nothing more precious than an innocent human being. Thus the *mulk ba'al,* the sacrifice of a child. Hucar understood and accepted this, but had been privately relieved when his own children passed beyond the age limit.

They waited beside a statue of Baal Hammon, in the aspect of a bearded man flanked by a bull and an eagle. Through the archway Hucar saw the general kneeling at the altar. Such devotions could not be hurried; they had to be done according to form, lest the gods be affronted.

"That is Hasdrubal?" the slave inquired.

"Yes," Hucar agreed absently. Surely it was time for the slave to go home, having delivered them safely to this site.

Minih screamed. Then the slave drew a wickedly long knife and charged into the sacred chamber.

"What—?" Hucar started.

"Stop him!" Minih cried.

Guards appeared from hidden crevices and ran after the slave. But they were too late. The slave dived at the kneeling man and plunged his knife into the general's neck. Blood spurted.

Then the first guard caught up. With one smart chop he split the slave's head and face into halves. The slave fell, dead. But General Hasdrubal was also dead.

Hucar and Anice exchanged a stare of absolute horror. They had brought that slave! He was an impostor, on a mission of Iberian vengeance. He hadn't cared about his own life, as long as he killed Hasdrubal. He had achieved vengeance for the execution of his chief.

What had they done?

When General Hasdrubal was assassinated in Iberia, in revenge for his execution of an Iberian chief, Hamilcar's son Hannibal was given the buckler and sword of Carthaginian leadership at the age of twenty-four. He had already served six years as a highly ranked military commander under his brother-in-law. He was well regarded by his troops, had a brilliant military mind, was an outstanding horseman, and as a soldier he excelled in all facets of the military existence. He dressed as simply as his troops, and had an Iberian wife. But he was of a more hawkish disposition than Hasdrubal. So perhaps it is not surprising that he led Carthage into the second Punic War with the powerful city-state of Rome, and consistently defeated the Roman armies, even in Italy itself, for fifteen years. The second Punic War lasted from 218 to 202 B.C., when Rome finally prevailed by attacking Carthage in Africa, forcing Hannibal to return to fight on ground chosen by the Romans. But even when Carthage was later destroyed, the Phoenician presence and culture remained along the southern Mediterranean region for centuries, as part of the Roman Empire.

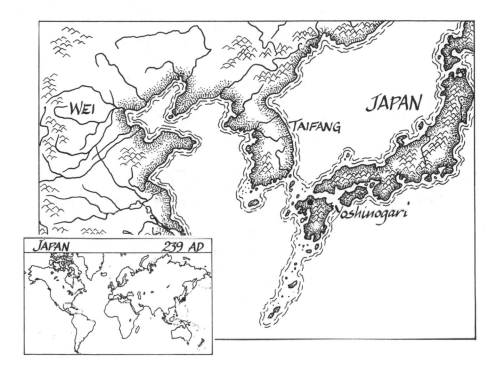

WEI

JAPAN

TAIFANG

Yoshinogari

JAPAN   239 AD

CHAPTER 13

YAYOI

At the southern tip of Japan, where it most closely approaches the peninsula of Korea, on the island of Kyushu, about thirty miles south of the modern city of Fukuoka, an ancient site is being excavated. This is Yoshinogari, a settlement once fortified by wooden fences and ditches, enclosed by a moat more than 900 meters long. It may have been the capital of the state of Yamatai, dominant in the Yayoi culture of 300 B.C. to A.D. 300. This is important in Japanese history because it was the time when the practice of growing rice in wet paddy fields developed. Rice was to dominate Asiatic food production for the following millennium and a half.

For three-quarters of a century Yamatai was ruled by kings, and was torn by wars and civil disturbances. Finally the people chose a queen instead: Himiko. She ushered in a period of peace and prosperity. She also practiced international diplomacy by sending an envoy to Korea requesting an audience with the Chinese emperor. The great Han Empire had by then fragmented, but its successor state in the northeast had considerable power. This mission occurred in A.D. 239.

HYU shook his head as he emerged from the paddy. This life was wearing him down, physically and spiritually. He was a musician, not a farmer. But what could he do? He was lucky even to be alive. He wore the tattoos of an elite entertainer, but his loss of status had brought him and his family to the lowest level.

It was dusk, and they had put in another grueling day weeding the rice. Hyu's feet were dirty and swollen in their wooden clogs, and his hands felt raw. He had a backache from the continual leaning over required. Ani and the children were no better off. They had gone from a fairly easy life-style to the most wearing life-style, and it weighed on them all.

Ani emerged from the muck and flashed him a smile. How he loved her in that moment—and always. She never complained about their situation, but simply made the best of it. But he hated to see her filthy and bent over. Her once-lustrous hair was now a dull braided mat. Instead of powder on her face and paint on her body to enhance her beauty, she now wore the caking of mud. She was a dancer, who should be making her exquisitely choreographed motions in a temple. How could such beauty be reduced to such a life?

Ten-year-old Chipo and eight-year-old Mini waded out of the paddy, and stood in their clogs on the land between fields. The paddies were below the normal ground level, divided by earthen embankments which served both as barriers to control the water flow and as paths. Now all the laborers were walking back toward the village, ready to eat and sleep and drag themselves up before dawn for the next long day.

An overseer came on a routine check of the fields. Hyu, Ani, and the children quickly stepped off the path to make way, and kneeled humbly until the man passed, in the prescribed manner for the lowly. The man was one Hyu knew, but he did Hyu the favor of pretending not to recognize him. Loss of status was a shameful thing. Hyu had considered killing himself, but Ani would not allow it; they had after all been blameless, the victims of bad fortune. She believed that in time the spirits would relent, and allow them to recover status.

Not far away were the palisades protecting the moat that surrounded the main village. Tall watchtowers rose inside it, so that the guards could get early news of any enemy's approach. The raised storage silos were in there, and the larger houses of the elite class. Of the men who could afford to have two or three or even more wives. In fact, the most important center of the village was additionally shielded by a water-filled ditch buttressed by two parallel wooden walls. But Hyu's family did not go there. Plebeians lived outside the defenses.

They passed a small grove of mulberry trees whose leaves were reserved for the valuable silk worms. But neither Hyu nor any member of his family wore silk; they could afford no better than long grasses and cotton for their clothing.

Hyu's house was made from thatch which sloped all the way to the ground. Above it was a second roof, whose thatch served to protect the house from the strong daytime sun; this shading had a significant cooling effect, and made the house a relative pleasure to be in. The second roof also helped keep the rain of storms out, so that there was not too much dripping inside.

Inside were four wooden posts. In the center was a clay pit hearth. A raised earthen bench supported by rough cut wood marked off the edge of the living area. This acted as a shelf for storage, as a seat, and as a barrier to water that seeped beneath the thatch. The house they had had before their cruel demotion had had wooden walls, was considerably larger, and had distinct rooms. But this one had to settle for flimsy room dividers.

Ani got to work making a fire and cooking a fish for supper, while Hyu brought out his bamboo flute and played a melancholy tune. The children fetched a basin with water and washed up. When they were clean and fed and in bed, Hyu and Ani would wash and talk a bit before sinking into their own resigned slumber.

"Why is it like this?" Chipo demanded rhetorically, trying to pick a quarrel with his sister as they used their fingers to pick out pieces of fish from their wooden bowls.

But no one could quarrel with Mini against her will. "It doesn't have to be," she replied.

"Just because we happened to be near when the stupid king died," Chipo said. "When they knew we didn't do it."

"Had they not known that, they would have slain us all," Mini reminded him.

"So they punish us anyway. Where's the sense in that?"

Hyu paused in his playing. "We are tainted by proximity," he explained. "There is nothing to be done about it."

"Mini said it doesn't have to be," Chipo reminded them.

That was true. "Why did you say that, Mini?" Hyu asked.

"I just know."

Hyu would have dismissed that, but for his daughter's uncanny certainty about things for which there was no natural explanation. But she couldn't answer questions that were not properly couched. "Is there something we can do to restore our social standing?"

"Yes," she said without hesitation.

He couldn't ask what, because that would leave her blank. But he might narrow it down. "Is there someone to whom we might apply for reprieve?"

"Yes."

And he couldn't ask who; that was too direct. But he was beginning to hope that there was something there. "An important person?"

"Yes." Mini answered immediately, without thought. That was the way it had to be, because doubt was a human quality, and what they sought was an answer from the spirits.

"A man?"

"No."

Now he was close enough to gamble. There was only one really important woman. "Queen Himiko?"

"Yes."

"But she won't talk to any man," Chipo protested. "She has a thousand maidservants, but only one man, and all he does is carry messages in and out of her quarters." He did not say what others did: that Queen Himiko was of mature years and unmarried; she evinced no personal interest in any man, and probably kept that one man mainly as a way to communicate messages to other leaders who were disdainful of women. Her whole effort seemed to be to avoid quarrels, even about the place of women.

Mini shrugged, not debating it.

"Maybe if your mother went to plead our case—"

"No."

Suddenly it came to him. "The queen is adept in shamanistic knowledge! She understands the spirits. And we have one here who—"

"Yes," Mini said, smiling. She had not understood it herself until he led her to it, but she recognized its truth.

"I wonder," Ani said thoughtfully as she brought a bowl of fish to Hyu. "If she gained an audience with the queen, and begged for some way to erase the cloud on our name—"

"Is there any harm in trying?" Hyu asked.

"No," Mini said. "She will agree."

There was no further discussion, but the matter was not forgotten. Mini's insights usually were correct in essence if not in detail. She had feared disaster for the family before it happened, without being able to define its nature, and it had come; now she anticipated relief.

When the children were in bed, Hyu removed his soiled headband and dropped his loincloth, and Ani slipped her dirty dress off over her head. She stood naked for a moment, glancing at him in a tacit query, but he looked away, not requiring sex this night. She was as lovely as ever, but they were both simply too tired. They washed their bodies, and then Ani rinsed their clothing and hung it up near the dying fire to dry during the night.

Hyu took her hand as she joined him in bed. "I would do anything to deliver you from this," he murmured.

"There is no need, as long as I am with you," she replied.

His love swelled and seemed to overflow the house itself. "If you are not the best wife a man could have, I can not imagine a better one."

She kissed him. "With you, I feel like the best."

Nevertheless, he hoped that Mini was right about their obtaining deliverance from the queen.

So it was that a few days later Ani took Mini to the royal house and begged an audience for the child. Hyu knew that if Mini managed to navigate the bureaucratic curtains and actually talk to the queen, she would make an impression. For in this respect Mini was unique: she really did relate well to the spirits. Hyu suspected that had Mini not been with them when the king died, their whole family would have been slain out of hand. But one deep look in the child's face was enough to give any person pause—particularly anyone who had more than incidental rapport with the spirit realm.

The queen had deeper rapport than anyone. She would be amazed when she met Mini. Hyu wished he could be there to watch, but of course that was impossible.

In due course Mini emerged from the house, and Ani brought her home. "What did she say!" Chipo demanded.

"Nothing," Mini said complacently.

"But—"

"But she listened."

It was not long before they learned how well the queen had listened. A lesser male official came to their house and spoke gruffly to Hyo. "The queen needs a man with mourning cloth for an extremely important mission. Are you that man?"

Hyu felt a chill. But there was only one feasible answer. "I am."

"Follow me."

And with that, without time even for preparation or parting from his beloved family, Hyu left his home to report for a mission from which he might never return.

❂

The ship was not intended for the open sea, but was the best that the queendom of Yamatai had. It carried as its cargo two ranking officials as envoys, four male slaves, six female slaves, and two rolls of fine cloth. And as protection from the spirits, one keeper of taboos: Hyu. He was forbidden to wash himself, comb his hair, rid himself of fleas, eat meat, or have contact with the opposite sex. He ate alone, and from the scraps left by others. He did no physical work, and seldom spoke to anyone else. His only task was to give the spirits his utmost devotion, so as to win their approval of the mission. If he failed, and things went wrong, he would be assumed to have been remiss. But if things went right, his reward would be great: the complete restoration of his status. The tainted reputation of his family would be forgotten, expunged from the records and from all human speech as a vile temporary error.

Mini believed he would be successful. But Mini was still a child, albeit an exceptional one already verging on beauty. She might have misunderstood the spirits. Still, the auspices were good; the bones of an ox had been baked, and Queen Himiko herself had read the pattern of the cracks the fire made in the bones. The presence of Hyu was the last incentive for success; he had excellent reason to desire it, and would influence the spirits on the venture's behalf if he possibly could. So the queen believed, and he hoped she was as correct about his influence as about his motivation.

The wind was fair and firm. It bore the ship northwest toward the enormous mainland of China. This was a good initial sign, for the spirits controlled the winds. But the spirits could be fickle, teasing mortals with favorable indications, then dashing their hopes. There was far more than mere traveling involved; if the emperor of China rejected the overture, they could all be doomed. The mission would not be done until they returned successfully.

They made it to the first interim island on the first day, and docked in a comfortable harbor for the night. The men made a bonfire on the shore, and the girl slaves entertained them with an appealing and suggestive dance. But that was as far as it went; these women were virgins, and would remain so until presented to the emperor.

Hyu, being a musician, was allowed to play for the dance. That was a pleasure, for him and for the others, because he was good at it, and had not played at any ceremony for some time. He hoped this was a signal of continuing success.

The scraps he was left were unusually generous this time. Protocol required that he dine on nothing better, but protocol could be bent if the leaders of the party allowed it. The envoys turned their backs, officially not noticing.

Hyu slept on the ship. It was uncomfortable and exposed, but this was his role; if he left it, something might happen to it, and the blame would be his by definition. The others had more comfortable lodging on the shore.

As he lay and looked at the stars, analyzing the constellations, he heard something. He did not move; instead he oriented on the sound, ready to act if he had to, though he did not know what he might do. It seemed to be a person, but not Captain Itti or one of the officials, because they would come boldly with lights. This one was trying to be quiet, and had no light, so was stumbling a bit as he moved. A slave? What could he want? There was nothing to steal, and everyone knew that Hyu was here.

The steps came up to the ship and paused. Then the figure spoke. "Hyu."

Hyu was surprised. It was a woman! One of the female slaves. "What are you doing here?" he asked.

"Do you not know me?" she asked. "I am Lee."

The name stirred a faint familiarity, but he couldn't place it. "I know you are one of the six beautiful virgin slaves destined for the emperor of China. I don't know any of your names."

"You played music at my village when I was a child. We have a distant family connection. I fell in love with you, but you had no interest. When my family later fell into misfortune, they had to sell me into slavery. Because I turned beautiful as I matured, I fetched a good price."

What was this? "You know me from before the taint on my name?"

"Yes. And before the ruin of my own family. I was thrilled when I saw you with this voyage. We have much in common."

This was mischief. But he did not want to jump to an awkward conclusion. "What is your purpose in coming here to the ship?"

"Just to talk with you. To let you know that I still desire you."

So he had not misunderstood. "I am the keeper of taboos. I may not touch a woman during this mission."

"Who would know?"

"The spirits would know! They would destroy the mission."

"Oh, who believes that nonsense? Nobody cares as long as the forms are followed. Let me come aboard and show you what I have learned beyond dancing."

The irony was that he did not believe that his role would have any effect on the mission. It would succeed or fail as it was destined to, and his reward or punishment would follow because of no credit or fault of his own. But he had undertaken to fulfill this role, and intended to do so. Since Lee obviously had no such concern, he gave her a different negation. "The emperor would know."

She laughed. "The emperor will never see any of us. We'll be taken by his lower officers. In any event, none of us are true virgins; it's merely a role we play, as you play yours. We are simply beautiful girls to be enjoyed. Everyone knows that. But seldom do we have opportunity to be enjoyed by one we really like."

Hyu had not known what she claimed everyone did, and distrusted it. But he was not in a position to refute it. So he gave his real reason. "I am married."

"I know. And you have no second wife. But you can have me for this journey—a temporary second wife, until we separate."

She was determined! But he had experienced an affair with some disturbingly similar elements, and been disgusted. He wanted no more of it. "I agree you are beautiful, and that you would surely be a delightful partner. But I took an oath to fulfill my role in this mission, and I shall do it. Please go quietly back to your associates and speak no more of this." He was being careful not to offend her, because he knew that an angry woman could cause as much mischief as a loving one.

"But there is so little time," she protested. "Only this night, and tomorrow, and perhaps another. Then we shall never meet again, and I will have lost my only chance to embrace the man I love."

She sounded so winsome that he was tempted in spite of his resolve. But he knew better than to yield. "I regret causing you distress. But so it must be. Leave me now."

She began to cry, but he remained firm. Finally she departed. He lay back again and stared at the stars, feeling like a fool. Perhaps it was a construction of his imagination, but he seemed almost to remember an association with her before, with her offering him devotion and sex, and him declining. But it surely hadn't happened in this life! Finally he succeeded in sleeping.

✪

Early in the morning the trip resumed. This time the winds were contrary, but the sailors made the best of it, sailing slantwise, one direction and then another, and managed to reach the next island by nightfall.

Again the others camped on land, while Hyu remained on the boat. Again the slave girl Lee came to beseech his interest. And again he turned her down, politely.

On the third day they made it to the mainland. There was a party there to meet them. They were guided to a town where they were given housing and required to wait while a messenger carried the news of the mission to the governor of the region, Liu Hsia.

In due course the governor's response came: bring the party to the capital. This was some distance away, necessitating several days of travel, but it turned out to be other than onerous, because the governor arranged for transportation. Now they rode in wagons instead of in the ship, with armed horsemen guarding them. Hyu wondered whether this was a show of honor, or a necessary precaution lest brigands attack, and concluded it was both.

There were no more nocturnal visits by the slave girl. Hyu knew why: the girls were now under the protection of the emperor of China, and were given no freedom to wander about by day or night. But he received an incidental additional insight on the matter from Captain Itti: "So you are constant, as I expected."

"Constant?"

"You are taking your role seriously. You sent the girl away. Twice."

"You knew of that?" Hyu asked, surprised.

"I should. I sent her to you."

"But why?"

"We made a bet. The envoys thought you could be corrupted. I said you could not. They said that any man can be corrupted by sufficient temptation and sufficient secrecy. That is, if there is something he desires, and he can have it without others knowing, he will take it, regardless of his oaths. So we put it to the test. I am pleased to say that I won a considerable wager."

Hyu was not completely pleased with this news. "You took a considerable risk! Suppose I had not been true to my vow? Not only would you have lost your wager, the mission itself would have been in peril."

Itti shrugged. "I am a believer in the fates. I have not observed the wind to change at the behest of men, though there are those who choose to believe otherwise. Whatever will be, will be. But if you are truly an indication of the auspices for this mission, then its fate has already been set, and the best we can do is confirm it early. That is, if you can be corrupted, then the mission is doomed to fail anyway. If I knew that was the case, I would act to spare myself the consequence of that failure. Since you were true, the mission is presumed to be fated for success, and that is reassuring."

"You believe that?"

Itti shrugged again. "The rationale will do until the confirmation. Meanwhile the others are reassured, and are proceeding with greater confidence."

So there had been more riding on the slave girl's proposition than Hyu had guessed. Was it a valid indication? His doubt echoed the captain's doubt, but he had to agree that a reassured envoy was better than one who expected to fail. Meanwhile, neither of them would be speaking of this matter elsewhere, and surely the envoys would keep the secret also.

But what of the girl, Lee? Now he knew that she had been put up to it—but would she have done it if he had agreed? What of his seeming memory of a prior encounter? Her statement that she had heard him play at her village, which he also seemed almost to remember? Were the spirits playing with him by providing a woman who really did like him, and a situation that would enable her to destroy him?

But if he believed that the spirits really were active here, then he had also to believe the certainty of his daughter Mini that the success of the mission was assured. That was more comforting.

✺

By the time they reached the palace of the governor, swift messengers had evidently already carried the news farther, because not only did the governor welcome the party, he had decided to accompany them to the Imperial capital himself. This meant a much farther journey, but it was also done in better style, for the governor was not one to allow himself to suffer the indignities of the open road. They rode in a caravan of closed coaches, with a small army of horsemen as guards. If there were any brigands in the area, they were careful to stay clear, because any attack on the governor's party would have been suicidal. At regular intervals they stopped for quite good meals, and always parked at night in protected camps.

However, Hyu himself did not have the best of it. The envoys explained his purpose, so he was tolerated, but he was largely confined to an isolated wagon where menial slaves congregated. He did not speak their language, but they took him for one of their kind, and treated him affably. On occasion he brought out his flute and played for them, and then they became quite pleasant; they seldom had entertainment of this level. He began to learn some of their words, so that the problem of communication diminished. When they learned his actual role, they thought it hilarious: he was actually of the elite class, being treated worse than a slave.

The journey north took a full month. Hyu saw the glittering curling roofs of the great city and its temple palaces, and wished he could inspect them closely, but only the envoys and their offerings were allowed to enter the city. In due course—after several days—the envoys returned without their offerings, but with a sealed scroll and some wrapped packages. They seemed pleased, but Hyu was not close enough to speak with them. Thus he remained in some doubt about the success of the mission, and his own fate.

Then something unexpected occurred. The chief envoy approached him. "The emperor has feted us in a manner beyond our expectation," he said. "We find ourselves embarrassed to be unable to respond in kind. But you are a fine musician; we know your reputation, and we have heard you play."

"I can not go near the emperor!" Hyu protested. "I must neither clean myself nor accept any benefit."

"But it is in your interest to forward the success of our mission. We do not ask you to accept any reward, merely to give, so that we may leave the emperor without the shame of inadequacy."

This made sense. "What do you wish me to give?"

"Your music. You must play your flute for the emperor."

"But—"

"We will put you behind a curtain, so that his eyes need never be soiled by the sight of your squalor, and we will surround you with perfumes to cover your odor. You will not speak. You will only play. One melody."

They had thought it through. "As you wish."

They bundled Hyu in a voluminous cape, completely hiding him from the view of others, put him in a wagon that carried him to the palace, then guided him through the labyrinth of the royal demesnes to a chamber formed of standing white panels. There they unwrapped him. The odor of perfume was so strong as to make him catch his breath. "On my signal," the envoy said, standing at the angled entrance of the chamber.

Hyu stood with his flute. He glanced up, and saw the enormous vault of the palace ceiling, more elaborate and majestic than anything he had seen in Japan. Awed, he studied its intricate painted ridges and angles, becoming lost in the intricacies of the pattern.

"Hssst!"

Hyu was jolted out of his reverie. The envoy was making the signal. So he lifted his flute and began to play. But his eyes returned to the marvelous ceiling, whose wonders seemed endless.

The melody floated out, filling the small chamber, reaching up to caress the lovely ceiling. Hyu felt the echoes of that surface, and adjusted his style and beat to accommodate it. It became a collaboration, and the ceiling enhanced his quality of tone, making the melody more than it could ever have been alone. The faint reverberations surrounded him, and guided him, and he played as never before. He seemed to be floating amidst the music, breathing it, loving it.

Then it was done, and he had to stop. The melody was complete, and could not be extended; it established its own boundary. But it had been an experience he would never forget.

He waited for them to come with the cloak to take him away, but there was a pause. Then a panel lifted, silently, making a gap in the temporary wall the size of a door. Hyu looked through the hole that appeared, all but his eyes remaining still.

There sat a man who could be only the emperor, surrounded by his courtiers. He wore a bright yellow robe with a dark dragon embroidered on the chest. His head was covered by a simple cap that covered his hair. His eyes gazed straight at Hyu.

Hyu did not know what to do. Had someone made a mistake, and opened the wrong panel? He in his filth was not supposed to be revealed to the emperor! Yet here he was abruptly exposed. And no one was giving any indication of his proper response; it was as if the entire city were frozen.

Caught completely unprepared, Hyu could think of only one thing to do: pretend that all was in order. Slowly he bowed his head to the emperor, making a token obeisance to the lord of China, hoping that this act was not insulting in its presumption.

There was absolute silence. Then the emperor, expressionless, bowed his head in return.

The panel came down, separating them. Hyu was suitably isolated again, and free to move. He turned to look at the envoy—and caught him standing open-mouthed.

❁

The trip back south took another month, and then several more days to the shore where their ship waited. They set off with a light cargo. Only then did Hyu get to speak again with Captain Itti. "The news is good. But we still must cross the sea. If a storm takes us out, all is lost."

The news was good. Hyu felt substantial relief. But exactly how good was it? That, too, made a difference.

The captain did not leave him in doubt. "The emperor—you never saw such finery!—met the envoys personally. I was allowed only to the adjacent room, but I got a peek at him. He seemed quite touched by their message and gifts. He strikes me as a vain man, and such a compliment to his authority encouraged him to a generous response. He met with them, then retired for two days while they were treated sumptuously, then met with them again and gave them the scroll. And unless it says to behead them upon their return, it means the success of the mission. We should all benefit handsomely."

"But what of the time I played?" Hyu asked.

"The envoys set it up," Itti said. "You played well. I have never heard such music! The emperor listened without apparent emotion. But then he indicated that he wanted to see the author of the music, and they could not refuse him. The emperor knew your situation. The envoy would have prepared you for the encounter, acquainting you with the proper forms, but no one knew this would happen."

"I think he liked the melody," Hyu said.

"The whole city was agog as we departed. The emperor did you great honor. He acknowledges no one without excellent reason. And yet all those who heard you play there understood. The spirits were surely with you."

"They surely were," Hyu agreed, gratified.

Later the clouds piled up to the south-southwest, directly in their path. "You didn't—?" Itti asked Hyu, his face lining with worry.

"I did not violate any part of my role," Hyu said. "Much thanks to you."

The captain ignored the irony. "Then that storm will slide past us harmlessly." He was not being humorous or casual; he really believed it, and thus his underlying faith was revealed. He might deny the influence of the spirits when there was no threat, but he was quick to accept it when there was a threat.

The storm loomed darkly, and its inflowing winds carried the ship swiftly toward it. But the storm was moving north, and by the time the ship drew close, the peripheral winds remaining in the route were manageable. In fact they made better time than they might have, because of the storm's boost. The spirits were teasing them, but helping rather than hurting. Soon enough they made it to land, and all was well.

The captain's judgment proved to be valid. The emperor had not only accepted the gifts, he had sent gifts of his own: blue silk, white silk, gold silk, dragon-embossed silk, pearls, valuable red pigment, and a sword almost as long as a man. He had also conferred high titles upon the envoys, and given them special awards. The scroll expressed his extreme pleasure, and Queen Himiko's own pleasure was not long in being felt.

Hyu knew what this meant to him and his family. Yet what remained foremost in his mind was the way the palace ceiling had enhanced his melody, and the emperor's slow nod. Surely Hyu's children's children would someday learn of that.

Himiko ruled securely until A.D. *244 before she had a problem with a neighboring king. She sent to the emperor for support, and he provided it. But Himiko died before the envoy returned. She was buried beneath a mound more than a hundred paces in diameter, and a hundred men and maidservants were buried with her. The Yoshinogari site is the oldest known large mound burial in Japan, making it seem likely to be Himiko's.*

A king succeeded her, but civil unrest followed, with assassinations becoming commonplace—exactly as had been the case before Himiko's ascension. Finally a thirteen-year-old girl named Iyo, a relative of Himiko, was made queen, and she restored order. The Chinese emperor supported her, and an exchange of gifts occurred. It seems that peace and prosperity remained until the time when men achieved power again, and the Yayoi culture disappeared. If there is a lesson here, it seems to have been lost on men.

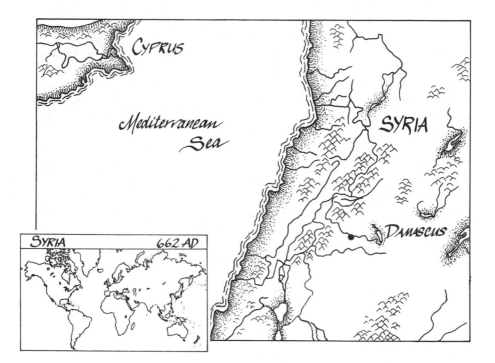

CHAPTER 14

MOSLEM

In the Year of the Elephant, according to tradition, or about A.D. 570, a boy was born in Mecca, Arabia. Orphaned by age five, Muhammad was raised by an uncle. At age twenty-five he married a rich forty-year-old widow, and it was a happy union. But he was disturbed by the corruption that flourished in the name of religion; there were 360 idols in Mecca. In 610 he heard bells and a voice enjoining him to recite the nature of Allah, a single god. Thus, in time, came to be the Moslem religion. The Prophet died in A.D. 632, having unified a number of Arab tribes by preaching and force of arms. His successors continued similarly,

securing all Arabia, then expanding operations to neighboring Palestine, Syria,
and Mesopotamia. In these regions there had been constant strife, weakening
their governments, and the local populace welcomed the forces of Islam as
liberators. Cities that surrendered without fighting were treated leniently. Thus
Islam spread rapidly, soon amassing globally significant territory. But by A.D.
655 the unity of the new empire was crumbling; factions were quarreling.
Muhammad's cousin Ali, who had married the Prophet's daughter Fatima,
became the dominant figure, but strife was constant. In 661 Ali was assassinated
—and became revered in death as he had not been in life. His supporters are
known today as the Shiites. Power then shifted to Muawiya, the governor of
Syria, a skilled statesman, who moved the capital from Mecca to Damascus and
established the century-long rule of the Umayyad caliphs.

O NCE the joy of Huo's return, and the family's restoration of status,
had been celebrated, they held a family council. The Bedouin Huo
had been implicated in the Caliph Ali's assassination by a poisoned blade,
but his pilgrimage to Mecca had established his piety, and new evidence had
absolved him. But Arabia was the region of his degradation, and he wasn't
sure he wanted to remain here.

First they went out as a family for the dawn devotion, prostrating
themselves in the direction of Mecca, the Holy City. Then they discussed
their prospects.

"But where else could we go?" An'a asked for the benefit of the children.
They had already discussed it privately, but preferred family unity.

"The Caliph Muawiya has invited me to play for him in Damascus," Huo
said. "He will even provide my family with good lodging."

"But you supported Caliph Ali!" Chi'ip exclaimed. He was eleven, and
knew what was what.

"But Caliph Muawiya fought Caliph Ali," Miina reminded him. She was
nine, and a midnight-haired beauty despite her youth. Huo knew that when
she had a body to go with her face, she would be a dancer like no other.

"So the fact that I may have had a problem relating to Ali's death does
not bother Muawiya," Huo said. "He suspects that though I supported
him, my position among his other supporters has been weakened because of
their attempt to implicate me unfairly. And he is right. I am no longer eager
to associate with them."

"The man is clever about such things," An'a remarked.

"He sure is," Chi'ip said enthusiastically. "When he fought Ali at Siffen,
Ali had 50,000 troops and was winning, until Muawiya's men tied pages of
the Koran to their lances, saying, 'Let Allah decide.' So they had to go to
arbitration, and Muawiya didn't get beaten."

"And when they wanted to call Ali's son Hasan the new caliph," Miina
said, eager to show that she knew about politics too, "Muawiya sent him a

note that said: 'Ask what thou wilt,' and enclosed a blank sheet of paper with Muawiya's signature on it. And Hasan took the money of the town treasury and went with his wives and harem to Medina, and renounced his claim to power."

Huo nodded. "Muawiya never uses the sword where the lash suffices, and spares the lash where his tongue is enough. He makes lavish gifts to his enemies, because a war costs infinitely more. He has an administrative staff made up largely of Christians, because they are competent and have no ambitions to weaken his power, on which theirs depends. Christians and Jews aren't truly unbelievers, because the Prophet named them 'People of the Book.' He is clever and devious throughout. So now should I join him on a similar basis—as a nonsupporter to whom he is being generous?"

"Yes, because our own kind did us dirt," Chi'ip said righteously.

But Miina wasn't so certain. "It's a long journey. What is Damascus like?"

"It was perhaps the wealthiest city of the Byzantine Empire," Huo said. "It surrendered to the faithful after a six month siege, so wasn't ravaged, and remains prominent. The Christians and Jews are allowed not only to remain, they can continue their idolatrous worship and run their businesses, as long as they pay their taxes. Any citizen can ask for and receive an audience with the caliph, and many do. So it is an interesting, cosmopolitan place."

"Even I could meet the caliph?" Miina asked, awed.

"Even you, I think," Huo agreed.

She nodded. "Then we can go."

❂

Damascus was indeed impressive. Mecca might be the Holy City, but Damascus was huge and beautiful. It had been left as it was, expect for one thing: the caliph was constructing a palace of green marble and painted ceilings. Here he would be able to hold court in style, sitting cross-legged on golden cushions, with his paternal relatives to his right and his maternal relatives to his left, all dressed in their silks and brocades. There would be plenty of room for the lawyers and secretaries and poets and guild masters, too, along with a plethora of minor officials. But at the moment the most splendid building was the enormous Christian church, where there were human figures painted on the walls. No Moslem Mosque would tolerate such forbidden art, of course, as it constituted the worship of idols, but allowance had to be made for those who didn't know better.

The apparel of the city folk was surprising too. Huo was of course garbed in loose trousers, loose shirt, loose jacket overall, and a turban on his head and scarf wrapped around his lower face, so as to keep the sun and sand out, and An'a was covered just as thoroughly. But the people of Damascus ranged from Bedouin style to garish Christian style, with many of them completely and shamelessly barefaced. Their clothing was of every color, and some young women exposed so much of their wrists and ankles that it was hard not to stare.

But all were unified at the five times for universal prayers. At dawn, noon, afternoon, sunset, and darkness all Moslems faced Mecca, went to their knees, and down on their faces, all together. It was a phenomenal synchronized display of the worship of Allah, the one God, and devotion to his prophet Muhammad. However else the city might be strange, this proved it to be familiar in the faith.

It was familiar, in a less comfortable way, to Huo. The left hand was considered to be a thing of impiety. The left was used in the performance of the cruder bodily functions, and the right for all elevated tasks. The difference between superficially similar hands was like that between the manners in which the body expelled air: a belch after a good meal was excellent form, while an inadvertent breaking of wind was a social horror of the grossest magnitude. Thus Huo had to eat and write with his right hand, though it was clumsy for him. Only when alone with An'a, who understood, and when playing music, where both hands were equal, could he relax. Often he wished he could be in some other culture, where he could be himself. But that was a pointless dream; everything that he valued was here in the land of the faithful.

But they could not spend too much time gawking at the wonders of the city. They had to locate the promised lodgings before nightfall.

A man approached Huo. "Are you the musician from Arabia?" he asked.

"I do answer to that description," Huo agreed cautiously.

"Here is a letter from the caliph." The man handed him a scroll, saluted smartly and departed.

An'a and the children stared after him. "A what?" she asked.

"I seem to remember that the caliph has established a postal service," Huo said, bemused. "And a system for archiving and protecting official documents. I had not expected to encounter it so quickly."

"What does it say?" Chi'ip asked.

Huo broke the seal and read the ornate text. "It says that we have been assigned a residence in the elite section, with a servant who knows the city to take care of routine matters. It gives the address, and requests an audience tomorrow."

"Who requests an audience?" An'a asked.

"It is signed 'The Barking Bitch.'"

Both children burst out laughing. But An'a was thoughtful. "Doesn't Muawiya's name mean that?"

"Yes," Huo said. "But I never thought he would use it himself. I fear that this may be a false message."

"Unless the caliph has a considerable sense of humor."

"I think we shall just have to check the address, and see what we can discover," Huo said.

They made their way to the lodging, and it was a nice section of the city, clean and without dangerous-looking people. Huo approached the door, and was met there by a young woman. "Are you the musician?" she asked.

"I am. I received a letter—"

"Yes. Come in with your family. I am your servant Mou'se. I will do your shopping, take care of your children, and guide you wherever you need to go. Tomorrow you must see the caliph."

"The letter was signed 'The Barking Bitch.' That couldn't be the caliph!"

Mou'se smiled. "It is the humor of the scribe. Caliph Muawiya is tolerant of such jests, so long as they are not uttered by powerful enemies. He is also called the brother of a bastard, and accused of having enormous buttocks. All true, of course, but—"

"But we shall not call him anything but Caliph," Huo said firmly, looking at his children, who were starting to giggle. They sobered immediately.

"What is your family, and how did you come to be assigned to this chore?" An'a asked Mou'se.

"Oh, I like helping folk," Mou'se said. "My family lived in the country, but the drought made us move to the city. So my father and mother, and my two older sisters, and my brother and his lovely wife Se'ed all came here, and we remember how hard it is to get used to at first. Even twenty years later. And I love music."

That seemed to cover it. They entered the house and Mou'se made them feel right at home. She had food ready, and quickly acquainted them with all the necessary things to know about the city. This was their first experience with a servant, but in just a few hours it seemed as if she had always been with them.

"Do the Bedouin still value eloquence, archery, and horsemanship above all else?" Mou'se inquired shyly. "I was only five when—but that is of no interest.

"The old values still hold," Huo agreed. "Our proverb states that the three great boons to a clan are the birth of a son, the foaling of a mare, and the discovery of a poet."

"I remember!" Mou'se exclaimed. "And music is like poetry. I hope I hear you play one day."

"Perhaps," Huo agreed, flattered but wary. It was true that his ability with the double clarinet had lifted him from the commonplace to the rare, and given him access to prominent families and courts. Until his implication in the death of a caliph, and banishment from recognition. Now his reputation had been restored, but he retained a certain nervousness about what could happen in a royal court.

In the evening they found themselves too tired to go back out into the city, but still too tense from travel and new experience to relax. The children were showing signs of becoming cranky, and An'a feared they were about to make a scene that would embarrass them in front of an outsider.

But Mou'se, alert to exactly that, stepped in. "Let me tell you a tale of Persia," she said. "It is a wondrous story that always enthralled my sisters and me."

Chi'ip looked doubtful, afraid that Huo and An'a might be planning to go out and leave him and Miina with the servant.

A tale of Persia. Huo found himself intrigued. "We'll all listen," he said, taking a comfortable seat. That reassured the children, and they relaxed.

Mou'se began the tale of "The Enchanted Horse."

❂

There was once, in times of yore and the passage of ages, a great and wise king of the Persians named Sabur. He had a son who was handsome and bold, and three daughters who were like three moons or three wonderful flowers in their beauty and delicacy. He had a great love of science, geometry, and astronomy, and encouraged these disciplines in his kingdom.

One day during a spring festival three sages presented themselves before King Sabur. They had come from several far countries, and each spoke a different language. The first was a Hindu from India, and the second was a Christian from Constantinople, and the third was a Persian from a distant province of the king's own realm.

The Hindu sage brought a truly royal present: a man formed from gold encrusted with diamonds, with a golden trumpet in his hand. "If you set him up at the gate of your city, he will be a sleepless guardian. If an enemy approaches, the golden man will blow a blast which will paralyze your foe with fear and alert your entire city to the danger."

"As Allah lives," cried the king, "if this is true, I will grant you your fondest wish, whatever it may be."

Then the Roman sage came forward, and presented the king with a basin of silver, in which was a peacock of gold, surrounded by twenty-four gold peahens. "Each time that an hour passes, of the day or night, the peacock pecks one of the peahens, and mounts her, with a great beating of his wings, thus marking the hours, until all the females have been mounted and the day and night are past. Further, when a month has passed, he will open his mouth and the crescent of the new moon will appear in his throat."

"If you speak sooth," said the king, "I will give you whatever you may desire, if it be in my power."

The Persian sage approached. He presented the king with a horse made from rare black ebony, inlaid with gold and diamonds, and with a saddle. "When this horse is mounted, it will carry its rider through the air with such speed that it covers a year's distance in a day."

"By Allah the Omnipotent, if this is true, I will reward you most splendidly!" the king exclaimed.

For three days thereafter the king tested the three marvelous devices, and all of them worked exactly as specified. "O illustrious sages," the king said, gratified, "now that I have proved the truth of your claims, I will fulfill my promise. Ask what you will, and I shall grant it on the instant."

The three replied that they wished the king to bestow on them his three daughters in marriage, for they had heard of the beauty of the damsels. The king agreed, and summoned the officials and witnesses so that the ceremony could be performed forthwith.

Now it happened that the king's three daughters, being curious by nature, were circumspectly witnessing the interchange. They were seated behind a curtain in the reception hall and heard what was said. Two of them did not object, for the sages were of fair countenance and mannerly, but when the youngest looked closely at the sage who would be her husband, lo, he was an old man, looking to be a hundred years of age, with his hair frosted, his forehead drooping, moth-eaten eyebrows, a nose like an eggplant, teeth jutting like those of a wild pig, lips like a camel's, and the rest of him less fair to behold. He was a compost of monstrous ugliness, supremely deformed. In truth, his aspect would have put a terrible demon of a haunted house to shame.

The princess, in contrast, was the fairest and most beautiful girl of her time, like a gazelle in her grace and symmetry, putting even her two lovely sisters to shame. She was truly formed for the games and works of love, outshining the full moon in luster. When she saw what was to befall her, she fled to her room, tore her robes, strewed dust on her head, and flung herself down in a dreadful fit of weeping.

The king's son, just returned from a prolonged hunting excursion, knew nothing of the events of the past three days, but happened to discover his sibling in her misery. His name was Prince Kamar al-Akmar, and of all the people in the world, he loved his little sister the most dearly. He was most grieved to find her in such distress. "What has happened, O my darling sister?" he inquired.

"O my dear and only brother," she responded tearfully, beating her fair breast, "I will hide nothing from you. Our father has resolved upon a foul thing, and I think I must flee this court forever, rather than suffer this odious union, for I would far rather die. Know that he has promised me to a vile senile ugly magician who brought him a gift of black wood." And she told him the whole story.

"This shall not be," Kamar said, and went to reprove their father.

He found the king and braced him forthwith. "What is this I hear of a magician to whom you have promised my little sister in marriage? What gift could be so precious as to warrant slaying her with grief? This thing must not happen." No ordinary person would dare speak to the king thus, but

Kamar was his prize, and trained to be decisive in the manner of one who would one day rule.

The Persian was nearby, and heard what the prince said. The words infuriated him, but he pretended nonchalance.

"My son," the king said, "you must see this marvelous horse. Then you will understand."

"I think I had better," the prince replied grimly.

They went to the court where the horse stood. The prince was amazed by its beauty. "I must try this steed," he said, and jumped into the saddle, for he was an accomplished horseman. He thrust his feet into the stirrups and spurred the horse forward, but it did not move.

"Tell him how it works," the king told the sage.

The sage wanted to be rid of the prince, so he took advantage of the young man's impetuous nature by telling him only part of the truth. "Do you see that gold peg on the right side? Turn that to make the horse rise."

Kamar immediately did so, and behold, the horse rose in the air with the quickness of a bird, for the prince had turned it too far for caution. In a moment the horse was far above the palace and soaring away, out of earshot.

"What is this?" the king demanded, alarmed. "How can he bring it down again?"

"O master, he did not give me time to explain the use of the peg on the left side, which governs descent. I can do nothing."

King Sabur was no fool, and he suspected the sage of deliberate mischief. But he was not sure. So he compromised by indulging a middle path: instead of slaying the man immediately, he had him beaten and thrown into the darkest dungeon of the city until such time as the prince should safely return. Then he cast the crown from his head, beat himself in the face, and tore out handfuls of his beard. He went to his youngest daughter, who was in similar state. "Indeed you shall not marry that vile sage," he said. "I rue the moment I considered such a thing, for now my son is lost."

The princess was quick to forgive her father, for she was of a sweet nature, and of course the loss of a son was a much greater affliction than the loss of a daughter. She consoled him as well as she could, but she grieved for Kamar herself, for she loved him as dearly as he loved her.

Meanwhile the prince found himself high aloft on the reckless steed, which would not respond to his directives. The peg caused the ascent to speed or slow, but would not bring the horse down. Kamar was impetuous, but also no fool; he realized that there had been malice in the sage's limited instruction. But since the sage himself was able to control the horse, there had to be a way. "Surely there is a second peg," he said.

So he felt all over the horse, and finally found a tiny peg, no more than a pin, easy to overlook. He pressed down on it, and the horse leveled, then began to descend rather too swiftly for comfort. The ground was rushing up, and the prince feared a crash.

But he experimented with the two pegs, and found that by touching them together with different motions, turning one slowly while pressing the other lightly, he could achieve complete control of the horse's elevation and velocity. Then he could affect its direction of motion by using the normal signals of his legs and feet. He was now in charge, and no longer in danger. He brought it to a gentle landing, and then caused it to rise again, going forward and backward, learning its nuances, until he was as expert with it as he was with a natural horse.

But he was now in a far realm, for the horse had flown most swiftly at the beginning, and that day was ending. He realized that he would not be able to find his way home in the dark, so decided to find a place to stay for the night. He rose high enough to gain a good view of the local landscape, and spied the lights of a sizable city surrounded by a formidable wall, and the turret of a palace in the distance. "That should be a good place," he said. "Surely they will have fitting food and lodging."

He flew the horse to the palace, and landed on a terrace. But now it was dark, and the lights here had been doused. So Prince Kamar left the horse and descended a stair in search of the proprietors, or at least some servants who could help him, for he was now quite hungry and thirsty. He came to a courtyard paved with marble and alabaster, and marveled at the intricacy and beauty of the building, but found no living person. "There is no help here," he concluded. "I had better return to the horse, and pass the night there."

But as he started back, he spied a light, which turned out to be a torch set in the wall. He went to it and found a huge black slave asleep on a mattress before a closed door. There was a bag of food beside the slave, so Kamar quietly took it, opened it, and found a loaf of good bread. He ate this with relish, then returned the bag and took the slave's great sword. He hoped that the slaves of his father's palace were not this careless, but was nevertheless thankful that this one was. He went to a nearby fountain and drank deeply.

Much refreshed, Kamar explored farther, and came to a second lighted door, this one not guarded. It was covered by a velvet curtain. He drew aside the curtain and entered, and discovered a great ivory couch, inlaid with pearls, rubies, and other jewels, guarded by four slave girls who slept around it. On it was a maiden of singular beauty, whose flowing hair served as her only covering.

Kamar gazed at her in wonder, for she was the loveliest creature he had seen, other than his little sister, and indeed was like a twin in the luster of her flower-white brow, anemone-red cheeks, and perfect symmetry.

The prince was overcome by emotion, for love was burgeoning in his heart at the sight of her, and he bent to kiss her right cheek. The girl woke, surprised. "Who are you?" she demanded.

"I am the slave of love," he replied. "For never have I seen a creature of such exquisite perfection."

The girl might have been frightened or angry, but there was something about the way the man expressed himself that appealed to her. She saw that he was handsome, and clothed in the manner of a prince. "Are you the one who sued yesterday for my hand in marriage, but my father rejected on the pretext that he was ugly?" she asked. "If so, I must say I differ from my father, for you are by no means ill favored in my eyes. I am the Princess Shams al-Nahar, called Sun of the Day, of the Kingdom of Arabia."

"I am not he," Kamar said. "But surely I shall sue likewise for your hand, for you are surely she who I thought existed only in my dreams of rapture. I am Kamar al-Akmar, Prince of Persia."

The slave girls woke, and overheard this exchange. "Indeed, this is not the one, mistress," one informed the princess. "For that one is indeed hideous of aspect, while this man is handsome."

"Then I choose to be with you," Princess Shams said, and stepped into Kamar's embrace. He welcomed her approach, and in a moment it seemed that they had exchanged a thousand caresses and compliments, being instantly in love.

But by this time word of Kamar's intrusion had spread through the palace, and Shams's father the king had been roused. He came charging into the chamber, sword in hand.

Kamar immediately separated from Shams and lifted the sword he had taken from the slave. It was apparent that he was younger, stronger, and bolder than the other man, and capable of slaying the other in short order. But Shams screamed, "No! It is my father the king!"

"How dare you sneak into my palace, take my daughter, and smirch my honor?" the king demanded with some irritation. "Is there any reason I should not have my slaves put you to the worst of deaths?"

This caused Kamar to hesitate. "Very well," he decided. "I will talk with him." He then approached the king, and said "I am Prince Kamar al-Akmar, and I wish to marry your lovely daughter. If you will not agree to this, I see two courses of action."

"Two?" the king asked, taken aback by the prince's audacity. He also noted his daughter's interest in the young man, and realized that she might never forgive him if he had her lover summarily put to death. Daughters could be touchy about such things.

"Either you should fight me now, and if you win you have redeemed your honor and saved your daughter; and if I win, I will have her and your kingdom. Or let me be this night, and in the morning I will fight your entire force, and—" Kamar paused, thinking of something. "How many are there?"

"Forty thousand horsemen, plus a similar number of foot soldiers and armed slaves and the slaves of the slaves."

"Very well. Draw them up before me in the morning, and if they kill me, you will have your vengeance, and if I put them to flight, you will know that you have found a son-in-law worthy of the honor."

The king was so surprised by this offer that he agreed to it, being certain that the morning would finish the matter. Then his daughter would not hold it against him, because Kamar himself had proposed the contest. So he gave orders to have the force drawn up ready for battle in the morning. Then he remained to talk with Kamar, being in doubt as to the propriety in leaving the virile young man alone with his lovely daughter, and was impressed with Kamar's handsomeness and manners. Had the prince come in the normal fashion, the king might have been inclined to grant his suit. He really did love his daughter, and desired her welfare.

Before they knew it, dawn came. There was the sound of the massed troops outside. "It is time," said the king, and the princess nodded sadly, fearing that the king had the better part of the deal.

"O King," replied Kamar, "how can I fight against all these horsemen, when I am on foot?"

"Choose any of my horses to ride," the king replied graciously. "All are well trained."

"No, I prefer to ride the one that brought me to your kingdom."

"Very well. Where is it?"

"On the terrace above the palace."

"What folly is this?" the king demanded. But he turned to the chief of his armies. "Go to the terrace and bring me what you find there."

So men went to the terrace and found the ebony horse. They brought it down to the ground before the palace, where Kamar stood before the cavalry and armies of the king. All were amazed by the wooden horse, and gathered around to admire it. "Is this your horse?" the King asked.

"It is," Kamar agreed. "I will mount and show you the marvels of it. In fact I will charge your troops and put them all to flight. But first your men must retire a bow-shot's distance, so that I have room to maneuver."

The king indulged him in this too, being intrigued by the continuing arrogance and mystery of the man. "Do what you wish," he said. "Do not spare my cavalry, for they will not spare you."

Then Kamar kissed the princess and mounted the horse. He set himself and touched the two pegs, and the horse responded by shaking, panting, pawing the ground, and leaping sideways in a remarkable manner. Then its belly filled with wind, and it sailed up into the air as quickly as an arrow, carrying Kamar away.

Suddenly the king realized that he had been fooled. "Catch him!" he cried, but it was too late; the prince had escaped them.

At this the Princess Shams wept for the loss of her lover, and smote her face and fell seriously ill. The king tried to console her, but she swore, "As Allah lives, I will neither eat nor drink until I am reunited with my love." The world darkened before the king's eyes, as he saw the case, and he fell into a melancholy.

Meanwhile Prince Kamar flew toward Persia, glad for his deliverance, but his mind was filled with dreams of the lovely Princess Shams. Then he reached his father's city and descended, landing on the palace roof. He went down into the palace, which was strewn with ashes, and found his father, mother, and sisters all clad in mourning raiment. "What's this?" he inquired. "Has someone died?"

There was a considerable commotion, and in a moment he was buried under the embraces of his family, especially his youngest sister, who lavished kisses on him and soaked his face with her tears of joy. Then he told them the whole story. The king gave orders for a great feast, distributed gold, and threw open the dungeons in a general pardon. It seemed he was pleased with his son's return.

Then Kamar inquired after the sage, and at his behest the king pardoned him too and released him from prison and rewarded him richly. But he would not give him the princess as wife, and so the sage still raged inside.

The king distrusted the ebony horse, and urged his son to stay away from it. But Kamar could not forget the Princess Shams, and longed to be with her again. The king tried to distract him by summoning a handsome handmaiden, skilled in playing the lute, and she played and sang most eloquently.

"Memory dies, but never my love for you
So I will die in your wonderful love so true
And in your love I will my life renew"

When the prince heard this, the fires of longing flamed anew in his heart. He went forthwith to the ebony horse and flew into the air. It was evening, but his passion was such that he did not care. He could find the way.

When the king realized what had happened, he was sore afflicted. "By Allah, if I get my son back again, I will burn that accursed horse!" Then he resumed his mourning, fearing that he would never see the prince again.

Kamar flew directly to Arabia, and landed unobserved on the high terrace as before. He went to the same room and found the Princess Shams al-Nahar, clothed only in her long hair, weeping unconsolably. He entered the room and made himself known to her, and she threw herself upon him, covering his face with kisses. "O light of my eyes, I have been desolate because you were gone from me! Had you stayed away longer, I would have died. How could you leave me? How can life be sweet to me, without you?"

"I could not stop longing for you," he replied. "But what am I to do, when your father will not suffer me to wed you?"

"Take me away with you," she pleaded, "rather than make me taste the bitter gourd of separation from you."

Amazed and pleased, he agreed. So the princess opened a chest and donned her richest and finest things, including expensive gems. Then she went out with him, her handmaids not daring to protest.

They went to the horse, and the princess mounted behind the prince, and clung to him most tightly. He turned the pegs, and the horse flew up into the air.

When the handmaidens saw this, they screamed, and the king was roused from his sleep and discovered what was happening. He came up to the terrace and called out "O king's son, I conjure you by Allah, do not take my daughter away!" But the princess urged him to continue, for she did not trust her father to allow them to marry.

They flew to a meadow, where there was a spring. They landed and drank, then mounted again and flew the rest of the way, arriving by morning. They landed on the upper terrace, and Kamar left the princess while he went to notify his father. "I know my family will welcome you in proper style." For of course a princess could not be brought in like some slave girl. Shams was glad to agree.

The king was overjoyed at his son's return, and made immediate arrangements to prepare a suitable palace for the princess to occupy. Then he made up a procession in honor of the visitor, a vast array of richly dressed nobles, and litters of gold with brocaded canopies, and many slaves with great feather fans.

Kamar went ahead to rejoin the princess. He hurried to the roof of the palace—and found that both princess and ebony horse were gone.

Soon he realized what had happened. The evil sorcerer had spied the horse, and flown it away. And somehow managed to take the princess with him.

And indeed, that was the case. The cunning sage, discovering the horse, had also smelled the sweet scent of Princess Shams, and gone to her and inquired as to her identity. She, thinking him to be a servant who had come to bring her to the welcoming ceremony, had naively agreed to ride the horse with him, though she had had to close her eyes against the indignity of his awful ugliness. He had caused the horse to fly far up and away from the palace. Only then did she realize the cruel trick fate had played on her.

"Fear not," the sage told her. "You will not be neglected. I will marry you, and you will live out your life in Christian Constantinople. It will not be difficult, after you give up your idolatrous faith in Allah." For though the sage was Persian, he knew that there would be no safe place in Persia for him after this, and he did have connections in infidel Constantinople.

Then Princess Shams knew she was truly lost, for she was a virtuous maiden who would die rather than live among the infidels.

But Constantinople was a long way away, and the old sage was uncomfortable traveling for an extended period, so he brought the horse down in a meadow near a great city. It happened that the king of that region was out hunting, and a member of his party saw the strange horse come down, and told him. So the king sent his slaves out to fetch back this oddity. They came upon the sage unawares, and brought him, the damsel, and the horse to the king. "What is this?" the king asked them, astonished at the old man's loathsome aspect and the ravishing beauty of the girl.

"She is my wife," the sage said.

But the princess gave him the lie, saying that he was a sorcerer and a heathen and a villain. So the king had the sage beaten and thrown into a dungeon, and brought the girl and the wooden horse to his palace.

Meanwhile Prince Kamar was riding out across the lands, searching for his lost love. He questioned everyone, and soon was able to trace the course of the marvelous flying horse, for people did tend to notice such a thing as it flew over them. He located the city where the horse had landed, and learned that a hideous old man and a beauteous young woman and a strange carved horse had appeared there. The ugly man had been thrown away, but the king was smitten with the girl and would fain marry her. Unfortunately she was mad, for she talked wildly, and sprang at the king as if to attack him, and screamed in animal rage when any man approached her. The king had offered an excellent reward to any healer who could cure her, but so far none had succeeded.

Kamar pondered this, and realized that the princess was feigning her illness in order to protect herself from the lust of the king. Therein lay his hope to rescue her. He made himself up to be a traveling healer, versed in the arts of Persia, and presented himself at the court. The king was a portly figure of middle age. "So you are a healer," the king said. "Can you cure madness?"

"Indeed, that is my specialty," Kamar said. "I believe I can help. But first you must tell me all the particulars of her situation, so that I know exactly what I am up against."

The king proceeded to tell him everything.

"A wooden horse?" Kamar asked as if in surprise. "This might be the cause of the mischief. Perhaps if I examine it, I will find something that will serve for the recovery of the damsel."

"By all means," the king said, and conveyed him to the place where the horse was kept. The people of the city did not realize its magic nature; they thought it a mere statue.

Kamar was overjoyed to discover that the ebony horse was undamaged and in perfect working order. "Surely some enchantment here," he muttered, accurately enough. "Now I must see the girl."

So he was brought to the presence of the madwoman. She was twisting her hands and writhing on the floor and tearing her clothes to tatters, as was her wont. She hissed as she saw his approach, for she did not recognize him in his disguise. Her hands and feet were tied, to prevent her from scratching or kicking.

Then he kneeled down beside her and whispered "I am Kamar. Do what I tell you, my beloved."

Shams recognized him, and cried out with excess of joy, and swooned. But the king thought that this was just another of her fits.

"I believe she has been touched by a thing of evil," Kamar said. "The evil is in that statue of a horse, which the ugly old man must have used to bewitch her. But perhaps I can use it to reverse its spell, and free her of the madness. Can you bring it here?"

The king immediately ordered it done, and the ebony horse was set up outside the madwoman's chamber. Kamar had the slaves carry her out to it and he placed her bound hands on its flank. "Now be cured—for an hour," he whispered.

Then he turned to the king. "I believe I have cured her, for a time. But the evil is very strong, and I am not sure how long my cure will last."

Then the king came somewhat hesitantly to Shams and addressed her. "Are you cured, fair lady?" he inquired.

"Welcome, sire," Shams said to him. "You do great honor to visit your handmaid this day."

The king was delighted. "Strike off her bonds and garb her as befits her station," he cried.

This was done, and soon Shams al-Nahar was as regal as the princess she was. The king approached her and kissed her on the cheek, and she bowed to him most graciously.

"But we must not presume too much," Kamar said warningly. "For the genie that possessed her has been merely stunned, and may return."

Indeed, as he spoke, the woman began to twitch, just slightly in her hands, and her eyes widened. The king, perceiving this, hastily stepped away from her.

"What is the matter, my lord?" she inquired dulcetly enough. But her hands continued to twitch.

"You must complete the cure," the king said to Kamar. "Abolish the genie completely."

"This I may be able to do," Kamar said cautiously. "But it will require more effort."

"Whatever it takes," the king said.

So Kamar had them place incense all around the horse, and draw magical figures around it, to contain the malice of the genie when it was exorcised. Then he brought the woman back to the horse. She was now twitching considerably, and spitting at folk, and her eyes rolled recklessly, but he managed to lift her onto the back of the horse, behind the saddle. At that she calmed somewhat, as if cowed by the contact with the demon. Kamar climbed into the saddle. "Now this may become somewhat violent," he warned, "for the genie does not want to be driven from the girl and forced back into the horse. It will struggle. But be ready, for once the exorcism is done, we shall have to flee the horse, and then you must burn it, so as to destroy the demon forever." This made no sense, of course, for genie were indestructible; if the bottles or other objects they were confined in were destroyed, they were freed for further mischief. That was why such bottles were normally thrown into the deep sea, where no one would find them. But the king did not know enough about Persian magic to realize that. He and the others stepped back, concerned that the genie might hurt them if they remained within its reach.

Then Kamar went into a spell of exorcism, and while he chanted it, he touched the two pegs on the horse, carefully. The horse pitched about, as if shaken by an evil spirit, and the madwoman put her arms around Kamar and clutched tight, as if being rent from within. She groaned piteously. The folk watching stepped back farther, alarmed. The smoke of the incense became thick, half hiding them.

"Hold tight," Kamar said. Then he twisted the right peg hard, and the horse shot straight up into the air so swiftly that no sensible person would have believed it. In moments the palace and city were so far below as to be of no account, and Kamar set the course of the horse for home.

There was great rejoicing when they arrived, and the happiest of all was Kamar's little sister. Indeed, when the two princesses stood together, it was hard to tell which one was lovelier, for they were like two moons on a warm spring night. Each had been threatened by the foul sage, and was relieved to be forever free of him. Kamar married Shams, and her father soon became reconciled, for the two kingdoms adjoined and made common cause against enemies. And King Sabur assured the future by breaking the ebony horse in pieces and burning them. And thus was their happiness, until there came to them the Destroyer of delights and Sunderer of societies. And glory be to Allah, the merciful and mighty, who holds in His hands the dominion of the worlds visible and invisible!

☢

Mou'se looked up. "And that was the tale of 'The Enchanted Horse,'" she concluded.

An'a fixed on something. "In your family—there was one brother and three sisters?"

"True," Mou'se agreed.

"Of which you were the youngest?"

"Yes. And my brother married the world's most beautiful woman. I envied Se'ed, though she had suffered privations." She smiled. "I always did like that tale, for some reason."

The others laughed. "It is a fine tale," Huo said.

"But I'm sorry about the magic horse," Miina said.

"Yes. It had no fault in itself, only serving its masters. But folk do not always distinguish between things and the uses to which they are put."

How true that was, Huo thought, thinking of the problem of his hands.

"We thank you for the marvelous tale," An'a said. "Now it grows late, and we must retire." Indeed, both children were obviously sleepy.

Mou'se helped in that too, seeing to the children's evening rituals while Huo and An'a saw to their own. "I could get used to having a servant," Huo murmured as they lay for sleep.

"Maybe you could take her for a second wife," An'a suggested. "She is unmarried, and a year younger than I am."

"She is twenty-five?" he asked, surprised. "She seemed younger."

"Perhaps because of her animation as she spoke of the youngest princess. She is overdue for marriage, perhaps not yet having found a good man."

He considered it. A man was entitled to four wives, if he could maintain them, as well as servants and slaves. The later wives were in effect the servants of the first wife, so often this strengthened a marriage. Mou'se did seem to be a fine woman, of pleasing physical aspect and personality. But it did not seem right for him. "One wife fills all my aspirations."

"So I am to have no relief in bed?" she inquired mischievously.

"None at all," he agreed, kissing her.

The kiss proceeded to more, to his surprise; he had intended to let her rest. Then he realized that she was the animating force in this encounter, and by this token knew that she was pleased with his decision. So they made love despite being tired, and it was as if they remained young and passionate, despite being in their mid-twenties.

❂

Next morning the family went for their audience with the caliph, who had insisted on meeting all of them, rather than just Huo. Muawiya turned out to be a potbellied old man of benign disposition, whose turban was slightly askew. When she saw him, Miina tittered. An'a hastily silenced her, but the caliph had noticed.

"Come here, child," he said.

Miina, suddenly mortified, come forward, looking woeful. But the caliph smiled. "Tell me the truth, child," he said. "Was it my appearance that made you laugh?"

She prostrated herself before him. "O great Caliph, I meant nothing by it!" she cried. "Please don't slay my family!"

"Oh, get up, child. No one will be slain. I know I am a funny-looking man, and anyone who says otherwise is trying to deceive me. You would not try to deceive me, would you?"

Wordlessly, she shook her head.

"In fact, my appearance is laughable. Is that not so?"

She started to deny it, but caught his look and nodded.

"So we have no quarrel, do we?" She nodded. "But you, in contrast, are beautiful. I think you must be a dancer." She nodded. "So I have made you laugh. Now you must make me smile. Dance for me." He looked around. "Have we a musician near?" Huo lifted his double clarinet. "Yes, so we do. I love the arts. Play for my dancer."

So Huo played, and Miina danced, at first cautiously, and then with abandon as she saw that the caliph was enjoying it. Indeed, she was good at it, and soon all the palace attendants were watching. After a while, the caliph signaled to An'a, whose lithe lines he evidently recognized, and she came out to join her daughter in the dance. They made a beautiful couple, the full-bodied woman and the almost-bodied girl.

"So there we are," the caliph said as they finished. "Now I think we are introduced." He snapped his fingers. "Bring pastries and milk for my guests and me."

Thus readily did they find themselves in audience with the caliph, who was exactly as reputed to be. Still, the informality surprised them. "We have never met before," Huo said. "You know we supported the Caliph Ali. How can you trust us so close, so soon?"

"I never met an assassin yet who brought his children along," Muawiya said. "And Ali was a good man. Just not skilled in negotiations. While he lived, your loyalty was to him; will it be to me, now, while I live?"

"Yes."

"I trust you because of your demonstrated loyalty. If you would not play him false, you will not play me false. That is more than can be said for those who put you under an unnecessary cloud."

"Yes!" Chi'ip exclaimed. Then he was abashed, realizing that he shouldn't have spoken.

But the caliph merely nodded. "The young express themselves more freely, therefore can be trusted. Tell me, young man: do you know the origin of the Arabs and the Israelites?"

"Yes, Caliph," Chi'ip said, surprised.

"Then advise me of it, for I seem to have forgotten."

"Two thousand years ago the patriarch Abraham left his home in Ur of the Chaldees and went to dwell in Palestine," Chi'ip said promptly. "His wife Sarah seemed barren, so she had him wed a slave girl named Hagar. Hagar bore him a son, Ishmael. Then Sarah had a son, Isaac. This caused trouble between the two women, for each wanted her son to inherit Abraham's wealth. So Abraham had to separate them. He took Hagar and Ishmael to the Valley of Mecca, which was then a lonely rest stop for caravans, and left them there with provisions, while he returned to Sarah."

"He left them alone in a far place?" the caliph asked, affecting surprise. "Was that right?"

"No," Chi'ip said. "Hagar had done him no evil, and had borne him his first son. But Sarah was his first wife, so he had to support her. It was very dry in Arabia, and Hagar was frantic; they were running out of water. But Ishmael dragged his heel through the sand, and there was water. It was a good spring, which became the well of Zamzam, which we revere today. Now it was possible to settle there, and so there came to be the great city of Mecca. Abraham visited Hagar, and helped Ishmael build the Kaaba, the shrine that is the holiest place in Islam, with a sacred black stone from the sky in its wall. Ishmael married a woman of the new settlers, and their children became the Arabs, while the children of Isaac became the Israelites."

"Ah, yes, I remember now," the caliph said. "And so we are of a single ancestry, and we Arabs recognize the prophets of the Israelites, and we recognize the Prophet Jesus of the Christians too. So there is no actual need for us to quarrel over the name of God, is there?"

Both children stared at him, uncertain whether he was testing or teasing. But he just laughed. "After all, do we not face toward the Holy City of Jerusalem five times a day in worship?"

"No!" the children said together.

"No? Where do we face, then?" He looked at Miina.

"Toward Mecca," she said promptly.

"But why?"

"Because it's the Holy City."

"And Jerusalem is not?"

That stumped them.

"I will tell you," the caliph said. "At first we did pray toward Jerusalem. But then the Israelites in Mecca supported a faction that opposed the Prophet Muhammad, and that annoyed him, so he turned the face of our faith away from their holy city of Jerusalem and toward Mecca, and so it has been thereafter."

They were amazed.

Muawiya looked at Huo. "So you see, I know you, through your children. They are loyal and well instructed. Now I have two situations available, and I do not know which is better for you. I need good musicians and dancers here in Damascus, for as you know the arts are dear to me, but I also need them in the far reaches of our expanding empire. There is an island called Bahrain that is to be settled by a contingent of the followers of Ali, and their need for cultural reinforcement is great. It is so far distant that contacts will be few, and those musicians and dancers that go there will be prominent. But because it is distant, and because of the uncertain alliance of the force going there, I prefer to have among them those I can trust."

Huo was chagrined. "You are sending us away?"

"By no means! I am offering you a choice. You may remain here in good favor, and perform among those who match you in skills, or you may go to some other settled region of the empire and be leading musicians and dancers, or go to the island and be the master performers of the region. I leave the choice to you. I will welcome what you choose, for I want you to be satisfied." And he sat back, awaiting their decision.

Huo looked at An'a. This sudden decision would affect the rest of their lives, and they had to make it immediately, lest they try the caliph's patience. They could be two among many in a rich city, or well favored in a lesser city, or leaders at the fringe of the empire. What should they say?

The power of Islam continued to expand, and today it remains one of the great religious and cultural centers of the world. At one time Islam controlled Spain and southern France, and at another time a significant portion of eastern Europe. Much of Africa, India, and Indonesia is Moslem, and there is a significant contingent in central Asia. The discovery of oil in the Moslem heartland brought riches to a number of nations. The Dark Ages of Europe were not dark for the sons of the Prophet, where a high level of culture was maintained throughout.

One of the monuments of literature is the framework of the Arabian Nights, by tradition a series of tales Scheherazade told to a king over a thousand nights to distract him from killing the women of his kingdom. They reflect the culture, with the added elements of fantasy and human frailties. "The Enchanted Horse" is typical of these entertainments.

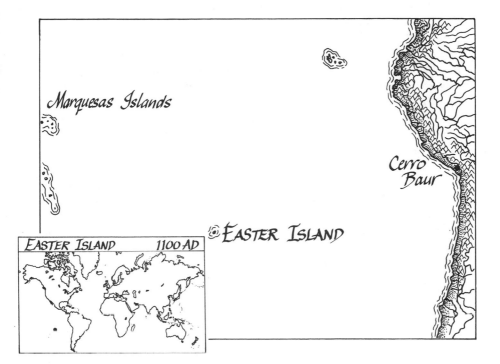

CHAPTER 15

MYSTERY

When the Spanish Conquistadors came to America they found several prominent cultures: the Aztec in the north, the Maya in the central, and the Inca in the south. They destroyed them all, though it would have been a different story had the native Americans understood the nature of the threat at the outset, instead of welcoming the strangers and their devastating diseases and greed. What is not as widely known is that American culture had been evolving for five thousand years, and in certain respects matched or exceeded that of the invaders. The Maya calendar was the most accurate known, and some of their pyramids

are more massive and elegant than those of Egypt. The Inca network of highways and aqueducts was reminiscent of those of the Romans, and their artistic metalwork was phenomenal. These achievements were built on those of prior peoples, which were less impressive but nonetheless solid. In South America things were in transition; the Moche state gave way to the Huari Empire circa
A.D. *700, and Huari gave way to Chimu, circa 1100, despite climatic disruptions following an El Niño event that destroyed Chimú's capital city at that time; Chimú would in another 400 years give way to the Inca empire that covered present-day Peru and Chile, approximately. Then the coming of the Spaniards would destroy it all.*

Considerable controversy surrounds the origin and mechanisms of the culture that made and erected the enormous stone statues of Easter Island, in the Pacific Ocean. These statues were up to thirty-two feet tall, weighing as much as thirty tons, and there were about a thousand of them around the island, some still in the quarry. How were they made, how were they moved, and why? For this was not the center of a vast empire. The volcanic island is sixteen miles long and nearly barren, though it once was forested. It is more than a thousand miles from its nearest island neighbors, and almost 2,500 miles from South America, the nearest continent. It was first colonized about A.D. *300. There is little evidence that it had more than two contacts with any other human population, in the course of 1,500 years. There appear to have been two major population groups: the long ears, who may have had red hair and white skin, and the short ears, who were darker.*

Some of the mysteries have been solved; some remain. Thor Heyerdahl of Kon Tiki *fame is amidst the controversy, arguing that the long ears came from South America, and the short ears from Polynesian islands to the west. Others believe that Polynesia was the only origin. There is persuasive evidence on more than one side. Here is the way it may have been, circa* A.D. *1100.*

This is a triple setting; the male view is on Easter Island, and the female view in the Andes of South America, and the slave view in the Marquesas of Polynesia. The first assumes that a given family traveled to a far isle, the second that it remained on the mainland, and the third that it found an intermediate location.

H UU kissed Aan and hugged Min. "We will return in five days," he promised. "You women keep working on your scripting." For the art of writing was part of the legacy from the old country, and it had to be scrupulously passed along to each new generation of long ears, and kept secret from all others.

"But who will feed us?" Kip asked. He was twelve, and verging on manhood. He was proud to be going on this important mission, but suddenly realized that there could be disadvantages.

"The slaves will provide, as usual."

"Who will keep you warm at night?" Min asked in her turn. She was ten, and her breasts were showing.

"What do you think girl slaves are for, dummy?" Kip asked her scathingly. Huu and Aan laughed; it was true that the short-ear women were invariably obliging. Unspoken was one of the reasons for this excursion: Kip was of age to have his first sexual experience, for which a slave girl would do, and mothers and sisters were not welcome.

"Yes, maybe that one I taught to dance four years ago," Huu said, "the last time I was away from your mother." He would never touch a long-ear woman, of course, but short ears didn't count. Aan did not expect him to sleep alone.

Then he took his wooden flute and his son and set off for the opposite side of the island. He didn't like separating from his wife, even for a few days, but a statue was ready to be moved into place, and it was time to train a new crew. Three long ears would train about fifty slaves, drilling them in precision maneuvers, so as to have them ready. Huu, of course, was the musician; he would handle cadence. The other two would handle directives and discipline. They would train with a dummy block, not risking a real statue, until they not only had it right, they had it without hesitation. The constant drilling would be dull, but there was no alternative. Slaves just weren't reliable unless thoroughly trained and supervised.

He thought about that. When the long ears first decided to erect really significant statues in honor of their gods, they had soon realized that a lot more could be done with less struggle if they had a better source of labor. It had taken years to complete and move the first statue, and there had been injuries and broken stone. So they had organized a slaving expedition, using the same giant reed boats they had used for deep sea fishing, and circled the island to come upon the encampment of short ears by surprise. They had known where they were, because some few short-ear craft had come to the island, blown by a storm, and taken over a section of the island. It had taken time to teach the survivors to speak in the civilized tongue, and to learn their origin. But it was apparent that this was a potential source of labor. So they had gone out and captured the short ears, together with their women and children. They had trained these as suitable slaves, encouraging them to breed so as to increase the work force, and in due course had enough for their purposes.

In fact they had more than enough. The short ears now governed themselves, in their section of the island, and were about to be assigned their first chief of their own number. The truth was that no long ear cared to struggle constantly with the necessary discipline of the unruly slave class, but the change was being presented as a step toward autonomy for the short ears. Their chief would answer to the long ears, but as long as he kept the discipline he would be allowed the privileges of ruling.

They walked south and east and south along the paved road. They were soon clear of the town and in the open country. The forest had been cleared back from the road, and short-ear farmers were tending the fields for their long-ear owners. The ones in the fields ignored the travelers, but those encountered on the road stepped off and bowed until the two long ears were past.

This reminded Kip of something. "Why are their ears so short?"

Huu smiled. "It is not that their are short, but that ours are long. If we did not use earplugs, ours would be as short as theirs."

"They couldn't be!"

"They could be. It is not nature, but status that gives us the privilege of beautiful ears. Don't you remember the discomfort of your early plugs as they stretched your ears?"

His son nodded, remembering. "But some pain is the price of nobility," he said, repeating the common sentiment.

"It is indeed," Huu agreed.

"Tell me how we came here," Kip said.

It was familiar history, but the boy never tired of hearing it. "The great god Make-Make saw fit to guide King Machaa after he suffered defeat in battle in the homeland. He built a huge reed boat and sailed for two months into the unknown sea, bringing along his wife and children and the families of his supporters. He came here to the Navel of the World, and settled and built the good roads. But he didn't stay. Then Hotu Matua in the homeland lost three great battles against the enemy, and he too had to flee to save his people. He sailed here and settled, and his people govern the island to this day."

"And my great-grandfather came with him."

"Yes. My grandfather, with his wife and children. They had been entertaining in Hotu Matua's court, and were invited along. Grandfather Huo thought about it a long time, knowing that his wife preferred to remain in the civilized country, but in the end concluded that it was better to be important entertainers in a new kingdom than routine ones in an old kingdom. So it is that we are here, instead of in the old land."

"But where did King Machaa's people go?"

"We aren't sure," Huu admitted. "When my grandfather arrived here, there were roads all across the island, extending from the stone quarry at Rano Raraku. There were many circular stone houses, and houses of other designs, unlike our reed-ship houses. Our people were so busy getting settled at first that they didn't have time for stone building, so we simply turned our ships over and propped them in place and used them for shelters. But the cleared fields were growing back into forest, and only a few people remained, so their stone houses hadn't protected them. Perhaps most of them were hiding in the forest. They spoke of a terrible storm, but it seems it was so long ago that the details of it had been lost. So we don't know whether the people found better islands and went there, or were lost in the storm."

"What about Min?"

Kip never tired of that story, either. "We thought we had found all the remaining people and taken them into our own kingdom," Huu said. "But some hid in caves, and we found them only by chance. Ten years ago, when you were only two, I was exploring for a suitable site for a better home, near the north cliffs, and I heard something. I thought it was an animal, but it was a newborn baby girl. The mother was dead, and the baby was crying. So I picked her up and brought her home, uncertain what else to do, and your mother—well, she was still nursing you, and said she had two breasts, so we kept the baby. That was Min. You see, when your mother birthed you, it was difficult, and though she seemed to recover, she never birthed another baby. I didn't know it was to be that way, but maybe she did, so she was ready to adopt. And I can't say it was wrong, because Min has been a good daughter."

"She is of the early folk," Kip said. "That's why she's so spooky."

"That must be it," Huu agreed. "The spirits must have safeguarded her, by summoning me there before she died. We buried her mother where she was, and we did not settle there, but every month we take Min there so that her mother's spirit can see that the child is well. And nothing truly bad has happened to us since Min joined us, though there have been some threats."

"Yes, we almost got banished when King Hotu Matua died."

"We almost did," Huu agreed. "But we had no hand in that, and that became clear in due course. In any event, he was very old. He was king for fifty years, ever since our people arrived here. Now we will erect a great statue in his memory, which is why you and I are making this trip."

"Yes, because we have the instructions written in the script," Kip said. "That's why we have to read. So we can remember how to make and move the statue." He had complained about having to read throughout, but now he was proud of his ability.

"And why the short ears don't read," Huu said. "That knowledge gives us power."

"Do the spirits protect me too?"

Huu backtracked a bit to catch the reference: the spirits protected Min. "Of that we can't be sure. But we hope so."

"She has always been there when the spirits helped."

"We don't really know that the spirits help or hinder us," Huu reminded him. "They may not care about ordinary people."

"No, Min can see the spirits," Kip said.

Huu didn't argue. He had never seen a spirit himself, but there was indeed something about Min. Even the bugs didn't seem to bite her as they did others.

The sun was high when they reached the quarry, and they stopped to eat their lunch of hardened sweet potato mash before climbing the slope to the quarry. Then they made their way up to the top of the mountain, where it opened out into a bowl-shaped depression. This was the quarry, where they were chipping out yellow stone. The real statue was being carved from the outside edge of the mountain, but the practice block was inside, where there happened to be unneeded stone. A number of short-ear children were crowding close, fascinated by the proceedings. One crew of their elders used hand axes to chip away at the rock beneath the statue. It was evidently tedious, wearing work, but there were many slaves, and when one man had to quit and leave the pit for fresh air, another immediately took his place. The long-ear supervisor kept the work constantly going.

The short ears were already hauling the practice block over the rim, so as to start it sliding down the slope toward the level ground. The long-ear foreman and his assistant were yelling constant orders. It wasn't going well, because the stone was extremely heavy and rough, and kept snagging, so that men with long poles had to pry it up. At the moment it was balking right at the rim.

"This is why they need us," Huu said. He brought out his flute and approached the foreman. "Music will give them strength," he said.

The foreman looked doubtful, but made the best of it. "Anything will be better than this."

Huu addressed the workers. "When you hear the music, pull. When it stops, you stop."

They smiled. They liked music.

They took hold of the ropes and got the slack out. The men with the poles got set. Then Huu played his music, and the men heaved on both ropes and poles.

The huge stone quivered, then moved. It tilted over the rim and came down outside, sliding so readily that the foreman's jaw dropped. Huu had to stop playing almost as soon as he started, because the sudden shift had changed the angle.

The foreman looked at Huu with new appreciation. In a moment the barrier that had balked them had been surmounted. All because of the strength lent by the music.

"They pull harder, and together," Huu explained. "Music coordinates them."

"Well, let's get this on down the hill so we can stand it up," the foreman said gruffly.

The next stage promised to be much easier, because the motion would be all downhill. At some places it looked almost steep enough for the block to slide on its own.

The slaves lined up along their ropes. The children collected, eager to watch the huge stone move. "Get clear!" the foreman yelled at them irritably, and most stepped back, but sneaked forward again the moment his eyes were off them.

"Help warn them back," Huu told Kip. "They could get in the way." His son, glad to get involved, went to enforce the clearance. He was young, but he was older than the slave children, and he was a long ear, so they paid attention.

Huu lifted his flute, watching the foreman. When the foreman nodded, he began to play. The slaves hauled vigorously on the ropes, and the polemen heaved behind.

The block nudged forward—then abruptly slid faster. The men had put forth the same effort as they had at the brink, but this was downslope, and the effect was much greater. The ropes went slack as the block moved on its own, its momentum increasing.

"Get clear!" the foreman shouted, and the men dropped the ropes and scrambled away to the sides as the block ground down upon them.

The children screamed, similarly scrambling. But one little girl stumbled, fell, and rolled back into the path of the surging block. Huu watched in horror, seeing her doomed. Then Kip launched himself at her, running in front of the hurtling block, hauled her bodily up, and hurled her ahead of him, out of the way.

And the block slid down on his trailing leg.

Kip didn't scream. He just sank down as the block crunched to a halt, looming over his body.

For a moment Huu thought his son hadn't been hurt. Then he realized that Kip's training had told: he would not admit pain before slaves. It was part of the protocol that kept the slaves in awe.

Huu and the foreman and several children arrived at the block together. A woman appeared to pick up the crying child.

Huu kneeled before Kip. The boy was face down, his jaw clenched. Huu felt down along his body. One leg was clear, but the other was pinned under the block.

The foreman shouted three names. "Dig him out! Carefully!" The three workers took their stone axes and pounded at the hard ground around Kip's leg, excavating widening holes.

Huu took his son's hand. "We are getting you clear," he said in a normal tone, as if this were routine. Kip looked at him, his face expressionless. Huu knew the boy was in terrible pain, but was locking it out.

Slowly the excavation around Kip's leg extended under the block. The pressure eased, and Huu was able to haul his son clear.

The foreman barked more orders. A pallet was brought, and the boy set on it. Four slaves carried him carefully down the slope to the temporary house there.

A woman approached Huu. "He saved my child. I know medicine. I will help him."

Huu nodded. Slaves could not always be trusted, but this woman had reason. She hurried after the pallet party.

When Huu rejoined Kip, he saw that the woman was already applying a poultice to the leg. Kip was unconscious. But he also saw that the damage was very bad. The leg below the knee had been severely crushed, and blood was everywhere. He doubted that Kip would be able to walk again.

"I have sent a slave to notify your wife," the foreman said. Huu nodded thanks. Like Kip, he was constrained to show no weak emotions before slaves.

When it was clear that all was being done for Kip that could be done, they returned to work moving the block. No emotion, no delay: long ears were always efficient. Only when the job was done, and the slaves were gone, would Huu be able to let his feelings out. So that afternoon he played his flute while the block moved, and they got the job done.

"But we'll need an anchor for the real statue," the foreman said. "It's bigger than the block, and more delicate."

"We can cut a big tree, and set the trunk in stone," Huu said. "Then ropes can be tied to it, to hold the statue back." They were learning as they proceeded; the practice block was turning out to be an excellent device.

But behind the mask of the job, Huu's thoughts were circling like seabirds. What was to become of Kip—and how would Aan react to the awful news?

❂

Min suddenly cried out as if in pain. "What is it?" Aan asked, alarmed. They were in their small garden by the bank of the river, picking bad bugs from their sweet potatoes. They could buy food at the town market, but preferred to grow their own when they could; it tasted better.

"Kip!" the girl cried.

Aan felt a chill. Sometimes Min imagined things, but sometimes she was right. "What about Kip?"

"I don't know. But it's bad. Very bad." Min began to cry.

Aan did not like this at all. She simply had to hope that it was a false alarm.

She looked out to the west, seeing the sea that led to the horizon. It made her wonder, as it always did, whether her grandmother had been right to remain here, instead of going with the expedition into the sea.

"Tell me," Min said, picking up on her mother's mood, as she always did.

Maybe the familiar story would break the deadly worry. "Fifty summers ago, my grandparents were musicians and dancers who entertained kings, in the great capital city of Chan Chan," Aan said. "But when our clan leader fought and lost, he had to sail across the great sea, lest his supporters be destroyed. My grandfather had played music, and my grandmother had danced at his court, and he offered them the chance to come with him. They considered it carefully, and almost decided to go, but Grandmother An'a concluded that it would not be a safe journey for her children, so they stayed. But there was still a shadow on our lineage, so they traveled south along the great road that follows the sea, a long, long way. Until they came here to Omo, where there was a great need for their talents and no great concern about the reputation of their clan. Here they settled, though it was part of the culture of Tiahuanaco, not Chimú. Here they worship the sun more than the moon, but our grandparents found they could accept that."

"It is good for me that they did," Min said. "Otherwise you would not have been here to find me when I lost my other mother."

Aan hugged her. "And how desolate our lives would have been, without you, for I will never have a blood daughter." Min knew that she had been adopted as a baby, but not the full circumstance of it: her mother had conceived her adulterously, and rather than face death by being cast off a raft far out to sea, or from a high mountain cliff, had left the newborn baby in the desert to die. Huu had happened to be in the area, and had seen the baby left, and picked it up and brought it home. They had adopted Min, though not then realizing that Aan had become barren. Thus it was, in retrospect, a better decision than it had seemed at the time, and Min had turned out to be blessed of the spirits, making it better yet.

As they returned to their house, they saw a slave hurrying toward it. "He is seeking us," Min said.

Aan's alarm returned. "What is it?" she called. The man was dusty, and must have traveled through the desert.

"Are you the Lady Aan?" he asked, and when he saw her nod, continued, "I am sent from Cerro Baul by Huu to tell you that Kip is injured."

"Oh!" Aan cried, her daughter's premonition confirmed. "What happened?"

"They were moving a big stone block for a statue, and a slave child fell before it, and Kip saved the child but his own leg was caught."

Aan started to ask how bad the injury was, but saw Min's face and stifled it. "We must go there immediately," she said.

"It is too late," the slave said. "It will be dark."

He was right. "Go to the slave house," Aan said. "Return here at dawn. You will guide us there."

The slave nodded and departed. The slave house wasn't much, but there was shelter and food there. Aan and Min entered their house. When they were alone, they both wept.

Then they made preparations for their journey. Huu and Kip had gone to Cerro Baul, which was an ancient city, now deserted, with many marvels of stone, for work on a large stone statue that was being prepared as a monument. Slaves would be doing most of the work, but qualified citizens of the culture had to supervise, and Huu knew the ritual music. He was acclaimed as the best musician in the region, so the honor had been his, and Kip was getting good experience.

For they were members of the elite class, and leadership was their role, whether in the arts or otherwise. They enjoyed the social privilege of wearing ear tubes, and of marrying among the lesser nobility, which was rare for artisans. Kip and Min were schooled in the manners of their class, so that they would uphold its standards without error.

There was time left before full night. Aan and Min composed themselves like the ladies they were, and went out to shop for supplies for the journey. Their stucco apartment was part of a larger complex within the elite quarter, separately walled; they had to go to the market section to requisition what they needed.

They got good cotton traveling cloaks, and heavy sandals for the rough trail. They got bags of dried beans and maize, for these were lighter to carry. And of course some coca leaves for chewing, to extend their endurance.

They returned to their sector, which was now lighted at intervals by torches so that they could see their way. The guard at the gate let them through without challenge, recognizing them. "You are traveling?" he asked, noting their supplies.

"My son has been injured in Cerro Baul," Aan explained.

"That is an ill-favored ruin. I will pray to the goddess of the moon that he recovers," the man said courteously. The moon goddess was Si, much more powerful than the sun god, because the moon could be seen by both night and day. Sometimes the two gods fought each other, and the sun would succeed in darkening the moon for a time. That was a terrible omen. But sometimes the moon darkened the sun, and that was cause for great celebration.

"Thank you," Aan said. The more appeals to Si, the better. She and Min would make their own before they slept this night.

❂

Next day they set out, following the trail along the mountain slopes. The region was paved with some good roads, but not where they needed to go. The slave carried most of the supplies, except for the coca; while Aan knew that Huu would not have sent an untrustworthy man, caution was best, and they would need to ration the precious leaves sensibly. They both carried hidden knives, as a further precaution, for they were a woman and a girl, going into the desert, and male slaves had been known to get notions. But the knives would be shown only as a last resort; as dancers they were tougher than they looked, and could probably avoid trouble without bloodshed.

The day soon became hot, and they paused frequently to dip water from the small streams they passed. The slave simply threw himself down and put his mouth to the water, but this was not appropriate for either elites or women; they used their own cups. In addition they drank singly, the other always alert. The same was true when they needed to perform other natural functions: one always guarded the other. Only at night did they both relax, sharing a blanket in the way station house, while the slave slept outside the door. Should the man choose to enter, they would hear and awaken immediately, grasping their knives.

"This is fun!" Min confided just before she slept.

Aan didn't comment.

In the morning they resumed walking, and made good progress; Aan could see that the slave was surprised. "We are dancers," she explained. "We are used to using our legs." That was true, but it was also true that this constant travel through the heat was wearing.

It was uphill, and the slope increased. That was inevitable, because Cerro Baul had been a mountaintop fortress-city, back in the years of empire. It had been established beyond the accepted limit of the Huari Empire, so had to be well fortified. But that had not done it much good, because it had been deserted for as long as anyone remembered.

At last they approached the empty city. It was a sharp contrast to Omo, which was really just a village, readily accessible, and not intended to be defended. Cerro Baul was solidly walled atop a mountain so steep that in some places the sides were vertical. Yet there were terraced fields around it, irrigated by a long contour canal from the neighboring mountain, where there was a spring. From the narrow connection between mountains a narrow trail led on up toward the city. They paused to dip drinks from it before moving on.

The final approach was guarded by walled terraces with parapets, with soldiers watching; it was unimaginable that such a city could be taken by storm. Min was openly staring, amazed by the ramparts. "How could this city ever be conquered?" she asked. For according to legend it had indeed changed hands on occasion.

"A long siege during a drought would deny water and food to it," Aan explained. "After a time, the spring would dry up, and the defenders could no longer fight; they would be dying."

"Oh. Ugh." Perhaps the girl had learned a significant lesson. No one strategy could prevail against every threat.

The path switched back and forth, limited to single-file traffic, leading up the face of the cliff. Aan affected nonchalance, but this seemed precarious to her, and she was quite relieved to reach the comfort of the main walls.

At last they were in the city proper. Nestled within its stout walls, it seemed ordinary, apart from its eerie silence, because they could not see out over the ragged landscape. But both Aan and Min were breathing faster, because the air seemed thin here, though perhaps it was just from their exertion. The slave guided them through the narrow avenues between stone buildings to the building where Huu and Kip were.

Huu met them at the entrance with a mixed expression. He was glad to see them, obviously, but apprehensive too. He didn't hug them in his usual fashion, but simply led them inside. Min clutched Aan's hand, shivering, and that made Aan more nervous. Min always seemed to know what was serious and what was not.

Kip was lying on a cushioned pallet, and Aan knew immediately that he was seriously ill. Sweat glistened on his forehead, yet he was shivering much as Min was. Aan glanced at Min, and saw similar sweat on her forehead. She was relating to the illness, in her fashion.

Aan fell to her knees, embracing her son. He felt her touch, and his eyes flickered open. He formed a tremulous smile. "Mother."

"Yes, my darling, I am here," she said soothingly. But she felt the terrible heat of him; he was shivering while burning. She knew that he had the fever of injury, the kind that killed wounded men, and he was only a boy.

"So cold," he said, and closed his eyes again. She hugged him closer, and kissed his fiery face, reassuring him by her closeness and love.

"I am here," she repeated. "I will make you well." But the fear gnawed at her core, as cold as Kip was hot.

She heard Min's sobbing, muffled by Huu's cloak. Then she knew that her son could not be saved. She had arrived only in time to give him comfort as he died.

❈

Scil followed the path along the rugged coastline, carrying her precious burden of breadfruit. The breadfruit tree fruited seasonally, and when the season was short, there could be famine. Life was hard, especially for those of the lower classes, and recent warfare had made it harder. She had hoped to marry well, but that had not worked out.

She came to the high square platform of fitted basalt stones that supported the house. Scev was there, wakened from his nap by her return. He ran to hug her, scrambling down from the higher level and around the red tuff slabs that divide their house.

Scil liked few folk, and loved none—except her three-year-old son. But she was practical, and knew that raising him without a father was not going to get easier. But she never told him that. Soon she had some breadfruit for him to eat.

Later, Baa entered the house. "The musician has lost his son," he said gruffly. "Now is your chance."

"I'm not giving him *my* son!" Scil said, glancing around to be sure that Scev was beyond hearing.

"You don't need to *give* him your son. Sell him."

"What?"

Her brother explained. Then, slowly, Scil smiled. This was the break she had been waiting for.

❁

Now it was time to walk the practice block to its destination. The real statue would be brought to the base of the quarry mountain, stood up, and finished on the backside—a process that would take some time. But the block needed no such attention, as it was of no account. They would use it until the drill was perfect, and by that time the real statue should be ready.

Huu's heart was hardly in it, but he had a job to do and a pretense to maintain. He had to demonstrate that even the loss of his only son and only natural child could not affect his composure as a long ear. No slave could be allowed to see him suffer.

So he lay in his shelter, alone, hoping to get enough sleep to enable him to put on the proper show of indifference in the morning, and to be able to play faultlessly for the practice sessions. Any tears he had, had to be now, covered by the darkness.

"Long ear Huu." It was a woman's voice, with the short-ear intonation. "I bring what you need."

"I need nothing," he replied curtly. Slave sex was the last thing he wanted at a time like this.

"It is Scil. I beg you heed me."

Scil—the wench he had used four years ago to warm the nights. She had been a luscious body, but he knew her to be a calculating creature, and he wanted none of her now.

"Depart."

"You must listen," she said, crawling into his shelter.

Anger flared at this violation. "I told you no!" He lifted his hand to strike her.

"I brought your son."

His hand froze in the darkness. She had interfered with the funeral preparations for Kip? "My son is dead. If you—"

"Your son by me. Here is his hand." She caught his hand in the darkness and placed in it a small hand, that of a child not far beyond walking age.

"You had a son by me?" he asked, astonished. "I know nothing of this!"

"I did not tell you of him."

He realized that it could be. He had had his pleasure of her several times. Then the mission had finished, and he had returned to Aan and needed no more bed warming. The wench had begged him to stay with her, but of course he hadn't. He had not seen her since. This child was the right age.

"Why?"

"Because when I had him in my belly, I knew there were three fates for him, and two of them I did not like. So I hid him instead. Only my people knew."

And of course her short-ear friends would not tell long ears what she did not wish them to. The short ears were as good at keeping secrets from long ears as the long ears were at keeping power from short ears. So he had never learned or even suspected. "Three fates?"

"You could kill him. You could take him into your family. You could leave him to me. I did not wish to lose him by either death or long-ear adoption."

"I would not kill a child!" Huu protested.

"But neither would you give him up."

He was silent, considering. She was probably right. Normally the offspring of mixed-class unions remained with the mother, but this was not fixed. He and Aan had adopted Min; they probably would have adopted a son he sired. Scil would have been powerless to prevent it, being of the slave class. "I would have taken him," he agreed.

"So I kept him, and I remained away from you despite my longing for you, because you would have seen by my breasts that I was nursing."

Also true. Long ears normally were clothed, but short ears usually wore only grass skirts. So that explained why she had disappeared, despite seeming to enjoy warming his bed those nights. She had just confirmed that she had liked it, and explained why she had come to him no more. He had thought she had merely lost interest, and though any long-ear man could claim any short-ear woman at any time regardless of her short-ear relationships, such as having a husband, he had not wished to have any woman against her will.

Then something else occurred to him. "Why reveal this now? I could still take him from you."

"Only at my price."

"Price?" This was not the way a short ear spoke to a long ear.

"I reveal him now because you are in need of a son."

Suddenly her rationale came clear. He had lost his son, and now learned that he had another. She was cynical, but that was in character. She had bided her time, hiding her son, until her opportunity came. But exactly what did she hope to accomplish?

"Price?" he repeated.

"Marry me."

"But I have a wife!"

"Divorce her."

The audacity of this demand stunned him. "You expect me to divorce my long-ear wife in favor of a short-ear woman?"

"She can never give you another son. I can. You may raise him as a long ear. I will oppose nothing—if you recognize me as your wife."

"Impossible!" Amazement was giving way to outrage.

"And I can warm you as well as any woman can, as you know," she said. She removed the little boy's hand from his and lifted his hand to her bare breast. It was no longer a nursing breast, but was marvelously full and firm, with a nice nipple. The touch stirred his groin.

But it was not enough. "I love Aan. I do not love you. I will not do it."

"Then I will not give you the boy."

"I will take him!"

"You will not find him. Already I have sent him back to hiding."

Huu realized that the boy had left them. At three years old, he could obey such an instruction. "How do I know he is mine?"

"If you saw him by day, you would know. Anyone would. He has fair skin and red hair. I have been with no other long-ear man."

She was surely right again. But she was mistaken in thinking that he would summarily dismiss his wife for the sake of a natural son. "No."

"I will give you time to consider," she said, stretching out beside him. Her warm body touched his along its length.

"No," he repeated. "I will adopt the boy, but I will not divorce my wife. I will not marry you."

"We shall see," she said. Then she drew away from him, and was silently gone.

Huu had thought that grief might keep him awake. Now he had two reasons, because the vamp had succeeded in arousing him, and had left him unfulfilled. Yet her demand remained impossible. He would not separate from Aan.

Yet how was he to get that boy, his son? He knew that Scil was too crafty to try to present a pretend son to him, and certainly she could have gotten the baby from their liaison of four years before. Taken now, the child could be raised as a long ear, and have his ears properly extended, and Huu's line would continue. That prospect was gaining in appeal. His grief for Kip still raged, but his sensible mind saw the advantage in replacing his lost son quickly.

What would Aan think of it? He knew she would accept it, because she had always treasured Min, who was no blood kin to either of them; she would be glad of a half-son.

None of which mitigated their agony over the loss of Kip. The boy had died with honor, upholding long-ear standards of conduct, but that did not alleviate the void. How readily he could have been saved, if only anyone had known what was about to happen! But it had been so sudden.

There was no profit in such thinking. Huu tried to turn his mind away from it. But then the thought of Scil's offer returned, and he did not want to dwell on that either.

He would ask Aan. She was grief-stricken too, for the same reason, but she would know what was best. Certainly he would not divorce her, but there might be some other avenue.

With that thought, he began to relax, and finally he slept.

❂

In the morning everything was ready. The slaves had been assembled, the ropes were attached, and the block was ready to walk. They had studied this in the script, and tried it with little models. They knew how to do it. But they had never before done it on this scale. There could be ugly surprises, just as there had been when sliding the block down the mountain slope.

The foremen was well aware of that. This was the practice block, but it was the same size as the statue, which meant that it stood twice the height of a man and would crush any man it landed on. They had already seen its power when it pinned Kip. There seemed to be a malignancy to it, as if its spirit was determined to wreak any mischief it could. The stone did not like to be moved from its home, and resisted their effort.

"Now here is how it goes," the foreman said. He brought out a much smaller wooden model. "We pull on the high rope until it tilts, like so—" He angled the wood block so that it was tilting on one side. "Then we pull on the low rope, so, and the other side comes forward." He demonstrated, making the block lurch drunkenly forward as it fell back into place. "That's one step."

The slaves murmured, beginning to appreciate how a statue could walk. Some of them tried it themselves, leaning to one side, then pulling stiff legs around to the front. It could be done.

"You will follow the music," the foreman said. "Don't watch me. Listen. You on the top rope: when you hear this, pull, slowly." He signaled Huu. Huu played a strident alternation of two high notes. "You on the bottom rope: when you hear this, pull swiftly." Huu played an alternation of two lower notes. "When your music stops, you stop. Instantly."

Then, to be sure they had it, the foreman demonstrated again with his wooden block. Huu played the high notes, and the man tilted the block to one side. Then Huu played the low notes, and the side jerked forward. "One step at a time," the foreman concluded. "Then we change the ropes to the opposite sides, so we can step the other side forward. Any questions?"

"Won't it take a long time to get anywhere?" a slave asked.

"No longer than it took to raise it," the foreman said. "But we'll get it done. Anyway, this is just one stage of it; the next lesson will be how to haul it on rollers, where we have room."

Then they went to work on the stone block. Men climbed ladders to its head section, and wrapped a reed mat around it for cushioning and protection. Of course there was no face there, but they understood that everything had to be the same on the practice block as it would be on the real statue, or there might be other deadly surprises. The high rope was attached to one side. Then they wrapped the base similarly and attached the low rope to the other side.

The men took hold of their ropes, ten to a rope. They stretched out in their two lines. "Remember," the foreman said, "you don't look at me or the statue. You listen for your music and pull. I will watch the statue, and the musician will watch me. So if the statue falls, it's my fault. If you do it right."

The slaves chuckled. They would be careful to do it right. They did not want to get blamed for a mistake, and they did not want to have to erect the block a second tedious time, under the supervision of an angry long ear.

"Crew—ready," the foreman said, and the men took good grips on their ropes. "Musician—ready." Huu lifted his flute, his eyes on the foreman. The man had made light of the task, but there was no question that precise timing was necessary, and if the statue fell, it would take another half month to stand it up again.

The foreman glanced around at his assistant and two slave spotters, who would judge the tilt of the block from each side and signal its direction and extent by the angles of their lifted arms. Kip would have been doing that, had he not—but Huu had to drive out that thought before it destroyed his concentration. Because he had to read the foreman's signals exactly. He would not be playing long at a time, or melodically, but he had to be just right.

The foreman gave him the high sign. Huu played the high tweedle. The men pulled on the high rope. Huu wanted to watch the block, but couldn't; his eyes were fixed on the foreman. He, of all people, had to get it just right.

The foreman gave him the low sign. Huu played the low tweedle. He heard the grunting at one rope abate, and begin at the other. He heard the crunching as the block moved. It was working!

The foreman gave him the stop sign, and Huu stopped. Now he could look at the block. It seemed unchanged, but as they went to it, he saw that its position had shifted. There was a wedge-shaped depression behind, where it had stood. It had taken one step, and half of it was standing on new ground.

"That was beautiful," the foreman said. "We got it right the first time. But that's only one step. We need to work on smoothness. I'm going to swap out one man on each rope each time, so he can watch it walk; then you'll all see what we're doing."

Thereafter there were always two slaves watching. And sometimes the angle was such that Huu could see the stone as well as the foreman. The thing lurched crazily, but it was indeed like a clumsy man walking. It was impressive to watch.

By noon they had walked the block twenty paces. The imprint of its track remained in the soil, making a hard path. The slaves walked along it during their noon rest break, endlessly impressed with this secondary evidence of their accomplishment. They had moved the giant stone so far!

But the corners of the block were wearing and chipping, because the rock of the mountain wasn't as hard as other rock. If they walked it a long way, it would wear down too far, spoiling the statue. They would have to brace it with a wooden base, to protect the corners for long walks. They were learning as they went.

In the afternoon the foreman trained another crew, because the labor was strenuous and fatiguing, and men who were overtired could make mistakes. But there was no substitute for Huu, because there were not many musicians on the island. That might have been just as well, because the constant concentration kept his mind off the death of his son. To a degree.

✪

Several days later, when the walking crews had been trained, Huu walked west across the island to the topknot quarry at Puna Pao. The main statue was of yellow stone, but it would wear a headdress of red stone, because Hotu Matua's hair was red. It would also have inset eyes of bright white shell with black obsidian pupils. The eye sockets would not even be cut until the statue was in its appointed place, but the eyes were already being prepared. It wouldn't do to have a statue that couldn't see.

And of course this would be only the first statue. There would be others when other kings died, and the gods would be represented. The head priest had determined a model which all statues would emulate. So this was merely the beginning of a great age of ceremony.

And his son Kip would never see it.

More than one topknot was being carved from the stone. They were almost as tall as Huu, seeming huge, but would be the right size when set atop their statues. These would not be as difficult to move, because they could simply be wrapped and rolled, then lifted by stone ramps to their places. It was Huu's job to select the particular topknot to grace Statue Hotu's head.

A short-ear man approached him. He looked familiar, but Huu wasn't sure of his identity. "What is your concern?" he asked the man.

"I am Baa, brother of Scil. We might deal."

What was this presumption? The only way long ears dealt with short ears was by giving them their directives for work. "What is your concern?"

"My sister has hidden her child. I can fetch him for you."

So the man knew about that. But Huu did not care to let him know the boy's value to him. "I instructed Scil in dancing, several years ago. She had a baby. She may do what she pleases."

"But the boy is yours, and now you have no other son."

A flash of irritation mixed with his grief. Huu did not like this man knowing about this matter. But of course he would know his sister's business. And if he could deliver the boy—"What do you want?"

Baa looked canny. "Your wife is beautiful."

"You suppose this is something I do not know?"

"In the dark of the moon, each month, send her to me."

What? This lowly slave wanted to touch a long-ear woman? This was worse than presumption! "Begone before I have you flogged."

"For the boy."

Scil might hide the boy from Huu, but she couldn't hide him from her brother. Scil wanted to trade the boy for marriage, displacing Aan. Baa wanted to embrace Aan one or two nights a month without denying her her status. It was an appalling prospect, but it was a better alternative than divorce. Huu did want the boy.

"I will consider," he said gruffly, turning away.

When he turned again, Baa was gone. He continued his business, checking the topknots, and made his selection. He marked it, and went to his tent.

There was a woman in it. Huu knew immediately who it would be. "Go away, Scil," he said. "I will not pay your price."

"Then have me this night for no price," she said. "I know you need warming."

"Warming becomes too complicated."

She did not move. "I told you I warmed you four years ago for the dancing you taught me. I lied. It was because I love you."

This made him pause. "Maybe then you will understand that I love Aan, and will not give her up."

"But she can never give you a son."

He wondered whether she knew about her brother's offer. "If I could have the boy without having you also, I might take him."

She laughed. "Of course. But I am the price of him. If you would love my boy, you must let me love you."

So she did not know. If he told her, she would hide the boy from her brother, too, and that deal would be void. But if he made that other deal, what would become of Scil? "What will you do if I make no deal?"

"You are actually interested?"

"Yes." Though perhaps not in the way she thought.

"Then lie with me, and I will tell you."

She wanted to lie with Huu, and her brother wanted to lie with Aan. Would she settle for Baa's price? "What if I were to lie with you only in the dark of the moon?"

"For my son? That is the kind of deal a man would make. I want more."

So it was status, rather than love of him, that drove her, despite her claim. "I will not give you more."

"You are as hard to bargain with as my brother," she complained.

"What of your brother?" he asked, suddenly alert.

"He wants to be the first short-ear chief."

Huu remembered. It was becoming cumbersome to administer the growing short-ear population directly, so a short-ear chief would be assigned. Candidates were now being considered, and the decision would be announced during the ceremony of the completion of the placement of the Hotu statue. "That decision is not in his hands. Three leading short ears will do it."

"Yes. One of them hates Baa, so will vote for someone else. But Baa hopes to marry me to another, so he will support Baa. That will give him an even chance."

"Your brother can tell you whom to marry?"

"He is the man of our family."

"Oh, of course. But how can you offer to marry me, then, without his authority?"

"You are long ear. He is short ear. If you married me, my brother could not stop it. And my son would be better off, because you would not mistreat him."

More of her rationale was coming into view. "The other man would mistreat him?" Huu had his own misgiving about that.

"He doesn't want another man's child. He would be happier if I came alone. But he will take me, because—" She reached up from where she lay to catch Huu's leg in the darkness. "You know why. I will show you again, if you have forgotten."

"I can see why you would prefer to marry me," Huu said. "If you have to pretend to love a man, it might as well be one who will treat your son well."

"Yes." Then he knew she was smiling. "But it would not be pretense, with you. I would warm you without price, were it not for my son."

"Then give him to me, and be free to marry the other man without fear for your son."

"Give him to you? When I could do so much better for myself? I think you want him enough to pay for him."

"I will not sacrifice my wife for him!"

"That may be your choice," she said indifferently.

"You seek to force me into something I do not want. Suppose I force *you* into something you do not want?"

"That is impossible, because with you I want it."

"Something else," he said grimly.

"Kill me," she said evenly. "And know that your son will die where he is hidden. You will never find him."

"Get out of my tent!"

She sighed. "I suppose the mood is spoiled. I will come to you another time." She got up and brushed by him, so that he could tell she was naked. The touch did stir his reaction, making him desire her, as she intended. She had been a remarkably apt warmer. Then she was out and gone, silently.

He lay in the bed that she had warmed. Scil knew how badly he wanted that boy, and was playing him in like a fish, to gain her way. But her demand was simply too much.

She had shown her callousness. It matched that of her brother. And her brother had a better offer.

Except for one thing. Baa wanted Aan, one night a month. Aan was unlikely to agree to that. But Huu would ask her, when he returned home tomorrow.

✸

Aan and Min went out to meet Huu gladly as he approached the house. He had been long away, and they had had to suffer their grief alone; now it was time to resume living. But Min had a caution. "Something amazing," she said.

"Anything is better than what we have been through."

"Maybe not." But there was no more time for discussion, for they had reached Huu, who hugged them both.

"Min says you have something amazing to tell us," Aan said after a moment.

Huu looked abashed. "I do. But it is awkward. There are—"

"Tell us, Daddy!"

He told them.

Aan stared at him, shocked. "You have a son? By a slave woman?" She had thought that nothing could push aside the shock of her grief for Kip, but she had never anticipated this.

"It seems I do," he said, looking rueful. "That bed warmer, four years ago, Scil. It seems she got a baby by me, but never told me. Now she has offered him to me, but at too steep a price."

"You must get that child! What price could be too steep?"

"She wants me to divorce you and marry her."

Shock on shock! Aan had to sit down, lest she faint.

"I told her no," Huu hastened to tell her. "I love you. I would never—"

"What about the boy? How can any son of yours grow to be a slave?"

"There is another way," he said, but he did not look easy. "Her brother Baa approached me next day, and said he would fetch me the boy. But his price—"

"Oooo!" Min exclaimed, her eyes as round as her mouth.

Aan glanced at her, suddenly apprehensive.

"He wants you, by the dark of each moon," Huu finished.

Now she looked at him, sharply. "You would allow this?"

"I would, before I would allow the other."

He would let her be with another man, rather than divorce her. At another time she might have felt complimented. But either was intolerable.

"There is more," Min said.

"We had better hear it," Aan said, feeling somewhat as if she had stepped into the spirit world.

Huu glanced at her, then shrugged. "Well, only that I learned that Baa wants to be chief of the slave tribe. But that does not relate to this, except that it explains why Scil is so eager to marry me. She wants to escape being used as a prize for one of the judges' vote."

"More," Min repeated.

"And to keep her son from a man who would mistreat him."

Aan stiffened. "She has a point." It was a special irony that Aan could not have more children of her own, because she loved them dearly. The thought of one being abused horrified her.

"I'll have another brother!" Min exclaimed.

Now Huu looked at her. "How can that be so, when we will not do what either slave wants?"

"I don't know. But he'll be here soon."

Aan exchanged a glance with Huu. Then he looked away. "Let me take Min somewhere," he said.

So Aan could get herself settled. She nodded, appreciating the thought. Huu took Min's hand, and they went out to consider the evening sky.

Aan lay down, but she did not rest. Her emotions had been roughly stirred by Huu's news. She could understand why the slave brother and slave sister would seek to capitalize on their situations, but did not see how to get the boy without paying an appalling price. She did want the boy, because he was Huu's, and because he might help fill the void left by Kip. She didn't care that the child had been sired on a slave girl; these things happened. Had they known about him before, they would have taken the baby immediately after weaning. It was a shock, learning about him now, but more of a favorable one than an unfavorable one.

Min believed that there was an acceptable way to get the child. What could it be? Aan focused on that, for it was a considerable distraction from her grief. How could they get that child without having to submit to the lusts of brother or sister?

Then Huu and Min were returning. "We thought of a way!" Min cried.

"A way?" she inquired guardedly.

"We can offer Baa something else," Huu explained. "He wants power in the slave realm. We can arrange for him to have our people's support. We control one of the three judges who will decide what man will be the slave leader. Baa means to marry his sister to another, and that will give him a majority. He surely craves power more than the body of a dancer. He will agree."

"Surely," Aan agreed, her feelings mixed. "But is he a man of honor? Will he deliver the boy when he gains his position?"

"He is not a man of honor, but I am," Huu said. "I will arrange the support after he delivers the boy."

"Then let it be done," Aan said with relief.

○

Days later, a slave with a bundle approached the house. "He's here! He's here!" Min exclaimed.

Aan was baffled. "It is only a slave, dear, not your father."

"My brother! My brother!"

The boy! Aan faced the slave as the man stopped before them. "What have you brought?"

"I made a deal with your husband," the man said. "You for this." He opened the bundle to reveal the face of a small child. Aan saw immediately that the child was kin to Huu; there were bones of the face she recognized.

"That was not the deal," she said with certainty.

"Your support for the child," he said, as if clarifying his reference. But she knew she had backed him off; he had hoped to deceive her into paying an additional price. That was surely why he had brought the child directly to her, instead of to Huu.

"How do I know this is the one?" she asked, though she was sure it was.

"Take his hand." The man set the child down, free of the covering.

Min stepped forward, reaching out her right hand to the boy. The boy reached out to take it with his left hand.

"Like Daddy!" Min cried, pleased.

Evidence enough. The child's mother would have known that he would have a difficult time in a normal family and a worse one with a stepfather who disliked him anyway. Here he would be allowed to use his hands as he pleased, and taught how to conceal his wrong-sidedness when that wasn't possible.

"What is he called?"

"She calls him Scev."

Aan saw the significance. He had given a term for left-handed son. It was exactly appropriate. "Scev," she repeated, and the boy looked at her.

"I have delivered him," the man said. "Keep him safe." He turned away.

The child saw that, and made as if to follow. But Min held him. "You are with us now," she said, hugging him.

Scev had been about to cry. Now he turned into Min, accepting her embrace. Once again Min's magic was working.

Soon they got to know the boy, in their separate fashions. Aan offered him food, and he accepted it somewhat warily; he knew that she was not his mother. He surely thought that his real mother would return for him in due course. And Aan was satisfied with that, for now, because she was not sure how she felt about him. She was adopting him because he was Huu's son; he was no blood relation to her. He was the child of a woman who had wanted to seduce Huu and replace Aan as his wife. That was not an easy thing to accept. Yet the boy himself was innocent of any such scheme; he deserved no censure. He did not know that he was the living evidence of her husband's infidelity. So how was she to approach him, emotionally?

Min had no such problem. She hugged the boy, she played with him, she helped him eat. He had not eaten the food Aan gave him until Min encouraged him. She called him brother. And, indeed, Min was no more related by blood to Aan than Scev was. And there, perhaps, was the key: Aan did love Min. Min had been the joy of her life throughout, as much a daughter to her as any birthing of her own could have been. Min had shown the way, just by existing; of course Aan could accept a child she hadn't birthed.

They made a bed for him, but Scev preferred to sleep with Min. Min was willing; she embraced him, and he slept immediately. Aan did not oppose it; the girl was evincing a side of her personality Aan hadn't seen before, because she had always been the little sister, not the big sister. She was taking care of the child, and this definitely made it easier for Aan, with her private doubts and adjustments. She realized that it could have been difficult, had she had to deal with the boy alone. Instead it was easy, because of Min.

Aan took time to sew a new outfit for the boy to wear, because he was in slave attire; that simply would not do. They would have to see about his ears, too, having them pierced for pegs. But that could wait a few days. She laid the clothing out beside Min's bed where she would find it when she woke. Then Aan retired herself, spending some time in a turmoil of racing thoughts before she was able to sleep.

She realized one thing, belatedly: she had hardly thought of Kip since Scev had arrived. That did not mean she did not love and grieve for Kip, just that Scev was a considerable distraction. And he was, perhaps, a son.

◎

Scil returned to her house to discover that Scev was gone. She knew immediately that her brother was responsible. He was trying to make his own deal, and he was trying to deprive her of her son.

She sought him out. She left the village and followed the deep valley to the Tohua, the large ceremonial center where he was working. The Tohua area was a rectangular, flattened earthen area surrounded by stone platforms of various levels. Some platforms served as temples, and others functioned as seating for the various levels of society: "valliol," visitors, old

men, women and children, and the priests each had their own sections. The
entrance was a low cleft between two high platforms, and often one of the
platforms held the long ceremonial drums. This was where the harvest
ceremonies occurred, and memorials, and rites of passages for the members of high-ranking families, and formal tattooing. It had taken a lot of
work to make the Tohua, and it had to be properly maintained. That was the
detail Baa was on today.

Now she spied him. "You took Scev!" she cried. "Where is he?"

"You are better off without that boy. It leaves you free to marry."

"Where is he?" she repeated, anger and fear sharpening her voice.

"I took him to the musician's house. We made a deal."

"You had no right!"

"You are my sister. I can marry you to whom I choose. I have a lot to gain
by this."

"We shall see about that." She stalked away.

She would have to get Scev back. Otherwise she would lose both her son
and her freedom. Only if she made her bargain her way could she escape
what Baa had in mind for her.

❂

It continued next morning. Min took Scev to handle natural functions, and
dressed him in the new clothing, and fed him breakfast. Aan stayed in the
background, ready to step forward when needed.

"Maybe we should get him a toy," Min suggested.

So they went out into the city to shop, and Scev clung tightly to Min's
hand, staring around at the houses he had not seen before. They got him a
rubber ball, and he was amazed and delighted with it. When they got home,
he played with it endlessly, with Min and alone, fascinated by its bounciness.
He was it seemed a cheerful child, ready to be entertained by things and not
quick to cry. He had evidently been well cared for, and that said something
about his mother. Aan understood that she was at best a well-proportioned
dancer—that went with the profession—and somewhat scheming and
heartless. But that could not have applied to her son, who had been neither
abused nor neglected. She must have devoted a lot of caring time to him.

Yet she had given him up to further her brother's career. That was not a
good signal. Aan would never have given up a child, for any reason short of
death—as was the case.

Suddenly the scene before her faded, and she was lost again in grief for
Kip. He had been just on the verge of manhood, trying so hard to measure
up to the standard expected. And he had succeeded—at the expense of his
life. Her tears flowed, blurring her vision, dripping from her chin. *Oh, my
son, my son!*

"Mother." It was Min.

Aan blinked. She shouldn't have let herself go in the presence of the children; it wasn't good form. "I'm sorry, dear. What is it?"

"She comes."

Aan looked around, but as her vision cleared she saw no one. "Who comes?"

"*Her,*" Min said urgently, her eyes flicking toward Scev.

It registered. Scev's mother, Scil. She must have changed her mind. Was she coming to demand her child back?

A cloaked figure appeared at the doorway. "Mother!" Scev cried, running toward her.

Aan remained sitting, the tears still on her face. She didn't know what to do.

The woman swooped Scev up, hugging him. Min came to join Aan, similarly uncertain. They watched the reunion.

Then the woman swung her gaze around to cover them. "You took my baby!" she exclaimed.

Aan, speechless for the moment, could only nod.

Scev wriggled to be put down. Scil set him on the ground. "Do you have any idea what it is like to lose your son?" she demanded angrily.

Scev, frightened by the tone, retreated.

Aan found her voice. "Yes." The tears began to flow again.

Scil paused. "Oh, yes. I forgot. But that doesn't mean you can take mine."

There was so much to say, but Aan found herself unable to utter any of it. Instead it was Min who spoke. "Your brother made a deal—to get me my brother. He brought him here."

"He had no right!" Scil flared.

Scev, frightened anew, went to Min for solace. The girl hugged him close. Min looked at Aan. Then her own tears started. "I guess he didn't," she said. "We thought he did."

Aan put her arm around Min.

"When I came home and found my child gone—" Scil said.

Scev began to cry. The ball fell from his hand, bounced, and rolled across the floor.

"Oh, my darling, I'm not angry at *you!*" Scil said to him, all her hardness and hurt disappearing. "You never did anything wrong. I have come to take you home. Come here."

But the boy turned to Min, burying his face in her robe.

Scil stared at him. Then her eyes took in the group of them: Aan with her arm around Min, Min with her arms around Scev, and the boy remaining with them, clearly of his own volition. All of them crying.

Then Scil's own eyes started flowing. "So close—in one day," she said. "And you got him a ball. What can I do?"

They couldn't answer her. They just waited.

Scil shook her head. "I wanted to be with him, so he would not be mistreated. But I think he is better off here than where I am going. Only—"

They still waited. It was her decision to make, and they could not oppose her.

"Only, may I visit him sometimes?"

"Oh, yes!" Min exclaimed, and Aan nodded.

Thus simply was it settled. Scil turned away.

"Mother!" Scev cried, disengaging. Min let him go. He ran to Scil and hugged her tearfully. Then she turned him around to face the others. "Fetch your ball," she said, and withdrew. By the time he had the ball, she was gone.

"She is still very angry," Min said wisely, "but not at us."

"At her brother, perhaps," Aan said. "Because he is marrying her to a man who doesn't want her child."

"So Scev will be happier with us," Min said.

"Yes. Scil may be a cynical, calculating woman, but she loves him. When she saw that we could love him too, she had to let him go."

"But what will she do to her brother?" Min asked.

Aan shook her head. "We don't want to know."

❁

Huu was glad it was almost over. They had finally walked the real Hotu statue to its stone platform, and set its white stone eyes with their round dark pupils into its eye sockets. They had placed the huge red topknot on its flat head. It was a singularly impressive monument, awing all who gazed upon it. Now all that remained was the ceremony of invocation, and then it would be done and Huu could go home to his wife and daughter. And son.

It began at sunset. A great fire was made before the statue, and a captured seabird was sacrificed on a stone altar. Then the elder long-ear men marched around it in their feather bonnets, and young short-ear women stepped out of their clothing and danced naked in the firelight, their arms uplifted over their heads. The rest sat around, the long ears in one crescent, the short ears in another, watching. The priests performed their rituals, dedicating the statue and invoking the spirit of Hotu Matua as a god who would hereafter look out for the welfare of the entire island.

"Hello," someone murmured beside him. Huu looked, and found the dancer Scil standing naked. It was an intermission for the dancers, and she must have sought him out.

"Your son is with us," he said. "Your brother brought him."

"I know. My new husband prefers it that way."

"You aren't angry?"

"I am angry," she said. "But not at you. You value your son. I saw Scev there. Now he has a sister."

"Min. She is adopted too. We love her."

"Yes. I saw."

"You saw?" he asked, startled, belatedly realizing what this meant. "You saw my family?"

"I went there to take back my child. But in one day they had already won him over. Your daughter is not your blood, but you treat her as your own. She will be a dancer."

"Yes. Min is special." Huu was nervous in retrospect about this woman meeting his family; she could have done much harm. But it seemed she hadn't.

"So I left him there. My anger is not toward your family."

"I am glad of that. I could not expel my wife."

"I understand that, now. She is a good woman. She will love my son as her own."

"Yes." But he wasn't sure that the matter was done. "What is your situation?"

"I showed my new husband two ways I could be," she said grimly. "One he liked very well. The other he liked not at all. I told him the price of the way he liked. He agreed to do my bidding."

Huu could imagine how different she could be, when she chose. She was a beautiful woman, but she had a hard edge. She no longer had to fear the possible abuse of her son, so there was little hold on her. He was still nervous about what she might do. "We honored our deal. Our man will support your brother."

"So my man will cast the deciding vote," she said. "Which I now control." Yet there was an odd stress on her statement. Then her tone shifted. "Your wife gave my boy a ball. She said I could visit him."

That surprised him again. He did not think that Aan would want any contact with Scil, or any chance that the woman might steal back her child. He was sorry again that he had not been able to be there. But the task of moving the statue had been steady, and his part vital.

Then it was time to name the new short-ear chief. The three judges stepped up to the altar and named their choices. The first, who was speaking for the long-ear preference, named Baa. The second named another candidate. The third, who had just married Scil, named—the other candidate.

There was a hush of amazement, for the people knew about the marriage and the reason for it. Had the man reneged? Baa looked stunned, then furious. But then Scil stepped up, still as gloriously naked as the other dancers, and linked her arm through her husband's. She was supporting his choice.

"What is this?" Baa demanded.

"You took my child," she replied, staring him down.

And that was it. He had taken her child, to make her available for this, and she had instead turned her new husband against him. The man had done her bidding. She had lost what she most valued, so she had denied her brother what *he* most desired. There was nothing he could do about it.

Baa stalked away. Now everyone knew how his ploy had failed. He had sought callously to use his sister's child for his own advancement, and paid a price. He had lost not only the position, but his reputation, for Scil had made a fool of him.

Yet Huu knew that she could almost as readily have made a fool of Huu himself, and cost him dearly, had her anger been directed at him or his family. She had gone to his home. Had she taken a knife to Aan—

He aborted that thought. Scil's anger could justifiably have been directed against him, because he had made the deal with her brother. But he had in effect offered what no one else could: a loving family for the child. That was what had saved him. Because Scil did love her son.

Was Easter Island colonized from South America? Legends of both the island and the continent can be interpreted to suggest that this was the case, and the presence of cultivated South American plants such as the sweet potato, the bottle gourd, the manioc, and the totora reeds from which they made their boats confirms that some contact occurred. There was also the giant palm, which grows on the coast of Chile and nowhere else—except Easter Island, before it and the other trees were destroyed by man there. One of those giant trunks seems to have been used as an anchoring post for ropes, to prevent statues from sliding down the slope from the quarry too rapidly. The presence of a written language, as yet undeciphered, in the island also suggests an origin on the continent, where legend speaks of a similar lost script. The appearance and blood group of the long ears may also associate with South America. There are representations of sailing craft, and one type of house emulated those same ships.

But there was also colonization from the Polynesian islands, because their racial type is also present, as the short ears. They brought bananas and chickens, but not much of their culture. One legend indicates that they served as slaves for two hundred years, then revolted and largely destroyed the long-ear power. At that point all work on the statues stopped, leaving hundreds still in the quarry. The subsequent island history was violent, with constant warfare decimating the population, and all the standing statues were eventually toppled. Later still slave ships abducted many islanders, and when some slaves were returned, they brought smallpox, which wiped out most of the rest. Catholic missionaries sought to stamp out all pagan evidences, so that invaluable wood carvings and tablets with writing were destroyed, leaving no one able to read those few that were salvaged. Could Polynesian origins account for all of the original colonization and culture of the island, except for chance vegetation carried by birds or sea currents?

Today Easter Island is faring better, as a tourist attraction, with many of the statues restored. But the debate continues whether there was any non-Polynesian colonization. What, for example, accounts for its lack of pottery, as there is a strong ceramic tradition in South America? What about its lack of sophisticated textiles of the type found on the continent? There was clay on the island for pottery, and fibers for textiles. Would they have brought sophisticated stoneworking technology, without similarly useful ceramics and weaving?

The picture on the west coast of South America is just as confused. Circa A.D. 1100 was between empires, and references seem to contradict each other. So it was difficult to establish exactly who was where, and harder to judge who might have sent the second mission to Easter Island. There isn't any credible historical evidence for such voyages. Yet there is similar statuary, and legends did correctly identify the location of Easter Island, suggesting that ships had not only gone there, but had returned, despite adverse currents. But there are Polynesian legends too, and certainly the ancient Polynesians had the sea traveling expertise to reach Easter Island.

What of the white-skinned, goateed, red-haired folk who became the long ears of the island? Continental legends have them arriving by reed boats from the north, bringing civilization with them. They taught the natives how to do things, then sailed away into the Pacific. Can this be believed? If so, where did they come from? Conjectures abound, but can become wild, such as tracing a group from Mesopotamia around Africa to Central America, across Panama, and down the coast, bringing their reed boat and stone carving technology with them. Yet part of the reason the Inca Empire fell was that the Incas took the Spaniards for these returning god figures. White skins and red hair don't generate in the tropics. Perhaps tissue typing will offer insights, in due course. Preliminary results suggest that the type is Basque, which may indicate that the legends of white men with ships stemmed from recent experience. Certainly the Basques ranged the Pacific in the sixteenth century, and if contacts with them were attributed to earlier times, that might be the explanation. The mysterious pictographic writing might also be a more recent invention, emulating the European scripts. Even the manner the statues were moved is in question; Thor Heyerdahl demonstrated that they could have been walked, but that may have been only for short distances, because the volcanic tuff wore down rapidly. They may have been hauled most of the distance on sledges, or even on tracks and rollers. And the red headstones and inset eyes may have been later innovations, not used at the time of this setting. So every part of it can be questioned, and the background of the settings seem to be cobbled together with spit and string, but the essence is intact: impressive works were accomplished by supposed primitives.

Overall, the mystery remains, with the apostles of the various theories seemingly more interested in supporting their chosen sides and discrediting rivals' claims than in the truth. But there is one lesson to be learned from Easter Island, regardless: a habitat with limited resources may not be wastefully exploited indefinitely, lest disaster strike. There will be more on that in the Author's Note.

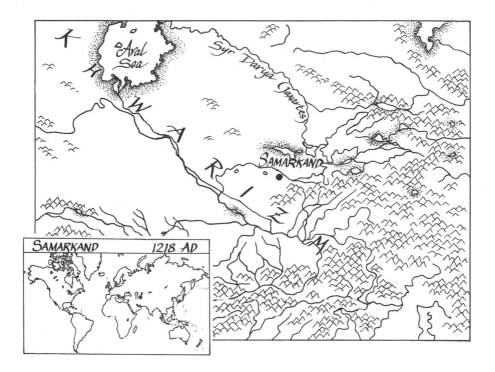

CHAPTER 16

MISTAKE

In A.D. 1218 in central Asia, east of the Aral Sea, the region of Transoxania ("land across the Oxus" River, later the Amu Darya River) was the border between two rapidly growing empires. To the west was Kwarizm, a Moslem state; to the east, Mongolia, a shamanistic culture that viewed the great religions of the world with tolerance as long as they presented no political threat. The Shah of Kwarizm, Muhammad, had largely consolidated his holdings; the khan of Mongolia, Genghis, was then in the process of conquering China, and preferred not to seek further quarrels elsewhere at the moment. The khan made a point of learning about the countries beyond his borders, and knew that Kwarizm was larger and richer than Mongolia, and could mobilize larger armies in this region, because of Mongolia's diversion to the east. Prudence seemed best. So he proposed that there be peace, with the river Jaxartes (later called the Syr Darya) as the boundary between them. He sent envoys with rich gifts to the Shah, with the friendly message that the khan would look upon the Shah as his son—that is, fondly.

Unfortunately, there was a slight misunderstanding that led to complications.

T RY this, Scevo," Huu said, setting the instrument down before his four-year-old son. "You are good on drums; this is better."

"A dulcimer!" Miin exclaimed, delighted. "Where did you get it, Father?"

"There was a barbarian at the bazaar who did not know its value," Huu said. "It was so cheap I had to have it."

"He probably got it from plunder," Ana said ominously.

"Don't be concerned; I wiped the blood off it."

Ana gave him a dark look and returned to the kitchen section, where she and the servant girl were preparing the afternoon meal. She was probably right; when rare quality artifacts appeared in the bazaar, they often derived from plunder. Soldiers and cavalrymen snatched whatever looked interesting, then dumped it for what prices they could get. The merchants cheated them shamelessly, but perhaps it was only fair, as they had probably killed the prior owners. The spoils of war were the main reason to join a military force, and lucky and unscrupulous mercenaries could do very well for themselves, if they survived. But Huu could not blame Ana for disliking this aspect.

"Where are the sticks?" Miin asked.

"He must have lost them," Huu said. "A barbarian wouldn't even recognize this as a musical instrument. I'll make a set." He got to work, quickly carving two fine wood beaters. Such was the force of habit that he looked warily around before starting the carving, and then faced a wall while doing it, so as to conceal the use of his left hand for the knife. His family knew all about his bad-handedness, of course, but he could never afford to forget the way outsiders saw it. In public his right hand was dominant.

Then Miin demonstrated them for the boy. "One in each hand, like this, and strike single strings, lightly, so." She struck a string, and a fine note came forth, augmented by the soundbox built into the base of the dulcimer.

Scevo's face widened into a huge smile. He took the sticks and beat on two strings, making two notes. He liked banging on things, especially when the things made interesting sounds. He beat on two more, making two new notes, and then two more. His happiness radiated in time with the sounds. This was a good instrument, because the child's own bad-handedness did not show; it was always played with both hands.

"Like this," Huu said after a moment. He sat behind the boy, reached around him, took the two little hands in his, and caused him to beat two notes alternately, making a primitive tune. Then he beat them together, making a primitive chord. "Can you do that?" he asked, letting go.

Scevo beat alternate notes, then chords. He was completely delighted.

"Now I will join you," Huu said, bringing out his double clarinet. "You play those notes; I'll play the melody."

The boy joyfully played the notes, and Huu went into a suitable melody. It worked well, for Scevo had good timing, and Huu had long experience that enabled him to adapt to almost any accompaniment.

"I think we have found his instrument," Ana remarked, relenting in her reservation toward it.

After a moment, Miin stepped out before them, dancing. At age eleven she was emerging as a beautiful girl with fine legs, her slenderness making her nascent breasts seem more. She swirled her long dark hair around and moved her hips lithely. Huu watched with appreciation tinged with concern; she was almost too lovely, which could put her at risk in another way. Her hands were normal, but there was a demand for loveliness for the harems of the wealthy or powerful, and some men did not take no as a suitable response.

Then Ana joined them too, moving her own mature body in the practiced ways of the experienced dancer. The two made a marvelous set, the woman and the girl, matching step for step. Huu elaborated his theme, and Scevo maintained the beat. The boy definitely had a talent for it; he had not missed a note, after getting it straight.

Huu completed his melody, and stopped, and Scevo stopped with him, aware of the patterning of it. "I think we have a family group," Huu said. "A troupe."

"I think we do," Ana agreed. "Now it is time to eat."

They went to the table, and the servant served them. Desert Flower was a girl of the steppes who worked for them to pay off a debt her family had incurred. She was thirteen, a pretty young woman in her own right, and very competent and loyal. In a few more months her service would be done, the debt paid. Then she could either go home, or continue service for pay. Huu hoped she would choose to continue service, because she got along well with Miin, was helpful with Scevo, and was always pleasant. She would surely marry well, in due course.

There was a sound outside, as they were finishing their meal, and a firm knock on the door. Huu went to meet the messenger from the palace who stood there. "Summons from the palace for service," the man said gruffly. "Music, dancing, within the hour."

"We will attend," Huu said. There was no other response he could make. He had done well in Samarkand, because of the favor of the palace; the nobles of Kwarizm liked his music and Ana's dancing. But he had to attend whenever called, day or night. The palace messenger would conduct them. This was nominally an honor guard, but also assurance that they would not delay.

"Hurry," the messenger said, not relaxing.

Huu re-entered the house. "Song and dance at the palace," he said. "We must both go immediately."

"We will all be there," Miin said, donning her veil. "Scevo too."

Huu looked at her, then at Ana, who shrugged as she veiled herself. The children had been close, ever since the adoption of Scevo, and the boy definitely preferred to be near his sister. Desert Flower could have taken care of the child during their absence, but it was now possible to claim him as a musician. It would be a novelty that might be appreciated at the palace. Appreciation could bring rich rewards.

So they took the children, with due cautions about remaining in sight of their parents, and silent. Desert Flower would keep the house in order alone.

They set out on foot through the city of Samarkand, Ana and Miin remaining fully cloaked and veiled in the fashion required of Moslem women. Huu wore the turban and distinctive robe of favored entertainer, which should have protected him from molestation on the street, but the messenger's sword was also clearly visible.

There was the sound of the horn: it was dusk, time for worship. All around them the people were facing toward Mecca and prostrating themselves on the ground. The four of them and the guard did likewise. Then they got up and resumed their travel, and so did everyone else, just as if nothing had happened.

There had been new construction recently, since the Shah moved his capital here. The smaller stucco buildings were being razed to make way for the grandiose structures of governance. But all of them were dwarfed by the palace, whose arches formed an arcade of golden brick. It was actually a complex of buildings anchored to the large enclosing wall, with many courtyards and connecting arcades. Above were domes and cupolas and small towers, perfectly symmetrical, catching the last beams of sunlight that no longer reached to the ground. The walls were decorated with myriad geometric carvings whose intricacy was amazing; an army of artisans had had to labor to fashion every detail. Seen from a distance, the palace was a marvel of architecture; seen close, it was a marvel of design.

Yet it was even more impressive inside. Ana had to murmur a word of caution to Scevo to prevent him from turning his head to gaze in open wonder. The impression was one of openness, of spaciousness, as if the palace were larger inside than outside. Now the interiors of the cupolas could be seen, forming patterns of cleverly fitted stonework, with inward projections reminiscent of the stalactites of large caves. Ornate columns descended to the floor, each perfect in its slender strength. The floor was tiled, with each chamber of a different design, some simple squares within squares, others so finely wrought as to dazzle the eye by their color and patterning. The walls were decorated with artistic inlays, notably of the finely glazed many-colored pottery called faience, forming flowing Arabic script: quotations from the Koran. Some walls were honeycombed with small alcoves, adding to the decoration.

Now they encountered one of the Divan, the corps of government officials. The name came from the couches set around the walls of the council hall in which they met. The master of ceremonies, Raay, hurried up. "I am really glad to see you," he said. "The sultan remains somewhat fatigued from his recent campaign in the west, and is in a foul mood. Heads will fly if it isn't eased." Muhammad, not content with the title of Shah, had assumed the title of Sultan, the Sword of Islam, and no one had the power to object. He also liked to be addressed by titles such as "The Warrior," or "The Great," "The Second Alexander," and "The Shadow of Allah upon Earth."

They were indoors now, but neither Ana nor Miin removed their veils or showed their faces. They would not let any man see them, other than the head of their household. Only infidels, such as Christian women, had the bad taste to show their bare faces in public.

"What set him off this time?" Huu asked. They had dealt with this officer many times, entertaining for lesser royalty during the absence of the Shah, and knew Raay would not report them for veiled uncomplimentary references. Those closest to the Shah tended to be somewhat nervous, because he was arrogant to the point of folly, and could take savage reprisals for trifling inadvertent affronts. There was a tacit conspiracy of silence about such things in the palace, and all the staff and artisans protected each other whenever they could.

For indeed, Shah Muhammad's rages were legendary. Only the year before, he had made a triumphal procession through Persia, accepting homage from all the lords and governors of his empire. During this travel he had come into conflict with the caliph at Baghdad. Muhammad had killed a holy man, a venerable sayyid, and as a matter of form asked for, then demanded, absolution from the caliph, the nominal spiritual head of the faith. The caliph had refused, and had some justice in his position, for the act had been reprehensible. Muhammad had then denounced the caliph and marched his mercenary army, complete with war elephants and trains of supply camels, westward toward the city. This was an act of outrageous presumption, but in the face of overwhelming power an accommodation was possible, and the caliph was about to be replaced. Actually the expedition did not reach Baghdad, because it had encountered the formidable Zagros mountain range just as a particularly harsh winter set in.

The Shah's forces were not inured to the hardships of a mountain passage in such conditions; horses starved and men froze. So, with bad grace, he had turned back. But the caliph knew that the mountains would not stop the Shah when spring came. The Shah had won his point, but had made an enemy of the entire spiritual establishment of Islam. The caliph refused to recognize Muhammad or to put his name in public prayers. There were those here in Samarkand who hated the Shah, for that reason, but of course none spoke aloud of it.

"It's the message from the Mongol," the master of ceremonies said. "The Shah has put out word to slay all Mongol sympathizers without hearings."

"That must have been an ugly message," Ana remarked.

"The odd thing is that it wasn't," Raay said. "It could have been taken as a gesture of friendship. But a single word gave it the lie. The khan called the Shah his son."

Huu coughed, and Miin put a hand to her mouth to stifle a titter. They all knew that in the language of diplomacy, sons were vassals, owing primary allegiance to their fathers. It was as if the Mongol had simply annexed the empire of Kwarizm to his own, making the Shah his servant.

"The impertinence of the man," Ana said. "And he couched it as a message of friendship?"

"Including gifts," Raay said. "For the good child." He made a droll expression; he was being ironic.

Now little Scevo covered his mouth. The Mongol's boldness of insult was amazing.

"I think the Mongols had better remain far from Kwarizm," Huu said.

"No, the fools sent a caravan. It is on its way now, moving along the Jaxartes River, approaching the frontier city of Otrar. It is said to have great wealth in gifts for the sultan."

"That might help," Huu said. But the matter bothered him. Why should the Mongol khan have sent such a caravan to likely extinction? Was the man a fool? He did not know much about politics, but he had never heard the khan spoken of as a leader without wit.

But there was no time to ponder the matter, because now the Shah was ready for his entertainment, and they were ushered to the meeting hall. It was called the Kapu, meaning the entrance to the sovereign's tent, but though the name reflected the more austere origin of the setting, the reality did not. This was the richest chamber yet, with marvelously woven Persian rugs hanging on its walls and covering much of its floor.

The Shah was seated on a comfortable couch, wearing a robe so fancy that its gems sparkled at every point. He was attended by the usual corps of courtiers, servants, and several favored wives from his harem guarded by a eunuch. Some were sipping sherbets from fancy mugs. The mugs, unlike the walls, were painted with human figures. Human statuary was forbidden, lest it be taken as graven images, but paintings were not icons and therefor not as restricted. The stricture against human or animal likenesses applied mainly to those things that "cast a shadow"—that were three-dimensional.

They did the same music and dance they had done at home, because that was the one they were sure Scevo could do without faltering. The woman and the girl were in costume now, dancing in a manner that had the courtiers watching with open relish, and the music was perfect for them. The wives focused especially on Miin, and that renewed Huu's nervousness; they were recognizing the girl's potential. A number of courtiers glanced at Scevo, evidently impressed by his command of the instrument, not knowing that this was the only accompaniment he could handle. Huu played carefully, making sure there was no slip, but could tell that the effect was being received very well. But none of that mattered, for there was only one person who counted.

The Shah watched and listened impassively. Then he smiled. Their act was a success!

Then they were ushered out, as the Shah retired to his harem. "You broke his mood," Raay said gratefully. "I think it was the novelty of the act. A woman and a girl dancing together—that was beautiful. And a man and a small boy playing music together. I think it was the boy who did it. He was so zestful."

A Persian clerk saw to their recompense: a generous payment in silver. Persians handled the organization and administration of the empire, as they had through the last several waves of Turkish conquest. Barbarians might be good at combat, but it required civilized folk to actually run things. Huu had understood long since that the arts and crafts were the most secure livelihood; the risk of injury or death was minimal, and the rewards could be both material and esthetic. That was why he was encouraging his children in the arts; dancing and music would assure their futures as well as any endeavors could.

Back home, they recounted their experience to Desert Flower. "The Shah liked Scevo!" Miin said.

"The Shah liked you, too," Huu told her, and she blushed as if never complimented before. That was a maidenly art she had practiced diligently.

"But that is a curious thing, the way the Mongol khan is acting," Ana said.

"The Mongol khan?" Desert Flower asked.

"He called the Shah his son!" Miin exclaimed. "Can you imagine! No wonder the Shah is furious. And now the khan is sending another caravan here."

"Why is the Shah angry?" Desert Flower asked, perplexed.

"That's the same as calling him a vassal," Huu explained. "He is nobody's vassal."

"No, it isn't," Desert Flower said. "It is a compliment. The khan dotes on his sons—even the one that isn't his."

Scevo looked at her, not so young as not to relate to this. For Scevo, like Miin, was adopted.

"One isn't his?" Ana asked, surprised for similar reason. She never spoke of it, but the loss of her elder son still pained her deeply, as it did Huu. The boy had been killed in an accident just before they adopted Scevo.

"His eldest," Desert Flower said. "The khan's wife was stolen just after they were married, and he didn't get her back for months, and then she was with child. But he accepted the child anyway. And he stands by his sons. Nobody crosses any of them. He paid the Shah a signal honor, calling him a son. This is how it is, with my people."

Huu exchanged a glance with Ana. "This is mischief," he said. "We shall have to get word to the Shah."

"Immediately," she agreed. "We did not know the steppe peoples' way."

Huu wrapped himself in his cloak and went through the night, back to the palace. He sought audience with the vizier, but the man had retired, and all he could get was an assistant. He explained about the misunderstanding, and how important it was to notify the Shah. But the man looked dubious, and Huu wasn't at all sure he understood. Yet it was all that could be done this night. Despondent, he returned home.

The next day he tried again, managing to reach the office of the vizier himself. He had to wait for some time in an anteroom, for the vizier was busy, but it was known that Huu was favored by the Shah, so he was put into the schedule. Two other men were waiting also, whiling away the time by playing a game of backgammon. At one point a slave passed through with a cheetah on a leash; the ferocious cat was a pet of the Shah's, and had to be kept in health by regular exercise. Later several serving maids scurried by on an errand for Muhammad's mother, Turkhan-Khatun. The formidable woman was much feared at court, being as temperamental and arbitrary as her son. The funny thing was that her worst malice was directed toward her own grandson, Jalal al-Din, who was the Shah's son and likely heir. He was a capable and courageous commander and a man of good will, a favorite of both his father and the court, but his grandmother loathed him and schemed constantly against him. Huu agreed with most others that things would be better if the vile grandmother were to come to a sudden end, but the worst that any of them could do was relay mischievous tales about her.

At last it was his turn to see the vizier, Biil, who was a somewhat harried man, not at all a warrior type. He had, according to Persian custom, been presented by the Shah with an ink pot when appointed to his position, and he always wore it on a fine chain, as the symbol of his office. Huu explained his concern. This time he got better news. "The Shah knows about that. It's an insult, but the khan is a barbarian, giving offense from sheer ignorance. Allowance has been made." His expression suggested that this had required some doing, however. "There will be peace and trade between the two empires."

Huu was relieved, realizing that the lower functionary had not been current on this matter. He apologized for bothering Biil about something that turned out to be of no importance. "By no means," the vizier demurred. "This could have been supremely important, and I am glad to know that had I not learned of it elsewhere, you would have called it to my attention. It demonstrates your loyalty to the welfare of the empire." That was the man's way of saying that Huu *had* wasted his time, but he didn't mind. Huu returned home with the good news.

But soon there was worse. The governor of the frontier town of Otrar, on the river Jaxartes, had arrested a Mongol caravan, confiscated the animals and their loads of treasure, and executed the Mongol in charge, together with all his attendants.

"But why?" Desert Flower asked, in evident pain for the deaths of her countrymen. "There was an agreement for trade."

"The governor claims they were spies," Huu said.

"A Mongol noble bringing gifts to the Shah?" she asked. "And all his attendants? There might be spies among them, because there always are, but that's routine. Don't the Shah's caravans have spies too?"

"They surely do," Huu agreed. "I suspect that the governor of Otrar, known to dislike Mongols, made up a pretext to rob the caravan, hoping that would excuse it."

"But the Shah shouldn't believe that," Desert Flower protested.

Huu shook his head. "It seems that the Shah believes what he chooses to believe. Now he is angry again."

"Couldn't you talk to him?"

"To the Shah?" Huu shook his head. "To the vizier, maybe. Why are you so concerned about this?"

"Because I know something of this man Genghis. He has made a reputation among my people. He is the smartest and most ruthless khan we've ever had. Killing his envoys will bring war, and the khan will win it. There will be terrible destruction."

Huu saw that she was serious, but she was only 13 and no expert in diplomacy or war. "We shall just have to hope it doesn't come to war, then," he said.

Still, the Shah did seem to be pursuing an inappropriate course. As time passed, Huu did talk with the vizier Biil again, who agreed that it was foolish to stir up a potential enemy without reason. It would result at best in the inconvenience of border hostilities, and at worst in open warfare, pointlessly draining the resources of the empire. But Biil thought that the Shah was slowly reconsidering the matter, because he did have many other concerns. For one thing, there was still the nest of opposition centered in Baghdad, that the Shah still wanted to deal with. It would not be expedient to get into quarrels both east and west. "There is another Mongol caravan coming here," he said. "Said to be the richest one yet. If the Mongol apologizes for his prior slur, and promises to send no more spies, peace may be achieved."

Huu reported that at home, and Desert Flower was comforted. She went about her work with greater cheer, and that had a beneficial effect on the family, for Miin and Scevo really liked her.

Meanwhile they sharpened their family performance. Scevo learned to play a second melody on the dulcimer, and a third, proceeding with enthusiasm. Miin danced, her body seeming to flesh out farther with each performance. Huu schooled himself to be objective, but even so it seemed to him that the two were quite good. At such time as age forced Ana to retire from display dancing, Miin would be ready to take her place. And Huu was already working out duets with Scevo that seemed to have real promise.

Indeed, their success as a family was flourishing. They were performing at the palace more often, and their status and economic situation improved accordingly. Their presentations satisfied the Shah in a way that most others did not. The outlook was good.

Then the Mongol caravan arrived. The vizier thought the Shah might be persuaded to accept peace, grudgingly. To improve the mood, he arranged for Huu's family to perform for the Shah and the Mongol envoys. If that mellowed the Shah sufficiently, all would be well. This time they had Desert Flower with them, to tend to their last moment preparations and remember any details they might overlook. This was not the time for any mistake.

They performed well, and it was plain that both the Shah and the Mongol leader were impressed. Then they retired discreetly, and the business of the occasion proceeded. But they did not go home; Biil kept them nearby, in readiness, in case there was further need for their services. Thus it was that they were in an antechamber, close enough to see and hear the discussion.

The spokesman for the Mongol mission was a noble of Kwarizm, so that no translation was required. He addressed the Shah forthrightly. "The Great Khan of the Mongols sends his greetings, and still regards you as a friend," the man said, carefully avoiding the word "son." But it didn't help; the Shah's scowl indicated that the term he heard was "vassal." Huu and his family held their breaths, hoping that no disaster would come of this. "The khan realizes that subordinates sometimes act without authority, generating mischief. Therefore he requests the extradition of the governor of Otrar, who—"

"Extradition!" the Shah cried. "Because he executed your spies? This is outrageous!"

"Oh, no," Ana murmured. It was falling apart.

"I'll show you what I think of such a demand!" the Shah continued grimly. He turned to the vizier. "Execute this traitor. Shave the Mongols' heads bald and ship them back to their master as a warning not to trifle with his betters."

"No!" Desert Flower screamed. Then she clapped her hands over her mouth, appalled at her outburst.

The Shah's head turned. He had heard.

"Depart the palace—swiftly and quietly," Huu said. He led the way.

The palace personnel assumed that the entertainers had been routinely dismissed, as had been the case before, and did not bar their exit. They made it out of the palace. But Huu knew that there would soon be pursuit, as Biil reluctantly obeyed orders. "We must flee the city—and the empire," he said tersely. "We must not even pass our home, for they will check that first."

"It's my fault!" Desert Flower said.

It was, but Huu saw no point in recriminations. They had all been upset by the senseless outcome of the Mongols' mission. "Can your people help us escape?"

"Yes," Desert Flower said. "I think."

So, suddenly, they were on their way to exile. Somehow the situation seemed familiar.

The Shah's arrogance had led him into rare rashness. In fact he had made a mistake of global proportion. The shaving of the hair and beards of the Mongol envoys was an insult beyond redemption. When Genghis Khan learned of it, he reacted with deceptive calm. "You have chosen war. The Blue Sky alone knows what will happen." Because the Shah had already alienated the caliph, he could not rally the forces of Islam to his banner in a Jihad against the Mongols. His armies were powerful, but lacked the force of spiritual unity.

The following year the Mongols invaded Kwarizm. The Mongol force was no massive horde; it was numerically inferior to that of the defenders, being 150,000 men, but that was no indication of its power. It consisted principally of cavalry, buttressed by a core of Chinese engineers whose arsenal of siege weapons was devastating, such as catapults hurling flaming naphtha bombs. The troops were the toughest known in Asia, and highly disciplined. The Mongol military intelligence was phenomenally competent. The generals possessed strategic and tactical genius that remains the subject of military admiration and awe even today. Taken as a whole, it was probably the finest fighting force ever assembled up to that time, and it was utterly ruthless.

In six months the empire of Kwarizm was destroyed, and the Shah killed. The governor of Otrar was captured, and molten silver was poured into his ears and nostrils: he had been given the wealth he evidently craved. Cities were completely razed, their populations shipped back to Mongolia as slaves or artisans, or killed. Pyramids of severed heads were formed. Central Asia may never have recovered from the fury of the Mongol invasion. Before it was completed, Mongol power expanded all the way to the border of Egypt, Russia was conquered in the only successful winter campaign against it, and an invasion of Europe was halted only by the coincidental death of the reigning khan. It became the largest land empire of all time. And its sudden, savage thrust westward may have brought gunpowder to Europe, which was to transform warfare in another way.

All because the Shah miscalculated.

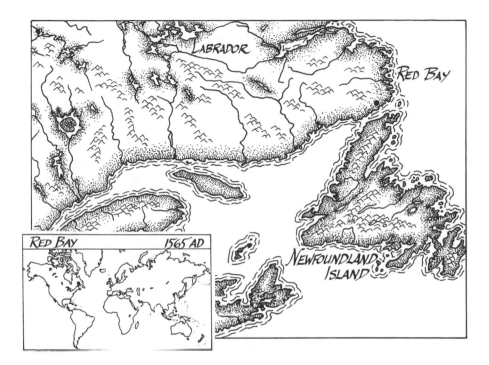

Red Bay   1565 AD

CHAPTER 17

TERRANOVA

The Basques are one of the very few peoples of Europe to have escaped the Indo-European linguistic conquest; their language does not relate to the others. This may have been because they were fierce mountain folk in the Pyrenees, in northern Iberia (Spain), hard to get at, and very protective of their culture. What is not well known is that they also went to sea. Soon after the European discovery of the New World, Basque whaling ships were operating there. The life and work were hard, but the pay was good, and they were up to it. They went to a fishing port they called Butus, in Terranova, which today is known as Red Bay

in the New World, on the Canadian coast just north of the island of Newfound-
land. There they caught and processed several thousand whales.

There is no evidence that women or children were on these voyages. But
perhaps there could have been a special situation, in 1565.

IT was infernally smelly near the tryworks, but the heat of its operation
was a comfort in the chill of early winter. Besides, Ana used its fire to
cook with. So they endured it. They knew it would not be much longer,
because the *San Juan* had a full cargo of whale oil and was ready to sail for
home. Tomorrow they would board it, and the following day be on their
way.

The tryworks was a firebox set into the ground, facing the island beach. It
was a square hole lined with stone, four feet across and just about as deep,
to hold the big steady fire needed for the rending of the oil from the
blubber. Wooden posts supported its red tiled roof. It was a constant job to
find and haul dry wood to keep several tryworks going all day. But without
this stage, the whalers would not be able to function, because the blubber
would not give up its oil before it spoiled. So the tryworks was really the
center of the operation.

"Father! A boat!" Scevor cried, pointing.

Hue looked. A *chalupa* was rowing toward them: one of the fast whale
pursuit boats from the ship. But instead of a harpooner, this one had a
lesser officer. Hue recognized him by his heavy blue woolen trousers
gathered at the knees and his red long-sleeved shirt. The craft landed, and
the officer stepped out and approached Hue. "Bad news," he said. "The
men voted to exclude you. They don't want women back on board."

"But we came here on the *San Juan!*" Hue protested. "We paid for the
privilege. You can't just leave us here to die."

The man shook his head. "This is not my choice, my friend. I am only
reporting on their decision. They say that they were not consulted about the
matter when you boarded, and that we had bad luck on the trip because of
you. Two women and two of the sinister hand—please understand, they are
frightened. It is not a personal thing. They refuse to risk it again. But we are
not stranding you. There is another ship. We are refunding your money.
Give it to Captain Ittai." He handed Hue several silver coins.

"Who may be just as superstitious," Hue said tersely. But he knew they
would have to try it, because it was clear that they would not have a
compatible berth aboard the *San Juan*.

"They may be unduly credulous," the officer agreed. "It is the way of
seamen. But I understand that Captain Ittai is not, and he will take you."
He turned smartly about and marched back to his boat.

Hue and Scevor returned to their temporary sod house. It had red roof
tiles which had been brought across as ballast for the empty ship. The
Basques were nothing if not practical. They had made their oil barrels from

staves on the way across. Nothing was wasted, not even time. So even their ballast had definite uses elsewhere.

"They won't take us?" Ana asked incredulously. "But we paid, and we've been working, *and* entertaining them!"

"They gave back the money. They're afraid. Of women and hands. But they say that we can go on the *San Pedro.*"

"We'll die if we don't," she said grimly.

Hue went back to work tending the cooling tub. This was the last stage in preparing the whale oil before it was barreled. The tub was made from a barrel sawn in half and partly filled with water. The hot oil from the tryworks was poured in, and cooled by the cold air and water. The oil quickly coalesced and floated on the water, and the impurities floated on the oil, where Hue sieved them out during the cooling. When the oil was clear and cool, he dipped it out carefully and poured it into a complete barrel. When he had several barrels, a boat would take them out to the ship. Making oil was a far cry from making music, but it was gainful work, and he didn't mind it any more than Ana minded cooking pots of cod and beans for the men to eat. It was part of the deal.

The deal was that they had paid to come as a family unit on this nonfamily business venture. It was highly irregular, but necessary for them, because they had had to flee Spain and get out of reach of the king, and the power of Spain was such that this desperate ploy was the only feasible way. The Basques had never liked being dominated by Spain, so had had some sympathy, but couldn't protect them. Instead they had signed them as crew members aboard the whaler *San Juan,* and the ship had then set sail for Terranova, one of the few regions of the world that the Spanish king could not conveniently reach.

The money had done no more than gain them the right to be on the ship; they had to haul their weight, as every crewman did. So Hue and Scevor had assisted the cooper on the voyage across, assembling hundreds of oil barrels from pre-fitted beech and oak staves. They used hoops of green alder to make the casks tight. Hue's musician fingers turned out to be similarly dextrous, not sinister, with the staves, and even five-year-old Scevor had a touch in matching stave to stave. Ana and Min had settled in as cook's assistants, and though the cook was reputed to be the grouchiest man aboard, he soon had to concede that they were good at it.

But there was one more aspect to the deal. They agreed to entertain the crew, in exchange for being left alone by the crew. In slow times they did music and dance performances on the deck, and the captain issued a standing order that any man who touched any of them, literally, would be keelhauled. He was a man of word and discipline, so the threat was meaningful. That meant that the men could look all they wanted, and say what they wished, but not one finger touched woman or child. The order was necessary because not all the men were married, and not all the married ones were faithful, and some had pederastic tastes. But all of them were tough, whether as workers or fighters or simply enduring the rigors of the weather. Thus the suggestive dances of the women were roundly applauded, and the boy at times became a dancer too, but all were off limits. It had worked reasonably well, but toward the end of the cruise across the big ocean there had been increasing grumbling and intensifying hunger in a number of eyes, and the officers had had to use the whip on occasion to maintain discipline.

So perhaps it wasn't surprising that the balance had shifted, and now the family was not welcome aboard the *San Juan*. Hue knew it was not a complete change, for there had always been a sizable minority that objected to their presence, and now there was surely a sizable minority that preferred their presence. Probably the captain had made the decision, for the sake of continuing discipline, not caring to risk even the slightest chance of mutiny.

However, the men of the *San Pedro* were fresher from Spain, so not as hungry for women, and Captain Ittai had a less harsh yet somehow more effective mode of discipline. So it did seem to be time to change ships. But Hue had a nagging tinge of uncertainty, because the *San Pedro* had already been unlucky, and might decline to risk any more of the same.

"There she blows!" the lookout on high ground cried. Hue looked, and saw the signs of one or more bowheads. Immediately men boiled out of their temporary shelters on the island and piled into their chase boats. Each *chalupa* had places for seven: four rowers, a helmsman, a harpooner, and the boat captain. They slipped through the icy water with astonishing speed, angling out to intercept the whales that were swimming near the land. One boat was too far to the side to catch a whale, but the other cut in immediately behind a whale, maneuvering to avoid the dangerous flukes. Its harpooner hurled his barb and scored on the whale's back. Then the men cast the drogue snake over the bow and hung on as the harpoon line went taut.

Now it was time for endurance, as the injured whale tugged the craft rapidly across the water, sometimes cutting back to charge the boat, sometimes diving deep, trying to escape the pain. This stage could last for hours, as the whale slowly tired, and became vulnerable to a stroke to a vital organ. Once it was dead it would be laboriously towed to a trying station on the shore. Then the flippers and tail would be cut away to facilitate rotation of the carcass, and three men would stand on top of it, cutting away long strips of blubber. They would cast these ashore, where a man covered with soot and fat would shovel lumps of blubber into a boiling cauldron. The boiling removed the oil, and fritters of exhausted blubber would be fished out. Then the hot oil would be poured into the cooling barrel that Hue was tending. The process was messy, stinky, but efficient.

In a few more days the *San Pedro* would have enough oil to return to Spain, though far short of a full load. The ship had suffered a series of misfortunes, losing a number of good men and a boat, and a mishap had caused a fair proportion of the casks of oil to be contaminated. That was why the ship was staying until the end of the season, when the very last whales passed, trying to make up the difference. It would not be a complete loss, because the ships worked for the same employer, and the incomplete cargo would be mitigated by the full cargo of the *San Juan*. Still, it was not a happy time.

There was a noise farther along the shore, and a cry. A cauldron had burst, dumping its valuable oil into the firepit, not only being lost but effectively destroying the tryworks. More bad luck.

Then another boat came from a ship, this one from the *San Pedro*. "This will be news from Captain Ittai," Hue said.

"Will he take us?" Scevor asked, concerned.

"Of course he will," Hue said. Because there was no alternative; it would be a death sentence for any people left here for the winter. The water was close to freezing already, and huge icebergs could be seen sometimes in the sea; it would be much worse in winter.

The boat arrived, and its passenger got out and approached Hue. It was Captain Ittai himself. "We have considered the matter, and we will take you," the man said. "Our luck couldn't be much worse than it has already been. But some of the men are against it. So I have suggested this challenge: board the ship now, and if our luck turns, we will assume that your influence is beneficial, and the matter will be at rest."

"And if your luck turns worse?" Hue asked.

"Then the naysayers win their bets, and will be satisfied. You will not be left here." He proffered his hand, and Hue took it. Captain Ittai had found a way to secure their passage, regardless.

Hue and Scevor went to tell Ana and Min. "We will be aboard the *San Pedro* tonight," he said, and explained why.

"I will feel safer there," Ana said, flashing him a weary smile. It was a bit more comfortable on land than on a ship, but now that there was a question about their return to Spain, the ship was attractive.

They finished their shifts at the tryworks and cooling tub, and got into the captain's boat. There were only two oarsmen now, because this was not a whale chase, leaving room for them.

They boarded the ship and went to the allocated cabin. And the mischief started. There was a shout from the tallest of the three masts: "Storm ahoy!"

That was the last thing they wanted. There was little a ship could do in a storm except try to ride it out, and it was not a pleasant ride. Those camping on land would be better off. At least they wouldn't have to endure the embarrassing threat of seasickness from the violent heaving on the waves.

Hue saw the crewmen looking at him. He knew they were regretting the presence of the family on the ship, taking the sudden storm as an omen. He hoped that their concern did not prove justified.

But Min caught his glance with her large eyes. "The spirits of the air are not against us," she murmured.

That reassured him. She had never yet been wrong about the spirits.

"But the spirits of the whales don't like the ships," she continued.

"That is hardly surprising." Hue found the slaughter unpleasant, but did not feel it was appropriate for him to object to the business of the ships that had given his family sanctuary.

The storm moved swiftly in, as if it had come into being with the sole object of striking at them. Dark clouds piled up from the horizon, blotting out much of the light of day. The crewmen scurried about the ship, tying everything down, especially the sails. They were going to ride it out at anchor, to prevent being blown onto the rocks of the shore. Storms were especially dangerous to ships near land.

Ana and the children retreated to their cabin, not liking this.

Hue looked across to the other ships, and saw that the *San Juan* was also battening down, as were the smaller two-masted vessels that served as messenger ships and transport between the main ships. Their bare rigging looked stark, as if the ships were naked. Columns of thick smoke still rose from the tryworks on land, as the important work could not be stopped just because of rain. That was why they were roofed. One coil of smoke was flattening in the wind and passing directly over the small cemetery, as if signaling the storm's intention: death to whalers.

The winds struck, whipping the sea into waves of increasing size and heft, with whitecaps forming. The *San Pedro* shuddered with the blast of air, and nosed around to face the storm, straining at the anchor.

Meanwhile the *chalupa* with the whale remained at sea, unable to return to land or ship unless it cut free. But it wasn't cutting free; a whale was too valuable to let go for any reason. The men were risking their lives to hold on to their prey.

Hue remained on deck, ready to help in whatever way was needed. But Captain Ittai spied him and yelled negation. "Don't tempt it, man! Get out of sight."

That seemed like good advice, for now a wave smashed against the hull and broke over the deck, sending a wash of bubbly water across to wet their feet.

Hue got out of sight, rejoining his family. Scevor was frightened, clinging to Ana, who also looked distinctly nervous as the ship pitched. But Min was at peace, holding on to the wall but staring raptly out the tiny porthole.

Hue joined her. It was a window to savagery, as the waves battered at the hull. Each shock seemed harder than the last, until the ship's timbers groaned with strain. The spirits certainly seemed angry!

Min put her hand on his, reassuringly. She seemed older than her twelve years, and her touch did shore up his confidence again.

The howl of the winds got worse. The masts made it sing, but it wasn't any nice song. Water dripped from above, signaling more washes across the deck. How big would those waves get?

The storm continued as the night closed, rocking the ship at irregular intervals. Whenever it seemed to be easing, an even more ferocious wave would strike. There was nothing they could do but wait, and try to relax.

They got together on the bunk, each with one or two hands hung on to it, and spread a blanket over them all. There was warmth as well as comfort in this family group.

"Why did we come here, Daddy?" Scevor asked plaintively.

"We unintentionally affronted the king of Spain, and had to flee his possible wrath," Hue said. "But when we return, after several months, we believe he will have forgotten the matter, so we will be safe." But they would try to remain inconspicuous, just in case.

Finally they slept, still bundled. Hue dreamed of the storm, of ships being smashed against the rocks of shore and wrecked. Such images came readily to mind as long as the storm held.

Some time in the night it passed, and all was calm.

But the morning brought no joy. For the *San Juan* was gone. The men in small boats quickly confirmed the worst: she had gone down in the storm.

"The women!" a crewman shouted. "The bad hands! They caused this!"

Others turned to face Hue and his family, their expressions turning ugly. Hue felt a chill that was not of the storm. But Captain Ittai overrode it. "You have it reversed," he proclaimed. "We were spared! We have had bad luck all along, and this one time good luck. While the *San Juan* had good luck as long as they associated with it — and the moment they left it, the luck turned. Had they brought us a curse, *we* would have been the ship sunk. They bring good luck, not bad."

The crewmen stared at him and at Hue's family, then at each other. He was right: the message of the luck was plain. No one could deny the precision of the storm's damage.

"Now get to work on salvage," the captain said. "We can help the survivors, and we can bring up most of that sunken oil. We will have our hold full after all."

Hue looked at Min. How right she had been about the spirits! They had spared the family, and struck at the ship with the most whale oil aboard.

Could she also predict their reception when they returned to Spain? He thought it better not to ask.

They did manage to salvage more than half of the barrels of whale oil aboard the San Juan, *and left the sunken hulk for archaeologists to discover almost four hundred years later, when the fact of Basque whaling in the region had been almost forgotten.*

The operation continued until the populations of right whales and bowheads was virtually extinct in that region. Then they moved on to Spitsbergen, north of Norway, where an undepleted stock of whales beckoned. Today a number of species of whales have been hunted almost to extinction, and several nations are eager to resume the slaughter. Whaling pays very well—until the whales are gone.

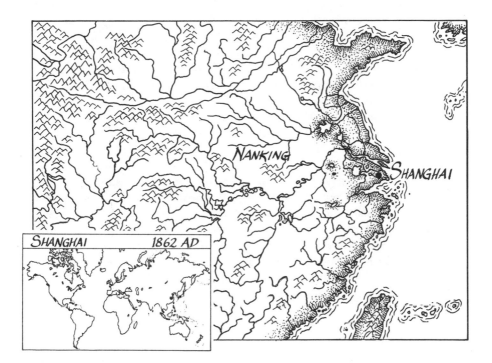

CHAPTER 18

TAIPING

The Mongols governed China for most of a century before a rebellion conquered them. The following Ming dynasty endured almost 300 years before being conquered by the Manchus of Manchuria, whose Ch'ing dynasty lasted almost another 300 years. But at times the government's hold seemed tenuous. It was a period of unrest.

In 1836 a young man went to Canton to take the civil service examinations, which he had failed before. He failed again, which was not surprising, as there might be only one position for a hundred applicants. He happened to be given a *pamphlet titled "Good Words to Admonish the Age," which explained the basic tenets of Protestant Christianity. A year later, after failing another examination, he had a nervous breakdown, complicated by physical illness. He suffered convulsions and delusions for four days, and was transformed by the experience. He became more confident. But in 1843 he failed the exam yet again, and this time was impressed by the pamphlet he had had for seven years. He realized that during his illness he had ascended to heaven and met with many angels, Jesus, and God Himself. God had charged him with the task of destroying the devils infesting the earthly kingdom. He changed his name, called himself the Noble King, and claimed to be the younger brother of Christ. He set out to establish the Kingdom of God on Earth. Disaffected people found this appealing.*

Militia units were formed to protect local interests. His early followers had brilliant organizational abilities, and in 1850 the movement grew into a full military rebellion called the T'ai-p'ing T'ien-kuo: Heavenly Kingdom of Great Peace. It had male and female armies, though the women usually had non-combatant roles. An early attempt to abolish marriage, because all people were brothers and sisters, did not work out. Military leaders were the East, North, West, and South kings, who sometimes conspired against each other, and in due course were replaced by other kings. Nevertheless, the Taiping armies of peace conquered much of China, and in 1862 they were moving to take the important port cities that had withstood their prior sieges. It looked very much as if these would fall.

However, there were European interests moving into China, because of the lucrative opium trade, and these viewed the Taiping encroachment with misgiving. It was ironic that Taiping, as a Christian force, should normally have affiliated with the Christian forces of Europe—but wouldn't, because Taiping abhorred opium. Thus these seemingly natural allies became opponents. The Europeans were concentrated in the worst of the ports, the one the empire let them have, because of its miserable climate, chronic plagues of smallpox, cholera, and dysentery, and common piracy and brigandage. In fact it was a notorious sinkhole of filth, crime, and foreigners that the Imperial authorities hardly cared about. The Manchu military forces there were ill-trained and unmotivated. This was Shanghai.

As the armies of the Heavenly Kingdom advanced on this stinking hole, it might have seemed that Shanghai was destined for conquest and enlightenment. But there were certain cautions. The foreigners' numbers were very small compared to those of the Taiping armies, but they had modern firearms, against soldiers armed mostly with spears. And they had an American adventurer named Frederick Townsend Ward who, with a few hundred disciplined mercenaries, had routed vastly larger Taiping forces. Now they were to be tested more thoroughly. The time was May, 1862.

T HE junk sailed into the port of Shanghai with its square sails half furled. Hu'o tried to conceal his nervousness. They had been away from China for the better part of a year, but there was no certainty that the Heavenly Kingdom had forgotten about them. If they could travel quietly to some far province of the Manchu Empire they would probably be safe, and they would be among their own kind instead of foreigners. It was a chance they had to take.

Captain I'ti approached. "It has been good to have you aboard," he said. "Your music has delighted us."

"Thank you." Hu'o suspected that the man had something on his mind, so waited politely.

"I understand that the city is under siege," I'ti said. "Sometimes this makes for complications."

"Surely so," Hu'o agreed.

"Your wife and daughter are both beautiful. This might be considered a liability in certain circumstances."

"Never to me." Hu'o glanced at both Ann and Mi'in, who were beside him. Ann had always been beautiful, and now Mi'in at age thirteen was coming into her splendor.

"Perhaps they might don male attire, until you are free of the city."

Now Hu'o understood. In time of war, pretty women were apt to become prizes for troops of either side. "This is a thoughtful notion."

"I have some clothing left by former hands. They would be welcome to it."

"We thank you most effusively," Hu'o said, bowing his head to the captain.

In short order the family of man, two women, and boy became a family of man, two striplings, and boy. Ann even rubbed some dirt into her chin as if it were considering a beard. She and Mi'in appeared to be rather slight young men, but that was surely better than to be rather comely women.

They were not the first to depart the ship. Hu'o preferred to wait, searching the dock for any suspicious character. There were a number of unsavory-looking men, but that was normal, considering the reputation of this port. All seemed to be in order.

They filed across the gangplank, little Skev following Hu'o. There was no way to conceal the boy's small stature; he was only six. But they tried to act nonchalant, hoping that no agent of Taiping was lurking. No one else mattered, really, for they could probably handle the routine cutthroats, especially if any of the ship's crewmen remained near. It had been an excellent trading voyage, and the crew had concluded that the presence of the family had brought the ship good fortune.

As Hu'o led the way from the dock, a young foreigner intercepted him. "I beg your pardon," the man said. He was British, wearing the odd clothing of the type: leather boots, belted trousers, buttoned jacket, white shirt with collar and tie, and, when he doffed his green turban, a thick head of short hair parted down the center.

Hu'o paused. He did not speak the foreigner's barbaric tongue, but perhaps the man spoke Chinese. "I do not understand," he said carefully.

The man shifted to a passable emulation of Hu'o's dialect. "Could I talk with you a moment? It may be important."

This did not seem to be a threat. "If you wish," Hu'o agreed.

"I see you have a child in your party, and two women garbed as men. This is unusual, for a merchant ship."

So much for their effort of concealment. "What is your concern?"

"Please, let me introduce myself. I am Wood, from England. I am attached to Commander Ward's unit. Perhaps you know of him."

Hu'o nodded. "An American soldier of fortune," he said. "Said to be very brave. Fighting the Taiping." Which was a good sign. "I am Hu'o, with my family."

"We believe that there is a Taiping spy in the vicinity, looking for someone, up to no good," Wood said. "Would you know anything of that?"

"We are afraid of that," Hu'o said. "We inadvertently gave offense to the Taiping leader, and had to flee for our lives. We hoped we had been forgotten."

"Then you are surely the people I am seeking," Wood said, smiling. "You see, we wish to capture that spy and interrogate her. It is no secret that our lines are spread extremely thinly, and we need all the information about the enemy's plans that we can obtain. If you are the ones she is after, we can offer our protection, and hope to benefit by it."

"The spy is a woman?" Ann asked sharply.

"Oh, yes, some of the most effective spies are women," Wood said. "They can sometimes infiltrate where men can't, and avoid suspicion. I have been especially alert for women who conceal their gender, lest one be her." Which explained why he had spotted Ann and Mi'in. "This one is adept at disguise, so that we have no idea what she may look like now. In fact we know her mainly by reputation."

"Do you know her name?"

"She has many names, but we call her Serilda, the 'girl of war.' She's about thirty years old, but still remarkably attractive and well conditioned."

"Is she a dancer?" Ann asked.

"Why yes, at one time she was; that perhaps accounts for her appearance. How did you know?"

"We know her," Hu'o said tightly.

Wood broke into a smile. "Wonderful! This is exactly what we need. Someone who can recognize her even in disguise. But by the same token, you must indeed be the ones she is after. We knew she was looking for someone or something that would arrive on a ship, but we knew neither what it was nor whom she was. I simply had to watch every ship, and hope to catch her when she found what she sought. I'm glad I checked with you. But something I don't quite understand is why they would send a lone woman instead of a male assassin, if they wish to be rid of you."

"Because she knows us," Hu'o said. "Maybe she means only to identify us, and then will report to the assassin."

"Yes, of course. How foolish of me not to realize that." Wood looked around a bit nervously. "I believe we can do each other some good. Will you come with me to meet my leader? Commander Ward can protect you, and maybe we can capture Serilda when she comes to identify you."

Hu'o exchanged a glance with Ann, then with Mi'in, who had a special perception about such things. Ann also looked at the girl. Mi'in nodded yes, but there was doubt on her face.

Wood picked up on it. "I see this is a family decision. I realize that I am a stranger to you, so trust is difficult. I'm not sure how I can reassure you that I am legitimate."

"It's not that," Mi'in said, meeting his gaze. Hu'o saw Wood's eyes dilate as he appreciated her young beauty despite the male costume. It would have happened well before this, if she had been dressed normally, and instantly had she wished to impress him. She was Chinese, and he was white-skinned British, but her magic transcended race. It wasn't just her developing beauty; it was her ambience. The spirits surrounded her, and showed in her eyes. That was why the family consulted with her when making important decisions; she had insights stemming from other than normal channels. "You are all right. But there is danger." She averted her eyes.

Only then did Wood shake himself back to ordinary matters. Mi'in had been looking beyond his face, perhaps into his soul, but in so doing she had held him fascinated. She had done it for good reason, because he was indeed a stranger about whom they needed reassurance. Unfortunately it was clear that the young man had not before encountered something like this, and his fascination of the moment could readily become a more abiding passion if they weren't careful.

"We will go with you," Ann said, appreciating the situation, as Hu'o had. "Take us to your leader."

Wood nodded, still a bit blankly, then turned. Ann followed, taking Skev's hand. Hu'o and Mi'in were last. Ann was arranging it that way, to protect the child, and so that Hu'o could question Mi'in privately.

"Danger?" he murmured.

"She is here," Mi'in said. "She has seen us. We can't hide from her."

"She wants Skev," Hu'o said. "Maybe she doesn't care what happens to us, but she wants to get Skev back."

"Yes. But it's more than that. I'm not sure Wood can protect us."

"It's better than being alone," Hu'o said. "She must have been watching for us all along. We had no chance to escape her notice."

She glanced at him. "Maybe she wants you, too."

That made him take stock. Serilda had been a special nemesis over the years. At one time, in circumstances he preferred not to think about, he had had an affair with her, and Skev was the result. He had managed to get the boy three years ago, and hadn't seen Serilda since, but there was always the lurking fear that she would reappear. Now it seemed that she had gone to work for the Taiping Rebellion, so had become immensely more dangerous. He could understand her antipathy to his family, though his family had never been at fault. He could understand her desire to recover her son, though she had agreed to the adoption at the time, because it had been to an extent under duress. But he had more difficulty understanding how she could still desire him, as he had made it plain that he did not desire her. Unless she simply wanted to have the victory—to take him over his own protest. She had always seemed to have a hankering for him, and he had at one time found her intriguing, but he had always preferred Ann. Maybe that was an intolerable affront to Serilda.

In any event, he wanted to be far away from whatever Serilda had in mind. Wood and Commander Ward seemed to be their best chance at the moment. But he knew how cunning Serilda was. She was all too apt to find a way to strike at them despite any protection they might have. "Keep an eye on Skev," he murmured.

"And on you," Mi'in said, smiling. It was a joke, but with its element of truth; she knew about Skev's origin. Then her face sobered, as did Hu'o's own, because thoughts of Skev's arrival reminded them of the loss of Hu'o and Ann's natural son, Chi'ip, at the same time. He had been two years older than Mi'in, her big brother for all her memory. Hu'o had never been sure of the effect that loss had on her, and had never cared to inquire. Certainly it had impressed on her the uncertainty of life.

They proceeded through the paved streets of Shanghai, which seemed ever narrower and filthier than before. The city thronged with people, most on foot, but some being borne along by hand-drawn rickshaws. The higher-class women preferred to ride, both because it showed their status, and because their tiny bound feet were not suitable for walking any distance. There were also people and animals coming to market on big wheeled wheelbarrows; they paused to let one pass by, the farmer sitting to the right side of the wheel, an alcohol-drugged pig tied to the left side, the indefatigable servant lifting and pushing from behind, a rope over his shoulders helping to take the weight of the wide handles. They passed a public square where a condemned criminal was caged for execution: his hands were bound, and his head was through a special hole in the top. He had the choice of standing on tiptoe as long as his feet held out, to relieve the pressure, or letting his body sag so that he strangled. This was an example for the innocent: the consequence of crime. Yet bystanders seemed more interested than appalled; indeed, some were making bets on the hour of his expiration. An official with a fancy hat was posing beside the cage to have his picture taken; he would probably savor that picture of justice in practice, the law and the condemned. Hu'o had no doubt that pickpockets and thieves were working this area as usual, each one supposing that he himself would never be caught, and if he was, well, it was mere fate.

His thought returned to one aspect: the bound feet. Ann's feet had been bound in childhood, and were attractively small, though when she danced too long they pained her. The smallness was attained by preventing the bones from growing normally; the feet were actually malformed. Mi'in, still a baby when the Taiping Rebellion started, had not had her feet bound, because this was a reform the reformers had actually instituted. And the truth was, her natural feet were not only considerably sturdier, they were not ugly. Ann had designed artful slippers that made them appear almost as small as Ann's own. So there was really no need for binding the feet. But it would be mischief to say that in Empire territory; the custom was too firmly entrenched.

Ward's station of the moment was in a regular old stone and wood house, distinguished from others only by its cleaner appearance. The British had a thing about dirt: they thought it unnatural, and tried to avoid it. This turned out to be a temporary hospital station; one of Ward's oddities was his insistence that his wounded men be treated instead of merely dismissed. Hu'o had heard that this made for friction between the commander and his Chinese backers, but it did seem like a compassionate idea.

There were armed Filipino soldiers at the entrance, all wearing deep green turbans, but Wood spoke briefly to them, and they immediately allowed him and his group inside. They passed through a room where a woman was rebinding a wounded soldier, and came to a small antechamber. "Please wait while I see if the commander is available," Wood said, and turned to go on down a hall. Then he turned back. "There is no need for concealment, here," he said. "If the ladies prefer to be themselves, that may be best." Then he moved away.

"We had best make a good impression," Ann remarked. She removed her peasant skullcap and let her voluminous hair show, working it and placing combs in it, and Mi'in did the same. Hu'o let his own long queue show and saw to Skev. In moments they all looked much improved.

Wood returned. "He will see you now," he said. "This way." He indicated the hall.

They followed him to a chamber no larger than the other. There stood a man in a plain blue frock coat, buttoned at the top, with a plain white shirt, and a kerchief tied loosely at the neck. He had a solid black mustache and a goatee. He held a rattan walking stick. Beside him was a dog: a huge black and white mastiff. Overall, Commander Ward had a considerable presence; he was clearly a leader. Yet, oddly, he carried no weapon, despite the formidable firearms available to him.

"Commander, this is the family who knows the female spy," Wood said deferentially. Then, to Hu'o: "This is Commander Frederick Ward."

Hu'o was uncertain of the protocol, so merely nodded without speaking. But Mi'in smiled at the soldier of fortune.

This had the usual effect. The man focused on her immediately, and visibly softened. He was a mature American, but few men of any persuasion failed to appreciate her qualities. "How do you do," he said. The left side of his mouth drooped as he spoke, distorting his speech somewhat and damaging the handsomeness of repose. Hu'o remembered that he had been shot through the cheek once, leaving him with a liability of expression. There was no doubt that this was the man he had heard about.

"We know Serilda by sight," Hu'o said. "She—this is her son." He indicated Skev.

Ward glanced at Skev, then to Hu'o, and nodded. "That explains much," he said. "She must have volunteered for the mission."

"We want merely to find a safe haven where we can play our music and dance, according to our training," Hu'o said. "But we may not have it as long as the Taiping leaders wish to destroy us, and Serilda can recognize us."

Ward smiled, lopsidedly because of his mouth droop. "Rest assured that if we catch her, she will not bother you further. But we shall have to offer her a seeming chance to approach you without revealing herself. Suppose we place you in a guarded house for a few days, and on the second night the guard falls asleep?"

So they would serve as a lure. Hu'o was not completely sanguine about the notion, but it did seem to make sense. If they caught Serilda now, they would not have to be concerned about her subsequently. He looked at Ann and Mi'in, who both shrugged, though Mi'in again seemed less than easy. By common consent they did not mention or glance at Skev, who was the most likely target. Skev, fortunately, was not paying attention; he was making friends with the big dog.

Ward looked at Wood. "I think you are right. This is our best chance to capture the spy. See to it."

So it was done. Soon enough that evening they found themselves in a reasonably tight house elsewhere in the city, with Wood himself standing guard at the door. After dinner Mi'in took Skev out to talk with him, so as to let the boy be seen from the street; she was sure that Serilda was watching. Wood was more than willing to have their company. Mi'in was now normally dressed, and her dark slender beauty was manifest.

"She is somewhat taken with him," Ann murmured to Hu'o. "And he with her."

He hadn't thought of that. Mi'in had had her effect on men even in childhood, especially when she danced, but had never taken any interest in any outside the family. He had assumed she was dazzling the young soldier just to facilitate things for the family. Yet she was coming of age, and so her interest was changing. "Is that wise?"

"Probably not. But maidens will be foolish, as I am with you."

Hu'o caught her hint: for now they were alone in the house. He took her into the bedroom. They were no longer young, each being thirty or thirty-one, but for a while they pretended that they were.

○

A day later it happened: Skev was gone. Hu'o knew it by Ann's scream. The boy was not in his room and not in the house.

"But no one passed the door," Wood protested. "We guarded it in shifts all night, and I myself pretended to sleep and even to snore, while watching."

"It is true," Ann said. "See, I sprinkled flour lightly just inside the door, and there is no footprint in it. But he is gone."

They searched the house again. This time Mi'in found a crevice in the wall of a closet, too small for a grown person to wriggle through,, but perhaps large enough for a child. It led outside, to the shrouded back of the building. And there, caught on a projection of the crevice, was a small strand of hair.

"It is hers," Mi'in said. "Left here for us to find. I feared this."

"She must have lured him out," Ann said. "He knows she is his mother. Maybe she told him she just wanted to talk to him for a moment."

"And I never thought to watch the back of the building," Wood said, chagrined. "There was no door, no window; I thought it had to be the front."

"We all thought so," Hu'o said. "But she knew this house better than we did."

"It can't have been long ago," Wood said. "We may yet intercept her, if we put out the alert for a woman and a child."

"There are tens of thousands of women and children on the streets," Ann said morosely.

"But few who would try to cross to the Taiping side," Wood said. "Those are the ones to check. We can ban all such crossings; that will keep them within the city. And we can search here. You can recognize the woman if you see her, even in disguise, or your son."

"Yes," Ann agreed, her mouth tight.

"Yes," Hu'o said.

"We will assign men to accompany you, to capture the women you point out. That will allow you to search separately, widening the range. I wish I knew what she looked like!"

"I will go with you, to identify her," Mi'in said.

Again Hu'o glanced at Ann, but neither protested. Three search parties were better than two. Wood was a decent young man, despite being British, and would treat Mi'in with chivalrous respect. He hoped that Mi'in would remember her common sense.

Soon Hu'o found himself with one of Commander Ward's trusted mercenaries: a Filipino who spoke no Chinese but who knew the mission. All Hu'o had to do was point out a woman, and the soldier would go after her.

Assuming he managed to spy Serilda or Skev. Hu'o had a sick doubt in his belly, but he was trying to conceal that from others. Serilda might have had hours to spirit the boy out of the city before the alarm went out, and he wasn't sure how effective that alarm would be anyway. There was not a battle line; there was merely the empire territory and the Taiping territory, with ordinary residents between them, trying to avoid getting hurt. Serilda would surely have connections to help her escape, or she could have a hiding place in the city where she could not be found among the myriad thousands of other Chinese women with children.

They went to a main avenue leading out of the city toward the Taiping sector. Ann and Mi'in would be checking two others. If Serilda had hidden for a while, and was only now departing the city, it should be along one of these roads. Most of the traffic was inward, refugees from the encroaching armies, which made it easier; few were going the other way. Still, the chances of—

Then he saw her. He had once been Serilda's lover; he knew her bearing, her walk, even after a number of years. And the boy was with her! "There!" he exclaimed, pointing her out. What amazing fortune!

The Filipino ran to intercept the pair. But almost at the same time, the woman realized that she had been discovered, and ran off the street, hauling the child along with her. She was not particularly fleet, because of her small feet, but moved well enough to be out of sight by the time they reached the place she had been.

There was an alley she had fled into. They went to it, and saw her disappearing at its other end. They ran there, but the woman and the boy were gone. They hadn't been quite fast enough; she had had time to escape into another alley or even a building.

They checked to see what door she might have entered, but all were closed tight. The citizens were not inclined to open their doors to strangers during war. So unless she had happened to have a contact here, which seemed unlikely, she must still be on the street. Hu'o peered down it without much hope—and saw her in the distance, with the child.

He cried out, and they resumed the chase. But again she was gone by the time they got there. They had to make another search, this time in an area ravaged by one of the prior battles; the houses were unoccupied, being mere husks amidst rubble.

There was too much to search. So they doubled their chances by splitting; the Filipino took the section to the left of the street, and Hu'o the section to the right. Both of them paused frequently, listening, in case the woman was trying to move again, or the boy cried out.

Hu'o's search was fruitless, as he had feared. So in due course he crossed the street to join the Filipino—and found him unconscious. He had been struck on the head with a brick. Serilda must have ambushed him!

Hu'o looked rapidly around, knowing that Serilda had to be close. Within brick-throwing range. What was her purpose? To kill him? Or merely to escape with the boy? He couldn't allow that.

So he moved rapidly, making himself a difficult target for thrown missiles, and searched all around the half-standing walls and columns. This was nominally part of the city, but a desolate landscape, with stones and bricks littering the ground throughout, and pits where cellars had been. He almost wished that more of the buildings had been knocked down, because what remained standing provided too much cover for an ambush. Yet one of the buildings was a ruined Buddhist temple, hardly more than a façade, with human statues still in their frames; he was not a Buddhist, but he was sorry to see the temple in such state. Buddhists, as a rule, did not practice violence; they tried to follow their eight-forked path.

But this was no time for reflections. Where was the woman? He neither saw nor heard anyone moving in the vicinity, and it was open enough, thanks to the destruction of warfare, so that he should have been able to locate any fugitives. Where was the one who had struck down the Filipino?

Then he got smart. Serilda had Skev. Unless she had the boy bound and gagged, Skev could be reached by voice. She had surely told him that bad soldiers were after them, so he had to be quiet and obey her implicitly. But the sound of his father's voice might overrule that. "Skev!" he called.

"Father!"

It was from the husk of a building, the walls forming a chamber open to the sky. Hu'o ran to it, alert for any sound or motion. But Skev ran out to meet him.

He swept up the boy. "Are you all right?" he asked. "She didn't hurt you?"

"How could I hurt my son?" Serilda asked from close by.

Hu'o jumped, whirling to avoid attack, thrusting the boy behind him. But she was not attacking. She stood there behind a low wall, where she must have ducked down to hide. She was dressed in ragged street clothing, like a farmer's woman, so that she would not be noticed on the crowded streets, but he could see that her body remained healthy and strong. She was a spy in enemy territory; she had to be ready for anything. She had used the boy to distract him. Yet she hadn't thrown a brick at him, or a knife, as she could have in that moment. She was merely waiting. Waiting for him to understand that she could have brought him down, and had not.

"What do you want?" he asked her.

"I led you here," she said. "When you lost me, I showed myself again, so you could follow. I did not even kill the mercenary; he will recover in due course."

Surely true; he should have been suspicious of the easy pursuit. "What do you want?" he repeated.

"I want my boy, and I want you. To be a family, together."

"I thought you were married."

"I am free of that now. You were always the one I wanted."

"You were never the one I wanted," he replied harshly.

"Then I will take my son from you."

"No. I have him now."

"Do you?" She looked at Skev, who now stood between them. "Will you go with your father or your mother?" she asked him.

Skev looked at her, then at him. "With my mother," he said.

Hu'o was astounded. "You mean Serilda? Not Ann?"

"My real mother," the boy said, stepping toward Serilda.

"You see, he is mine," Serilda said. "Come with me, and you will have him and me, and the others you have known will be spared, because I will not tell Taiping of you. Remain behind, and—" She shrugged.

"Unless I kill you now," he said. He had a knife, and he could throw it before she could throw a brick.

"No!" Skev cried, running to her.

Hu'o realized that he couldn't do it. Not in front of his son, and perhaps not anyway. She was the boy's natural mother, whatever else she was not.

Then Skev tripped on a stone and stumbled toward a hole in the pavement. He was about to fall into one of the cellar pits!

Hu'o lunged for him, but knew he was too far away. He saw his son stepping at the brink, beginning his tumble. Just out of reach, in the time available.

Then he saw Serilda leaping over the wall with the athleticism of her dancing experience. She caught the boy by the shoulder, hauling him back.

Hu'o arrived. He caught Serilda. She writhed within his grasp, turning to face him, her body tight against him, her mouth seeking his. She kissed him with startling passion.

His first impulse was to shove her away. But his second was to hold her close: as a captive. "I have you," he said.

She did not struggle. Instead she moved her torso so that he could feel its slenderness and its softness. "You always did," she said, trying to kiss him again.

He turned his face away. "You are a spy for the Taiping Rebellion. You will be confined."

"I could have gutted you," she said, drawing away just enough to show him the knife she held in her right hand. "I kissed you instead."

He realized that she was right, again. She had caught Skev, he had caught her, but she could have kneed him or stabbed him. He had not truly overpowered her. "Why?"

"How do you kill the man you love?"

She was serious. She had been sent on a mission to execute him, and could have accomplished it, having successfully led him to this isolated spot. But she had not even tried. Still, as long as she was free, the other members of his family were in danger. "You are still a spy."

Then he saw a figure. "Well spoken," Wood said. The man had a pistol pointed at Serilda. Mi'in stood behind him; she must have guided him here, using her uncanny awareness. "Commander Ward will interrogate her." Beside him was the Filipino mercenary, evidently somewhat dazed, but functional.

Serilda did not remove her eyes from Hu'o's face. "You know what they do to female captives?"

"No!" Skev cried. Hu'o had forgotten for the moment that his son was standing close.

Serilda stooped to enfold him. "You will not have to watch," she said. "Return to your—your other mother. She will be out of danger now."

"No!" Skev repeated tearfully, hugging her.

"What did you tell him?" Hu'o asked as Wood approached with a length of cord in the hand that did not hold the gun. The gun did not waver; the man was ready to fire at the first sign of trouble.

"That if he did not come with me, you and your woman and the girl would be slain by the Taiping," she replied without looking at him.

That explained why the boy had so readily gone with her: to protect his family. Yet it was clear that he had not forgotten his first mother.

Wood held out the cord, and Serilda held out her hands. Wood gave Hu'o the rope. Hu'o began to tie her hands together. But her remark clung to his awareness. What was normally done to spies was interrogation by torture, and execution. An attractive female spy would also be raped. Serilda would submit to it all, and die without divulging anything she did not choose to.

Hu'o paused. "I don't think I can do this," he said.

"You won't have to," Wood said. "Commander Ward will take care of everything. Your family will be out of danger, and we shall have our information."

"She—I caught her because she saved my son—her son—from falling in that pit," Hu'o said. "She could have ambushed me, as she did the mercenary. She could have killed me even then, but she didn't."

"What are you saying?" Wood asked sharply.

"I—I am not without concern in this matter," Hu'o said with difficulty. "I do not love this woman, but she may love me, and she is the mother of my son. I can't see her hurt like this."

"We have to interrogate her," Wood said. "Lives depend on the information she has. Perhaps the very success of our mission. We must know what she knows."

"I won't tell you anything," Serilda said.

"Oh, I think you will," Wood replied grimly. "The commander has ways."

"They won't work on her," Hu'o said. "I know this woman. What you contemplate is pointless. All you can do is make her death ugly."

"No!" Skev cried a third time.

"No," Mi'in echoed, looking directly at Wood. Hu'o knew that she might as well have pointed a gun at him. Hu'o had felt that look himself, and he was no longer a romantic young man. Wood would not be able to go against her.

Wood looked uncomfortable. He wrenched his eyes away from hers and addressed Hu'o. "I realize this puts you in an awkward situation. But we must have that information, and we can't let her go to make more mischief. If there were any other way, I would gladly embrace it." Then he looked flustered as his gaze crossed Mi'in's face again. "That is, avidly pursue it. I mean, warmly espouse it." He couldn't find a nonsuggestive phrase. Even Serilda smiled, faintly, recognizing the beauty of the girl. Serilda herself had used her charms many times to befuddle men and school them to her will. How well Hu'o knew!

Hu'o understood the logic of the soldier's position. But there was nothing in this he liked.

More figures approached: Ann, with her soldier. "We have her," Hu'o told them. "But—"

"Of course," Ann said, taking in the embrace of boy and woman.

"Come, Skev," Mi'in said. The boy disengaged from his mother and sought the girl's embrace.

Serilda's eyes widened. Then her face set. She knew she had lost the boy, regardless what else happened. Mi'in's magic was strongest on her little brother.

"We can't let her go," Wood said, looking more uncomfortable. "We must have that information."

"Yes you can," Mi'in said. "She will tell you."

Serilda's face turned to the girl. Their eyes met. "My, you are something special," Serilda said, feeling the power herself.

"She will tell you, if you let her go," Mi'in said, glancing significantly at Wood. The man looked as if he had been struck a body blow, as duty warred with inclination.

Hu'o jumped on that, using the opening the girl made for him. "My daughter can tell when someone speaks a lie," he said. "Make a deal: let the spy go unharmed, if she tells you all she can. It's the information you want, not her pain or death."

"This is highly irregular," Wood said, wavering. It seemed he was not hard-hearted, despite being a soldier, and Mi'in had surely had impact on him.

"Take her to Commander Ward, and let him make the deal," Hu'o said. "Then it will be out of your hands."

"Yes, of course," Wood said. "But I can't promise—"

Hu'o looked at Serilda. "You have no loyalty to Taiping. You're a mercenary yourself. You signed onto this mission just to recover your son—and perhaps more. If you tell the enemy what you know, you will not be able to return to Taiping; they would execute you. So we will be safe. Exactly as we will be if they kill you. And your son will not have to know you are dead."

Serilda considered. "Do *you* ask this of me?" She was soliciting his confession of emotion. His agreement would constitute a commitment of some indefinite kind. It seemed that he had effect on her similar to what Mi'in had on Wood.

Hu'o looked at Ann. She nodded, almost imperceptibly. "Yes," he said.

"Then I will do it," Serilda said.

"Yes!" Skev cried, returning to her to hug her around her bound hands. There were tears on Serilda's cheeks. Hu'o wasn't sure he had ever seen real tears on her before.

"Then it appears we have an agreement," Wood said, looking relieved. "Provided the commander accedes."

"He will agree," Mi'in said. Then she stepped up and kissed him. This was a very forward act for a Chinese girl, but she was not bound by ordinary rules. "Then we will go our way, and you will go yours, but maybe we will remember each other."

"Yes, of course," Wood agreed, dazed.

Now Hu'o was relieved in another way. His daughter had just signaled that the limit of the relationship had been reached. She recognized that there was no future in it. So the two would remember each other with fondness, but marry elsewhere. This was of course the way it had to be.

The Taiping siege of Shanghai in 1862 was foiled largely by the valiant efforts of Ward's tiny force. General Li divided his forces so as to control each of the towns within a thirty-mile radius of Shanghai, driving out the imperial garrisons and cutting the city off from the surrounding territory. This strategy came close to success. But it meant that Li had fewer than 100,000 men remaining to besiege Shanghai itself. Ward's defenders were even more thinly spread, and were strictly defensive. But thanks to determination, boldness, and perhaps special information, they managed to keep the Taiping force at bay until an imperial army arrived to drive it back. The imperials besieged the Taiping capital of Nanking, forcing Li to return in an attempt to save the Heavenly Capital, somewhat in the manner Rome forced Carthage to defend its home city instead of rampaging farther in Italy. Ward himself was wounded in battle fifteen times, sometimes grievously, but survived until September 1862 when an injury finally killed him. But the tide had turned; in two more years the Taiping Rebellion was crushed.

The devastation of this (to some views) pointless combat over ideology was phenomenal; ten to twenty million people died of slaughter, disease, and starvation, and central China was impoverished for decades. Yet it was just one of many rebellions, of which perhaps only the Boxer uprising of 1900 is well known to Westerners. All of them cost the nation heavily. There is another irony: in 1862 America was hardly paying attention to the enormous grief of China, being preoccupied by its own far smaller concern of the moment: the War of the Rebellion, popularly known as the Civil War, where half a million died.

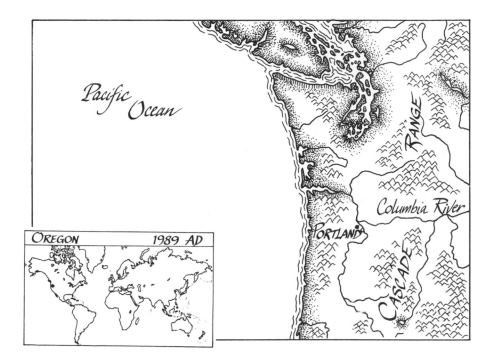

Pacific Ocean

OREGON   1989 AD

RANGE

Columbia River

PORTLAND

CASCADE

CHAPTER 19

EARTH FIRST!

Wherever mankind went, destruction of the wilderness followed. New territories flourished, then faded as their natural resources were exhausted. The New World was one of the last bastions of the natural globe, but was relentlessly plundered in the name of jobs, of progress, of civilization. Yet there were those who became conscious of the likely consequence of this sequence, and began to take up arms in defense of the wilderness for its own sake. They faced, however, formidable opposition. The place is Oregon, the time 1989.

Y OU want to what?" Hugh demanded of his daughter.
    "Daddy, it's just a weekend camping trip with Billie," Minnie pro-
tested innocently. "And some of his friends."
    "Billie is seventeen," he said. "You are fourteen. You hardly know him
yet. Does the term age of consent have any meaning for you?"
    "Oh, Daddy, don't be a fuddy-duddy! Anyway, he's only sixteen. How
well do you expect me to get to know him in only three weeks? And the first
two it was his sister Faience I was getting to know. She's my age. It's a nature
trip. Didn't you bring us out here to enjoy nature?"
    Sixteen. The age Chip would have been, if he had lived. But he couldn't
dwell on that. "It's the 'nature' of Billie's interest that bothers me. You are
one—" He caught himself. "One precious child. We don't want to risk you
in the wilderness."
    "You think I'm sneaking off to have sex!" she accused him with a fine
emulation of indignity. "You're afraid I'm *not* a child."
    Hugh knew better than to get into that argument with her. She would use
all the terms he shied away from. But it was exactly what he feared. "Yes."
    "Then why don't you have it out with Billie, if you don't trust me?"
    She was trying to put him in the wrong no matter what. So he trumped
her ploy. "I'll do better than that. I'll have it out with his dad."
    "What's his father have to do with it?"
    "The same thing I have to do with you." Hugh picked up the phone,
hoping she would lose her nerve and call off the excursion. "It's time I met
him, anyway." He opened the phone book.
    But Minnie wouldn't bluff. "Here's his number." She repeated it slowly
from memory. There was nothing Hugh could do but punch it in.
    Bill Senior answered. He placed Hugh in a moment. "You're the father of
that lovely little girl with the midnight hair and the noon-sun smile my son's
seeing."
    "Yes. She's 14, and—"
    "I can guess. One look into those huge dark eyes almost knocked *me* for a
loop, and I have a daughter her age. No wonder Billie's smitten! Look,
Hugh, why don't you come over here, and we'll talk about it? Minnie knows
where we live."
    Bemused, Hugh agreed. The man obviously appreciated the problem.
He hung up, then went to explain to Anne. "I'll go with you," she said. She
knew the importance of presenting a united front, particularly if they were
up against a permissive laissez-faire attitude.
    "We'll all go," Minnie said. "You'll like them. Bill's the smartest man I
know."
    Hugh didn't need to exchange a glance with his wife. It was inherent.
Minnie was getting to know these people too well, too fast. So they piled
into the pickup truck and headed for their neighbor, who lived two miles
down the road.

Soon they pulled into the neat log cabin. Bill came out to meet them, hand extended. He was a man of Hugh's age, but thinner, and he wore glasses. There was an odd familiarity about him. "Have we met before?" Hugh asked as the shook hands.

"Could be. I meet so many in my business, I can't remember them all. I'm in computers—AI design. Used to be in upper management for a large corporation, before it got taken over by a corporate raider. I got disgusted, moved to the country, and went native. You?"

That was reasonably close to what Hugh had done. "I'm a musician."

Bill laughed. "Must've been two other people, then. Come on in and meet the family."

All this was surprisingly compatible. Hugh found himself liking Bill. It did feel as if they had known each other before.

"Fay, this is our new neighbor Hugh," Bill said as they encountered a woman in an apron. "And his wife—"

"Anne," Anne said. "And our seven-year-old son Scevo. I think you know our daughter already."

"Sure do!" Bill agreed. "And here's Bill Junior, and my daughter Faience. Minnie must have told you about them."

"Yes," Hugh agreed as they settled in the living room. He looked at Fay more carefully. She, too, seemed oddly familiar. Not as a casual acquaintance, but almost as a former lover. But of course that hadn't been the case. And though the daughter wasn't familiar, there was something about her name, which meant pretty pottery, that also nagged him. What *was* it about this family?

"So let's cut to the chase," Bill said affably. "We're going on this weekend camping trip, and Minnie wants to come along. You have social or religions objections?"

"A family trip!" Anne said.

Bill glanced at her. "You thought we'd let the kids go out alone? Nuh-uh! They could get into trouble out there."

For sure. Hugh was becoming reassured. "It does seem there was a detail she omitted. Still, we are not entirely sanguine about her being with folk we don't know well, no offense."

"That's readily solved," Bill said. "Why don't you come along too?"

But Fay glanced warningly at her husband. "That may not—"

"Oh, I forgot." Bill smiled. "There's a condition. We don't know you well either. You must swear never to tell anyone else what you see."

"Never to tell?" Anne asked, puzzled. "There are rare birds or something?"

Bill laughed. "Or something! We take nature seriously. Everything is precious. Fauna and flora and minerals in their natural state. We want to leave them all that way. Minnie says you are folk of your word, and we believe her."

Minnie was right, but Hugh was uncertain of this. "We moved out here to get away from the strife and squalor and politics of the big city. We were overseas for a while, and decided then to get out to the country when we returned. If there are rare animals here, why should this be secret?"

"We can't say," Bill said. "It may be that you don't approve of what we do. But we want your word."

"If you're doing something illegal—you're not growing marijuana?" Hugh asked, concerned. "We don't like the drug trade."

"No drugs!" Bill said. "Nothing like that. I think you'll approve. But if you don't, then go your way in silence. I think that's a fair compromise."

Hugh looked at Anne, then at Minnie. "Do it, Daddy," she murmured.

Hugh shrugged. "Okay. I hope we don't regret this."

"So do we," Bill agreed. "You have sleeping bags? Come here Friday afternoon, and we'll hike into the forest together. It's not far. There's a river, so water's no problem. We have tents." He paused. "You're a musician? What instrument?"

"Orchestral clarinet."

"Can that be played in the forest? If you care to bring it along, we can serenade the sunset. That should be nice."

"I have spare instruments; I can bring one," Hugh agreed. This camping trip was becoming quite intriguing.

"Bring the special one!" Scevo cried. Smiling, Hugh nodded. He had several, but the special one was mainly a novelty, though the children loved it.

"See, I knew you'd like them," Minnie said as they drove home. "When I met Faience it was like I'd known her before, and then Billie." Her eyes turned dreamy. "Like we were destined for each other."

"That's odd," Hugh said. "I felt the same about Bill and Fay."

"As if you and Fay are destined for each other?" Anne inquired with a lift of a brow.

"Don't tease me, wench. It was more as if I'd been close to them in the past, a long time ago. I remember his intelligence, and her—" The memory took an illicit turn, forcing him to break off.

"No, let's have it," Anne said. "I know you aren't contemplating anything. This may be important."

"It's not something I care to discuss in front of the children."

"Ooooh!" Minnie and Scevo groaned together, perfectly synchronized. Then they went into their routine.

"Our conservative parents are at it again," Minnie said in a hushed tone. She had learned early that "conservative" was a bad word in the political sense.

"Thou shalt not hear a thing about the Forbidden Subject," Scevo said in the same tone.

"SEX!" all four of them cried, as the parents joined in.

"All right," Hugh said, with mock bad grace. "It's as if I remember having sex with Fae." He realized that in his mind the spelling of her name had changed, but that didn't matter. "This weird image suddenly came to me: the two of us in a rocky field in a hilly wilderness, she childlike but also womanlike, frightened, relieved, and very friendly. She clung to me, and kissed me, and we became one. I think we married, but it didn't last. Then I met you, Anne, and that lasted. But it has to be a false memory, because I never had sex with any strange woman in any field."

"A dream," Anne said. "An old adolescent wish-fulfillment dream, perhaps."

"A great one," Minnie said. "Maybe Billie and I will find a rocky field."

"Not funny," Anne said sharply.

"I thought it was," Scevo said.

"Well, you're a little troglodyte," Minnie said, smiling, displaying a new word.

"I'll bet you think I don't know what that means," he said in a challenging tone.

"Yes."

"Well, you're right. I don't know it means caveman. But I'm proud to be one. Maybe we'll find a cave with a bear in it."

The adults had to smile. He had trumped her. But later, when they could talk privately, Anne had more to say. "They seemed familiar to me, too," she confided. "No memory of sex; you were my first and only, in dream as in reality. I think I came into existence when you found me, existing only for you. But it was as if we knew them as a couple, and their children, a long time ago. We lived in stone houses by a cold sea. A curious image. But in that picture they were good people, as they seem to be now. I suspect Minnie could do worse than Billie. He's Chip's age, you know."

"I know. That may explain her attraction to him. She hasn't spoken of Chip, really, since he died; she has devoted herself to Scevo. But perhaps it is time for her to look outside the family."

"None of us have spoken much of Chip. And speaking of losses, I wonder who Minnie's natural parents were?" Anne said musingly. "We adopted her, but got no information. I think she deserves to know her origin."

"If she chooses, she can sign the registry," he said. "If her natural mother signs too, they will introduce them. But let's wait for her to decide."

"Maybe she will have a mysterious dream, too," she said. "Meanwhile, keep an eye out; she's a sensible girl, but if she suffers anything like the memory flashes we've been having, she may do something with that boy that we'll regret."

He laughed. "Something like this?" He kissed her and touched her intimately.

"Or even worse," she agreed, meeting his interest with her own.

"What do you think Bill's secret is, that we must not tell?" he asked as they proceeded to make love.

"Probably a rare species of butterfly they don't want lepidopterists to learn about, because they'd pin it to a board. They seem to be ardent ecologists."

"That works for me." Then their passion squeezed out further dialogue.

❂

On Friday they arrived at Bill's house, complete with sleeping bags and other supplies. Bill had a heavy knapsack, which he wore without seeming notice. It didn't contain camping supplies, because Fay and their children were well loaded with those.

They set off for the forest, following a path Bill's family knew. Minnie quickly fell in beside Billie, who seemed more than glad for the company. Soon the way became devious; it seemed that they were looking for a region not reached by any obvious route. There were brambles and prickles; it was a good thing they had boots. But the scenery was interesting; they were making their way into the heart of an increasingly ancient forest. Fortunately they were not trying to scale any high peaks; their route was more or less level, following contours where possible.

The trees near the road were small, but the farther into the backwoods they got, the larger the trees became, until they were among white pines and Douglas firs of truly impressive size. They were so tall as to make normal trees resemble dwarfs, and some of them looked to be six feet or more in diameter at the bases. These were the giants of the wilderness, standing silently in their glory. Hugh almost expected to see elves hiding among them.

At last they reached their campsite: a glade by a trickling brook. The children were delighted. The two girls went first for drinks, giggling as they splashed each other with the icy water. They were like twins, one with bright yellow hair, the other with black hair, worn at similar length. But Faience, despite her pretty name, was an ordinary girl, while Minnie with the ordinary name was a beauty. Their friendship was probably doomed, unless Minnie's relationship with Billie changed the girls' association.

Hugh helped Bill set up the two tents. Scevo, for the moment left out because of his sister's distraction with the other youths, approached. "Daddy, want me to find firewood?"

"No fire," Bill said quickly. "This is a state forest. They're on chronic edge about fire. I don't blame them. They'd be on us in minutes if they spied smoke. We brought food that's good cold."

"Oh," Scevo said, disappointed.

"But there's plenty else to do," Bill said. "We need to make little trenches around the tents, in case it rains in the night. We don't want to get soaked. Can you help me do that?"

"Sure!" Soon the boy was busy with stick and trowel, while Bill dug.

Billie approached, with the girls tittering behind him. "Sing 'The Frozen Logger,' Dad," he said.

"Okay." And Bill sang, adequately, with his son and then the girls joining in.

> "As I sat down one evening, within a small cafe
> A forty-year-old waitress to me these words did say:
> 'I see that you are a logger, and not just a common bum,
> 'Cause nobody but a logger stirs his coffee with his thumb!'"

They continued the song of her love the logger, who forgot his mackinaw, but didn't miss it, as the temperature was only forty-eight below. The weather grew colder, and at a hundred degrees below zero he buttoned up his vest. But it froze through to China, and to the stars above, and finally managed to freeze him at a thousand degrees below zero. Fortunately he wasn't wasted; they made him into axeheads to chop the Douglas fir. And so the waitress lost her logger, and waited at the cafe for another man who stirred his coffee with his thumb.

Hugh laughed. "But you know, that pays no respect to the trees," he said. "All over the world the trees have been cut, the land stripped, until it is bare. In England they think it's supposed to be like that, with bald hills, not remembering how Britain was once heavily forested. Now it's happening in America. I think we have something like a tenth of our original forests left, and those are being cut now."

"Oh, we have a good deal of forest left," Bill said. "Just not old growth."

Hugh gestured across the glade. "How much like this?"

"Not a lot," Bill admitted. "But these trees will last some time."

Hugh doubted that, but didn't want to argue, so he dropped the subject.

They ate at dusk: army rations Bill had saved, that were indeed good cold. Minnie was sitting contentedly beside Billie, now and then murmuring to him or exchanging a glance. She had his whole attention. Billie's fate was probably already sealed. Faience, increasingly isolated, was making the acquaintance of Scevo, who was glad for the consideration. Indeed, Faience seemed to be a tomboy, itching to climb bull spruce trees or wade in cold water; she would get along with Scevo well enough despite being twice his age.

Then Hugh brought out his clarinet, the special one.

Billie stared, distracted momentarily from Minnie. "What is that thing? I never saw a clarinet like that."

"Contrabass," Hugh said with a smile. "Some folk mistake it for a double bassoon, but it's a single reed instrument, not a double reed like the bassoon or oboe. They come in a variety of styles; my kids like this one because they find it weird. It's the extra loop on it. It's a good instrument; I got it at an auction sale, thinking it would be junk, but was pleasantly surprised. It has became a family favorite."

Then Hugh played, and the soft, low, round notes wafted out like floating soap bubbles and drifted through the glade to the big trees.

"Oh, there's that sound," Anne said. "You know what that does to me." She got up and started to dance before them, her body almost invisible in the closing darkness.

"Oh, I want to see this," Fay said. She fetched a gas lamp, and set it farther in the glade, to illuminate Anne from behind. Now she appeared in silhouette, resembling a goddess, her motions accentuating her lines.

Then Minnie got up and joined her, matching her move for move, resembling a nature sprite. She was not yet as well fleshed as Anne, but Hugh realized that she had completed her transformation to woman form and was as lovely as any maiden could be. It was past time to stop thinking of her as a child.

"No offense," Bill murmured, "but I think they both could dance among those trees forever, and no one would know they were mortal."

"Yeah," his son agreed, rapt.

"Yeah," Scevo echoed.

Hugh played several melodies, then let it rest. The women made elegant little concluding bows and left the gladelight.

"That was some show," Bill said. "And you are some musician."

"Well, it is my business." But Hugh was pleased.

Then they retired to their two family tents. "Are you going to marry Billie?" Scevo asked Minnie.

"Maybe," she said. "But you'll always be my brother."

"Okay." He settled down to sleep beside her.

Anne's hand squeezed Hugh's hand as she joined him in their double sleeping bag. They both know that teen romance was apt to be fleeting, but if Minnie got serious, Billie would have no choice. Billie did not seem bad, so far, but there was a good deal yet to be learned about him and his family.

Anne kissed his cheek. She was tantalizingly soft and warm beside him. He was suddenly tempted to make love to her. But of course this wasn't the occasion, with the children so close.

She kissed him again. Then he realized that the idea had originated with her rather than with him. Her dancer's body enabled her to do remarkable things in perfect silence, without miscues. So he turned into her, and soon had such joy as only she could give him. Who needed paradise? It was right here.

✪

They were all up at dawn. The womenfolk went to the stream to wash, sending back chilly screams. Then the menfolk went, taking turns under poured dipperfuls. The water seemed twice as cold as the day before, but Hugh enjoyed it as a ritual of the outdoors. Then, braced for the day, they returned to the camp, where the women had milk and raisin bread ready.

After breakfast Bill glanced at his son. "It's time," he said. He turned to Hugh. "This is where we may part company, but you have pledged your silence."

"Yes," Hugh agreed, his curiosity burgeoning. Bill's family had seemed quite normal so far; what was this secret? Surely they weren't into ritual animal sacrifice or anything like that.

Bill lifted his heavy knapsack. He brought out a hammer and huge long nails. The hammer had webbing over its head as if to muffle it. Billie got out what looked like a shearing tool. "It's best that we don't speak of this even now," Bill said. "Just watch, and you should understand." Then he and Billie crossed the glade to one of the large fir trees. Hugh and Minnie followed, bemused.

Bill lifted a nail to head height and applied it to a crack in the bark. He tapped it with the muffled hammer. As it caught, he hammered harder, driving the nail in. Was he making a hook to hang a sign on? But he kept on hammering until the nail was almost flush with the wood.

Then he stopped, and Billie lifted his tool. He cut the head off the nail. Then Bill resumed hammering, until the nail was entirely embedded in the trunk of the tree.

They walked around the tree and started the process with another nail. Baffled, Hugh and Minnie followed. "What good do buried nails in trees do?" she asked quietly. "They aren't useful for anything, and if anyone tries to saw up that tree for lumber—" She broke off, staring at him with sudden surmise.

"Tree spiking!" Hugh said. "They're tree spiking! So when the sawmill saw cuts that wood, the saw hits the metal and gets dulled or broken."

"To save the trees," she agreed. "They're radical environmentalists."

"I think the operative term is eco-warriors."

"Eco-warriors," she echoed. "I like it."

"But you know it's illegal."

"What about destroying the environment?" she asked rhetorically. "Isn't that a crime?"

"Not according to the government. Japan pays good money for those trees. It's good for the economy."

She made a pooping sound with her tongue and lips. "I want a hammer."

"You'll be breaking a law," he said warningly.

"So you made an oath not to tell."

"So I did." He walked with her back to the camp. "Do you have another hammer?" he asked.

"And some big nails?" Minnie added.

Wordlessly Fay indicated the knapsack. They went to it and got a muffled hammer—the kind that didn't make a lot of noise, he now realized—and some nails, and another shearing tool.

Hugh looked around. "Where are the others?"

"Taking a hike, circling the region," Fay said.

"Looking out for Forest Service officers," Minnie said, realizing. "They caught on before we did."

"Maybe Faience blabbed to Scevo."

"Yes, I told him to snoop if he could."

He punched her lightly on the shoulder. "If you had decent looks, you'd be dangerous." It was another standard family joke.

"Go high," Fay said, as if describing a path. "Loggers cut low; sawmills cut high."

They walked back across the glade. "I thought I liked this family," Minnie remarked. "Now I know I do."

They chose a tree somewhat removed from the section Bill and Billie were working, but in sight. "High—so it doesn't hurt the logger when it hits," Hugh said. "So it breaks up an expensive big circular sawmill saw and disrupts business until they get it fixed."

"Hurt machinery, not people," she agreed. "Hit them in the pocketbook. That's what corporations understand."

"They can probably locate the spikes with metal detectors, but it's still expensive."

They got to work hammering in nails, removing the heads so they couldn't be readily pulled out again. They tried to fix it so that there was no visible evidence of what they had done. They were rapidly learning to be effective criminals.

But it was wearing work, because they were not used to hammering such big nails so deeply. Before long they had to take a break. They sat in the glade, looking around.

Bill and Billie came across. "Just resting," Hugh said.

Billie looked at Hugh. "Sir—may I kiss your daughter?"

"Watch where your hands go," Hugh said.

"Oh, shut up, Daddy," Minnie said. She put her arms around Billie and kissed him firmly on the mouth.

"I guess they're going to get along," Bill said.

"This—I understand why not much should be said," Hugh said. "But speaking hypothetically, if there were a—a club that liked a certain type of activity—let's make it something innocent, like doing designer drugs or wife-swapping—how would a person get in touch?"

Bill smiled. "Speaking purely hypothetically, I'd say there probably wouldn't be much organization, because that leads to conformity and lack of change. Have you noticed how many big, established, reasonably wealthy environmentalist clubs there are—and how the cutting of the last old growth forests continues almost without pause? With the attendant loss of biodiversity and habitat for all plants and creatures mankind thinks he has no use for? Extinctions are occurring at a rate that rivals that of the termination of the dinosaur age. Because nice folk are trying to discuss the issues, without giving offense, while the logging, mining, overgrazing, polluting, river damming, and destruction of wilderness never pause. That's what happened in Europe, and elsewhere, as you mentioned. It occurred to some people that maybe there comes a time when the politeness has to end, and the compromising has to stop. That maybe it's not enough to be socially respectable, it's time to act to save what counts. Time to put Earth first."

"Earth first," Hugh repeated, recognizing the name. "No organization?"

"Nothing formal. No membership rolls, no dues, no officers, no constitution. Just folk with a mission. Not even like-minded folk. They come in every color, faith, economic situation, politics, gender, age, and they don't agree on anything. Except that Earth needs to be preserved for its own sake, not for the use of man. And that when the law is against the Earth, the law is an ass."

"That must be quite a collection of people," Minnie said.

"Unreasonable people," Bill agreed. "Because it is time to get angry at what the human cancer is doing to Earth. Time to cry Enough. To make no truce, no cease-fire, no surrender, because there is no other Earth after this one. If the medicine is too strong for one person's taste, let him stand aside and make way for those who can handle it."

Hugh frowned. "This theoretical club believes that the ends justify the means? That is a treacherous doctrine."

"No. There are limits to the means. No people should be hurt, just equipment. No shooting with guns—but maybe sand in the gas tanks of the big log haulers. No property destroyed, but maybe road markers removed so trucks get lost or mired. When trees are spiked, a notice goes out, warning the authorities that it has been done. Their sensible course is to leave those trees alone. Just let them grow. And leave the creatures they shelter alone; they have as much of a right to exist as we do. Ethical means to support a single god: Earth. Nothing else. No power trips, no riches, no applause, just getting the job done. Earth first!"

Hugh nodded. "Maybe if you ever hear of a meeting of such a group, let us know."

"Maybe," Bill agreed.

Then they went to spike some more trees.

❂

Sunday morning the nails were gone and it was time to go home. They broke camp, erased all evidence of their temporary presence, and began the trek back, using a different route. Hugh wondered why, as this took more time, but it wasn't long before events demonstrated why deviousness was best.

Suddenly there were men in their way. They were dressed in combat fatigues and carried automatic rifles. "Oh, no," Bill murmured as the men forged toward them. "Pot commandos."

"What?" Hugh asked.

"Three years ago the National Forest Drug Enforcement Act of Congress set up a force to combat the cultivation of marijuana on public lands. It was effective; now most of the pot is shipped in from elsewhere. So they beefed up the force and turned it against the radical environmentalists. Naturally we wouldn't know anything about that."

The pot commandos reached them. Two trained their weapons on the campers while the third faced them menacingly. "Whatcha doing here? This section of the forest is closed."

"Closed?" Bill asked mildly. "We understood it was open to camping."

"Rotating closure, idiot. You're off limits."

"Then perhaps you will tell us where the new boundary is," Bill said. "So we can get on its right side. We'll gladly go there."

"Just get the hell out of the area," the commando snapped. "You know what we mean."

"We will," Bill said. He started to step forward.

"Wait a minute, asshole. What's in that pack?" Without waiting for an answer, the man put his hands on Bill's knapsack, opened it, reached in—and found the hammers. He whistled. "Got a live one," he announced.

"Tree spikers," another said with deep disgust.

"Where'd you spike?" the leader demanded.

Bill shrugged, not answering.

"That does it," the man said. "I'm arresting you."

"Then identify yourself and name the charge," Bill said evenly.

"I'm Lieutenant Baabub of Forest Service Enforcement. You're in custody for maliciously damaging public property and being in violation of closure." He looked angrily around. "All of you."

Then the man's eye fell on Anne, and lingered. Hugh did not like that look at all, or the way the other men looked briefly at Faience and more persistently at Minnie.

The two families were herded under guard to a Forest Service security trailer, where they were held until evening, then questioned individually, including the women. Hugh was quite uneasy when Baabub took Anne alone into the trailer for an hour, but he knew she could handle herself. Then it was his turn. "Okay, we know you were doing it; your wife confessed," the man said. "You just sign a corollary statement, and we'll let you go until your court appearance."

"I will sign no statement," Hugh said. "And I'm sure Anne didn't either."

"Oh, you figure it's okay to vandalize national forests and kill people when their saws get smashed by those spikes?"

"People have been killed?" Hugh asked with surprise.

"Don't play the innocent with me! You eco-terrorists don't care who gets hurt or how many jobs are lost. You're probably all Communists."

"Who was killed?" Hugh asked evenly. He did not like this man at all, and doubted his veracity.

"Cloverdale! I'm talking about Cloverdale. Remember that? You damned Earth First!ers spiked that redwood log and damn near killed that mill worker. That's what you want for the nation?"

"No," Hugh said, shaken. "I don't want anyone hurt. But you know, no one has to cut those big old redwoods. They are of more value to our country as tourist attractions and sanctuaries for wildlife. After the last trees are cut down, where will the jobs be then?"

"I'm not here to argue with you about the value of trees, joker. The question is, do we tolerate vandalism and law breaking? Do we let innocent people get maimed because you terrorists got a bug up your ass about a stupid owl? Now where were you spiking?"

"That's a funny attitude for the Forest Service," Hugh remarked, knowing it would make the man angrier than ever. "It is my understanding that that owl represents the top of a food chain, which means that if it survives, so do all the creatures below it, and we know the system is sound. So it represents not so much an end in itself, but a bell marker, an indication of the health of the forest ecology. I should think you would be the first to protect its habitat."

"So you'd take a worthless owl over the jobs of human beings!" the man said righteously. "You don't care at all about the big picture."

"My picture is bigger than the temporary convenience of local loggers who will soon lose their jobs anyway, because they are heedless of the principle of sustainability. Or of companies that don't care at all about the future welfare of our nation, so long as they get their profits today. They are killing the goose that lays the golden eggs."

The man shook his head. "Now you're getting into fairy tales. You're really weird."

The dialogue continued, but got nowhere. Hugh was finally let out, to make way for the next subject for questioning, Minnie. He knew that Baabub would get nowhere with her, either.

As they waited, Hugh asked Bill about Cloverdale. The man laughed. "That was a celebrated episode two years ago. A band saw hit an 11-inch spike in a log. The saw shattered, and a piece of it struck a worker in the face, breaking his jaw and knocking out several teeth. They put up a twenty thousand dollar award for information leading to the arrest of the Earth First! spiker who did it. Big outcry."

Hugh was perplexed and disturbed. "You don't seem concerned."

"It turned out to have been done by a conservative Republican in his midfifties who owned property next to the logging site. Seemed he was annoyed by the heavy truck traffic, noise, and erosion resulting from the cutting. Earth First! had nothing to do with it. Turned out that that saw that broke was cracked, wobbly, and due for replacement; it wouldn't have flown apart if it had been good. It was the mill proprietor who was careless about the safety of his workers, not the eco-warriors. There have been no injuries from Earth First! tree spikings. We always warn the folk concerned, so they know the risk before they start cutting a spiked forest. It's the inconvenience and financial loss that really annoys them."

So there had been no deaths or injuries from "legitimate" tree spiking. Hugh was relieved.

The separate interrogations didn't accomplish anything for the Forest Service, which was clearly operating on suspicion rather than proof, and had no real case to make. But the experience drew the two families closer together. Especially Billie and Minnie, who seemed to be enjoying enduring adversity together.

Finally all eight of them were cited for trespassing, trucked to a remote trailhead miles from any house or phone or vehicle, and released at midnight. They had a long, hard hike ahead.

Somehow they didn't mind it.

Earth First!, founded in 1980 by Dave Foreman, who had formerly been an issues coordinator for The Wilderness Society, was the most notorious of a number of ecological activist groups. They were known as tree spikers, but practiced many types of interference to logging, mining, damming, overgrazing, road-building, poaching, and other wilderness-damaging activities. Some were quite imaginative and daring. In 1989 four activists dug a ditch across a logging road, filled it with cement, set their feet in it, and let it harden around them. Pot commandos used sledgehammers to get them out. But there were other episodes. The authorities, responsive to special interests, fought the activists constantly, but could not be fully effective against guerrilla action. As the quality of the soil, water, and air deteriorated, the general public's awareness of the environment increased, leading to tacit support for the activists. But as the pressure of burgeoning population increased, such efforts to protect the remaining wilderness areas seemed doomed. Most people did put jobs before owls.

Yet the question remained: should mankind be allowed to obliterate all other uses of the Earth? The Warriors for the Earth fought on.

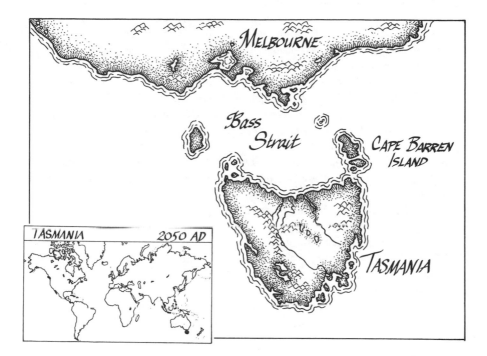

CHAPTER 20

TASMANIA

In the early twenty-first century great mischief came to the peoples of the world, as the last forests were destroyed, species extinction was wholesale, climate changed, deadly pollution saturated air, earth, and sea, and the overstrained food supply collapsed. The population plummeted, the hard way. Only at the somewhat isolated fringes was the disruption minimal. One such fringe was Tasmania, south of Australia—or more correctly, several smaller islands off the north coast of Tasmania known as the Furneaux Group. The second largest of these was Cape Barren Island, named for its barrenness, whose unique history perhaps led to its eventual success in survival. Tasmania had been reputed to have the cleanest air in the world, but in time the pollution spread even here.

The colonization of Tasmania by the white man was no kinder to the aborigine natives than it was elsewhere. De facto genocide was the rule. It was also used as a penal colony for Australian criminals. The natives were seemingly rendered extinct in 1876, but a number had been deported to the Furneaux islands. British sealing expeditions found this region to be rich with seals, and some sealers settled there, taking native wives. This mixed-breed settlement endured despite the hostility of the government, and finally was allowed to exist in peace. It maintained awareness of its aboriginal identity. Its physical and cultural isolation from European Tasmania seemed in the twentieth century to be a liability, but in the twenty-first emerged as an asset. Nevertheless there was an influx of contemporary science, as the people adopted what proved useful, without sacrificing cultural values. The resulting society was unlike either the European or aboriginal origins, but stronger than both in the changed world situation.

The time is A.D. 2050; the place is Cape Barren Island.

HUGH played his clarinet while Minne danced. The patrollers were rapt. She was only 15, but perhaps would never be prettier in her shaped slenderness and joy of nascent maturity. When the dance ended, the applause was enthusiastic.

Captain Ittai of the ferry approached. "I remember when you were a tyke only seven years old," he said to Minne. "You showed promise then, when you danced aboard my boat, and you have realized it now. Your mother trained you well."

"Thank you, Captain," she said, flashing him a warm trained smile. She had learned to take compliments in stride, but she clearly valued this one, for Ittai was an old family friend. He had often taken them from Cape Barren Island north to Flinders Island or south to Tasmania for their gigs, and sometimes even to Australia, more than a hundred and fifty kilometers northwest.

Chief Joe came up to thank them personally. "It is good of you to stay to catch the late shift," he said. "The men really appreciate it. Now I know you have to get home. I'll see you out the gate."

"Thank you," Hugh said. "We don't want Anne to worry."

They walked out in the darkness to the fenced car lot. "It's in there," Joe murmured almost inaudibly.

"Understood," Hugh said. Then he and Minne got into their car, and he started the motor. It revved up almost silently, as Joe walked to open the gate by hand. Fuel cells were used for all powered machines, producing electricity to light houses and propel vehicles, leaving a residue of clean water. The island's solar, wind, and hydroelectric plants provided the power for the preparation of the hydrogen fuel and the limited manufacturing industry; when those free resources failed, people simply existed on less. They would not touch wood or any fossil fuel, because the wood was too valuable for other purposes and the others were nonrenewable and polluting. Sustainability was the key, here and everywhere. The bad old days of heedless exploitation were gone, because those who had continued to practice it had doomed themselves to an unspeakably ugly demise.

"Dad, you forgot to turn on the lights," Minne reminded him reprovingly.

"Tonight we drive without lights," he said. "And without radio."

"But that's not allowed," she protested. "All cars have to be tracked."

"It is allowed tonight."

Joe swung the gate open—the wrong direction. Instead of clearing the way to the coast road, he gave them access to the forest road. Hugh drove his dark car through the gate and into the forest. He moved slowly, peering ahead.

"This is a mission!" Minne said, catching on. "You're after the poacher!"

"Yes. Joe put a rifle in the car, and will cover for me. It's the only way to catch a man who knows the guard schedules, watches cars, and monitors the radio. He's taken two trees in the last month, and Joe thinks he'll strike again tonight."

"A rifle!"

"The forest is supposed to be clear this night," he said grimly. "No one has any legitimate business in there. So if I see anyone, I'm supposed to shoot him and get out immediately. Joe will send guards to investigate."

"Just for a couple of trees?" she asked. "When there are thousands in the forest?"

"Yes. Because it's a controlled wilderness. If we allow one person to take a tree, another person will want a tree, and then everyone, and the forest inevitably will be decimated. That is what happened to Earth in the twentieth century. When all the trees were gone, and the other natural resources, civilization collapsed. Now that we are forging a new, sustainable society here at the edge of the world, we mean to protect it in a way that others did not. Our fathers planted these trees where there had been only grazing land before; they enhanced the soil, channeled water, and protected it from predation. Now we have a healthy forest where none used to exist, that can sustain itself, as long as it is left alone. That means no poaching."

"I know all that," she said, a bit impatiently. "And I know how we're descended from mixed white sealers and black aborigines who escaped the war and starvation of the rest of the world. Because we were isolated, and had our own community, here on a small island off a big island off a continent that was far from population centers. And I know how we latched onto the best that civilization had to offer, such as perfect contraception and completely nonpolluting engines. But shooting a man just for a tree? There must be a better way."

"I can't say that I like it myself," Hugh admitted. "But I trust Joe's judgment in such a matter; the decision is his, and I am acting as his representative. All I ask of you is that you say nothing about this to anyone."

"You won't want to tell the world your act of citizenship?" she asked acidly. "Shooting a stranger without warning?"

"It's the way Joe wants it. So folk will know that poachers are likely to be anonymously shot. That should discourage repetition."

She became thoughtful. "Wasn't it Machiavelli who said that fear was a better motivator than love?"

"I think so. For those who aren't motivated by love of the welfare of the community, fear may be a better tool. It would be nice if all people always had the best intentions, but unfortunately some don't."

"Like when Bubba tried to get you booted from Cape Barren Island because you're left-handed? So he could court Mom, for whom he's had the hots for years despite her advanced years?"

Hugh was surprised. "How did you know about that? We have never spoken of it."

"Serilda told me, when she was visiting Scevor. You know, Dad, I think she's still hot for you, too, after all these years, unbelievable as it may seem for anyone your age to have an interest in sex."

She was teasing him. She knew that he and Anne were thirty-two and physically fit. She knew of the situation that had led him to have an affair with Serilda, from which Scevor had resulted. Serilda had had to give up her son when she married an heir with two children of his own, and Hugh, having coincidentally lost his own son, had been glad to take him. Then Serilda's marriage hadn't worked out, and she had divorced and returned to live with her brother Bubba, who was that family's heir. As a divorced nonheir her prospects for remarriage were slight, and Hugh could tell she would have liked to marry him. But he wanted none of her; Anne had always been his love. Fortunately Anne knew that, so had no concern. "Sex? I don't think I remember that word. What does it mean?"

She ignored that. "But sometimes I worry about Mom. I mean, I'm adopted, and Scevor's adopted, and so she has no real children. But she seems perfectly satisfied. She couldn't be a better mother to either of us even if we had been hers. Is that normal?"

"No," he said seriously. "It means that's she's as fine a woman as exists, and a model for all others. You can see why I love her."

"What," she said with mock amazement. "You mean it's not just sex appeal?"

"How could it be, with us so anciently old?"

She bopped him on the shoulder with her small fist, reprovingly. Then she got serious. "I want to marry Bille."

He was braced for it. "Minne, you're a year shy of nuptial age. You can't marry him yet."

"We could mock marry."

There was her real desire. Modern society was rigidly structured, with family limits enforced. No person married before age sixteen, and no couple had more than two children without special dispensation from the community as a whole. This was because of the disaster of uncontrolled human population increase that had destroyed most of the rest of the world, leaving it largely barren. Here, ironically, on an island named for its barrenness, they had a viable, sustainable community—because they had implemented the lessons of the past. Zero population growth was not an ideal, but an absolute. This had certain social consequences. But more was tolerated in the mock system.

"That could be complicated," he said.

"It's like this, Dad," she said persuasively. "We're in love and we know we'll marry. We just don't want to wait a whole 'nother year." Her tone made it sound like something clinically equivalent to eternity. "So we'll mock marry now, and then marry for real when I'm of age."

"Let me elucidate the complications," he said. "First, you can't have children—"

"We don't want them yet, Dad. We just want the sex. We'll apply for the antister dose when we ready."

She was referring to the medication that countered the airborne contraceptive they all breathed. The atmosphere of the world was foul, and clearing with glacial slowness, so a filtration plant purified it for the island, and introduced the contraceptive. Anyone who got good air was sterile. That was the real control on population: the fact that only with community permission could anyone get the antisterility treatment, and while this was routine for married couples with fewer than two children, it was complicated beyond that.

"And since both of you are heirs, and two heirs can't marry—"

"But there are no limits on mock marriages," she countered. "No restrictions at all. Mocks can be any ages, any status, any gender. Look at Bubba and Serilda—they can't marry, being brother and sister, but they were mock married when she got pregnant with Scevor. When the time comes for us to true marry, I'll give up my heirship to Scevor."

Only one child, normally the firstborn, could inherit the family lot; that was the designated heir, duly registered in the community records. The nonheir had to find an heir to marry, or be excluded from reproduction. Some nonheirs left the island in search of better chances, but this was a bleak prospect, because other communities had similar restrictions. Most settled for mock marriages, accepting the semblance of propriety in lieu of the reality. That was the necessary give in the rigid system. Mock marriages could be dissolved without delay by either party, if a real prospect developed. And it was true that there were no limits, since the marriages weren't real. Yet the parties were accepted, socially, as being married, and of course they cohabited. That was what made the convention so popular, and often necessary. Mock marriages were often for mutual convenience rather than love.

"And where would you stay, since each family is already quota'd on folk of your age bracket?" A family lot sustained six people: nominally two grandparents, two parents, and two children. No one could live where there wasn't a place, because neither law nor feasibility sanctioned it. A lot's garden, carefully tended, had a limited production. Though there was a brisk trade in food, custom enforced the limit: six occupants and one pet animal per lot.

"I'll stay with Bille's folks," she said. "And you'll mock adopt Faience."

Hugh shook his head. "You have it all figured out! Naturally you have cleared this with Scevor and Faience? They don't mind becoming mock brother and sister?"

"Naturally," she agreed. "They love the notion."

"And that is why you seek our permission—which you don't need for a mock relationship—because we have to accede to our own part in it," he said. "We have to mock adopt Bille's sister, so you can move in with Bille."

"You got it," she agreed. "Well?"

"Why didn't you broach this first to your mother? She's the heir in our generation, you know; it's her parents we share with."

"Because you're the softer touch, and once you agree, so will she, being the perfect wife."

And he would agree, because he could deny his daughter nothing that was within law and custom. It was a standing joke that was true: Daddy's little girl did bend him around her little finger. "Okay, Minne. Mock marry him."

"Great, Dad!" she exclaimed, leaning over to plant a fervent kiss on the side of his face. He liked that, too, more than he cared to admit. There had always been something special about her; she really did seem to be blessed by the spirits. Bille was one supremely fortunate young man.

They were now well into the forest, moving slowly and silently. Hugh was peering left, and Minne right, their eyes accustomed to the darkness. He hoped they would find nothing, but he was sure Joe had reason to check the forest this night.

"I see him," Minne said. "Around the next curve."

Hugh braked the car, peering ahead. "Are you sure? I don't see anything."

"Use your scope."

He opened the door, got out, and reached back to take the rifle, moving deliberately so as to make no noise. He lifted the rifle to his shoulder and sighted through its infrared scope.

There was a man, using a muffled handsaw to cut a medium tree he had already felled. This was the poacher, without doubt.

Hugh lifted the rifle and aimed. The scope made it easy. When he had the figure centered, he fired, once. The man jumped and fell.

Hugh quickly put the rifle back into the car and got in himself. He turned it and drove away. He had done his job, perhaps murdering a man. He felt numb, and feared the time when that numbness wore off.

"It's Bubba," Minne said. She had sharper eyes than he, even without the scope, or perhaps some other way of knowing.

Bubba. Hugh was not surprised. The man had been bad seed throughout. But he was glad that he had not known the man's identity, so that he could reassure himself that it had not been a vengeance shot. It had been ugly duty, no more.

The drive back seemed much shorter than the drive in, though the car moved just as slowly and carefully. Neither of them spoke again. When they approached the gate by the guard complex, it opened. Joe was there.

"Done," Hugh said grimly. "Midforest."

"Thanks, stranger." Then Joe opened the other gate, and they drove onto the coast road. They paused only long enough for Joe to reach in for the rifle. Then they moved out, no other words spoken.

"So we're anonymous," Minne said. "No one will ever know who did it."

"Or admit what they suspect," Hugh said.

Once they were sufficiently on their way, he turned on the headlights. Then they could travel at full speed.

"But maybe tell Serilda."

He hadn't thought of that. But she was right. Serilda surely knew what her brother was up to, but would be technically innocent. She was not as bad as Bubba, but couldn't stop him from his way. And she was Scevo's natural mother. He owed her that much.

When they came to the town, he drove first to Serilda's address. He parked the car, got out, and went to the door. The woman evidently saw him coming, because Serilda opened the door as he approached it.

Hugh just stood there, unable for the moment to find the necessary words. But she knew them anyway. "Oh!" she said, and turned away, closing the door.

Hugh returned to the car. "She knows."

"I thought she would."

They drove on home. Hugh parked, and they entered. The dog didn't even bark, knowing them by sound and smell.

Anne was waiting for him. "Trouble?" she asked, because they were late returning.

"Minne wants to mock marry Bille," he said. "We talked. I agreed to adopt Faience, if you do."

"Of course," Anne said softly. Then Minne went to the room she shared with Skevor, and Hugh and Anne went to theirs.

Then, in bed, in darkness, he told her. "I shot Bubba in the forest. I let Serilda know."

"Of course," she said, and kissed him. Then she held him while he suffered his reaction, stifled until now. She knew they would never be able to speak of this. Bubba, if he survived, would be banished to the penal colony on Tasmania, and his sister would become their heir, provided there was no evidence suggesting her complicity. They knew there would be none, because his warning had given Serilda time to cover any traces.

They had repaid her for Scevor. Perhaps that was why Joe had selected Hugh for this mission, suspecting who the poacher was.

❂

It was a nice ceremony of mock marriage, next afternoon. Hugh played his clarinet, and eight-year-old Scevor his dulcimer, and Anne danced, for the first time doing it not for credit as entertainers, but for their own folk. Bille was suitably handsome, and Minne was stunning in the dress she had made for herself. They kissed, and it was done, to general applause.

There was a refreshment and dance break before the second ceremony. Bille and Minne danced together, then split to dance with guests. Scevor went to join Serilda, who had been invited. Scevor had joined the family in a real, not mock, adoption, so his natural mother had no further rights, but their relationship was no secret. Serilda, however, had distractions, because she was now of greater interest to men, having become an heir. There had been no announcement yet, but such news traveled invisibly at light speed.

Hugh talked with Bill, as one father to another, as they gazed on the proceedings. But their dialogue was not what others might have expected.

"They found Bubba slumped over the tree he was poaching," Bill said. "One bullet through his side. Not fatal, but he'll be some time recovering. No question of his guilt. They're tracing down his contacts now."

"Any notion who shot him?" Hugh asked.

"Maybe one of the guards. Joe won't say, as a matter of policy, but he's obviously pleased. There probably won't be any more trees poached for a long time."

So if Bill knew, he wasn't letting on. Bill was concerned because he was the forester. When he discovered trees being poached, he had taken the matter to Joe, and Joe had handled it. That was the usual quiet way of such matters; the real leaders did not advertise.

Someone laughed. It was Serilda, because of something Scevor had whispered to her. "She does like that boy," Bill remarked.

"He's a good boy," Hugh said. "Instead of her having a bad influence on him, he has had a good influence on her."

Then it was time for the second ceremony. Hugh joined Anne, and Bill joined Faye. Their fifteen-year-old daughter Faience stepped up to stand before Hugh and Anne. She was a lanky, freckle-specked blond girl with barely a trace of the beauty of Minne, but universally pleasant and fun to be with. Scevor liked her almost as well as he liked his big sister, because she would roughhouse with him and had a sense of mischief. Hugh knew she would be no trouble, and of course she had made it possible for her brother to mock marry, by agreeing to mock adopt out. She had done it because of her friendship with Minne, but it showed her nature.

Hugh's sister Bea did the honors. "Hugh and Anne, do you accept this girl Faience as your mock daughter, to live with you on your lot?"

"We do," Anne said, speaking as the heir of the pair.

Bea turned to the boy. "And do you, Scevor, accept this girl Faience as your mock sister, to share your room?" For he had rights too, especially as a prospective heir.

Scevor stood up straight. "I do not," he said clearly.

Bea blinked. Others glanced at him, surprised. "I beg your pardon?"

"I'll mock marry her instead," Scevor said. "And she'll mock marry me. Ask her."

"Yes," Faience agreed. "We'll marry instead."

There was a round of chuckles. Now Hugh understood what had made Serilda laugh: the boy had confided his secret to her. The two youngsters had cooked up a surprising, but viable alternative. For they could indeed mock marry, age being no barrier. The net effect would be similar: Faience would come to live with Scevor. Their mock rights with respect to each other would be broader, but it didn't really matter. They would be referred to as man and wife rather than as brother and sister, and would have to have an announced mock divorce before Faience could marry elsewhere for real, but such things were easy enough to do. Children did mock marry on occasion, making their point, such as when their parents did not agree to mock adoptions. Children did have rights.

So there was a second mock marriage ceremony instead, with Faience donning a white dress that did lend her some appeal, and Scevor acting his part flawlessly. Hugh knew it would be some time before the news of this event became passé. And it might even eventually be that their mock marriage would become a real one, for there was no barrier there either, once both parties were of age. The two did like each other very well, and Scevor would be an heir, and Faience was not the kind to bedazzle men. Friendship marriages were becoming as popular as romance marriages or convenience marriages.

"Worse could happen," Anne said, knowing his thought.

Overall, Hugh liked the look of the future.

And so a sustainable society came to Earth, with absolute population control, and fanatic protection for the world's remaining resources. The unrestricted increase in human population had been a disaster, and the heedless destruction of all the Earth's natural resources, both wilderness and civilized, was the shame of man. It had to stop, but only in the outlying fringes was a balance found, where pollution wasn't as bad and the plants and animals had not been ravaged as harshly. A stable, nonpolluting, nondestructive life-style was the ideal, and perhaps at last it had been achieved. Maybe, as the Earth recovered, similar societies would spread.

THIS is the second volume in the Geodyssey series, this time covering eight million years of prehuman and human history—twice the range I expected. It represents my response to the kind of history teaching I deplore, which is filled with names and dates and obscurities that make it an aversive chore to assimilate. History in its essence is fascinating, representing as it does the lessons of the past that signal our future, if we just pay attention. The third volume, *Hope of Earth,* should follow another family through a similar chain of different settings, interacting with the first two volumes as this one interacts with *Isle of Woman.*

As before, I used my quarter century collection of books on history, archaeology, anthropology, and human nature. I got fed up with having to search for half an hour for a book I knew I had, so this time we got my home library organized. Now all my reference books are marked according to the system used by the Library of Congress, and listed in a computer file; I can locate any one of them quickly. As before, my research assistant Alan Riggs struggled to keep up with the vagaries of my settings. Again, the University of South Florida was kind enough to let us borrow research books whose specialization went beyond what I had. And as before, I found that the sublime themes and aspects of history I wanted to explore got shoved aside by the mundane necessities of reality and plotting.

For example, I had this lovely scene in mind for Chapter 11, "Philistine," wherein a man in a swan suit raped a girl on stage, to the delight of the spectators. Leda and the Swan is a famous incident of Greek mythology; after being raped by Zeus in the form of a swan, Leda duly laid two eggs, from one of which hatched Helen, antiquity's most beautiful woman, who later made her fame in connection with the Trojan War. In addition, by sheer coincidence the name Leda fit exactly into the name pattern for a woman who plays a role in my protagonist's life: Le, Lee, Lea, Leda. Beautiful; it would look like genius writing. But Alan's research indicated that this was a later myth, tacked onto the Trojan War story perhaps as an afterthought, and was not current circa 1000 B.C. Helen herself had started as a nature goddess, rather than as the wife of a Greek king. Since this fiction is historically accurate wherever I can verify the material, that myth could not be used, and I had to substitute something that was at least arguable. Thus Helen and Baal the Bull. But I did name the actress Leda, thus salvaging just a whiff of the original vision. History could not deny me my fictional character. But anthropology did deny me another thing I had wanted: to show how mankind's recovery of color vision gave him a significant advantage in finding ripe fruit and berries to eat. I could not verify when he had ever lost color vision, or whether he had; it seems to have existed throughout the period of this novel. So my throwback character with the color vision had to be scratched. Ouch. There were a number of such disappointments, as I gradually replaced supposition with information. Writing any novel is a learning process, and this is especially true in the Geodyssey series.

For this volume I did research on left-handedness, and that proved to be fascinating. I noted even as a child that those things I was taught to do, I did right-handed, while those I taught myself I did left-handed. Later I tried switching over by playing Ping-Pong (my one competent sport) left-handed, writing left-handed, and eating left-handed. Though my left had learned a great deal more rapidly than my right hand had, I saw in due course that the left hand did not then excel the right hand in these things; the velocity of learning seemed to stem from my prior familiarity rather than inherent talent. So I concluded that I am after all naturally right-handed, and I retained left-handedness only in eating, because it seemed prudent not to have all my skills invested in one hand. What, then, of my self-taught things? They were two-handed tasks, like picking berries, where perhaps the dominant hand chose the first aspect—holding the can—and left the second aspect—the actual picking—to the other. But I learned that few people are completely left- or right-sided; most have some things they happen to do "wrong." That would account for me. But the matter left me with an interest in handedness, and I thought it was time to explore it. Hence my left-handed protagonist.

My research taught me intriguing and alarming things. Actually people are not only handed, they are footed and eyed and perhaps eared. That is, they are right- and left-sided. Their brains are right- and left-sided too, but despite popular wisdom, it seems that this aspect does not relate consistently to physical sidedness. It is true that the right brain controls the left side, and the left brain the right side, but this is generally true regardless of handedness. There do not really seem to be right-brained and left-brained personalities; our brains coordinate so that every person has both aspects. It appears that sidedness stems from the fundamental wiring of the species, and that it developed most significantly when mankind lifted the forefeet from the ground. Since the hands are most obvious, I will orient on them.

Four-footed creatures must use their limbs for locomotion, and they have particular patterns of leg movement, so that the legs don't go in opposite directions or bang into each other. There just isn't much place for left and right; the sides alternate so that the body doesn't fall to the ground. But with two limbs elevated, choice is possible. It seems that our species soon oriented on the right, and that became the template. Mankind is a right-handed species.

What, then, of the roughly 10 percent of people who are left-handed? That has been a riddle long in the fathoming, and doubts remain. There is no compelling evidence for heredity; some families do run to left-handedness, but even there, the majority are right-handed. A left-handed mother may have a left-handed child, but there seems to be no correlation to fatherhood. Thus it was coincidence that Scevor (the name means "a left-handed son") followed his father's way in this respect. It seems that lefties are damaged goods: something happens at a certain point during their gestation that stifles or diminishes their natural rightness, allowing leftness to develop. They may be more likely to have other defects, as stifling may be a generalized situation. (This is intended as a clinical, rather than a value judgment; I am not casting aspersions. Some of my best friends, etc.) And they pay for it. A survey showed that lefties are at risk of death, in our rightie culture. For example, power saws are made for right-handers; use one with the left hand, on the left side, and the blade is next to the body instead of away from it. That's dangerous. Tools are commonly right-handed, if there is differentiation, so are awkward for lefties to use. Even our motor traffic conventions favor the majority, so that when startled a rightie is "fail-safe," while a leftie may swerve into opposing traffic and crash. And this does lead to a greater incidence of fatality for lefties of about one percent a year. That may not seem like much, but think of it this way: of every hundred lefties, one dies each year, on average, from causes that don't affect righties. By the time a leftie reaches retirement age, by such crude math, he has perhaps a two-thirds chance of being dead. The average leftie dies nine years younger than the average rightie, and there are very few old lefties. I'm not listing my research sources for this volume, but will make an exception here, to forestall the letters of disbelief and outrage I will otherwise receive: *The Left-Hander Syndrome* by Stanley Coren, published by Vintage Books in 1993. Another interesting book, though it doesn't address this aspect, is *Lefties* by Jack Fincher, republished in 1993 by Barnes & Noble. Thus not only have lefties been consciously discriminated against, on a sporadic basis, through human history, the current physical bias against them is deadly. I think of it as an aspect of the shame of man.

Another aspect I wanted to explore more thoroughly, but couldn't quite define, is the full nature of language. Perhaps this will never be completely clarified, but I'll keep searching. I remain fascinated by the connections between language and art, perhaps because I regard myself as an artist with words: I shape images and moods without paints or music, while appreciating all the other arts. Storytelling may be the most ancient art. But even when it is viewed as straight communication, there are mysteries about language. For example, Noam Chomsky suggests that the human brain is preprogrammed for particular syntax: when children of diverse linguistics are thrown together, they develop new languages with a set variety of syntax resembling that of the existing languages of the world. At first they use pidgin, which is a polyglot assemblage of words from all over. This evolves into a creole, which is an actual new language with syntax. The importance of syntax is unquestioned in this novel; I believe it is what separated mankind from Neandertal man. But is it wired in? I believe it is not— because there has been no actual test of this, no clear indication. The children who formed their pidgin had words borrowed from the several languages of their parents, and also the pattern of syntax from the same source. Naturally they used it in their new language. Thus both individual words and the common syntax were culturally inspired; there is no need to assume hard genetic wiring, and no reason for it to have evolved. But the matter has not yet been settled; if there is some future test that eliminates the cultural influence, the truth may yet come clear.

Similarly the truth of dreams has yet to be understood. My conjecture that they represent part of the sorting and classification process for memories is my own; I think it is safe to say that this is not presently accepted doctrine. The human brain, during its sleeping downtime, may be methodically calling up all the memories of the past day and seeking their affinities, however farfetched, in the manner of a computer search for particular combinations of symbols. When a match or partial match is found, it is as if a light flashes, and the two memories are compared in greater detail. Probably the background sorting and comparing is constant, and after affinities are evoked, the sorting is done again to see what new alignments have come into being in the light of that discovery. Most things stay in the background; only when new connections are forged is the dreaming process necessary. Then consciousness is invoked, as when a person checks the match the computer has found and put on the screen, and judges in what ways it makes sense. So our dreams do make sense—in ways we are doomed to forget. It is the startling juxtapositions that may be remembered after we wake, but this is like noting the coincidence of a crack of thunder just as a person invokes God's name: probably not meaningful, but nevertheless memorable. I suspect that most dream analysis, whether psychiatric or amateur, is worthless, because it mistakes the purpose of dreams.

Also as before, I tried to focus on aspects of history that are not currently fashionable, in an effort to broaden my base. The standard model I was raised on suggests that civilization started in Egypt, spread to Greece, advanced to Rome, and then collapsed into the Dark Ages until the Renaissance, British world dominion, and modern America. That model is an ignoramus. A whole lot was going on in the rest of the world throughout, as these volumes show, and the subject has hardly been addressed. I believe that the roots of civilization reach into many parts of the globe, and that much of what we have called progress has been an ongoing ecological disaster. For example, agriculture is commonly hailed as one of the greatest breakthroughs of mankind, because it enabled our species to control its food supply and prosper. But cultivation of human food crops destroys the natural plant and animal life of the region, helping to impoverish the diversity of the world's life. Similarly the use of wood has to a considerable degree governed the power and prosperity of human cultures, because it is so useful for housing, ships, and fuel. But deforestation is destroying the vitality of the land, leading to erosion and climatic change. Industry has multiplied human efficiency of accomplishment, but left in its wake the pollution of air, earth, and sea. Everything has its price, and the wasteful use and destruction of Earth's natural resources is the shame of mankind, for it is destroying the viability of the natural world and imperiling future human existence. Species extinctions are proceeding at a rate that promises to rival that of the holocaust of the dinosaurs—because of mankind's heedless exploitation of the world. Whether it is the endless destruction of war, as when the Mongols ravaged Asia; or China's Taiping Rebellion killed up to twenty million people and impoverished the nation; or hunting local whale populations to near extinction as the Basques of Terranova did; or leveling the forests of entire continents, as occurred in modern times; or wiping out the American Indians or the aborigines of Tasmania and elsewhere—we are doing it as we always have, everywhere across the globe. For shame.

Mankind is a species running amok. The qualities which enabled our species to prosper are now sending us to doom. Our intelligence and adaptability enabled us to prevail over other creatures and the rigors of the world's climate; they removed our limits of geography and season. Our ability to procreate enabled us to populate the world. Now those same qualities enable us to squeeze out all other life, and to overpopulate the world so badly that little remains ahead but disaster. Because a quality for which we had no prior need is now desperately needed: restraint.

We may already have seen it happen in a microcosm. Chapter 15, about Easter Island, focused on the mystery of the origin of its stoneworking inhabitants: did they come from Polynesia, or South America? The question may be summed up by POT: the lack of POTtery suggests the former, the presence of sweet POTatoes the latter. But if we focus on their later history, the implication is appalling. When mankind came there, the island was covered by forest, a paradise of its kind. But the human population increased without restraint. At one time the island supported several

thousand people, and was making and erecting giant statues at a phenomenal rate. Other arts may have flourished similarly: woodworking, feather
working, rock art, tattooing, and specialized cloth making. Civilization, by
local definition, was at its peak. But the resources of the land were being
squandered. All the trees were taken, leaving the isle bare. Then there was
no more fresh wood to make boats, so that no one could seek new land, and
deep-sea fishing could no longer be done. The denuded land suffered
erosion and loss of fertility. Thus at a time of greatest industrial progress,
the food gave out. The statue erection abruptly halted, and the population
crashed as the survivors fought over the diminishing resources. Only an
impoverished remnant remained, even before the depredations of the
Europeans occurred. Thus do we conjecture that paradise became hell—
because there was no foresight and no restraint about the exploitation of
natural resources.

There are persuasive computer models suggesting that something similar
is now happening to the whole of Earth. Common sense agrees. We are,
after all, the same species that did it to Easter Island. Famine may be our
future. In the prior volume, *Isle of Woman,* I conjectured that cannibalism
would occur on a global scale as the food system collapsed. This volume
evades that issue by focusing on the fringe, where the population never rises
as high, so has less distance to fall. But even so, Draconian measures are
likely to be required, with rigid control of population and protection of
natural resources. Thus the six-person family lots of the final chapter,
absolute control of births, and nonpolluting fuel cells whose residue is
water, used to power vehicles and other devices. Thus death or banishment
for those who willfully violate such strictures. Because if the lid is not kept
on, the overpopulation and pollution and destruction of vital resources will
resume, and that can not be tolerated. Gaea has been harmed too much
already.

We are living in an age of disastrous pseudo-affluence that will soon
enough be curbed, one way or another, as it was on Easter Island. I hope
that this time sanity comes before destruction. Otherwise the shame of man
will also be the doom of mankind.

Call 1-800 HI PIERS
for a sample newsletter and catalog of
Piers Anthony titles available by mail.